The camera view swung left, then right. Spacer caught a glimpse of a silvery something glistening in the moving beams of illumination. For a moment, it looked like a man in an e-suit.

He heard Maricia's sharp intake of breath. "God!" Then, "*Questar!* Can you see any of this?"

"I wish I didn't," Jarrett said. "Careful, Maricia! Don't touch a damned thing!"

"Believe me! I won't!"

Both cameras finally held steady. Five man-sized shapes appeared to be hanging in the air, suspended midway between floor and ceiling in a broad semicircle. As Maricia moved closer, her helmet lamps focused more tightly on one shape alone, the one hanging in the middle of the array.

Spacer and the others leaned closer, trying to see. As details became clearer—silvery fabric, corroded fittings, faded red helmet—he suddenly realized what he was looking at and jumped. "*Damn!*"

A human skull, still part̲⎯⎯⎯⎯⎯⎯ the rags and tatters of lon̲⎯⎯⎯⎯⎯⎯⎯⎯⎯⎯⎯⎯ ⎯outhed from behind th⎯

THE HARBINGER TRILOGY

DIANE DUANE

VOLUME ONE:
STARRISE AT CORRIVALE

VOLUME TWO:
STORM AT ELDALA

VOLUME THREE:
NIGHTFALL AT ALGEMRON

ON THE VERGE
ROLAND GREEN

ZERO POINT
RICHARD BAKER

STARFALL
EDITED BY MARTIN H. GREENBERG

GRIDRUNNER
THOMAS REID
(SEPTEMBER 2000)

TWO of Minds

William H. Keith, Jr.

TWO OF MINDS

All characters in this book are fictitious. Any resemblance to actual persons, living or dead, is purely coincidental.

This book is protected under the copyright laws of the United States of America. Any reproduction or unauthorized use of the material or artwork contained herein is prohibited without the express written permission of Wizards of the Coast, Inc.

Distributed in the United States by St. Martin's Press. Distributed in Canada by Fenn Ltd.

Distributed to the hobby, toy, and comic trade in the United States and Canada by regional distributors.

Distributed worldwide by Wizards of the Coast, Inc. and regional distributors.

STAR*DRIVE and the Wizards of the Coast logo are registered trademarks owned by Wizards of the Coast, Inc.

All Wizards of the Coast characters, character names, and the distinctive likenesses thereof are trademarks owned by Wizards of the Coast, Inc.

All rights reserved. Made in the U.S.A.

Cover art by D. Alexander Gregory
Maps by Robert Lazzaretti
Interior art by Corey Macourek
First Printing: July 2000
Library of Congress Catalog Card Number: 99-69278

9 8 7 6 5 4 3 2 1

ISBN: 0-7869-1558-7
620-T21558

U.S., CANADA, ASIA, PACIFIC, & LATIN AMERICA	EUROPEAN HEADQUARTERS
Wizards of the Coast, Inc.	Wizards of the Coast, Belgium
P.O. Box 707	P.B. 2031
Renton, WA 98057-0707	2600 Berchem
+1-800-324-6496	Belgium
	Tel. +32-70-23-32-77

Visit our web-site at **www.wizards.com**

My thanks to Dave Plottel for helping me run the numbers and to Heather Foutz for her ever-valiant help with preparing the manuscript.

In addition, my very special thanks and appreciation to everyone who attended my world-building panel at Confluence '98 in Pittsburgh and who helped with the genesis of Storm.

TRIBON

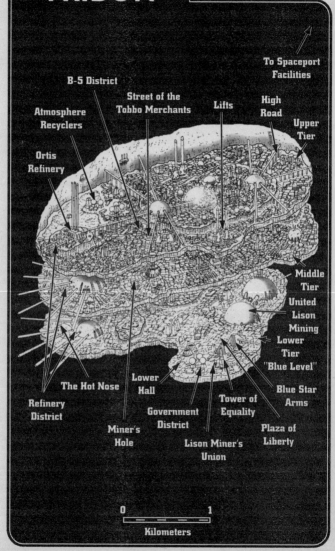

To Spaceport
Facilities

B-5 District

Street of the
Tobbo Merchants

Lifts

High
Road

Atmosphere
Recyclers

Upper
Tier

Ortis
Refinery

Middle
Tier

United
Lison
Mining

Lower
Tier
"Blue Level"

The Hot Nose

Lower
Hall

Blue Star
Arms

Refinery
District

Tower of
Equality

Miner's
Hole

Government
District

Plaza of
Liberty

Lison Miner's
Union

0   1
Kilometers

Chapter One

SPACER ROUNDED THE corner at a jog and hit the chain-link fence full on, the impact startling him almost as badly as that near-miss with the Tribon plexwatch a couple of weeks back. When the grep had they put *that* up?

He took a few steps to the left, then to the right, looking for a way around, over, or under the thing, but the fence had been welded all the way across the entrance to Downtunnel Twelve. There was no way through and no time to find a different tunnel access.

With a deep groan, Spacer steeled himself and reached out to the fence. Nothing. At least they hadn't thrown up a power fence . . . though he suspected that this alteration to the Tribon Spaceport's decor was strictly a temporary measure, one intended to block off the downtunnels until something more permanent and less obtrusive could be erected instead.

"Ah-ha!" a fat man in the gold-and-black livery of the Tribon Watch shouted from the other side. He was leaning against one wall, thumbs hooked into his waistband beneath a generous paunch. "Another squeakin' little plexrat, scuttlin' out from under his rock and lookin' for table scraps! Might as well go back where ya came from. Your kind ain't welcome here with your betters!"

"Hey! What's the idea, goldie?" Spacer said. Reaching up, he grasped the steel links with both hands and gave them a shake. "What's with the fence?"

"What's the matter? Ya can't read?"

He drew an ugly black stun baton and gestured with it at the signs attached to the fence above Spacer's head. There were several of them, with messages in Standard, Fraal, Françaislison, Rigunmor, and Nariac. He could only read the first and third of these, and that with halting, letter-by-letter difficulty, but the gist was something about authorized personnel only, about passes being required for admittance at specific screening gates, about passes being obtained with a permit from Tribon Low, down in the Government District. . . .

"Ha!" The watchman chortled. "I keep forgettin'! You plexrats can't read!"

"I can read, goldie," Spacer said, "but what's the point, huh?"

"The government's sick and tired of you plexbangers goin' where you're not wanted, mixin' with your betters and feedin' off the tourists like a bunch of damned scuttlegrabs."

Spacer glanced at his tattime, numerals showing on the skin on the back of his left hand. Less than four minutes left!

"Aw, c'mon, goldie!" he said. "I'm not gonna hurt nothin', honest! Let me through!"

"Not a chance, kid. Scram."

"I'll tell your fortune!" He reached for the red cloth bag he always kept tied to his belt beneath the hang of his shabby looking gray arm-cloak. "I'll tell you a *good* fortune! Just let me—"

The watchman jabbed his baton against the fence. There was a flash and a snap, and Spacer felt the tingle of the charge through his hands . . . not painful, dispersed that way through the links, but sharp enough to startle.

"I said scram!" the watchman said. "Beat it, before I come through there and burn your skinny plexbanger tail!"

That caught Spacer's interest. There was a way through?

He glanced at the crowd swarming in the Main Concourse beyond. There still might be time. . . .

"Don't make me laugh, you greppin' goldroid!" he called. "You rent-a-cops spend so much time sitting on your fat behinds narfing sugar rings and pastries, you couldn't haul your butts out of a gravity well with a Number Ten inductor drive!"

The trooper's eyes narrowed to dangerous, piggish slits. "Izzatso? I'll show *you* a fat behind. You're gonna kiss it!" He touched his uniform cuff, tapping out a code on a comm processor embedded in the weave. One portion of the chainlink fence suddenly separated from the rest, rolling itself up like a parchment scroll.

So! A magnetic lock! That was worth knowing.

But then the trooper was crowding through the narrow opening, brandishing his shockstick in front of him like a sword. "Let's see how you like eating volts," he snarled. "I'm gonna ram this prod right down your throat and switch on the juice!"

Spacer could feel the man's anger like a hot flame. He took three steps back, hands raised. "Aw, jeez, goldie! I didn't mean anything! Don't hurt me!" He let his voice rise to a thin whine. "*Please! Don't!*"

"Maybe next time you won't have such a smart mouth, plexrat! C'mere!" Grinning, the trooper advanced on him, stun baton extended. Spacer did his best to look terrified, glanced left as though getting ready to run, then dived to the right, brushing past the trooper and slamming hard against the man's shoulder with both hands.

Knocked off-balance by the sudden attack, the trooper tried to swing the baton, but Spacer was already past him, sprinting for the still open gateway in the fence.

"Stop!"

The trooper stabbed at his uniform cuff, trying to close the gate, but Spacer dived through the opening just as it started to scroll shut, hitting the floor on his shoulder and rolling back to his feet. In the very next instant he'd plunged into the crowd.

*   *   *   *   *

Tribon Spaceport's Grand Concourse was bathed in golden light. Crowds of people surged and mingled in a colorfully clashing sea of costume, dress, and decoration. Rich folk . . . tourists . . . business people . . . human women and men of half a dozen different stellar nations, not to mention a scattering of mechalus, some fraal, and even a pair of t'sa—eerie, eager shapes, heavily scaled and tattooed, as flickeringly quick in their movements as liquid mercury. The high walls of the Concourse trapped, amplified, and echoed the deep-rumbling tones of hundreds of moving people, threaded through murmuring voices, children's cries, and the harsh bray of a loudspeaker announcement repeated in five languages. Checking over his shoulder every few moments to see if he was being followed, Spacer worked his way across the traffic lanes, eliciting occasional protests when he stepped on a man's dress-booted foot or jostled a woman's elbow.

It was the farthest wall opposite the mouth of Down-tunnel Twelve that Spacer was most interested in. That entire vast expanse, twenty meters high and inward-leaning across a long, arching curve that stretched almost eighty meters from the port entry locks to the security and customs checkpoints, was a huge vidscreen set to show the planet's topside.

The effect was that of a titanic window . . . not that any building on or in the world would risk that thin and uncertain a barrier between so large an inner space as the Concourse and the deadly environment of Lison's surface. All of the inner workings of Tribon Spaceport were safely buried deep beneath the radiation-baked surface of the world, and the view displayed above was that relayed by armored and automated cameras.

The surface itself was barren and heavily eroded—an

acid-seared, wind-scoured desert stretching to the black mountains on the horizon. The sky, cloud-mottled and brassy with the golden light of the never-setting sun, presented a majestic and ever-changing panorama of light and color. The clouds were spectacular—rust-brown and red, limned with liquid gold and silver, constantly shifting and tattering under the constant gale of Lison's daywinds, while the sky itself was a luminous yellow, fading to green to deepest blue at the zenith. The Tribon port beacon rose in stark silhouette against that glorious sky. Spacer had heard that the tower, all ceramics and polymelded duralloy, had to be replaced at least once each year, so corrosive were the wind-blasted rains of topside.

His eyes weren't on the sky, however, or on the golden light. In the middle distance, a pit gaped a kilometer across, rimmed with anti-erosion ceramics. Guide lights strobed and pulsed from the guide towers, as if in anticipation.

Spacer checked his tattime. Less than a minute to go. . . .

He glanced back over his shoulder. A disturbance was making its way through the crowd, a parting of the colorful waves heralding the approach of the plexwatch.

He glanced down at his clothing. Deliberately muted, it actually stood out against the color and bustle of the crowd. Travelers aboard interstellar transports tended to wear their finery, even when visiting a hole like Lison. Spacer's garb—black trousers and boots, white pullover long since faded to dingy gray, and gray and black arm cloak—were common enough in the tunnels and the lower levels among other Lisoners, but he was as visible here in the Concourse as a roach on a dinner plate.

But perhaps . . .

He reached up and undid the clasp on his cloak, which hung from his left shoulder, concealing that side of his body down to the knee. Reversing it, he pulled it over his dirty blond hair, with the black-and-gray inner lining facing out, letting the tail hang over both shoulders and down his back, like a cape. A hard touch and turn of his fingertip in the corner, and the lining changed colors, the gray brightening to white, the black fading to a zigzag

pattern of orange and electric blue. He kept moving, too;
everyone in the Concourse was moving, and he had to
blend in.

The cape was one of the two most valuable things he
owned. It was stolen, of course. He'd lifted it from the
back of a couch in the lobby of the Galactic Arms Hotel
when its owner had become distracted by a carefully staged
collision between Hookie and a pretty but unsuspecting
member of the hotel staff. Spacer and Hookie had split the
contents of the wallet they'd found, but he'd kept the cloak
and had worn it for so long that it was beginning to fray.
Its circuitry was powered by the body heat of the wearer
and could cycle through twenty different colors and patterns, inside and out. Spacer would never have been able
to afford such a garment, not in ten solid years of pickpocketing and fortune-teller cons, and it had saved his tail
already more than once.

Walking swiftly and deliberately, he kept his back to
the plexwatch and kept staring up at the window that
looked topside.

It was time. . . .

The ship appeared, sliding down clouds and sunlight.
Half a kilometer long, painted black and forest green, it
gentled out of the cloud-choked blue and green sky on
hard-driven inductors. Spacer saw a sudden flash of lightning as the ship bled off an accumulated static charge.
She was fighting that wind, which must be keening like
banshees.

Nearing the gaping pit in Lison's surface, the vessel
slowed to a near-hover, still slipping along the curve of
inductor-bent space. *Star Traveler* was picked out in gold let-
tering at her prow, and the logo of Concord Starlines was
visible on the swelling of her port-aft main inductor sponson.

Spacer had watched this liner on previous visits to
Lison and knew every line, every curve, from bulbous
prow to the delicate curves of her aft inductor sponsons,
knew them as a lover knows the lines of his beloved's face.
Someday, he thought, and his hands clenched at his side so
tightly the nails bit skin. Someday . . .

The *Traveler* shuddered a bit in a heavy gust of wind, still descending. As the liner dropped beneath the port access rimwall, however, she entered the shelter of the ceramic walls. Dust-laden daywind blasted across the rim, dragging tattered ocher clouds across the green and lemon-yellow sky above, but the ship's massive bulk gentled into the calm of the rim's windshadow.

Near the bottom of the vid, inset windows showed the view inside the port entrance from cameras around the entrance ring. The liner was entering Lock One, the largest of Tribon Spaceport's receiving docks and the only one large enough to handle a ship of *Star Traveler*'s bulk. The outer lock access panels slid open like the wedges of a pie, revealing the landing dock hidden below. Lights glared against her belly as the *Traveler* eased into the main lock chamber. A moment later, as the pie wedges began to slide shut, she was bathed in a cascade of white spray, jets of water exploding across her hull from all sides as they started running the decon routine.

Spacer had stopped moving and hadn't even realized it. He stood there on the Concourse, transfixed, heart pounding as he watched the liner's approach, and the crowd flowed around him.

Star Traveler's passengers would begin debarking any moment now. He wondered if it would be worth it to try tagging a mark now that he was here. If the Authority's new security was high enough, it might be a while before he could get up here again.

He looked around at the crowds of people surging across the Concourse, feeling again the old excitement that drew him up here nearly every day. The place was always crowded, throbbing with activity and movement and color. All of the big ships arriving at Lison grounded at Tribon Spaceport, since it was the only port facility big enough to handle major cargo loads coming in or big ore shipments going out. As a result, the capital was the busiest transport and shipment hub on the planet, with small packets and freighters and commercial transports arriving and departing constantly.

As for offworlder vessels, at any given moment, there were at least one or two big liners in-port on Lison, plus dozens of smaller commercial transports, and Spacer tried to know them all. Hookie and Squint and Cutter all had warned him more than once that his lust for ships . . . no, his lust for those far-off worlds those ships could take him to, was cutting into business.

Spacer didn't care. Business was, well, just *business*, a means to an end, and the end was survival. A pocket picked here, a scam run there, a quick con on an offworld mark. Nothing violent. Nothing dangerous. He had enough money to get by, and the goldies left him and the other plexbangers in his cube alone, for the most part, so long as they didn't get too greedy or hit too fat a mark.

The authorities must have once again decided that crime was becoming a problem though, at least where the rich tourists were concerned. That had to be why they were trying to fence off the downtunnel entrances to the Concourse. There were other ways up from the Deep Warrens, of course, but longer, less convenient, and more under the eyes, electronic and organic, of the plexwatch. Spacer decided he'd have to do some exploring later to see how many of the minor downtunnels, conduits, and maintenance passageways had been sealed off in this latest crackdown.

Slowly, he started moving again, though he continued to glance longingly toward the vid wall. He knew the port schedule well. Another ship wasn't due in for another fifty hours . . . and the next launch wouldn't be until *Star Traveler* herself upshipped for the void, sixteen hours after that.

It was the launches Spacer loved best, the sight of a great liner rising above the wind barriers of the port entry, hovering for a moment as she took her bearings, and then accelerating for the empty sky, static bleed fields crackling blue with the high-speed passage through atmosphere.

Someday, Spacer thought, I'm gonna be on one of those ships. I'm gonna get off this rock and see some place besides downtunnels and warrens, passageways and public locks and Authority plexwatch troopers. *Someday . . .*

An amplified voice began calling from the Concourse speakers, announcing the arrival of passengers from the Concord Lines passenger vessel *Star Traveler*. A fresh influx of people began spilling from the arrival portals at one end of the Concourse, making their way across the hall toward the Security Check and customs. Some stopped to admire the view in the vid display, but most pressed ahead, eager to be the first in line for lifts or tubecars to Tribon's deep warrens or elsewhere in Lison.

Why *anyone* would want to visit this literal hole-in-a-rock was beyond Spacer.

Three goldies burst through the crowd twenty meters behind him, looking in all directions. The fat watchman he'd fooled at the fence was urging the other two along, staring at the faces in the incoming throng. A trio of AIs floated slowly above the crowd as well. Spacer wondered if they were in on the hunt or simply carrying out a general programmed surveillance for Tribon Security.

Spacer kept walking, trying to put some distance between them and him. The change in his cloak might throw them off for a moment, but they would be looking for someone of his age and description, someone alone . . .

Alone . . .

Ahead, he saw a man, a rich tourist by the look of him, standing next to a guide kiosk. He was wearing a cloak similar to Spacer's, the zigzag pattern set to green and pink. Increasing his pace and putting on his best smile, he walked up beside the man, who was studying the kiosk's three-dimensional display, one hand on his hip, the other scratching his head. Spacer wasn't sure, but he thought the man was one of the new arrivals off the *Traveler*.

"Feeling a little lost, sir?" Spacer asked. "This place can be awfully confusing to a first-downer."

The man looked at him with pale, squinty eyes showing just a hint of suspicion and possibly of fear as well. He was thickset, bordering on fat, with expensive thumb rings, brooch, and earrings, and some pretty sophisticated skin circuitry on the back of his left hand. The quality of his tunic and neon-striped breeches definitely marked him as strongly Concord dollar positive. "First-downer?"

"First time down on Lison, right?"

"Ah. It's that obvious?"

"Lissies don't need maps." He turned the word into a sneer. "And repeat visitors usually know where they're goin'. So, where ya headed? Maybe I can help."

Definitely money here, Spacer thought. He could smell it . . . probably in the cloak, in the hidden inner pocket designed for a man's secretary. He could nearly always sense where a mark kept his stash, just by watching the way he held his body, a kind of sixth sense that came in real handy for a promising career in pickpocketing.

He could see the guy trying to decide whether or not to trust him. "Uh . . . the Blue Star Arms."

Spacer's eyebrows ratcheted up a couple of notches, as did his assessment of the mark's wealth. "Not a problem, then," he said easily. "I could take you there."

"What . . . are you a guide? Licensed, bonded, all that?"

Spacer spread his arms, and gave his most disarming smile. "Me? A professional? No way! Those plexrats'll strip you to the bone faster than the daywind, y'know? I'll take ya for five CD. It's a bargain!"

It might also give him his chance at the guy's hidden pocket.

The man glanced right, then left. There were a couple of beads of sweat on his forehead, and Spacer realized the guy was scared. Of him? That didn't seem likely. Those three watchmen were in plain sight fifteen meters away now, standing off to the side as they scanned the crowd. It would be easy for this mark to yell, to raise a hand, and then the plexwatch would be all over him.

Spacer thought he saw someone watching the two of them, though, a tall, almost cadaverous man in black . . . but he looked away as soon as Spacer glanced at him. Coincidence, probably. Damn. The mark's nervousness was catching!

"You know," the mark said after a lip-chewing moment, "that would be an excellent idea. They told me I could take a High Road tubecar from the port straight up to the hotel, but I figured the place had to be pretty close to the arrival dock. But this map," he waved at the holodisplay, "has me all turned around. I can't even find the hotel!"

"That's because you're looking for it on the upper level," Spacer explained. "And you don't want to go *up* to the hotel. It's *down*."

He moved his hand through the control field, adding layers one at a time beneath the red, wire-frame diagram of Tribon's spaceport and upper level. The layers were color-coded, from red at the top through orange and yellow and all the way to deep blue at the bottom. Another hand movement, and the upper levels vanished, leaving only the Deep Warrens. "See? Here it is. The Blue Star . . . Blue Level. Close by the Tower of Equality and the Lower Hall." He grinned. "Seven kilometers down! That's definitely Tribon's high-rent district. Way up here, right under topside, you're still in the Tribon plexslums!"

"Good heavens! I had no idea!" He peered at the slow-rotating diagram. "Back on Earth, the fancy places tend to be high up, as far above the streets and undercities as they can get. No wonder I was turned around!"

Earth! Spacer's eyes widened at that. He was actually talking with a man from Earth! . . .

"Grep," he said and snorted. "All of Tribon is an undercity, you know. And the closer to the surface you are, the cheaper it is!"

"Why is that?"

"Man, you know what topside is like?"

"I know your world always keeps the same side to the sun."

"That's just to start! It's broiling on dayside and cold on nightside, so the wind is always blowing up there, sometimes a much as three, four hundred klicks per hour. The atmosphere's poison, the rain is acid, and the dust will scour flesh from bone in minutes. And the radiation . . ."

"All right, all right," the man said, holding up a pudgy hand. "I'd heard the climate on Lison was bad." He cocked his head, studying Spacer. "What's your name, son?"

"Spacer."

His brow furrowed. "That's your name?"

A shrug. "It's what they call me. How 'bout you?"

"Thorne," the big man said. He extended a hand. "Sennis Thorne."

It took Spacer a beat to realize that he was supposed to grasp Thorne's hand in reply . . . some sort of greeting ritual, he guessed. He took the hand and was surprised by the strong grip. His estimation of the man's wealth went up another couple of notches as he noticed Thorne's jeweled rings.

"A pleasure to meet you, Spacer," Thorne said. "I'll tell you . . . I could really use your help. I'm here to meet some people, but I'm not sure how to go about finding them. I'll pay you whatever the going rate is for guides here."

Spacer smiled. Offworlders were so damned naïve, sometimes! How was this fat mark going to know what the going rate was?

The offer, though, was tempting. Which would be better, Spacer wondered, to lift the mark's stash and be gone, or string him along for a while on the chance of getting something more?

His left hand lightly brushed against the pouch beneath his cloak. He wished he could do a reading now, but that would have to wait.

"So," Thorne said, looking about. "Where do we go?"

Still smiling, Spacer took the man's elbow and turned him toward the signs on the far wall that read HIGH ROAD in several languages. Most of the arriving passengers were moving toward the tunnel opening beneath, passing through the Concourse security checkpoint. A light touch . . . and Spacer had confirmed that the man was carrying a secretary, right where he'd known it would be.

He didn't take it, though. Not yet. He had a feeling about this guy. . . .

"You got bags?"

"They're being sent on to the hotel from the ship." Thorne was sweating, his face florid. "Damn! The gravity here is *killing* me!"

Spacer smiled. The man was fat and out of shape, an easy mark. "We don't have to walk all the way," he said. "We'll grab a tubecar once we get through lock security and customs."

They joined a queue and walked through the tube, allowing the security techs behind the screens to scan them right down to their bones. Air Guardsmen—Lison's military elite—stood watch on all sides in their black and white Tiger Mod 6 power armor. Each held a hefty mass rifle, and a point-defense robot equipped with a variety of antipersonnel weapons hulked above the crowd nearby.

"You folks take security pretty seriously," Thorne called back over his shoulder.

"Have to," Spacer replied. "Life in Lison is kind of on the edge, y'know? A saboteur could kill thousands of people if he hit the air recyclers or blew out a lock."

"Why would he want to?"

He sounded genuinely puzzled. Offworlders, Spacer thought with a snort. A strange bunch.

They were stopped at the far end of the scan tube. Thorne was asked to produce his secretary and dataslate, while Spacer had to reveal the contents of his pouch. "I'm with him," Spacer said when a tech looked at his cards and asked dubiously if he was a new arrival. They were waved through.

Spacer watched Thorne's dataslate vanish back into a holster at his belt, and he wondered if he could lift that as well as the wallet. Nah. Probably better not to push his luck. It was tempting, though.

As they walked onto the tubecar platform, Spacer chanced a look back over his shoulder. No goldies in sight. It looked like he'd lost them.

There was something else, though . . . a tall, rather gaunt man, his face all harsh planes and angles, stepped through the security checkpoint, holding up an ID of some sort and being waved through by the techs without a question or a second glance. He wasn't in uniform, though. He was wearing a rather severe-looking black garment that included a complex left gauntlet and a lot of visible circuitry.

Spacer had the impression he'd seen the guy at the kiosk when he'd first approached Thorne.

A plainclothes cop? Or something else?

"I think," Thorne said, as though reading Spacer's mind, "that we're being followed."

"Yeah," Spacer replied.

"Can we lose him?"

"We can try. It'll cost extra, though."

"Money's no problem," Thorne said.

"I like the sound of that! C'mon!"

The next tubecar in line slid silently up to them on its maglev guides, and Spacer hustled Thorne in through the sliding door. "High Road to the Warrens!" he called, touching the command screen with his palm. "Stops at A-7, B-5, and C1!"

As they took their seat, the car glided off, moving through an airlock that passed them into a vacuum tunnel, then accelerating rapidly into darkness. Spacer reached into his pouch and extracted his deck of holotarot, shuffling them with practiced ease.

"Don't worry." Spacer told the nervous-looking Thorne with a grin as he shuffled. "We'll lose 'im."

"I hope so," Thorne said. "You have no idea how important this meeting is."

Spacer extracted a single card from the deck, flipping it over and staring into the soft glow triggered by the card's microcircuit projectors.

"Oh, I think I do," he replied.

The card he'd drawn was the Star.

Chapter Two

THE WOMAN KNELT beside a pool of water, gloriously and uninhibitedly nude, a pitcher in each hand. One pitcher emptied in a steady cascade into the water, the other upon the earth, representing dreams and imagination on the one hand, the material universe on the other. In the sky above, a dazzling star shone bright, casting eight scintillating rays as seven lesser stars glowed brightly about it. A bird, a sacred ibis, sang in a tree, representing the mind, its chirps rising from the card like the faint tinkling of bells. The entire scene was tranquil and melodic, an image of peace and the faith that things would improve with time.

Spacer's heart thumped hard and fast as he stared into the glowing, three-dimensional animation projected in the air above the card as it lay flat on his upturned hand. The Star! An auspicious draw . . . especially since he'd long ago made the Star *his* card, the one symbolizing his own hopes and aspirations.

The Star represented hope and faith, tranquility and improvement. Drawn alone, rather than as part of a spread, it was still a hopeful sign. Spacer decided to accept its appearance as a good omen for whatever he decided to do.

"What the hell is that?" Thorne wanted to know. He was seated opposite Spacer in the tubecar, leaning forward against his seat harness to see the holoanimated display.

Spacer flipped the card over, and the image vanished. "Holotarot," he said. He'd been about to run a quick card reading on himself but was suddenly aware that he didn't want an audience. Not for that.

He eyed Thorne speculatively. "How about it? Want a reading? I'm pretty good."

Thorne made a face. "I don't think so."

"Not a believer, huh?" Spacer chuckled. "Neither was I, but I tell you, these cards know the future!"

"Those cards," Thorne said, leaning back in his seat and folding his hands across his generous paunch, "are sheets of polylam layered with microcircuitry and embedded with nanoelectronics. They're not complex enough to support AI and can't *know* anything. The appearance of any particular card is dictated by chance, and its meaning is entirely dependent on the reader's interpretation. And you, my young friend, don't know me nearly well enough to interpret anything for me."

"So, you know all about it, huh, Mr. Thorne?"

"I know reality, Spacer. And I know that *those*"—he stabbed a fat forefinger at the card deck—"can't know my destiny!"

"Maybe not," Spacer said, "but they can reveal it." He shuffled the cards quickly and handed the deck to Thorne. "Here."

"What?"

"Shuffle them. And cut."

"This is preposterous. Superstitious nonsense!"

"Then think of it as a game. Or a proof. Look, I usually charge fifty CDs for a reading. For you, right here, right now, it's free."

"And to what do I owe this incredible largess?"

"Let's just say it's your chance to prove the cards are superstitious nonsense, like you say."

Thorne blinked, then laughed. "You're on! But no giving me some sort of fuzzy, feel-good generalization. If it's my future you're reading, make it specific, to the point, and precise!"

"I don't control the cards, Mr. Thorne." Spacer touched a release, and a tabletop unfolded from the arm of his chair, locking into position above his lap. Spacer took a moment to formulate the question in his mind. *What's in Sennis Thorne's immediate future?* He tried to focus on the precision of the answer, on the need for specific information.

"We'll try a three-card reading, with you as the querent," Spacer said. He glanced at the time readout high on the curving, inner wall of the tubecar. "We don't have time for a longer, more specific one."

"So we get fuzzy, is that it?" Thorne grinned and shook his head. "It never fails to amaze me how we can be a technological, starfaring species and still have a part of us mired in this kind of superstition."

Spacer didn't answer, but drew the first card and laid it on the table.

The first card was the Five of Wands, indicating struggle. Five men stood in a barren field, each brandishing a wand, a heavy, four-meter staff with leaves budding from living wood. The five were fighting among themselves, a scene of complete confusion. One man would be struck and fall, only to rise from the swirling dust and strike back. There was no particular focus, no organization, no teamwork, no sides . . . only chaos and a mindless scattering of energies. Their shouts and the clash and clatter of their fighting rose above the roiling dust, tiny and distant.

"Opposition or a struggle of some sort," Spacer said, interpreting the scene. "You, or people you're working with, are about to be caught by surprise. You might have to protect yourself from an unexpected attack of some kind."

Spacer wondered if he should focus the reading on Thorne himself or expand it to include the people he was planning to meet . . . obviously a group intent on some specific business or planning. The question had been centered on Thorne, and he decided that that was how he should shape the interpretation. Still, he had the feeling at a deep-seated, almost gut level that this reading involved more than just Sennis Thorne.

"The reading is for you, personally, of course," he told Thorne, "but this struggle almost certainly involves the other people you're with."

He turned over the next card and laid it beside the first.

The Seven of Swords. A man plucked five of seven swords standing upright, point driven into the ground, and with exaggerated stealthiness, he quietly slipped away. In the background was a military encampment, banners fluttering from the tops of colorful tents.

Spacer was a bit startled by that one . . . but then, he thought, he shouldn't have been. The Seven of Swords usually suggested that things weren't going as planned . . . worse, that someone was being deceptive or planning on stealing something from the querent.

"Unreliability," he said, trying to keep his tone neutral. "Someone you know may be holding out on you, Mr. Thorne, hiding the truth from you or not telling you everything. It could—"

"What?"

"It could also mean someone's stealing from you."

Thorne chuckled. "Or running a slick con on me?"

There was no way to answer that. Spacer drew the third and final card, turning it face up beside the others.

The last card was Death. A skeleton in black armor sat astride a white horse, riding toward a priest, a woman, and a child. Beneath the horse's feet lay the figure of a fallen king, his crown on the ground nearby. Snapping in an unfelt breeze, a banner fluttered from a staff in Death's hand, bearing the five-petaled rose signifying regeneration and the Roman Numeral XIII, while in the distance, the sun rose in yellow fire between two towers. The card's name, DEATH, showed at the bottom of the scene.

"Death?" Thorne asked. "Is that supposed to be my future?

"No," Spacer said quickly . . . a little too quickly, perhaps. "No, not at all! Death represents regeneration, transformation, a total change in your life. It leads to new growth, new ideas. Out with the old, in with the new, like that. Of course, it *can* mean physical death, since that's a change in your life too."

"About as big a change as I can imagine," Thorne said, grinning.

"But the way *I* would interpret this reading is that you or your group are engaged in some sort of struggle, and you may be taken unawares, soon. Someone is trying to steal something of value from you, and that theft will lead to a major change of direction in your life. Maybe a new goal. Maybe new ideas. I can't say without knowing just what you're looking for and doing a more detailed reading."

Thorne was laughing now. "Very slick, Spacer. *Very* slick!" he waved his hand above the cards on the table, each displaying its small holoanimation of his destiny. "Don't you see? It's like I was saying! The interpretation is yours, not the cards, and it lets me put any meaning on them I choose! You tell me there's trouble ahead, but hell, what enterprise doesn't face difficulty of some sort? You tell me someone's trying to steal from me . . . but what? My money? My ideas? My project? And you twist *that* morbid little thing"—he pointed at the slow-riding figure of Death—"into something so vague and agreeable it could mean anything! Of *course* our lives are going to change! Change is what life is all about!"

Spacer shrugged as he deactivated the cards and shuffled them back into the deck. "Think what you want, Mister Thorne. I can't give you a detailed reading without more time." He glanced at the time readout. The tubecar was slowing now, approaching the A-7 level stop. They cycled through another airlock, entered the passenger boarding area, and the door hissed open. Thorne started to rise, but Spacer stopped him with a hand on his arm. "Not here," he said."

"Why not?"

"I set three destinations. If someone is following you, he won't know what level you got off on. We'll get out at the next stop and get another car. You wanted to lose them, right?"

"I did indeed. Very clever, Spacer. You've earned your pay."

And your trust too, offworlder, he thought. At least, I hope so.

Spacer could have lifted Thorne's secretary any of a dozen times already. Each time he'd touched the man in the past half hour, it had been an open invitation to slip a hand unseen and unfelt beneath the cloak and pluck the device from its pocket, but Spacer wanted more. This man, he sensed, could be the key to more than just a few hundred Concord dollars downloaded from a secretary.

The question was how to go about opening that particular door. He wished he could consult the cards, wished he could run a more detailed reading on himself and Thorne than a quick three-card array, but he couldn't take the time now. No matter. He was used to winging it, to catching life on the fly. He had Thorne's confidence now—enough at any rate to get closer to him and his friends later. He wondered who those friends were, and whether they had money too.

He found himself under Thorne's careful scrutiny. "How old are you, son?"

"Twelve."

Thorne's eyebrows raised. "You look a lot older than—"

"That's twelve *Lison* years."

"Ah." The man nodded. "That would be . . . what's the conversion? How many days in a Lison year?"

Spacer choked back a guffaw. Offworlders were so *damned* peculiar! "I have no idea. We don't have days in Lison. We have cycles of twenty-four hours."

"S'okay," Thorne said, reaching into his cloak pocket and extracting the secretary. "I've got it here." He punched in a couple of keystrokes and studied the screen. "Lison's year is 536.7 standard days. That makes you about eighteen standard."

"If you say so." Spacer could see no reason why the information would be relevant.

Thorne replaced the secretary. "I've done a fair bit of traveling, but I guess I'm still a bit of a provincial. Things

like that always trip me up. Different worlds. Different
customs. Even different ways of measuring something as
simple as a man's age. Takes some getting used to, you
know. You ever been offworld?"

Spacer shook his head, not trusting himself to speak.
Offworld! How he wanted to leave the close, crowded,
stinking caverns of Lison and see the Galaxy! To see
romantic and far-off places like Earth!

Spacer wondered if this man could really be from
Earth. There was such opportunity here. . . !

Moments later, they pulled into a second station,
Number Five on B-Level, and this time they unstrapped
and got out. As they exited the tubecar station, they were
plunged suddenly into the *real* world of Tribon, the
crowded, dark, tangled reality of the vast but tightly packaged underground city. An explosion of noise, smell, and
confusion assaulted them.

Parts of the floor beneath their feet were metal grating
or sheet steel; other parts were bare rock. To either side,
buildings crowded into the narrow lumen of the corridor,
each at once shabby and dazzling with vividly animated
holographic come-ins, tantalizing aromas, clashing music
and competing soundtrack pitches, all clamoring for, bick-
ering over, *demanding* the attention and the money of the
passers-by. Here a naked woman three meters tall promised a relaxing massage and other, more intimate favors
behind the garishly lit facade of the Pressure Point. There
a pile of wraithlike bars spilled onto the walkway outside
the Beginner's Luck Casino. A trio of women danced invitation to the Miner's Rest, where one low price purchased
a room for the night, and a higher one stocked the room
with live entertainment.

Tattoo parlors and drug dens, tobbo shops and feelers,
massage rooms, nude shows, restaurants, fruit markets
and liquor stores, survival outfitters and schools in every
thing from esoteric martial arts to cooking to commercial
computer art, skendle gamies, jack parlors, raunch halls
and pornemporiums all crowded in colorful, bawling,
brawling spectacle to every side, some actually engulfing

the street so that pedestrians had to pass through some
shops and their clutter of wares and offerings just to continue on their way.

Chaos mingled joyfully with free enterprise of every
stripe. Memory stores huddled side by side with memory
erasure clinics. Plexbangers sold peppers, diehards, and
growlers outside the front steps to the local Watch HQ. A
Chinese restaurant rose next to the sprawl of a grill promising the best in alga-culture protein. Girls in paint and
flashy plastic briefs or wispy, holoprojected nothings
paraded their wares in front of the Church of the Pure
Stellar Light. A high-tech cyberprosthetics warehouse
crowded incongruously close to a Hatire Temple, where
a brother used a powermike in a floater chair to boom out
his harangue against the evils of technology. And everywhere, everywhere, there were people, crowding in
against one another, jostling, bumping, yelling, cursing,
begging, holding aloft their wares at two or three for the
dollar, a bewildering swirl of color, noise, and movement. Above it all, holosigns and animations flashed,
winked, glared, glowed, and strutted in endless come-
hither array.

Spacer led Thorne with practiced ease through the
crowd, threading past the B-Level Bazaar and through the
Tunnel of the Beggar, a shortcut he knew to Lift Three.

"We'll take a lift down to the Deep Warren," Spacer
told the bewildered Thorne. "Whoever was following you
won't know which stop you got off at and won't know if
we've taken a lift or not."

Thorne looked about nervously. The crowd swarmed
and murmured, jostling closer with each step. Spacer
watched the mark closely as they moved through the
crowd, wondering if he was detecting a trace of claustro-
phobia. He'd heard about claustrophobes, people who
couldn't stand being shut up in small spaces, and agoro-
phobes, who couldn't stand the press of large crowds.
Spacer couldn't understand either concept.

People like that had no business coming to Lison and
deserved whatever they got.

"This way, Mr. Thorne." They ducked left, squeezing through a narrow opening in the cavern wall between a ropet store and a dopestick seller. The glare of overhead light panels gone, the only illumination was the gentle spill of light from either end. This new tunnel was empty, smooth-walled, and smelled of dust and empty eons.

"What the hell's this place?" Thorne wanted to know. He was puffing hard, unaccustomed to Lison's heavier gravity.

"Most of the tunnels in Lison were burned out by humans," Spacer replied, hurrying toward the glare of light up ahead. "A few were here when we arrived, though. Some folks think they're natural. Others think there was another race here a long, long time ago when Lison had a breathable atmosphere and a decent climate. Maybe they built the old tunnels. Either way, most Lisoners stay away from them."

"But not you?"

"I don't believe in that superstitious nonsense about ghosts and ancient aliens, no." They passed several branchings in the tunnel leading off and down into darkness, emerging instead through a narrow crack in yet another cavern wall, this one encircling a broad courtyard centered on a massive black pillar running from rocky ceiling to polished cavern floor. They joined a handful of Lisoners gathered by the doorway in the pillar's side and entered when it opened.

The lift took them swiftly down the last kilometer to their destination, the bottommost cavern known to Tribon's inhabitants as the Deep Warren.

Seven kilometers beneath the surface, the Deep Warren was a vast, open space crowded with buildings, most of them the structures associated with Tribon's government and commerce. Tribon's main business district was here, along with most of the major hotels and the most exclusive restaurants and shops. The Tower of Equality declared Lison's de facto victory over Rigunmor in their fight for independence, while nearby, bathed in light, was the truncated pyramid of the Lison Miner's Union. A clutter of interlocking cubes and domes housed the main government buildings in the complex known as the Lower Hall. In the distance, near one of the cavern walls, brooding spires marked the Ortis Refinery, where the rhodium that was Lison's lifeblood was processed. It was always day in these caverns, but the light came not from above, where rocks lost themselves in shadow five hundred meters overhead, but from the buildings below, which dazzled the eye in brilliant constellations of regimented lights and gleaming windows.

This was the heart of Tribon, bustling and gargantuan, as crowded as the upper halls and warrens but with a sense of space in the arching, vaulted ceiling of the rock-bound cavern. The crowds were nearly as tightly hemmed in here as above, but more of the people they encountered were businessmen, mining executives, and stylishly cloaked government bureaucrats. The holoadverts were a little less intrusive here, the buildings larger, more substantial and more monumental in character, the streets broader and less susceptible to encroachment by surrounding structures. Spacer continued leading Thorne along the Plaza of Freedom.

"That's the Blue Star, right up ahead," he told Thorne, pointing. "Is that where you're meeting your friends?"

"Yes, but I'm not sure whether or not they've arrived yet."

"I'd have thought they could have met you in the Grand Concourse."

"There . . . are reasons"—he glanced about at the passing faces in the crowd—"that we can't be seen together, just yet. Not in public." He stopped, still looking about. "In fact, it's probably not a good idea for you to come any farther, son." He reached inside his cloak, extracting his secretary. He opened it and removed a pay card, a flat plastic card with a small numeric display screen, and used a stylus to make an entry. "This is your fee for guiding me down here," he said, "and a tip."

Spacer pulled out his own government-issue pay card and let the man press the transfer patches together,

activating it with his thumb print. Spacer, faced suddenly
with the realization that he wasn't going to get to go back
and meet the others, had to abandon his idea of running
some sort of con on the group and decided to settle for the
secretary instead. As Thorne completed the data transfer
and put his card back in his secretary, Spacer's right hand
clasped Thorne's elbow.

"It's been a real pleasure doing business with you, Mr.
Thorne," he said, drawing out the moment. As soon as
Thorne replaced the secretary, Spacer slipped his hand
beneath the cloak and plucked it from its pocket.

The mark never felt its passing.

Spacer stepped back into a side alley, watching
Thorne's receding back. It was just as well, he decided. He
didn't know what sort of game Thorne and his mysterious
associates were playing, and a con would have been
damned risky. Probably the best he could have hoped for
was an introduction and additional gofer jobs, and to hell
with *that*.

He looked at the figure now showing on his pay card's
account, and his eyes bugged wide. Two hundred Concord
dollars? He looked after Thorne again, but the man was
already out of sight. The guy had just given him more
money than he'd ever held at one time in his life!

Swiftly, he fumbled the secretary open, checking the
ready payment memory. Another fifty, and that was all.
Thorne had given him almost every dollar he had in ready
access. Spacer suddenly felt bad about taking the secretary
as well.

It was like . . . a betrayal.

Well, of *course* it's a betrayal, he thought to himself,
angry. You tunneled your way into his confidence, got him
to trust you, and picked his pocket. Survival of the fittest,
that's all it is!

But he felt bad, nonetheless.

Thoughtful, he was about to close it again and slip it
into his own cloak when he noticed a message flashing on
the secretary's inner screen. He tapped the display icon,
and a starship boarding pass appeared.

The pass would admit him on board the *Star Traveler* when she departed for Earth, three days from now.

A starship boarding pass!

Spacer's knees very nearly gave way, and he had to brace himself against the wall at his back and slide slowly to the pavement. With this pass, he could leave Lison once and for all.

He could see the stars. . . .

Reality reasserted itself. Suppose he did get on board. Suppose the goldies weren't waiting to pick him up as soon as he tried. Thorne would report the theft, after all, as soon as he knew the secretary was missing. "Grep!" The curse was bitter and heartfelt. There wasn't a damned thing he could do with the boarding pass. Nothing that would do him any good, at any rate.

He sighed. Anyway—and assuming his meals during the long voyage would be covered by the price of the original ticket—how far could he get on Earth with two hundred CDs? How long before he had to start stealing to live?

How long before he ran afoul of Earth's laws?

He knew next to nothing about Earth, nothing except what everyone knew . . . that it was home to fifteen billion people and all of them were fabulously wealthy, that the sidewalks were iridium and the buildings floated in the sky on antigrav inductors. Damn. He would have loved to have seen that. . . .

Although he rarely listened to it, Spacer did have a conscience. It was squalling in his mind now, demanding that he do the right thing and return the secretary.

Why bother? Thorne was an offworlder and deserved whatever he got.

But the man had been *nice* to him. . . .

For a horrible moment, Spacer teetered on the razor's edge of his moral dilemma. He was safe and free. Once Yapper or one of the other e-fencers he knew cracked the secretary's thumbprint security, he might find bank account gridlinks or other codes in Thorne's secretary he could use, even if he couldn't use the boarding pass. At least he could snatch that last fifty CDs.

But . . . Thorne had been nice to him, had treated him like a human being.

It was more than any of the people Spacer knew ever did. Here in Tribon, he was just another plexbanger, even to other plexbangers like Hookie, Cutter, and Squint. To Thorne he'd been a *person*. That was worth a lot in Spacer's estimation.

Arriving at a decision, Spacer swung back into the street and started walking quickly toward the Blue Star hotel. Maybe he could catch up with Thorne and return the secretary. He wondered if he should make up a face-saving story about how Thorne had dropped it . . . or admit he'd stolen it and then changed his mind. Maybe he could claim that he'd taken it to teach the offworlder a lesson. Don't trust anyone in Lison, or they'll steal you blind.

A few moments later, as he hurried toward the main entrance of the Blue Star, he spotted Thorne.

The man was not alone, however. Three other men stood with him, very close to him, and one had a hand on Thorne's elbow as though to keep him from running. One of the men was the tall, gaunt figure that Spacer had seen on the Concourse. As he slowed his pace, not sure what he was getting into, Spacer saw the gleam of a weapon in the tall man's ungauntleted hand.

There was no time to think. They were already leading Thorne at a brisk walk away from the hotel's main entrance and around the corner into a kind of narrow alley that led to the hotel's delivery doors. Spacer looked about wildly. Where were the damned goldies when you actually *needed* one?

He picked up the pace again, trotting ahead. Maybe these were the guys Thorne wanted to meet? But he was pretty sure that Thorne had seen and recognized the gaunt man on the Concourse and that he was the one they'd been trying to lose.

Thorne looked terrified. Even from fifty meters away, Spacer could see his pale face, his staring eyes. And there was that gun—it looked like an ugly little flechette pistol—pressed now against Thorne's right kidney.

Grep, grep, *grep*! What could he do? Spacer was
unarmed and certainly not very formidable. He had to go
find help . . . but he was held transfixed by the sight as the
three men slammed Thorne back against the alley wall.
One of the men, a wiry little guy with frizzy hair, was
shouting at Thorne, but Spacer couldn't catch the words.
Rough hands tore the cloak from his shoulder, pawing
through it as though searching for something.

Thorne abruptly tried to break away, running down the
alley toward the back of the building. The tall man raised
the flechette pistol with almost arrogant negligence and
squeezed the trigger. Spacer heard the shrill hiss of the
flechette cloud . . . and the thuttering wet snap of dozens
of tiny, high-velocity projectiles shredding cloth and
flesh. Some flechettes struck sparks from the stone wall
at his side.

Thorne's arms went up, his legs folded in mid stride,
and he struck the alley pavement, bouncing once then sliding to a stop in a fast-spreading puddle of his own blood.
The three muggers trotted over the still body. One nudged
it with his foot, while the frizzy-haired one stooped and
went through Thorne's pockets.

Spacer took a step back, his breath catching in his
throat. He'd seen some rough things in the streets and tunnels of Tribon, but never anything quite so cold and non-
chalantly evil. His heart was hammering loudly enough
that Thorne's attackers were sure to hear. . . .

As if on cue, the gaunt man turned and stared directly
at Spacer, face hardening as their eyes met.

Spacer gasped then turned and ran, ran as hard as he
could, ran as if all the devils of hell were baying close at
his heels.

He didn't stop until he was safely back in his own
neighborhood, two kilometers up and five over from the
grisly murder of the man who'd befriended him.

Chapter Three

DIANE RADLEVICH STOOD on a broken, jagged plain, a tortured landscape intermittently visible through the rain and the incoming purple-black, lightning-charged storm clouds. She felt the wind shrieking across the world's tortured surface, but only as a steady, gentle pressure, not as the deadly bullwhip's lash of hard-driven grit and ice crystals that it should have been. The readout in the window visible at her lower right indicated a windspeed of over one hundred kph, a full gale, with a temperature of five degrees Celsius. A mix of rain and sleet was falling . . . though perhaps "falling" was a misleading term for precipitation that was essentially moving parallel to the ground.

Then, with the suddenness of a wide-flung door, the storm clouds overhead tattered and broke, their edges limned with dazzling pink light. Red-gold sunlight glinted off crystal from the distant glaciers and the flooded lowlands. Beyond, bulking huge and vast, the flattened and turbulently banded crescent of Salamanca loomed ponderous in a deep green and purple sky, as falling stars spilled from heaven in flashes and streaks of gold. . . .

"Storm's clearing!" Diane shouted to be heard above the din. "My God . . . it's beautiful!"

"Don't shout," Ta Shaa Ta's voice said, soft but easily heard in her ear. "We can hear you easily."

"Okay." She lowered her voice. "Okay, sorry! This seems so . . . real!"

Ahead, shimmering shapes—immense, crystalline forms just visible through the vanishing storm—reared into the mist. Monoliths, each ten meters high. There were twenty-three of them, arranged in a vast ring half a kilometer across on that barren, sleet-swept plain.

Diane drew closer to the nearest of the monoliths, close enough to reach out her hand and touch it. The stone felt rough and slightly chill to her hand; it looked like granite, but it was shot through with veins of crystal, like quartz, but each line and thread was aglow with a soft, inner blue radiance.

Lightning stabbed, blinding, followed instantly by the crash of thunder.

"I'm touching one of the monoliths," she said. "It definitely looks like it's been artificially shaped. The placement is certainly artificial, though I can't tell if I'm looking at the ruin of a larger structure of some kind, or if this is more like a monument, or maybe a stone ring for some religious or astronomical purpose, like Earth's Stonehenge . . . or the Sacred Circle on Ixax. It looks . . . it looks like the builders might have deliberately shaped some of these crystal veins, though. They have a polished look to them, and there are places where some of the overlaying granite has been ground or chipped away to reveal underlying crystal veins. I can't see any particular symmetry or design to the overall patterns of the veins, however. The light is . . . fantastic . . . beautiful! I've never seen anything like it!"

She took a deep breath. According to the readout, the atmosphere was essentially oxygen-nitrogen, but was also thick with carbon dioxide, sulfur dioxide, ammonia, and carbon monoxide—a witch's brew of noxious gases that would have poisoned her if the breath she'd drawn had been a real one.

Standing beneath the monolith, she looked around, watching as the rain receded and the mountains—fantastic, jagged shapes made surreal by eons of wind and water erosion—emerged from behind the gray mist. It was hard to realize that she was not, in fact, standing on that storm-blasted surface. The illusion cast in her mind was that real.

"No sign of inscriptions on the stone," she said, continuing her survey. "No sign of tools or other structures anywhere in sight. No dwellings." She took a step and felt the rolling surge of another quake. Shards of stone cracked and snapped, thrusting skyward a few meters away. On the horizon beyond the glacier, a volcano squatted ominously beneath a pall of rising black smoke and ash. The quake grew worse, wave after shuddering wave passing beneath her feet. "The footing here is very uncertain," she added. "I don't quite see how the individual stones of the ring remain standing."

"Is there any indication of age?" Ta Shaa Ta's voice asked her.

"No. None that I can see here, anyway." She reached out and lightly stroked the monolith again, tracing one of the crystal veins, feeling the slick, cool hardness of the glassy surface on her bare skin. "There's no patina or oxidation on the crystal at all, and the faceting of the exposed edges is so crisp and sharp I imagine I'd cut my hand if the program allowed it. And I don't see anything else around here that looks artificial—nothing we could date through this program, anyway."

She looked up again. Salamanca's crescent was rapidly vanishing behind a boiling, black-green wall of incoming clouds, but she could still see the mysterious flicker and turn and pulse of the Lights deep within the purple-dark of the gas giant's night hemisphere. As she watched, the gas giant vanished completely behind the veiling clouds. It began to rain again as the wind picked up and lightning flared.

Nearby, a section of wet, hard-packed ground churned as though alive, and something glistening and bright, stiff and bronze and wire-thin like the bristles of a wire-hair brush, poked up from beneath the mud. It was joined by another . . . then a forest of them, trembling with the wind and the still-shuddering ground.

"Fulgivores," she said, "and pretty close." She knew she was in no physical danger, but things were going to get pretty interesting around here very soon. She could have frozen the program, but the idea for this descent into the Storm met-plan files was to get an idea of the dynamic of the place. Closer, more leisurely scrutiny could come later.

Lightning stabbed and flared, so brilliant and close it was blinding. Bleeds from the main bolt played across the forest of bronze-colored stems, crackling and hissing ominously, and more fulgivores began sprouting a few meters away.

She wondered if the guy who'd recorded this data had survived the experience.

"I'm coming out, now," she said. "I don't think I can learn any more like this. End program."

Lightning flashed once more, and then clouds and broken rock and wind-lashed rain were gone, replaced by the tranquil hum of electronics, the dark, curved, metallic interior of a v-sphere, and the cool, slick pressure of her gridsuit snug across her body. One side of the sphere was open. Diane unstrapped herself, swung her legs off the couch, and stepped out of the device.

"Welcome back, Di," Maricia Strang said, smiling. "You didn't see any of the natives in there, did you?"

"No, but I didn't call up that part of the program," Diane said, unfastening her gridcaster helmet and placing it, with its attendant tangle of wiring, back on the seat inside the v-sphere. Her red hair, blonde-streaked and impossible, as always, after its confinement, clung to her scalp and her face in a sweat-soaked embrace. "I thought we'd agreed this run would just look at the artifact."

"Of course, of course," Maricia replied. "I was just wondering if the file you'd tapped was general or limited-specific."

"Definitely limited." She brushed at the front of her gridsuit, half expecting to find herself drenched and chilled by the rain. The virtuality-sphere's simulacrum provided most of the advantages of being on that other world, and none of the disadvantages. "There was so much going on with the weather and the environment, I didn't want to be distracted by the local reception committee."

"Virtual reality," Ta Shaa Ta said quietly, "is no substitute for the reality we will face on Storm."

Diane nodded at the fraal, the only non-human in the room. Tall and painfully slender, the humanoid had pale skin so delicate it appeared almost luminous. His large, dark, unblinking almond eyes took in everything while giving nothing away.

"True," she said, "but it sure as hell will help keep us from being surprised."

"Not necessarily," Ta Shaa Ta replied. "A recorded simulation can in no way account for unforeseen circumstances."

Not wishing to argue semantics or philosophy with the fraal, Diane let it drop.

They were standing in the suite they'd rented in the Blue Star Arms on Tribon's lowest level. The rooms were ostentatiously spacious for Lison—luxurious appointments for well-to-do offworld visitors, though they seemed to Diane as cramped as her quarters on the liner *Golden Nebula* had been during her long passage from Kaventaar. They'd paid extra, a *lot* extra, for a suite equipped with a v-sphere. The open, silver-gray capsule, built into the common room wall opposite a bubbling algal pool, dominated the small room.

Maricia Strang, dark-haired and sharp-featured, watched with Jarrett Aylen from the small sofa by the vid wall. Ta Shaa Ta sat on the rim of the algal pool next to the waterfall, while Rom Verdoss sat at the workstation desk.

"So Dr. Radlevich," Verdoss asked, "was Storm as advertised?"

"It was . . . interesting," Diane said. "It's no wonder it was passed over during earlier explorations of the region. At first glance, there's not much there."

"Hard to imagine a place with conditions worse than Lison," Jarrett said.

"I don't know," Diane replied. "In some ways, it's not as extreme as Lison. I wonder if any Lisoners would be willing to hire out as guides—someone used to harsh, violent conditions?"

"Might not be a bad idea," Jarrett said. "Trouble is, every planet is different. Each one is unique and has its own way of killing you. Survival techniques on Lison wouldn't help us on Storm."

"Thank you, Mr. Verge Ranger, for those comforting words," Maricia said with a laugh.

Diane reached to her throat and pressed hard at the touch-release on her gridsuit, slitting it open from throat to groin. Designed like a padded wetsuit with layered microcircuitry, temperature gel cells, and feedback sensors, it peeled off her bare skin like rubber. Diane was well aware of the two men in the room and of their frankly sexual gaze as she peeled the thick garment from her shoulders, arms, and torso.

"Have yourselves a good look, boys," she said, grinning at them as she bent over to drag the gridsuit down off of her long legs. The hotel suite included a bathroom and two other bedrooms where she could have retired for privacy, but the sleeping areas were more cramped than the lounge, and the bathroom with toilet, sink, and vertical coffin of a shower was too small for these kinds of acrobatics.

Besides, she'd never felt much need for personal modesty, not after years of xenoarchaeological field work in wilderness camps where privacy was nonexistent. In any case, Ta Shaa Ta was always present, a definite inhibition to any rampant human libidos.

Kicking the stinking, wet gridsuit into the wall laundry chute, she reached for the towel she'd left on a nearby chair and began to scrape the sweat from her body. Hell, the way she smelled right now, any turn-on Verdoss or Aylen might feel in her presence would be decidedly short lived. She wished she had time for a shower, or better yet, an old-fashioned hot soak for a couple of hours.

That, unfortunately, would have to wait.

"What was your overall impression of Storm?" Rom Verdoss asked. "That, after all, was why we paid extra for the v-sphere. What effect will the local conditions have on our operation there?" He was a big, heavy-set man, hard muscle beginning to give way to fat, with ebony skin and snowy hair. His tunic, glittergold and black synthsilk, was stylish, elegant, and just short of ostentatious, as was the monocular he wore over his left eye—a direct link to stock quotes from the local Grid. The elaborate gold filigree edging his tunic and his money-conscious manner fairly shouted, "Rigunmor Consortium."

Diane hoped that wasn't going to be a problem on Lison, a world once ruled by the Rigunmor Consortium and still rumored to be on their short list for reunification. She still wished that they'd been able to leave Verdoss behind.

"Well, it's obvious we're going to have an interesting time just getting around there," she replied, shifting the towel's attention to her hair, scrubbing it dry to a frizzy red nimbus about her head. "The weather reminds me of what little I've seen of topside here on Lison—windy, stormy, and uncomfortable, but with a hell of a view. It' no wonder they named the place Storm."

"Is there going to be a profit from those crystals, do you think?"

"That," the other man in the room said, "is something we'll have to settle once we're there." Young, sandy-haired, and good looking, Jarrett Aylen was an operative of the Verge Confederation, a liaison ranger assigned to the Radlevich-Strang Expedition as guide, mentor, and watch-dog. Originally born on Aegis, he knew as much about the Verge and the political currents surging through that iso-lated corner of known space as anyone, and Diane was glad he'd been assigned to the party. Besides, he was cute, without the macho frontier bluster so many Vergers affected, and she rather liked him.

Dry at last, she dropped the towel in the chute and began dressing, donning the leather torso straps, leggings, and briefs she'd been wearing before her virtual descent into the local Grid.

Her session on Storm had been informative, well worth

the voyage to Lison. While the data from the old Rigunmor
expedition to Storm should have been available through
the Grid—and therefore accessible anywhere in civilized
space—in reality there were a lot of odd corner pockets
and backwaters of information stored on the Grids of various Verge worlds that could not be accessed from elsewhere. That had been why they'd all rendezvoused here on
Lison, knowing that old Rigunmor records must still exist
here, forgotten, unwanted, and unused since the Second
Galactic War.

Rom Verdoss had started things moving when he'd
turned up data entries on Bazaar in the Consortium, men-
tioning the Loman system and the world of Salamanca,
and its crazy, almost unknown moon called Storm. Those
entries suggested that there were reasons to give Storm a
second look.

The file she'd accessed was a met-planetological survey
conducted by the Rigunmor explorer team that had first
visited the Loman System in 2348, early in the Second
Galactic War. It seemed a little strange that in the nearly
two-hundred year history of the Verge, no one had taken a
close look at the Loman system, but there were so many
stars, any of which might contain several worlds. So far,
the human outreach into the frontier known as the Verge
had claimed the more pleasant, habitable worlds like
Aegis, and those worlds with definite commercial value,
like Lison. Loman, a typical red dwarf twenty light-years
from Lison, simply had nothing of obvious value to draw
commercial interests.

In fact, the Rigunmor expedition to the place had
reported that there was nothing there of value, no reason to
invest more time, effort, or lives there. Those reports mentioned that five Rigunmor surveyors had been killed
during their brief stay on Storm, and the expedition's leaders had never bothered staking a claim.

However, they also mentioned a native, nonhuman
race—primitives unknown elsewhere in human space—
and strange, crystalline ruins.

"Where's Thorne?" Maricia asked, glancing at the time

implant on her hand. "His ship grounded two hours ago. He should've been here by now!"

"Maybe he got lost," Jarrett said. "Tribon can be pretty confusing for a newcomer."

"I knew we should have met him," Diane said. "We still haven't seen any indication that we have . . . competition."

"Caution was indicated," Ta Shaa Ta said. "I sense a growing concentration of . . . awareness."

"Aw, don't give us that mindwalker woo-woo," Verdoss said with a grimace of distaste. "It's enough that we take ordinary precautions against being seen together here, simply because we can't afford to be careless."

"I think the cloak and dagger is all a bit much," Maricia said.

"Oh?" Verdoss gave a pallid smile. "Here we have Dr. Radlevich, a well-known xenoarchaeologist, already notorious—not to mention wealthy—after her celebrated work on the lost Finders Keepers cache. A celebrity, no less! And Dr. Strang, one of the Stellar Ring's leading xenoculturists and linguists, the woman who translated the T'sa *Saga of the Restless Souls* into Standard. Another celebrity! Add to that a noted Verge Liaison explorer-guide, famous throughout the Verge, as well as Thorne and myself, two relatively wealthy individuals with a certain shared interest in alien artifacts and art objects, all coming together in one place on this God-forsaken frontier. If certain groups, if certain *individuals* see any of us in public together, they're going to notice. They're going to start wondering about why we're out here and just what it is we're looking for."

"Okay, okay, point made," Maricia said. "Though that any other interested parties know what we look like, are here, and are looking for us. Even if they did, so what? We're pursuing legitimate research."

"Legitimate research for you, perhaps," Verdoss reminded her. "I'm in it for the money, a return on my investment. And I *don't* like the idea of having to share with anyone else. I'm the one who started this expedition, don't forget! It was my research that made it possible."

"How can we forget?" Diane said. "You won't let us."

The tension in the tiny room was uncomfortably high. Diane wondered, and not for the first time, if this expedition was going to end up a sacrifice to either politics or greed.

"Perhaps," Ta Shaa Ta said quietly, "it would be better to direct our efforts along more productive lines. I am growing concerned about Sennis Thorne. Dr. Strang is right. He should have been here by now."

Leave it to Ta Shaa Ta to find a way to short-circuit a growing internal conflict and get all of them thinking in the same direction. She looked at the fraal, grinned, and winked.

Strange, though. As long as she'd known him, she still didn't know if he understood those distinctly human facial gestures. He was a mindwalker, could read her thoughts right down to her soul if he chose to do so . . . and yet she could never be sure that he truly understood what he saw there, any more than she could ever truly understand him.

Still, she wished she knew the other humans in the group as well as she knew her fraal friend.

"Well, we could check with Lison Security," Maricia suggested. "They would know if he'd gotten sick and been transferred to a hospital or something."

"The less we interact with the local authorities, the better," Verdoss said. He caught his lower lip between his teeth. He seemed worried, almost agitated, as though not knowing what course of action to take.

"I can make inquiries along those lines," Jarrett said. "I'm on pretty good terms with the Lisoners." He grinned. "And they're not likely to react to me the way they would with you, Mr. Verdoss!"

"Not everyone on this damned rock hates Rigunmor," Verdoss replied. "As I recall, a majority of the population voted to rejoin the Consortium a few years ago."

"That was before they found out you people planned to take them back to the old days," Maricia pointed out. "I don't blame them for nullifying the results of that referendum."

"Ingrates," Verdoss growled. "Traitors and vandals. We *created* Lison out of bare rock and sweat."

Diane was about to reply that the sweat had been that of the people the Rigunmors had tricked into coming to this God-forsaken rock in the first place, but Ta Shaa Ta spoke first.

"That is not the issue here," the fraal said, again diverting the conversation. "We are not here to redress the wrongs committed on this world by either side. We are here to investigate Storm, and to do that, we need to make contact with the last member of our unusual group."

"I'll check with the authorities," Jarrett said. He reached for a small, portable gridcaster on the workstation desk, positioning it over his head and switching on the holofield in a thin, glowing band across his eyes. For a simple call, the full virtual sensorium of the v-sphere was neither necessary nor desirable.

Diane smiled at Ta Shaa Ta's designation of the group as unusual. His assessment was true enough, certainly, if a bit understated. She was worried about whether they would be able to work together at all.

The varied political interests alone put a considerable strain on the operation. Diane worked for the Terran Xeno-archaeological Institute, which, despite the name—a hold-over from its founding three centuries before—operated as part of the Galactic Concord. Ta Shaa Ta was her colleague, but he worked for himself, working with her, she was pretty sure, only because the partnership served his interests for the moment. Dr. Strang was from Skai in the Orion League, a fellow of Yin-Farrow University and one of the founders of the Universal Translation Project. Verdoss was Rigunmor. Thorne was from Earth. Jarrett, of course, was a Verger. While the expedition was technically being sponsored by the TXI, Thorne and Verdoss were the financial backers. Diane and Maricia were the expedition's leaders in name only; Thorne and Verdoss were calling the shots, because their money was making the venture possible.

Diane detested politics, especially when it came to research and field work.

Verdoss, as the Rigunmor never failed to remind them
all, had gotten things rolling with his original discovery of
the records on Bazaar. He'd approached the TXI, which
had in turn offered the expedition to Diane and Maricia,
who'd worked with the Institute before. Diane's boss back
at the TXI's branch offices on Kendai had warned her that
the political ramifications of an expedition to Storm would
likely be a problem. Thorne and Verdoss, clearly, were
pursuing agendas of their own, though they hadn't shared
any details with her yet.

It made her uncomfortable, this working for people
with motives unknown.

Still, the possibility of examining a new nonhuman culture, one unknown as yet to the rest of humankind at large,
was too wonderful to pass up. Diane's particular area of
expertise was Precursor races, those cultures which had
attained starfaring technologies thousands or even millions
of years in the past, then vanished, leaving nothing behind
but the empty shells and detritus of a long-vanished civilization. There was no reason to think that the ruins on
Storm were Precursor. Almost certainly they belonged
to Storm's mysterious autochthons.

Understanding those ruins on that bleak, storm-swept
plain, and the beings who'd built them, would tell Diane
about the entire dynamic of civilization, about what made
a species reach for the stars . . . or turn upon itself, cancer-
like, and plunge to extinction.

For Maricia, contact with a new species would give the
linguist another insight into the diversity of culture and
mind. Diane knew Ta Shaa Ta's motivations as well. The
fraal was interested—one might almost say obsessed—
with the idea of finding clues to the location of the long-
lost fraal homeworld.

Sennis Thorne, senior vice president for one of Earth's
largest import-export firms, was an avid collector of alien
artifacts and technologies. No doubt he was interested in
the Storm natives and what they might have that was new,
intriguing, and potentially profitable.

As for Rom Verdoss . . . well, he was clearly looking for

profit. Exactly why he was so keenly interested in Storm—
a world his own people had declared worthless—was still
unknown. Diane had asked him several times for more
specifics, but he'd never answered her directly. She'd considered asking Ta Shaa Ta to probe his mind for answers,
but she knew how the fraal disliked probing another sentient's mind without good cause.

Verdoss was going to have to confess soon, though. If
he had any additional information about what the expedition was going to find on Storm, they would all have to
know. A new and alien planet was no place to go blunder-
ing blindly.

She wished Sennis were here. Verdoss was driven
by . . . something beyond the normal Rigunmor obsession
with profit and loss, and it was a bit scary to think of the
expedition being run for his personal benefit. Sennis, at
least, had transparent motives. When she'd last talked to
him, he'd seemed willing to accept that the scientific ele-
ment of the expedition would need to operate with a measure of independence. As the other of the expedition's two
main financial backers, Sennis brought a measure of balance to the project's administration, balance that was
sorely needed if they were going to function as a team.

Diane touched a tabletop control, switching on a wallvid
looking out over Tribon's Deep Warrens. The Tower of
Equality rose from light toward darkness less than a hundred meters away. They were high up on the Blue Star's
main tower, and the rocky, shadowed ceiling seemed closer
than the brightly lit avenues, domes, and buildings below.

"Damn it all, *where* is Sennis Thorne?"

Chapter Four

T̲H̲E̲ M̲O̲O̲N̲. I̲T̲ hung against black night, glorious and golden and somehow disturbing; the craters and maria splotching across its glowing surface suggested the face and scowling features of a chubby man. Tiny flames fell from the sky, each a burning, minute tongue. Below, in front of a pair of square-cut towers flanking a winding road, was a pond where a strange, joint-legged creature, all claws and legs and antennae, was crawling onto the land. On the shore, a dog and a wolf howled at the moon. The sound, their mingled bayings, ululated through the night, a paean of infinite loneliness and mystery. . . .

Spacer placed the card on the red cloth he'd spread out on the floor before him, positioning it below the Star, the nude woman pouring her two libations into earth and water. His hands felt clammy, and his heart was pounding in his chest. The moon signified inner disturbance or disquiet, foreboding, even dread, and suggested a changeable and possibly deceptive turn in his affairs. Those tongues of flame, his grandmother had told him, were tiny images of a letter in a very ancient alphabet; the letter was called Yod and represented the hand of God.

The card's position was that of foundations . . . where he was coming from.

He'd already drawn the Five of Pentacles, its placement to the right of the Star indicating his past and the factors that had been holding him back.

Poverty. A boy and a girl in rags trudged through ankle-deep snow, the boy on crutches, the girl in a filthy, ragged cloak and dress. Behind them, unseen or ignored by the pair, through windswept snow and sleet, a brightly lit church window glowed with warmth and hope. The stained glass image depicted a tree with five radiant pentacles—five-pointed stars within circles. The wind moaned and howled, echoing now the howls of the dog and wolf in the foundation card.

The Five of Pentacles suggested either physical or spiritual poverty. No surprises there. Spacer had almost nothing but the clothes he wore and the holotarot deck given to him by his grandmother just before she died. He lived in an empty foamboard packing box in District B-5 on the Upper Tier, tucked away in one of the warrens of old mining tunnels branching off from the main levels of Tribon.

He took a moment to look up and down the Street of the Tobbo Merchants, which, as was usually the case, was crowded with people, mostly the local residents shopping or working in the street markets. Most were miners, with a heavy scattering of algae wranglers, toppers, and even a few surface runners. The thugs who'd killed Thorne weren't in sight. Neither were the goldies. He wondered, though, if he should have come back to the box he called home.

Spacer ducked back into his box, squatting above the square of red cloth on which he was playing the cards. The array he was using was a very old one, called the Celtic Cross. His grandmother had told him the Cross was almost as old as the cards themselves and was derived from Old Earth itself, though Spacer wasn't sure he believed that.

Earth? What must it be like? For a long time, he'd questioned whether there even was such a place. Sennis Thorne, though, had claimed to be from there.

He drew another card, placing it face up above the Star, the position indicating hopes, fears, and aspirations.

Eight of Swords. A black-haired woman in a scarlet robe stood in a muddy field, surrounded by eight swords plunged tip-down into the soil, forming a glittering, steel enclosure. She was blindfolded and tightly bound, her hands tied behind her back. She struggled desperately against the ropes binding her arms, legs, and torso, but was unable to break free. In the distance, a castle brooded on a mountaintop, beneath a sullen gray sky. . . .

An inability to cope with the changes going on around him. Helplessness and indecision. A need for advice. But overall, more than anything else, *fear*. . . .

An uncomfortably close fit, that one. Fear? Yeah. He was still shaking from what he'd seen outside the Blue Star Arms. Careful not to disturb the cards, he crept forward again to look out into the street to see if the gaunt man or his accomplices had somehow managed to follow him. Nothing.

Returning to his place, he pulled the next card from the deck, laying it to the left of the Star, indicating the near future.

The Three of Machines, reversed. Spacer turned the card upside down as he flipped it over and placed it on the cloth. The projected holoimage of three barefooted, barebreasted women in fluttering, translucent gowns, holding aloft a trio of tiny, complex mechanisms of some kind, was inverted. In that position, the women appeared to be plunging headlong into a black abyss, their mouths opened wide in shrill screams. . . .

Spacer shared his grandmother's distrust of the so-called new suits of the tarot, the cards added to the traditional deck of seventy-two only within the last few centuries. Still, he knew the imagery of those cards, and only rarely culled them from the deck before a reading. This one seemed to have a bearing on his life right now.

The Three of Machines reversed could mean a disagreement, an argument, or a betrayal of some kind. It could also indicate the break-up of a group of people working together.

Spacer knew what *that* was about. For the past five years he'd been a member of the Ejees, one of the hundreds of plexgangs roaming Tribon's mid and upper levels. The gang name was slang for *egistron*, a deadly, nocturnal flying hunter native to the Verge world of Alaundril in the Tendril system. The name fit, at least so far as they were concerned. They considered themselves the supreme dark-adapted predators of Lison's tangled warrens.

Lately, though, Spacer had been feeling out of place, as though he simply didn't belong. There had to be more than hardscrabble, tunnelrunner existence, more than marks and picked pockets and a few Concord dollars at the end of it all, most of which went to pay the "taxes" levied on the gang by the authorities. Everyone in Lison, even tunnel rats and plexbangers, had to pay for the air they breathed and the water they used.

The Star was definitely his card, speaking of the future, of faith, of what could be, and more, of life with a point, a sense of meaning.

The next card would indicate the forces arrayed against him, and would be placed across the Star.

The Six of Machines. A man in white struggled with a black-cloaked figure who'd grabbed him from behind, his arm circling the man's throat. A jeweled dagger flashed in the assailant's free hand. In the distance, just visible in the night by the silvered glow of the moon, a pyramid was flanked by paired sphinxes. On the ground at the men's feet, six small orreries with glittering eyes at their centers clicked and buzzed, watching and somehow malevolent.

As the card dropped crossways across the Star, entering that card's holoprojection, the two scenes interpenetrated then changed, mingling. Now it was the woman grabbed from behind and threatened with the knife, her water containers fallen to the banks of the pond, empty now. Her hands clawed at the arm of her attacker across her throat.

In the sky, the Star's blue light dimmed and wavered, its hope now uncertain. The six mechanisms clicked and ratcheted at her feet as machine eyes impassively watched the struggle. . . .

Spacer's breath caught in his throat. The Six of Machines could mean a sneak attack, a betrayal of some kind, or an unexpected setback. The usual interpretation, though, was that there were powerful and unseen forces set against him . . . a bureaucracy, hidden enemies, the government, or other official powers. To have that card come up as the indicator of forces arrayed against him was disturbing in itself. Taken with the other cards that had come up so far . . .

Spacer was terrified. Leaning back against the rough stone wall of the tunnel, he closed his eyes and sighed. "I want off this rock."

The next card would tell him the immediate future, and any new factors that would be influencing him. His fingers brushed the top of the card, trembling slightly, then he drew back.

No, he thought. Sometimes it's better *not* to know.

But could he not look at all? Wasn't it better to be prepared?

Spacer was trying to decide whether he could summon the will to look at that fateful card when a shadow fell across the mouth of the box, startling him. He crouched, moving back, fists clenched.

"Spacer!" a familiar voice cried, tight with urgency, and maybe some fear as well. "What are you doing *here*?"

It was Hookie, one of the senior members of the Ejees. He was a heavy-set, chunky youth with the threadbare beginnings of a beard. His left wrist ended in a crude, steel and plastic prosthetic, the result of a cave-in in Mine 935 where he'd been working as a pitchboy three years back.

He used the hook now to snag Spacer's left arm and drag him toward the mouth of the packing crate. "Man, you gotta get outta here!"

Spacer swept his hand across the cards so carefully laid out in the first stages of the Celtic Cross, scooping them up, suppressing their holoimaging glow. He didn't want Hookie or anyone else to see the uncomfortable future he'd been revealing for himself there. Stacking all of the cards together, he wrapped them swiftly in the red cloth, grabbed his cloak, and let himself be pulled out into the street.

"What's the idea, Hookie?" he said, tucking the red bundle into his belt pouch and adjusting the cloak to conceal it. "You scared me to death!"

"Yeah, well, you outta be scared. They're after you, man!"

The gaunt-looking man . . . "Who? Who's after me?"

"The goldies, washbrain! There's a general call out for ya, and they *know* where ya live! C'mon!"

Spacer hurried through the crowded street close on Hookie's heels. They made their way down the Street of the Tobbo Merchants, then hung a left and a down toward the Miner's Hole.

The Miner's Hole was a huge bubble in the solid rock, once a major shaft head above a rich iridium-rhodium vein. When the vein was tapped out, the offices and supply caves ringing the bubble were converted to dwellings and thousands more were added. The walls of the bubble were now pocked from floor to ceiling with cave mouths, some brightly lit from within, others dark, and across them all wound a spider's web of stairs and scaffoldings affording access. At the center of the bubble, within a ring of shops and market stalls, was a thirty-meter algae pool, green and bubbling, surrounding a central kiosk with a nullhead newsvid.

Normally, the newsvid would have been projecting some random burbling of color and light in abstract display. Now, though, the holoprojector was displaying Spacer's head, a titanic image ten meters high, slowly rotating at the center of the cavern like the image of some vast, primitive deity.

As they emerged from the descending tunnel, a voice was booming from somewhere in the cavern rocks overhead. ". . . is considered armed and dangerous. All citizens are urged to cooperate in his apprehension, but extreme care must be exercised. He has killed at least one man already.

"Repeating. This man is Kai St. Cyr, a tunnelrunner and banger who has frequently operated on the upper levels, preying on offworlders through pickpocketing, robbery, and con. Two hours ago, he broke through a security fence on the upper level and entered the Grand Concourse."

As the voice spoke, windows opened beneath the slow-turning image of Spacer's head, showing scenes recorded by security cameras or, more likely, goldie floater eyes. He saw himself barging past the goldie at the gate, saw himself walk up to Sennis Thorne at the information display, saw himself following Thorne through customs and security.

"St. Cyr apparently gained the confidence of an off-world businessman, led him to an alley in the lower plex levels, and murdered him with a flechette pistol. The apparent motive was robbery.

"St. Cyr is twelve years old, with blond hair and gray eyes. He is 175 centimeters tall and masses 68 kilos. The Tribon Authority has posted a reward of five thousand Concord dollars for information leading to his capture. Kai St. Cyr is considered armed and dangerous. All citizens are urged . . ."

"I didn't kill anybody!" he said.

"Isn't that you up there with the offie?"

"Yeah, but I didn't *kill* the guy! I saw who did it, though. Three guys—"

"Huh! They're gonna believe that!" He snickered, then added, "Mr. *St. Cyr*."

"What are you laughing at?"

"That's some name! No wonder you took a handle like 'Spacer'!"

"Abort, Hookie. Leave it alone."

"Yeah, yeah. Anything you say, *Kai*." He snorted, then added, "We gotta get you outta sight, kid. Maybe even outta the plex!"

"But I didn't do it!"

"So? You think the goldies give a crawlie's tailhole what you have to say about it?" He pointed at the image. "This is coming out of the Tower, you know."

The Tower of Equality, down on the lower level next to the government complex, served as the communications nexus for all Tribon, broadcasting news and allowing Tribon's citizens to link with each other and with their government representatives. Right now, most of Tribon's citizens would be seeing his face and hearing that message on their secretaries, personal workstations, gauntlets, or directly through their skull jacks. And for nullheads—all of those citizens of Tribon too poor to own a secretary, a gauntlet, or a skull jack—there were nullhead newsvids like this one throughout the cavern complex to make sure *everyone* got the message.

Soon, there wouldn't be a single person in all of Tribon who hadn't seen Spacer's face and heard that he was a murderer. Spacer had always prided himself on his anonymity, his ability to blend away into camouflaged invisibility. It was how he'd survived for the majority of his twelve years.

He found he didn't care for notoriety at all.

"Grep, why'd you have to pick a vip offie like *that* guy?" Hookie asked as they crossed the Miner's Hold courtyard and entered another downtunnel.

"I told you, I didn't kill him!" Spacer insisted. "He paid me to lead him to his hotel, and I did." He decided not to admit that he'd lifted Thorne's secretary when they'd parted. That little piece of incriminating evidence would just convince Hookie that he had killed the guy. Spacer's breath caught at his throat. Grep! He would have to get rid of the secretary and fast. If the goldies caught him with that on him, nothing would save him from lock-out.

Spacer's hands were shaking now, and he was sweating heavily. Murder was a serious crime on Lison, despite the fact that life was cheap in a world where casualties in the mines ran to well over a thousand a year from cave-ins and pressure seal breaches alone. Lison depended on offworld businessmen simply to survive—people who came to trade, to build new businesses, to invest, and most of all, people who came to buy the rhodium that fueled Lison's economy. Spacer didn't know what kind of businessman Thorne was, but he was definitely wealthy. If the authorities caught Spacer and were convinced of his guilt, they just might decide to dispense with the niceties of a trial and get straight to the sentencing. A crime like this was a sure ticket to lock-out: loading the prisoner aboard a surface crawler, taking him to a designated area, and unceremoniously shoving him out the vehicle's airlock.

The prisoner's best hope was that he suffocated in the oxygen-depleted air before he suffered too much from the searing acid rain or the sandblasting effects of Lison's day-winds. Rumor had it that before the sentence was carried out, they sealed a lightweight breathing mask to the faces of the worst offenders with an instant bonder. The mask had a couple of built-in high-pressure O_2 cylinders, good for maybe two or even three hours topside . . . long enough that your death became a race between the acid, the grit, and the intense surface radiation . . . unless you were willing to suicide by literally tearing away part of your own, acid-burned face.

Well, Spacer knew that if they did that to him, he would go out the hatch fighting, but damn it, he shouldn't have to go! All right, he might have to pull some community service or draw some hardtime hauling rocks in the deep mines for the theft, maybe even be put on a lox-runner detail topside, but he hadn't done anything worth a lockout!

"Look," Hookie said as he led the way down the new tunnel. "I got connections, see? With Kind."

"Yeah?" Spacer was never sure how to take Hookie's name-dropping. He claimed to know most of the pirates, rogues, and major criminals in Tribon, but nothing ever seemed to come of it.

"Yeah! I got it all set up, too. Kind's people are willin' to smuggle ya out of Tribon and get ya to Raphal. You'll be safe there, if you stay low and keep out of sight."

Raphal was another city in Lison on the other side of the planet. The place was said to be largely controlled by gangs and criminal groups, most of which owed some sort of allegiance to Thomas Kind.

That was when the alarms started going off in the back of Spacer's mind.

You had to watch yourself in any conversation with Hookie. He was a grade-one guy, fun to hang with and a good brawler to have at your side in a fight, but his story could shift and change from one sentence to the next, morphing to what he thought you wanted to hear rather than the hard facts. He'd talked his way out of more bad spots with goldies than Spacer liked to think about, but you could never be sure whether he was telling the truth or not.

What had alerted Spacer was a shift in Hookie's story. A few moments ago, he'd said something along the lines of maybe getting him out of the plex. And now, a few moments later, he was talking about how a deal had already been set up with Thomas Kind.

A couple of things about that just didn't ring true. For one thing, Spacer was damned sure that Hookie didn't know Kind personally. Kind was the Oberon system's most notorious pirate and rhodium smuggler, a man said to be on speaking terms with President Kevik and other high-ranking government officials in Lison. What interest could such a man possibly have in a tunnel rat like Hookie?

Even if he did, how could Hookie have cut a deal so quickly? Only a couple of hours had passed since Thorne's murder. And . . . what had Hookie used for money? The likes of Thomas Kind didn't smuggle people out of Tribon for free, and Hookie wasn't much better off financially than Spacer.

What was really making the alarm bells sing, though, was the partial reading Spacer had been laying out before Hookie found him. Several of those cards had spoken of a betrayal . . . both the Three and the Six of Machines, especially.

They were offering a reward of five thousand Concord dollars for his capture. That was a very great deal of money to a tunnel rat who made his living by stealing a few dollars here and there by smuggling small quantities of rhodium or tech, or running the occasional con.

Hookie was going to turn him over to the goldies and claim the reward. Spacer was certain of it.

"Where we going, Hookie?"

"Down to the lower level. Kind's people will meet us at the Ortis Refinery."

Not that far from the Lower Halls and the Lison Authority Headquarters. That settled it. He wasn't going *anywhere* with Hookie.

They emerged from the tunnel and were instantly plunged into the surging, shoulder-to-shoulder chaos of the crowded lower level. Spacer hung back a bit, letting Hookie get ahead, then took his chance to turn right and plunge through the crowd at a dead run, scattering pedestrians and shoppers as he raced down a side passage. Fifty meters in, he took another side street, and then another after that, cutting through one of the domes belonging to the headquarters of United Lison Mining, then slowing his pace to what he hoped looked like a leisurely stroll and walking across the Plaza of Liberty toward the Blue Star Arms. There were security cameras everywhere, and plenty of goldie flying eyes, too. If he ran, he was certain to attract the wrong sort of attention. He adjusted his cloak to show a fairly conservative green and maroon pattern, pulled it up over his pale hair, and tried to look like a government clerk or lower assistant out for a mid-cycle walk.

The big question on his mind was whether Hookie had brought in any of the other gang members. He hadn't seen any, but that didn't mean they weren't there, hanging back in the crowd as a back-up measure, just in case Spacer spooked and ran for it. Fortunately, Hookie wasn't that bright, and it might well be that he didn't want to share the reward with the rest of the gang.

Twice, Spacer ducked into shops or side streets and watched to see if he was being followed, and once he even doubled back on his own track a ways, searching the crowd for Hookie, Dueler, Squint, or any other Ejees. Satisfied at last that he'd given Hookie the slip, he began to look for a place where he could get off the streets for a while, and maybe think about what to do next.

The Blue Star Arms rose just ahead, a green and black tower of glass, plastic, and iridium-steel alloy.

The place where this nightmare had begun.

Now that he thought about it, though, that just might be a decent place to hide. The goldies wouldn't expect him to come back to the scene of the crime, nor would they look for a tunnel-rat plexbanger to hide out in the lobby of one of the most expensive hotels in Lison. He needed a bit of time to sit and think . . . and he decided, to take a look at the secretary he'd lifted from Thorne. He knew he had to get rid of it, and that he couldn't dispose of the thing through the fences he normally used, but just maybe, there was information in the thing that he could use.

With the fancy dress cloak as camouflage, he walked through the main door of the Blue Star and entered the lobby, a spacious area for Lison, with vaulted ceilings displaying holos of Lison's gold, blue-green, and scarlet-orange day sky. There was also a parklike effect with waterfalls, various imported dwarf trees, and bubbling algae pools interspersed with clusters of sofas, chairs, and computer station ensembles. Walking with businesslike briskness past the front desk and two men in civilian clothing who were almost certainly hotel security, Spacer found an out-of-the way niche among the pools and trees, slouched back in a sofa, and withdrew his prize.

The screen still showed the blinking icon that led to the starship boarding pass. Gods of the galaxy, if he could only take advantage of that!

The secretary, as he'd guessed, was an expensive model, a definite step or two above the dataslates most people carried. This one allowed a continual gridlink for communications and newsfeeds, full-vid telecom service, and . . . grep! *That* icon was labeled "AI," and that gave Spacer pause.

A personal AI! That was going to be trouble. Personal AI secretaries were limited in both scope and intelligence. Small enough to fit in a palm-sized case, and without the usual servos and remotes employed by the big Grid AIs, they were neither self-aware nor truly intelligent, but they could present a passable imitation of their owner over Grid communications channels and were sharp enough to screen calls, handle appointments, and fulfill most other secretarial tasks a busy businessman might require.

This one wouldn't know him and wasn't about to open files at his request, not without a password or proof that he was Sennis Thorne. In fact, it might very well use its gridlink to report him to the authorities. Spacer felt a chill. What if it knew it had been stolen and had already called for help? That would be a logical security safeguard, especially for a wealthy businessman. The goldies could be tracking its signal at this moment, closing in on him to pick him up for Thorne's murder.

It would be best, he thought, if he simply left the secretary here in the lounge and quietly walked out a back door. The goldies would find it and return it to Thorne's friends.

Thorne's friends . . .

They were in this hotel, somewhere. He wondered if they knew yet that Sennis Thorne was dead.

He decided to take a chance and check some of the other, unguarded files first. As long as he didn't trigger the AI by touching its icon or asking a direct question, it should be okay. At least, it couldn't do any more damage than might have already been done.

The next icon was labeled simply "Notes." He touched that one and blinked as a long series of paragraphs scrolled up the screen. He couldn't catch it all, but it was talking about a planet called Storm, about unknown alien intelligences and ruins, about the possibility of VoidCorp knowing about the Rigunmor data. . . .

He snatched as much from the screen as he could. Another world! He'd never heard of Storm or its star, Loman. There were several references to an expedition being organized to go there, and something about the Rigunmor Expedition of 2348. Five Rigunmor explorers killed. . . ?

What was this all about?

Later. No time now. He returned to the main menu and touched the icon labeled "Contacts." The screen lit with a list of names—Maricia Strang, Diane Radlevich, Rom Verdoss . . . None of the names were familiar. The address of the Blue Star was also listed, along with a room number—Suite 84C—and a reservation confirmation number.

Was that where Thorne's friends were now?

The information suggested a possibility . . . a risky one. What to do? Leave the secretary here and walk away, or . . .

Spacer reached beneath the cloak and pulled out the cards, carefully unwrapping them from the red cloth. He didn't have the time for a full reading now, and he would attract unpleasant notice if he tried, but he could draw a single card and see what it suggested. He used the single-card method lots of times when he needed to make a decision.

He shuffled, focusing on the need to know what to do next, then pulled a card at random.

The Knight of Cups: A knight in armor rode a white horse slowly across a plain, approaching a swiftly flowing river. He held before him a large chalice.

Anytime a knight appeared in a reading, it meant that a long-term condition was about to change. Drawn in isolation like this, the Knight of Cups suggested that he wanted something badly, so badly he could almost taste it. There was a hint, too, of wanting to move elsewhere . . . whether physically, spiritually, or literally. *That* was true enough!

The knight's cup. He was being offered something—a chance, perhaps, to fulfill his deepest wish, *if* he could reach out and take it. Or was it a chance to escape his more pressing problems?

No matter. He knew now what he had to do.

Chapter Five

SHE STOOD ON Storm's broken, muddy surface, watching the procession approach in stately, measured single-file. Maricia Strang, visible as a slightly glowing, translucent form, stood nearby, to her right. There were at least twenty of them, majestic beings moving with a steady, rhythmic grace. Diane Radlevich felt herself sweating, felt her breathing quicken.

The sky overhead was a mind-numbing complexity of blue, brown, red, ocher, and dazzlingly silver clouds, twisting, tattering, and changing shape against a greenish sky. The worst of the storms were past now as the world swung around its huge primary, but the winds were still fierce. Salamanca hung low in the sky, a ringed and banded giant in half phase. A scattering of golden meteors flashed, flared, then faded from view. To the north, a golden ocean heaved and rippled as though with a life all its own, ablaze in red-orange daylight. The volcano on the horizon, beyond the mile-high glacier wall, rumbled and brooded like a huge, purring cat beneath its pall of ash and smoke.

Despite the rumble of the volcano and the tug of the incessant wind, Diane focused her full attention on the Storm natives. She'd seen holostills of them in the Rigunmor Expedition reports, but this was her first encounter with them in a virtuality session, as close to the reality of meeting and knowing these creatures as it was possible to get without actually standing on Storm's surface.

They were known as Stormies or Stormers, or simply as Storm natives. If they had a name for themselves in their own language of pulsing, throbbing, modulated hums and growls, it was unintelligible to the Rigunmor survey team who'd recorded them. Each stood nearly three meters tall in Storm's point six gravity, and the single tentacle rising in whiplash flickerings from the top of the oddly shaped and thick-ridged "head," if that was what it was, extended for another three meters easily, though the stormies never seemed to extend the thing straight up. Evolved in a relatively low gravity field, they looked slender, graceful, almost fragile, but their stolid tripedal stance gave them a feel of solidity and firmly balanced stability as well. Their skins were soft and rubbery looking, richly colored in smeared patterns of black and dark blue-green. A trio of gaping, triangular mouths gaped around the base of the tentacle, but there were no other obvious sense organs . . . no eyes or ears or other recognizable features. Below the mouths, midway down the body toward the willowy legs, the sleek surface was broken only by what looked like a puffy ring of loose skin. Their feet mounted long, curved, and partially retractable claws. The tentacles, half again as long as the creatures' torsos were tall, were in constant, agitated motion, whiplashing back and forth, touching everything, as if the beings were feeling their way.

"Is that them talking to each other?" Diane asked. She could easily hear the bass hum and rumble of their calls, deep pulsings interspersed with occasional piercing chirps and shrills that grated up her spine like fingernails across a chalkboard. Each creature seemed to be speaking in several voices, a trilling symphony of harmonies and discordances, ranging from bass to almost inaudible chirps. Diane had the impression that the creatures were howling at the sky as they strode forward in their peculiarly graceful one-two-three rippling gate. "Or are they trying to talk to us?"

"Well, not to us," Maricia pointed out. "This recording was made by a Rigunmor planetological research drone. They might be talking to it. It's hard to tell just how sophisticated they are. They appear to have a fairly primitive culture, not even tribal, really. Just a loose association of some kind."

"That's what I meant. Those sounds . . . they give me the shivers."

"Infrasonics," Maricia replied, "has that effect on the human nervous system. The Rigunmor survey established that much of their speech, if that's what it is, stretches from infrasonic all the way up to ultrasonic ranges. The only way to talk with these beings was with some pretty sophisticated hardware that can record a broad range of the sonic spectrum, then translate the sounds with a tongue cracker."

A tongue cracker, Diane had learned, was a powerful AI program designed to handle translations of mutually alien languages. That, of course, was why they had Maricia along on the expedition. She was currently writing the AI software that would let them talk with the Storm natives on an almost realtime basis.

A good thing, too. A century and a half ago, the Rigunmor Expedition had managed to translate some of the language through painstaking trial and error . . . and had recorded far more than they'd ever been able to translate. Maricia's program, built up from the foundations laid down by the Rigunmors, was slowly filling in some of the gaps in understanding. With a bit of luck, the program should make mutual comprehension at least feasible without months of preliminary work.

The operative word was *should*. There were no guarantees with the unknown. Never. It wasn't even certain that the stormies were sentient, though their behavior and speech seemed to suggest they were. From the bits of translated exchanges that Diane had heard so far, the problem wasn't so much the translation of the basic words themselves, but understanding the minds behind them.

"So, what are they saying?" Diane wanted to know.

"Here, I'll cut in the translation subtitles," Maricia said. "It's pretty raw, though. Don't expect to get much out of what they say. What we're trying to pick up on here is the *feeling* behind the words."

Words appeared in Diane's line of sight, scrolling across the top of her visual field.

. . . FOOD . . . MOVEMENT IS <UNKNOWN> SOUNDS/HEARS/ UNDERSTANDS REFLECTIVE<?> HARD . . . WHAT? <UNKNOWN> IT IS WHAT <QUERY?> <UNKNOWN> <UNKNOWN> NO SOUND/ FEELING/KNOWING <UNKNOWN> IT IS AS IT IS <?> HARD FOOD/ NOT FOOD <?> TOUCH <QUERY?> . . .

"My God," Diane said. "How do you make sense of *that*?"

"We've been running it through a fuzzy-logic hyper-routine, trying to shake out specific patterns that aren't susceptible to straight-on machine logic."

"Well, you can't get any fuzzier than *that*," Diane said. "Why the garble?"

"Language isn't just words that can be translated back and forth. It's a window into the speaker's background, attitude, environment, senses, how he sees the universe . . . everything. The more alien the speaker, the more alien his worldview, and the harder it is to make sense of what he's saying."

Diane studied the aliens a moment. "No eyes."

"That's right. They *literally* can't see the universe, much less see it the way we do."

"Then how do they sense their environment?"

"Several ways that we know of . . . and maybe a few that we don't. Hear those high-pitched rattling sounds?"

"Yeah."

"Sonar. Like moabs on Derelliger or dolphins on Earth. At those frequencies though, you or I would probably be mostly transparent to them. If they actually do pick up an *image* from the reflections instead of just an echo—and we don't know yet that they do—they would probably see our skeletons and pockets of air in our digestive tracks and lungs most clearly." She laughed. "They might even be able to tell what you had for breakfast this morning."

"No breakfast, just coffee. Charming thought."

"See those faint lines in their skin, running from their heads down each leg?"

"Yeah."

"We'd have to do a medical scan or even an autopsy to know for sure, but we think those are lateral lines, used in sensing changes in atmospheric pressure. They could probably tell if you just walked into the room . . . or even sense your breathing. We also suspect they can sense electric and magnetic fields."

"That would be useful in that environment, I imagine."

"Definitely. Watch that one over there . . . see?" Flickering things seemed to unfold from the puffy ring on the creature's body, like the petals of flowers. "See the body pouch open up?"

"I'm not sure what I saw."

"Those skin folds cover a number of what are probably different sense organs—smell and taste, possibly various chemosenses. That would be like taste or smell, but probably far more discriminating, more sensitive. One researcher I've talked to about this thinks they might create an odor map of some kind and actually "see" by the odors given off by everything around them, from other stormies to a wet rock.

"We think they are . . . well, for lack of a better word, herbivores . . . but the plants they eat are organisms like the fulgivores you saw in your first virtuality session. The plants attract lightning strikes and store electrical energy in organic batteries. The stormies find the batteries, dig them up, and eat them."

"With all three mouths?"

"Those aren't feeding mouths. They're for breathing and for projecting sound across a three-hundred sixty degree arc. There's a single cloaca down between the legs that serves as both mouth and anus, complete with a prehensile tongue they use as a feeding tentacle."

Diane made a face behind the embrace of her gridcaster helmet. "How pleasant."

"The tongue might also be a sex organ, though we don't yet know how they reproduce. We're not even sure if they're sexual."

She watched the blind, howling creatures a moment longer, before her gaze strayed from the nearest of the stormies to the dramatic sky behind them. It seemed like the cruelest of ironies that these beings should live in such a spectacularly beautiful place and not be able to see that beauty. Sound waves might paint images of rocks or other stormies or even falling rain, but they could never leave Storm's atmosphere to reveal the spectacular beauty of vast, ringed and banded Salamanca, or the huge, bright-glowing ember that was Loman.

Still, if what Maricia said was true, the stormies might have a richer and broader range of senses than humans. Diane wondered how keen their thought was, how sharp their minds.

. . . FOOD WHERE<QUERY?> <UNKNOWN> <UNKNOWN> IS GOING <UNKNOWN> EMPTY/NOT/NULL <UNKNOWN> HARD/REFLECTIVE<?> GROUP/GATHERING <UNKNOWN> DIG <EXCLAMATION!>

Two of the creatures moved across the muddy plain to a patch of fulgivore bristles and began digging with their large, curved claws. They appeared to be working together. At one point, they intertwined their head tentacles together in order to brace one another as they deepened the hole. In a few moments, they'd uncovered a clump of what looked like potatoes or tubers of some sort. The creatures rooted them out with delicate swipes of their feet. Other stormies began gathering around, and Diane saw one use its tongue-tentacle to pass tubers around to others before drawing one fat one up into a pouch at the bottom of its torso.

Cooperation. Social behavior. Communication.

62   WILLIAM H. KEITH, JR.

They would have to assume that the Storm natives were at least as bright as humans, even if the nature of that intelligence was radically different.

"We'd better pull out," Maricia said. "It's getting late, and . . ."

"And Sennis still hasn't showed," Diane added. The people outside the simulation would have broken in and alerted them if Thorne had turned up. "I'm beginning to think we should—" She stopped, holding up her hand. She'd taken a couple of steps toward the nearest stormie but encountered some sort of invisible barrier. It wasn't solid like a wall but had a rubbery, yielding feel to it. She reached higher, then to either side, feeling the stubborn, invisible resistance to her touch. "Hey, Maricia? What's this?"

"I don't know." Maricia had encountered the barrier as well. "Strange. There aren't supposed to be any barrier routines in this file. We should be able to just walk up and touch a stormie if we want to." Maricia leaned forward, taking another struggling step.

"Maricia, I don't like this," Diane said, stepping back. "It doesn't feel like part of the program."

"It might be a simulation of some defense the stormies have," Maricia said. "It almost feels like some sort of magnetic field, except, of course, that we're not—"

A sharp, audible pop sounded, and the invisible barrier collapsed. Something hit Diane, hard, a savage blow snapping out of nowhere. A moment of dizzy blackness, and she found herself sitting in the mud several meters away, head throbbing. At first, she thought she'd been struck by one of the stormies. Their head tentacles, lashing about, would make formidable weapons, but visitors to a v-sphere's simulation couldn't be injured unless the sensitivity parameters were set to allow it, and that blow had *hurt*. Her head was ringing and felt as though someone had just whacked her with a club. She started to get to her feet. Maricia lay nearby, face-down in the mud, unmoving. The stormies continued to move, probe, and howl, unaware of their virtual observers . . . or of the unexpected attack that had knocked them down.

Diane heard something behind her and turned. There was something there . . . almost impossible to make out, a whirling, crackling something on the edge of visibility, like a tight little knot in space, distorting the shape of the landscape behind it as it moved relentlessly forward.

Diane put up her arms. She had no idea what the thing was but knew instinctively that *this* was what had just attacked them. Or rather, attacked her shadow. . . .

Diane watched the thing's approach, breathing hard, feeling the tickle of the sweat gathering on her forehead. It was hard to keep in mind that she wasn't *really* on this alien plain surrounded by alien beings. She and Maricia both were safely inside the v-sphere in their hotel room in Tribon, watching the interactive display of recordings made a century and a half ago. Their cyberpresence shadows were in the Grid, but not their physical bodies. What was happening here could not really hurt them. . . .

The spinning knot of distortion struck her full-on and everything went black for an instant. She was lying on her back five meters away, blinking up at a green, brown, and orange cloud-tortured sky. She tried to move but found she couldn't. A window opened in one corner of her vision, displaying a cascade of raw, coded data, letters and numerals scrolling past too quickly to follow. Something was wrong with the simulation, but she didn't have the training to know what it might be.

She had to get out. They *both* had to get out. She struggled to a sitting position and saw the knot of twisted distortion hovering above Maricia's body. Even without true form or substance, it radiated a sense of implacable malevolence, almost of evil. . . .

The image of Maricia's luminous shadow-body was beginning to dissolve, flickering into the hovering vortex and vanishing into nothingness, pixel by pixel, as though the thing was *feeding* on her.

"End program!" Diane cried. Her gridcaster helmet ought to pick up those words and activate the emergency disconnect. She looked down. Her own body was beginning to dissolve, flowing away in a stream of glittering, luminous chaff.

She screamed, "End program!"

She was lying inside the cold embrace of the v-sphere. The space was cramped and confining, with Maricia's gridsuited body squeezed in on the couch next to hers. Maricia was between Diane and the sphere's open side, and she appeared to be unconscious.

"Help us!" Diane yelled, tugging at her helmet, dragging it off her head. Dropping it in her lap, she wiggled around and started pulling Maricia's helmet off as well. As she dragged it free, she saw a trickle of blood coming from Maricia's left nostril.

The helmet jumped in her grasp. There was a crack and a bright flash, followed by the thin, burnt smell of ozone and overheated circuitry. An identical flash crackled in her own helmet at the same instant, and wisps of smoke rose from the damaged helmets.

Jarrett's body filled the opening, casting both of the women into shadow. "What is it?" he said. "What happened?"

"An . . . attack . . ." Diane said, her slurred words thick and clumsy in her mouth. "Something . . . something hit us in there. Help me with Dr. Strang!"

Together, they got Maricia's unconscious body out of the v-sphere and onto the floor, and Diane was able to clamber out. Her knees were shaking, so weak she could hardly stand, and she had a diamond-drill headache chewing into the center of her forehead.

Ta Shaa Ta knelt at Maricia's side, spidery fingers hovering outstretched above her face, as though sampling her aura, her thoughts. "She lives," he whispered. "I do not believe she has been seriously damaged." The fraal looked up, meeting Diane's gaze with his large, dark eyes. "I believe you broke the connection in time."

"Thank God."

"We'd still better have a doctor look at her," Ta Shaa Ta said. "I can't be sure she has not suffered brain damage, and there could be physical complications I cannot detect.

We should have *both* of you checked." Rising, he turned and walked to the suite's workstation and began keying in a vidlink to the hotel desk.

"What happened in there?" Verdoss demanded as he entered the room. "We heard you scream."

"I think . . . I think it was a shadow attack," Diane said. "Something, some*one* on the Grid didn't want us in there." She described what she'd seen and felt, the spinning knot of distortion, the sudden physical blows.

"Sounds like a gridwipe," Jarrett said. "Probably hooked up to a booby trap or a shadow-triggered virus."

"That invisible wall we encountered."

"Yeah. Breaking that broke the virus program's shell and made it execute. Somebody doesn't want us in there." He held up one of the burned-out gridcaster helmets. An exposed, partially melted lead was still sparking in fitful cracks and hisses. "And they meant business."

"You mean someone tried to kill us?" Diane asked.

"Looks that way." He hefted the helmet. "I doubt that they could have through one of these, but look how the power surge shorted that circuit. If you'd been hooked in with a direct neural interface, it would have fried your brain."

"It hurt bad enough as it was," Diane replied. She touched Maricia's face lightly. The woman's eyes fluttered, and she blinked herself back to consciousness.

"What . . . oh, my head hurts," Maricia said. "What happened? The last I remember . . ."

"Looks like the Rigunmors don't want us snooping around in their old files," Diane told her.

"That's just not true!" Verdoss said. "These files were left here by the survey team after they visited Storm. There was no reason to booby trap the data, and it's been lying here in the Lison Grid, in storage and forgotten, for the past century and a half! There's no reason my people would have put a trap in there!"

"Yeah?" Diane said. "Someone did. If not your people, who?"

"A doctor is coming up," Ta Shaa Ta said, returning from

the workstation, "and a Grid technician. Perhaps he can tell us more about the attack. As for who left the trap in the first place, perhaps someone else is interested in Storm, someone with a competitive interest."

"Interesting idea," Diane said. She looked at Verdoss. "You know, Mr. Verdoss, you still haven't told us why you're so interested in Storm, a world your own survey expedition wrote off as unprofitable and forgot about."

"I . . . have my own reasons," Verdoss said, "but I assure you no one else could know about Storm. I suspect you two triggered some sort of security response within the local Grid."

"We were inside the Rigunmor Survey file," Maricia said, rubbing her head as she tried to sit up slowly. Jarrett helped her. "There's no way we could have triggered *any-thing* outside that file! The virus, or whatever it was, was in there waiting for us. Or anyone else who got too close."

"It must have been the Lisoners," Verdoss said, "the Lisoners and their insane paranoia about the Rigunmor Consortium's intentions here. They must have found the old data and decided that only Rigunmor agents would come back and try to access it, so they planted a virus to attack whoever showed up."

"I don't buy that," Diane said. "Hell, they could have just erased the files. Why go to so much trouble just to—"

"Because they're vindictive bastards," Verdoss said, interrupting. "*All* of them."

"That doesn't make any sense."

"I agree with Dr. Radlevich," Jarrett said. "Yeah, granted, a lot of Lisoners have no love for the Consortium, but what happened here happened before the Second Galactic War, over one hundred fifty years ago. In fact, most of them voted to have the Consortium come back during the referendum a couple of years back. It was Kevik and his government that overturned that vote. They wouldn't have any reason to—"

"Do madmen need a reason for anything they do?" Verdoss demanded.

"Even madmen are rational in their own assessment,"

Ta Shaa Ta said. "Whoever planted that trap had good reason to do so. In their opinion, at least."

The door chimed.

"The doctor," Jarrett said.

"I doubt that," Ta Shaa Ta said. "I called only seconds ago."

Verdoss walked to the door, squeezing past the people still huddled about Maricia on the floor beside the v-sphere. He tapped the flatscreen on the door and the imager switched on, showing a young man with dirty blond hair and an expensive-looking shoulder cloak standing outside. The cloak, somehow, clashed with the rest of the boy's garments, which looked dirty and a bit threadbare. He kept glancing to the left and right, as though he were nervous.

"Who the hell is that?" Verdoss said. "*Not* hotel staff, surely!"

"Open the door and we'll find out," Diane said.

Frowning, Verdoss palmed the release and the door slid quietly open, revealing the boy standing in the hall outside. "Who are you?"

The boy started and took a step back. "Uh . . . excuse the interruption," he said. "Are you guys friends of Sennis Thorne?"

"Where is he?" Verdoss demanded. "Do you have a message from him?"

"Uh . . . not exactly."

"Let him in, for God's sake!" Diane called. "Stop interrogating the poor guy in the corridor!" She glanced at Ta Shaa Ta, who was staring at the boy with a peculiar intensity. "Whatcha got?" she asked him.

"Interesting," Ta Shaa Ta replied, his eyes narrowing.

The boy stepped past a glowering Verdoss, brushing against him in the narrow entryway, and entered the room. "Uh . . . my name's Spacer," he told them. "I mean, that's what they call me, anyway. Look, I got some neg feed for ya. Mr. Thorne didn't send me. He's, well, he's dead . . . I saw them kill him, right outside the hotel!"

"What?" Verdoss snapped. "Killed! Who did it? Who was it?"

"Give the boy a chance!" Maricia said. "Spacer, is it? How do you know Sennis Thorne?"

"Well, he hired me to guide him down to the hotel, see? And, well . . . grep! You people haven't seen the local newsies?"

"The newsfeed?" Jarrett said. "No. We turned it off. Why?"

Spacer took a deep breath, as though bracing himself. "It's like this, see? I—I lifted this off Mr. Thorne." Reaching inside his shoulder cloak, he extracted a small, gray case, which he held out toward Diane.

She took it, flipping it open. "Thorne's secretary," she said. "You're telling us you stole this?"

"Yeah, but, well, I know this is crazy, but I was gonna return it. Really! But when I followed him to the hotel, I saw these three guys stop him right outside! One of 'em, I think, was following him. We saw him up on the starport concourse, earlier. He must've known Mr. Thorne was coming to this hotel, and they came down to grab him when he showed up. Anyway, they took him around to an alleyway beside the hotel. Looked like they were searching him for something. That secretary, maybe? Then he broke away and tried to run, and one of them shot him."

"How long ago was this?" Jarrett asked.

"A . . . a couple of hours, I guess. I ran away, see? Didn't know what to do! Then I found out the authorities are looking for me! They think *I* killed Mr. Thorne! But I didn't! Really! I didn't know what else to do, so I looked inside that secretary and saw the names of the friends he said he was meeting here . . . and this room number. The only thing I could think to do was come up and tell you what happened!"

Jarrett was standing by the workstation. He touched a key, and a holographic image appeared above the algae pool . . . Spacer's head, slowly rotating. ". . . the confidence of an offworld businessman," a voice said from hidden speakers, "led him to an alley in the lower plex levels and murdered him with a flechette pistol. The apparent motive was robbery. . . ."

"What's the real story, kid?" Verdoss demanded. "You didn't come all the way up here out of the goodness of your heart! Or to return property you stole." He reached out and plucked the secretary from Diane's hand. "Maybe you figured to run a con on us, huh? Get Thorne's security codes, maybe? Or get us to—"

"He tells the truth," Ta Shaa Ta said quietly.

Verdoss scowled at the fraal. "That mindwalking crap is getting on my nerves. You don't know humans, fraal. You don't know Lisoners like this tunnel rat! He could be lying up one side of the Galaxy and down the other!"

"No!" Spacer said, scared. "I'm tellin' the truth! Straight shaft and pure grade!"

"Perhaps," Jarrett said, "you should tell us a bit more about what you saw, about the people you saw with Thorne. Would you recognize them if you saw them again?"

"Huh? Sure!"

"Describe the man who shot him."

"Grep! I won't forget *him*! He was tall . . . taller than you. A real thin face, like skin over bone. Hardly any flesh at all, except his nose, which was long and kind of sharp. Don't remember his hair. I think it was real short, like a dark bristle on his scalp. Real dark eyes, far back in his head. And kind of a gray color to his skin. Gave me the crawlies, I tell ya!"

Jarrett looked at the others. "He's either telling the truth or he's a damned good actor."

"Sounds overly melodramatic to me," Verdoss said. "Look, we should call the local authorities. They're looking for this . . . person. We could get into trouble if we don't."

"Oh, man! Don't hand me over to the goldies!" Spacer cried. "They'll lock me out if they think I deleted an offie!"

"If you're innocent," Verdoss told him, "you have nothing to worry about."

"How long you been in Lison, man? The authorities don't care about plexbangers! They'll lock me out and figure they're ahead on their air quota for the cycle!"

"We're not handing you over to anyone!" Diane said sharply. "Mr. Verdoss, if Ta Shaa Ta says he's telling the truth, that's good enough for me. I say we let him stay and see if he can tell us any more about the people who killed Thorne."

"Agreed," Maricia said. "I'm starting to feel a little bit like a target. Someone killed Sennis . . . and they tried to kill us, too, inside the simulation."

"The two aren't necessarily connected," Verdoss pointed out. "I still think the Lisoners put that virus in the file."

"You're a Rig, ain't ya?" Spacer said, staring at Verdoss.

"I'm a citizen of the Rigunmor Consortium, yes," he growled. "What of it?"

"Nothin', 'cept maybe that you don't like Lisoners, much."

"That much is obvious," Ta Shaa Ta said. "What I am curious about is what you are trying to hide from the rest of us, Mr. Verdoss."

"Nothing!"

"Something, I think," the fraal replied, "something you've been carefully trying not to think about. I can't quite see it. . . ."

"Get the hell out of my mind, you fraal freak!"

"Maybe this is what he's trying to hide," Spacer said. He held his hand out, palm up, revealing a glowing gemstone of some sort. "I lifted it when I squeezed past him a minute ago."

Diane's eyes widened. She'd never seen a gemstone like this one . . . a translucent crystal as long as Spacer's thumb, twice as thick, and glowing with a rich blue, inner light. It was oddly shaped, with numerous facets reflecting the room's lighting . . . but most of the illumination appeared to be coming from inside that magically beautiful stone.

"That's it!" Verdoss shouted. "I'm calling security!"

He lunged for the jewel, face twisting into red-masked fury.

Chapter Six

SPACER WAS CAUGHT off guard by the man's sudden lunge. Clutching the gemstone tightly in his fist, he was picked up, carried, and slammed against the curved shell of the v-sphere at his back, the impact driving the air from his lungs in a heavy, painful *whoosh*.

"Hold it right there, Verdoss!" the other man in the room shouted.

Reluctantly, Verdoss released Spacer. The other man—the young, sandy-haired man who'd asked Spacer to describe Thorne's murderer—was holding a small but wicked-looking laser pistol, and he was aiming it squarely at the Rigunmor.

"You're making a big mistake, Jarrett," the Rig said, breathing hard.

"Maybe." Jarrett replied. He held out his hand. "Let me see that, kid."

Spacer handed the gemstone over.

"How'd you know he had that?" one of the women asked. She was pretty, with red-blonde hair. More importantly, she'd already stood up for him against the Rig's bullying.

Spacer shrugged. "I dunno. I can nearly always tell where a mark's got his stash, y'know?"

"The boy has considerable potential," a whispery voice, dry as dust, said. It was the fraal. Spacer had been startled by the sight of the nonhuman, and he was still having some trouble adjusting to his presence. He'd seen aliens before, certainly . . . but never this close up.

"You think he reads minds?" the second woman asked.

She was older than the first one, with dark brown hair, and she had a smear of what looked like blood on her upper lip. Both women were wearing gridsuits, and he wondered why one of them was bleeding. What the grep was going on here, some sort of virtuality duel? There was no explanation for offie tastes.

"Not consciously," the fraal replied. The alien was looking at Spacer, and those large, dark eyes felt as old as the Galaxy, old and wise and deep. Spacer felt himself shaking a bit beneath that gaze. "No . . . not consciously, but he could have considerable talent."

"For picking pockets," Verdoss muttered, "and maybe murder too, huh?"

"Shut up, Verdoss," the blonde woman said. She turned to Spacer. "Are you okay?"

"Yes," he said, rubbing the back of his head. "High grade."

"I'm Diane Radlevich," she said. She pointed at the others. "That's Dr. Maricia Strang. Jarrett Aylen. Rom Verdoss. And over there is Ta Shaa Ta."

"Uh . . . good to meet you." He felt totally out of his depth with these people, especially when the fraal's eyes were on him. He'd come here hoping to keep control of the conversation, to win their trust and get their support against the goldies, but things hadn't exactly been going according to plan.

The one called Jarrett was turning the crystal over in one hand, while he held the gun on Verdoss with the other. "I've never seen or heard of anything like this," he said, "but I'm guessing that this is the little secret you've been

hiding from us, and that it has something to do with Storm.
Am I right?"

Some of the bluff and bluster seemed to go out of Verdoss. His shoulders slumped. Ignoring the laser aimed at
his chest, he turned and walked over to the sofa, slumping
down into the cushions. "You're right," he said. "I was
going to tell you."

"Uh-huh, right," Maricia Strang said. "We believe
that."

"It's true! I swear!"

"Why don't you tell us the whole story?" Diane suggested. "The Rigunmor Survey to Storm didn't turn up as
dry as we've been led to believe, did it?"

"Officially . . . it did," Verdoss said. He looked up at
Jarrett. "Look, either shoot me or put that thing away. I'm
not very dangerous, and you hardly need to keep me at
gunpoint. I thought everybody had to surrender weapons
when they landed on Lison, anyway."

"Verge Rangers are authorized to go armed just about
anywhere," he replied. He clicked a switch on the
weapon's side, cutting off the thin whine of a power gen-
erator, then made it vanish somewhere beneath the long-
hemmed tunic he wore. He tossed the gemstone in the air,
where it flashed in the light, then caught it again. "This
came from Storm?"

Verdoss nodded. "It was found by one of the members
of the survey team," he said. "A planetologist named
Grigor Verdoss."

"Verdoss?" Maricia asked. "Any relation of—"

"My great-great-grandfather. It seems there was some
. . . disagreement among the survey crew, and he didn't
report what he'd found."

"Or he thought he could make more of a profit if he
helped certify the planet worthless, then came back
later with an expedition of his own," Jarrett said. "Is
that it?"

"Maybe." He sounded defensive. "It's not really important now, is it? Grigor Verdoss was killed at the Battle of
Calliope, early in the war. My great-grandfather and my

grandfather were both killed later in the war. And my
father was crippled in the fighting at Megalen.

"I learned about old Grigor's part in the expedition
about ten years ago, when my father died and left me the
passcode to a private bank vault on Bazaar. The contents
included a list of computer passwords and file names, the
location of some specific computer records, a printout of a
letter Grigor had left before leaving for the War . . . and
that crystal.

"I had it analyzed. I knew an assayer I could trust. The
stone is . . . unique. Grigor says in his letter that he thought
it was a fulgurite, though we haven't been able to confirm
that. The inner light appears to be generated by some
weakly radioactive isotopes that have been subjected to a
powerful electrical discharge of some kind."

"Fulgurite?" Jarrett asked. "What's that?"

"A mineral formation formed by lightning," Diane told
him. "If lightning hits certain compounds in the ground,
they can be fused into a crystalline mass. I've never heard
of one that looks like that, however. Usually, fulgurites are
kind of crusty and ugly looking, kind of like a fossilized
tree root."

"My friend said he'd never seen anything like it," Verdoss went on. "It may be quite valuable in certain engineering and electronics fields . . . but he said its value
simply as a gemstone—its beauty, its rarity, that unusual
light effect—all but guaranteed it would be priceless on
the open market."

"One of a kind artifacts usually are," the fraal pointed
out.

"We call them stormfires," Verdoss said. "There should
be an absolutely incredible demand for these, just within
the art and jewelry markets alone. And if they turn out to
be lucrative on the electronics markets too, so much the
better! My friend said that a half metric ton of crystals
might be worth as much as three billion."

A shocked silence hung in the air. Spacer blinked. Had
he heard right? Three . . . *billion*? As in Concord Dollars?

"That's a hell of a lot of money," Jarrett said softly.

"And a hell of a big temptation," Maricia added. "Why didn't your family cash in on that before?"

"We *couldn't*." Verdoss's mouth twisted, a sour expression. "The War kind of interrupted things."

"Wars have a way of doing so," Ta Shaa Ta said.

Rom glared at the fraal. "Yeah, well, Grigor said in his letter that most of the records were located in the Oberon Grid and could be accessed from Lison. That was an obvious move back then, of course, since Lison was a Rigunmor mining colony. Our people were just getting things up and running here, in fact. That was probably the main reason nothing much was done about Storm then. Oberon and the rhodium deposits discovered on Lison and on Leen were far more profitable in both long- and short-term. I gather the survey ship returned here from Storm and stopped to repair some damage. Grigor duplicated a lot of the expedition records and left them here on the local Grid. The records you've been running in those sims, Dr. Radlevich. That's why that virus you encountered couldn't have been left in there by him. He left those records for *me*, or at any rate, for one of his descendants. And he didn't say anything about trapping them!"

"So Grigor planted those records," Maricia said, "then went back home to Bazaar, figuring that if he couldn't come back, his son would."

"Yes. Only the War went on a lot longer than anyone figured it would . . . and he was killed, his son was killed, and *his* son was killed. My father knew what was in the family's storage vault. He tried to organize an expedition almost thirty years ago, but he was crippled at the end of the war and then couldn't raise enough money. The family business, you see . . . that's Periapsis Systems, the family business wasn't doing well. He desperately needed money, a lot of it, to maintain the Hold."

Spacer had been keeping quiet, unwilling to call attention to himself, but he turned to Diane and whispered, " 'The Hold'? What's that?"

"Rigunmor culture sets a lot of store by wealth," she told him. "A family's position in Rigunmor society is determined by how much money they have . . . especially as it's expressed by the family holdings, what they call the *Hold*. Isn't that right, Rom?"

"Close enough," he said. "Ettelkep, our Hold, the Verdoss estate you would call it, was in danger. We've kept Periapsis Systems going, but we desperately needed a new infusion of capital to put it solidly back into the black and to rescue Ettelkep from our creditors.

"Karpis, my brother, and Anjera, my sister, both came here four years ago to find the computer records on the Oberon Grid Grigor had talked about. They intended to raise another expedition." He shot a black, hard look at Spacer. "They waked right into the Reunification Revolt. Both of them were missing after the fighting . . . and presumed dead."

Maricia looked puzzled. "I thought that affair was almost bloodless?"

Jarrett chuckled, a harsh sound, like breaking ice. "The key word there is *almost*. A couple hundred Rigunmors were killed when the tapes were broadcast. Most were military personnel, but a few business people got caught in the crossfire."

Spacer listened, fascinated. They were talking now about recent history, history he had actually lived. He'd heard only rumors about the Second Galactic War, but he'd been there during the riots that followed Kevik's release of the Rigunmor Tapes.

Back in the Dark Years, a century ago or more, Rigunmor had run Lison like a vast slave labor camp, freely spending workers' lives for rhodium dragged from Lison's crust under almost primitive conditions. Many of those workers and their families had been lured to Lison by the Consortium's deceptive advertising, the *lies*, to put it bluntly, that had promised good working conditions and high pay. During the War, the communications relay connecting the Verge with the rest of human space had been destroyed during the Battle of Kendai, and Oberon had largely been left to its own devices. The Rigunmor Consortium had managed to keep a tight hold on their valuable

colony . . . but at the cost of relying more and more on
local crews to man the defending warships. In 2373, Lison
had revolted, and many of the ships assigned to keep the
planet in subjugation had changed sides rather than fire on
family and friends.

As strange as it seemed now, there had been little ill
will toward Rigunmor a century later when the War ended
and the Verge was again in contact with the rest of human
space. The events of a century ago were facts in history
texts, not a matter of immediate experience. In a referendum held in 2497, a substantial majority of Lison's population—suffering from unemployment and high inflation
rates—had actually voted to restore their status as a Rigunmor colony.

Somehow, though—the details still weren't known—
President Kevik had managed to get hold of a recording of
a planning session by Rigunmor Guilder representatives
en route to Lison. He had it broadcast all over the planet
shortly after the results of the referendum came in. Lison's
citizens had learned what Rigunmor's moneyed political
elite thought about Lison's people and their egalitarian
society, and how they planned to force a return to an efficient and *productive* colonial economy.

When the riots had ended a few days later, the results of
the referendum had been overturned, three of the thirteen
stellar nations of the Stellar Ring had recognized Lison's
independence, and Rigunmor's would-be caretakers of the
new colonial order had been sent packing.

So said the history sims. In point of raw fact, events
hadn't been quite that orderly, clear-cut and clean. The
riots had been brief, but they'd been savage and bloody,
fire and screaming in the night . . . and a nightmare threat
to Tribon's main air purification plant.

Spacer had been in the mob that had stormed the
Lower Hall and lynched a Rigunmor trader they'd caught
in the Justice Dome. His grandmother, who'd taken care
of him since his mother had died five years earlier, had
been crushed in the press of the crowd the day before,
during a confrontation in Miner's Hole between pro- and

anti-Rigunmor mobs. The rise of the United Lison State had been made in blood and fire. The fighting hadn't lasted long, but what fighting there had been had been especially vicious.

Civil wars—and that was what the Reunification Revolt had been—always were.

Spacer found himself looking at Verdoss with new interest. The man's brother and sister had been here that night. They might even have been part of the mostly native Lisoner mob that had killed Grandma. They'd died here in the fighting? Good.

So far as Spacer was concerned, the only good Rigunmor was a *dead* one.

And the history helped explain the Rigunmor's hatred of him in return.

Others were talking, and Spacer tried to bring the focus of his attention back to what they were saying.

"So, with Lison free," Diane was saying, "you weren't able to get the records you needed directly. Is that why you approached the Institute?"

"Of course. I'd already met with Sennis Thorne on Earth and convinced him to advance some venture capital on the expedition. He agreed to back me for a share of the profit, but we needed a ship and personnel. The stormies offered a good *scientific* reason for going back to the Loman system."

"And the ruins," Ta Shaa Ta said, "those monoliths, which could be the work of the Precursors."

"Yes, of course. You scientists get to study your ruins and your aliens." He pointed at the crystal in Jarrett's hand. "And I get enough of *those* to save my Hold."

"Is there even going to be a Storm Expedition now?" Maricia wanted to know. "I mean, with Mr. Thorne dead . . ."

"Of course there's still an expedition!" Diane said. "We have the ship, or we will tomorrow when they finish rigging her out. The funding has already been taken care of, hasn't it, Mr. Verdoss?"

"Eh? Yes, it has. Of course it has."

"What's the matter?"

He sighed. "If the expedition doesn't go as planned, I'm ruined. It's a simple as that. I'm ruined. My family is ruined. Don't you people see? We *must* go!"

"But to study the Storm sentients," Maricia pointed out, "not to save your precious Hold."

"What . . . what is this Storm place you're talking about?" Spacer asked in the long and somewhat uncomfortable silence that followed. "I never heard of it."

"Not many have," Maricia told him. "It's a moon in the Loman system, twenty light years from here. It's a hellish place and not many humans have ever been there."

"As hellish as Lison?"

Jarrett chuckled. "The kid's got a point there."

"Do"—Spacer swallowed—"do you think I could come too?"

Verdoss swore. Jarrett looked startled, then laughed. He glanced at Diane. "What were you saying earlier about hiring Lisoners as guides?"

Spacer perked up at that. "I can be a guide! I'm a *good* guide!"

"I don't think so," Jarrett said, shaking his head. "Storm is a pretty nasty place, and it *is* like Lison in some ways. But it's also different. More different then you could possibly imagine! And those differences could get us all killed."

"Have you ever been to the surface of Lison?" Diane asked Spacer.

"Huh? You mean topside? Uh-uh! You can get *killed* up there!"

"There, you see?" Jarrett said, nodding as though everything was now finally settled. "What we were talking about was finding someone familiar with surface conditions, who could help us all apply survival techniques he's learned here in the new environment. If you haven't even been up there—"

"Well, I haven't been topside, sure," Spacer said, "but I know what it's like. It's kind of drilled into every Lisoner's head from the time he's a baby, y'know? Besides—"

"Besides what, Spacer?" Diane asked. She had the most beautiful gray eyes he'd ever seen.

"Well, just because I've never e-suited and locked out, it's not like I ain't studied up on it, y'know? You get tired of the same old, gray tunnels, cycle after cycle, and you end up studying things that you see beyond the walls."

"You've not dreamed of going topside, however," the fraal said softly.

"Huh? No. 'Course not! That's a shortcut to suicide! What I really dream about is getting off this greppin' rock. Going someplace. Going to the *stars* . . ."

"That's all well and good," Jarrett said, "but it's no help to us."

"I *can* help," Spacer told him. He looked at the others, trying to hold down the intensity of his desire so that he could speak and not sound foolish. "Look, someone is trying to stop you. Maybe they're after those gems. Maybe they want something else, I don't know, but I saw them follow Mr. Thorne, and I saw them kill him." He pointed at the secretary, which Verdoss had tossed carelessly onto the workstation desk. "I think they wanted that. They didn't find what they were looking for, so they're going to try again. If they killed once, they're willing to kill again."

"He's right," Maricia said.

"You need me," he told them, "because I know what his murderers look like."

Diane looked at Ta Shaa Ta. "Do you think we should?"

"Hey, wait a minute!" Verdoss said. "You people aren't seriously considering—"

"Why not?" Diane said. "He could help a lot, simply because the environments are similar."

"Not similar enough, Diane," Jarrett said. He nodded at Verdoss. "I hate to agree with *him*, but I really don't think this is a good idea."

"The more people who know about this expedition," Verdoss said, "about what we're trying to find out there . . ."

"What do you think, Maricia?" Diane asked.

The woman shrugged. "We were already short-handed as it was, and now Sennis is dead. He can't provide the financial backing we've lost, but his brawn will be welcome, believe me! And, I don't care what Rom says. Someone tried to kill us in that simulation. I'm willing to bet they're the same people who killed Sennis. Anyone want to take odds on that? No? Then what he says is right. We need him for our own security."

Diane looked at Ta Shaa Ta. "It looks like you cast the deciding vote, old friend."

"I fear I still do not understand the human fascination with democracy and decisions by numbers."

"Two say he should come, and two disagree," Diane said. "Your vote breaks the tie, old friend, whether you understand us or not."

"Now wait just a minute!" Verdoss said, rising from the couch. "I'm still not convinced that this boy didn't murder Sennis himself! If you don't want to turn him over the authorities, fine, but we can't have him along on the expedition! We could all be murdered in our beds!"

This guy, Spacer thought, is trouble. Maybe more trouble than would make signing up with these people worthwhile.

No . . . Grep! They were actually talking about letting him come along, about a ticket out of Tribon, about rising up out of the docking pit on induction thunder and boosting for the sky, away from Lison.

Twenty light years away.

He wondered if that was a long way. The farther away the better, so far as he was concerned.

He remembered the Knight of Cups he'd just drawn down in the hotel lobby, and he thought of long-term conditions about to change, of a dream, a goal that he wanted so badly, had wanted so badly for so very, very long that it was a fire burning through from his soul.

The chance to seize what he wanted was here. He *knew* it.

But how to grab hold?

The fraal walked over to him, facing him, staring deep into him with those obsidian eyes. Spacer wondered if it were true what they said about fraal, that they had no emotions but could read you down to the deepest, blackest recess of your mind. One hand, the fingers spread and impossibly slender and delicate, raised and hovered just before his face. Something stirred behind that gaze, something cold and penetrating.

There was an unspoken question, however, a request for permission, asked without words and immediately granted. In that moment, Spacer didn't think there was anything he could refuse that emotionless face staring into his.

Spacer felt a small, cold tickle somewhere deep inside his brain. The cold spread, seeping from the front of his head to the back, a chill, burning trickle, like mingled ice and fire.

He tried to relax, tried not to fight.

A long time later—it might have been as much as ten seconds—the fraal dropped his hand and turned to face Verdoss. "The boy is no murderer," he said softly. "On this I place my thought, my heart, my reputation, my craft. What proof would you have, human, that *I* speak the truth?"

Verdoss gaped at the fraal, as though searching for words. "I wasn't calling *you* a liar."

"You were. Names, however, are not important. Realities are. Young Kai speaks the truth."

"Kai?"

"His name. His *real* name. Kai St. Cyr." Ta Shaa Ta looked at Spacer. "Is it not?"

Spacer nodded, feeling suddenly awkward, and wished he could disappear. "I—I never use that name, though," he said weakly.

"You may trust us both," the fraal told Verdoss, "or reject us both. There is no other ground."

Spacer couldn't understand why the fraal was siding with him so strongly.

"Just because he's not a murderer doesn't make this a good idea," Jarrett said, unconvinced.

"Well, *I* think he should come," Diane said. She hesitated then touched Spacer's arm. "That's if *you* want to."

"Huh? *Do* I!"

"I will interpret that as assent," the fraal said. Spacer had the impression that Ta Shaa Ta was laughing, though the dry and alien face was as empty of recognizable feeling as ever.

"We can't pay you, as such," Diane told him, "but we'll provide room and board, and if there is any profit to be made, you'll get a share."

"You'll certainly see something other than the tunnels of Tribon," Maricia added with a musical laugh.

"It sounds . . . fine."

He didn't care about money. He didn't even care about Tribon. At that instant, Spacer was aware of only one thing in the universe.

He was going to the *stars!*

Chapter Seven

"So," Diane told the others, "do we try using the simulacra again, or do we assume the next virus bomb we stumble across won't be as forgiving as the last one?"

It was hours later. The doctor had arrived, complete with a robotic assistant, and checked both Diane and Maricia carefully before pronouncing them whole and healthy. A repairman had come up as well, tsk-tsked over the burned-out circuits in the v-sphere, and then replaced them and the damaged gridcaster helmets. After a quick test, he'd pronounced the equipment good as new . . . and asked the group not to ride it *quite* so hard in the future.

Diane was simply glad he'd not added the cost of the repair to their bill.

"There is information in there we must have," Verdoss insisted.

"You want it?" Maricia asked, looking at him hard. "*You* get it, Guilder-boy. You couldn't pay me enough to go in there again."

"You could use the lightweight gear," Jarrett said,

waving a hand at the workstation. "You wouldn't be able to immerse yourself in the data like you can with a grid-suit, but you could see it, at least."

"I think we're going to have to do that," Diane said. "Damn. It was good getting to really experience what conditions on Storm were like."

"Someone is out to get us," Maricia said. "I, for one, don't care to make it easy for them."

The workstation alert chimed. Jarrett touched a key, and a holograph appeared in the air above the projector bar. Spacer jumped as the image steadied into the hard features and gold and black uniform of a Lison plexwatch officer. Spacer was out of the communicator's pick-up field, but Diane could tell he was trying to work his way farther back and out of its range. She reached past the boy and opened the door to one of the bedrooms. With a grateful nod, Spacer ducked inside.

"Ms. Radlevich?" the officer said, "or Ms. Strang?"

"I'm Diane Radlevich," she said, stepping into the pick-up field. She was pretty sure the police were calling about Thorne. They'd reported his disappearance shortly before Spacer showed up, and she imagined they were calling now to tell her they'd found the body.

Still, it was possible that someone had seen Spacer coming up to this room on a security camera. The poor kid was obviously terrified of being picked up by the local authorities.

"Ms. Radlevich, my name is Lieutenant Grady, and I'm afraid I have some bad news. *Serendipity* has been denied clearance to boost."

It took a moment for the statement to filter through her preconceptions. What did a ship chartered by the Institute for their voyage to Storm have to do with either Spacer or Sennis Thorne?

"Wait a minute," she said. "What are you talking about?"

"Your ship has been impounded and the crew placed under arrest. The routine customs inspection discovered a rather substantial quantity of uncleared rhodium aboard.

Nearly five hundred kilos. Rhodium smuggling is an extremely serious offense on Lison, you know."

"*Rhodium* smuggling!"

Jarrett stepped into the pick-up field next to Diane. "I'm Jarrett Aylen," he said, "Verge Liaison for these people. What seems to be the trouble, here?"

"Ah. Mr. Aylen. As I was telling Ms. Radlevich here, our customs people found four storage canisters in *Serendipity*'s engineering spaces, containing a total of four hundred ninety-one kilos of high-grade, processed rhodium ingots—almost half a ton. The ship's crew is now under arrest, and the vessel has been impounded, pending an investigation."

"That's ridiculous!" Diane said.

"Does that mean you're placing *us* under arrest as well?" Jarrett asked.

Grady looked uncomfortable. "Well, the matter has come up, actually . . . but no. The rhodium was found in an area normally kept off-limits to passengers. The customs warrant requested your arrest . . . but my department refused the request on the grounds of insufficient evidence. However, we have suspended your party's exit visas. I'm going to have to ask that all five of you remain in Tribon for the time being. We may need to question some or all of you . . . and there's always the possibility that some of you were in collusion with members of the ship's engineering crew." He smiled unpleasantly. "You'll be our guests here for the time being. We have quarters available in the Lower Hall, if you'd rather not continue paying the Blue Star Arms's prices for the next few weeks. I *am* sorry for the inconvenience, but this is a serious matter, and I must insist on your compliance."

"Did you say the next few *weeks?*" Diane asked. "That's outrageous!"

"I'm sorry, Ms. Radlevich. We're short-handed and our criminal caseload is backed up pretty far. There's really nothing I can do." He hesitated, as though he was about to add something, then changed his mind. "You have my number on your comm log. Call me if you have any questions or wish to make a statement. Thank you for your cooperation."

"Wait a minute!" Diane cried as he reached for a cut-off key. "What about Sennis Thorne? Have you found anything out about that, yet?"

"What about it, Miss Radlevich?"

"We reported him missing hours ago! Now it's all over your public broadcast network that he's been killed! Why didn't you tell us first?"

"I really have no information on that. Sorry." The holo winked out.

"Things have gotten somewhat inefficient here since the Consortium left," Verdoss said.

"I don't believe this," Maricia said.

"Captain Applegate has been with the Institute for twenty years," Diane said. "I can't believe he would have anything to do with smuggling. And his engineer! Kazuko Tamaguchi makes a straight arrow look crooked, and she wouldn't have anything on her engineering deck that didn't belong there. It doesn't make sense!"

"It sounds like a set-up to me," Jarrett said. "Like Maricia said earlier, someone out there doesn't want us going to Storm."

"Come, come," Verdoss said. "You're saying someone planted half a ton of rhodium on your ship, just to block the expedition?"

"You have a better explanation?" Jarrett asked. "Diane's right. One of *Serendipity*'s people would not have been involved in something like this. They would lose their transport licenses if they were caught in something like this." He looked at Verdoss, thoughtful.

"What're you staring at?" the Rigunmor demanded. "I wasn't trying to smuggle anything off this damned planet."

"Half a ton of rhodium must fetch quite a bit on the open market," Maricia pointed out.

"Not enough for what I need," Verdoss replied. "Not by a factor of three. And I resent that implication."

"Does this mean we're not going to Storm?" Spacer

asked. He was standing in the open bedroom door. He looked desolated, as if he'd been struck hard in the face.

"It doesn't look like it," Maricia said. "Damn! If it wasn't someone in the ship's crew, and it wasn't one of us, then someone *had* to have planted that metal. I'm betting it's the same people who tried to fry our brains in the simulation."

"And who killed Sennis," Diane added. "The question is, who's behind it?"

"Pirates," Verdoss said. Then he looked at Spacer. "Or local ruffians. Half of them are tied in with the major pirate gangs in this system anyway."

"I'm no pirate," Spacer told him, "and I don't know no pirates."

"We're not saying you do, son," Jarrett said. "Verdoss, you'd better let up on the kid. You want to hate Lisoners, fine, but do it on your own time and keep it to yourself. I have a real short tolerance for bigots."

"Even if he did have a connection," Diane said, "we've been talking with Kind's people anyway. They get paid if we make it safely out-system and back. Doesn't make sense for them to try to keep us here."

"Unless they know about the stormfires," Verdoss pointed out. "If anyone other than us finds out about them, they might try to beat us to Storm and get the stones for themselves."

"I'm sure there are enough to go around," Jarrett said.

"Not according to Grigor Verdoss. His letter indicated they were pretty hard to find."

"Doesn't matter," Jarrett said. "It is possible that whoever is out to get us is allied with pirates. Thomas Kind has the best-organized band in the Oberon system, yeah, but there are others. There's a lot of rivalry between some of the gangs. They don't play well together. One of Kind's rivals might be trying to block him by blocking us."

"What can we do about it?" Diane asked. "We can't pay off every pirate in the system!"

"No, but I can make some inquiries."

"I . . . I might be able to help," Spacer said.

Diane looked at him. He was holding something in his hand . . . a bundle wrapped in a bright red silk cloth. "What have you got there?"

Spacer opened the cloth. Inside was a deck of cards.

"We don't have time for games now, son," Jarrett said.

"This isn't a *game*." Spacer removed a card and laid it on the workstation desk. There was nothing on the upturned face but a tight, dark pattern of what looked like printed circuits, but as soon as the card hit the table top, an animated, holographic scene appeared in the air above it. Diane leaned closer, trying to see what the scene was. She could make out the figure of a seated man.

The Four of Pentacles. A man—a king, judging by his crown and the red and blue robes he wore—sat upon an elaborate throne. A city with towers and walls lay in the background. The image was strangely dominated, however, by four symbols, line drawings of five-pointed stars drawn on golden circles. One rested in the king's crown, and one was beneath each foot. He clutched the fourth to his chest with both arms, as though he would never let go of what was his.

"You want success and material reward," Spacer told Diane, "security and stability, and you're thinking about the impact of a new relationship or partnership on your venture."

"Holotarot?" Maricia said, one eyebrow arching high. "In *this* day and age?"

"Wonderful," Verdoss said. He laughed, a harsh bray. "Now he's a fortune teller! Superstitious nonsense!"

Jarrett reached out and picked up the card. The hologram winked out. "Very nice work," he said, studying it. "They look old. Where did these come from?"

"My grandmother gave them to me," Spacer replied, "a long time ago. She taught me to read them, too. She got them from her mother . . . and I guess they were just handed down in the family, going back to before they signed on with the Rigunmors and came to Lison. She always said they'd come from Earth, originally. And they *are* old—twenty-second, maybe early twenty-third century."

Jarrett dropped the card on the table again, and the man with the four pentacles reappeared.

Spacer swept up the card, dropped it back in the deck, then shuffled the cards swiftly and drew another.

The Nine of Cups. A fat, contented-looking man sat with arms folded, smiling. Above and behind him, on a curved arch, rested nine golden chalices.

Spacer looked at Maricia and said, "You have a particular interest in some highly-charged emotional events. You want personal fulfillment, though there's something in the way. With faith, you'll win through. Trust your self-confidence, your intuition. This one is called the wish card, sometimes. If it comes up in a reading, it's supposed to mean you'll get your wish."

Another shuffle, and this time he looked at Jarrett as he laid the card down.

The Ace of Wands. A hand, the hand of God, emerged from the clouds above a peaceful looking landscape—trees, a river, a castle on a hill. The hand clutched an upright wand, a living branch, budding with leaves and flowers that seemed to glow and pulsate with an inner light or energy.

"Ah!" Spacer said. "New beginnings! A *very* good sign. You want a new direction in life, a fresh start, either in business or in love. There may be a financially rewarding trip in the immediate future."

"Goodness," Jarrett said, grinning. He winked at Diane. "Now how would you be able to guess *that*?"

"This is garbage!" Verdoss said. "The kid's making up anything he can think of."

Spacer shuffled again, but paused, looking at Ta Shaa Ta. "I've . . . I've never tried reading for a nonhuman before," he said.

"Please proceed," the fraal replied. "I am most interested in this."

Spacer drew a card, his eyes widening when the image developed.

The Magician. A man in white, with a flowing red robe, stood behind a table and a profusion of wildly blossoming red and white flowers. On the table were his tools, represented by tarot symbology. There were six symbols—the four traditional ones: a chalice, a sword, a pentacle, and a wand; and the two new ones: a glass-eyed mechanism or mechanical device, and a glowing, white-hot star.

The Magician pointed at the ground with his left hand and held a short staff or baton aloft in his right. Roses and white lilies hung from a bower above him. The symbol for infinity turned and twisted above his head . . . or was it instead the numeral eight, representing strength?

"Wow," Spacer said quietly. "A major arcana card like this always means an important event or idea, something to pay attention to, and this one means something great is about to happen. It means new beginnings . . . and creative power, and that you have the power to create your own reality."

Throughout the reading, Ta Shaa Ta had been watching Spacer rather than the holoscene on the table. "Interesting."

"And for you," Spacer said, looking at Verdoss as he shuffled. He flipped out another card.

The Devil. A monster—a nightmare chimera with a scowling goat's head, a man's body, beast's legs, claws, and outspread bat wings—crouched atop a squared-off pedestal in the darkness. A reversed pentacle glowed above the beast's forehead between curving goat's horns. Its right hand was upright, as if in blessing, revealing a cabalistic sign—the ancient h-shaped symbol of Saturn—tattooed in rough flesh. Its left hand held a torch, the burning end thrust toward the earth. Before the beast stood a man and a woman, both completely naked, both chained by the neck to the pedestal at the Devil's clawed feet. Neither seemed bothered by their slavery but stood quietly, as though awaiting the bidding of their infernal master. Both had short horns growing from their heads and sported long, twitching tails ending in odd shapes—a bunch of grapes or some kind of fruit for the woman, a leaf shaped like fire for the man—as though their bondage had already changed them. There were mingled sounds of crackling flames, cries in the darkness, and clinking chains.

"Good God!" Verdoss gasped.

"Not quite," Maricia said.

"You do know how to win friends and smooth over difficult situations, don't you, kid?" Jarrett said through an incredulous smile.

"It wasn't me," Spacer said. "The card just came up!"

"What's it supposed to mean?" Maricia asked. Her eyes glittered with amusement. "What does it tell us about our Mr. Verdoss?"

Spacer took a deep breath. "That he's chained to material goods or possessions. That he's in a cycle where nothing seems to be going right, and there are unexpected delays or problems, or possibly major financial loss or trouble. It can mean bondage to something like fear or sex or possessions. It can also mean a wrong use of power, or maybe deceit of some sort."

"Tell me something," Ta Shaa Ta said. "If the Devil card had turned up for me instead of the Magician, what would you have told me?"

"But it didn't come up for you."

"Suppose it had?"

"It still means what it means. I can't change that. Bondage, materialism, deception, fear . . ."

"Do you really believe in those things?" Jarrett asked.

"Of course!" Spacer looked uncertain.

"Come on. Truthfully, now."

"Well . . . I know they seem to work, usually. I don't know why."

"Starships, artificial intelligences, contact with alien minds and civilizations," Maricia said, shaking her head, "and we still have people who believe in this stuff."

"Maybe it just means we're looking for something more in life than high tech miracles," Diane suggested. "Fortune telling cards, astrology, divination . . . that sort of thing always means a lot more about *people* than about the gimmick itself, no matter what it is."

"But it's such a waste!" Maricia insisted. She picked up the Devil and turned it over in her hand. "Look at this! Printed microcircuits. A projection lens the size of my little fingernail. Powered . . . how? By the your body heat?"

"And light and movement," Spacer admitted.

"Enough computer memory to hold not only a complete, three dimensional animated image with sound, but probably to create new images when you put several cards together."

"Yeah."

"Each card must have . . . what? Maybe half a gig of storage? Incredible technology for three hundred years ago. Hell, it's pretty slick even by today's standards. And it's being used *how*? For fortune-telling?"

"You do Spacer an injustice," Ta Shaa Ta said. "You misunderstand this device completely."

"Oh?" Jarrett said, chuckling. "Do the fraal have tarot cards?"

"Not as such, no, but we have devices that allow us to sense the current and flow of events within the universe, especially those that touch upon ourselves. We have devices that help us know our own minds. We are less interested in knowing our futures than are humans, and more interested in understanding who and what we are."

"Wait," Diane said. "You're saying that tarot cards are real? That they work?"

"These cards speak through symbols," Ta Shaa Ta said, "as does the human mind in dreams." The fraal reached out and plucked a card from Spacer's deck. He dropped it on the table.

The Two of Minds. A man and a woman, both nude, stood back to back in the deepening twilight, as though about to walk away from one another. Each held one hand out, and a small light, like a blue-white flame or bright-burning star hovered above each hand, illuminating their faces and casting sharply wavering shadows.

"Appropriate," he said. "In a sense, you humans have *two* brains . . . the left and right hemispheres of the cerebral cortex. You process language, math, and numeric skills, rational thought and decisions with your left brain. Intuition, feeling, and emotion tend to come from the right. This isn't universal, of course . . . and human women tend to be better integrated than men, which explains their greater reliance on intuition and feeling.

"Psionic powers in humans tend to be centered in the right brain . . . the primary reason that they do not submit well to statistical or scientific analysis. By speaking through symbols, which the right brain understands, it is possible that the cards act as a kind of focus for some extrasensory powers."

"How about you fraal?" Jarrett asked. "Do you guys go in for this left-brain, right-brain stuff?"

"Actually, we have three cerebral sections. The midbrain serves as a conduit and coordinator for the other two parts and is also the center for our psionic awareness. Our processing, you see, is organized differently than in humans. The model I've just described does not work well for fraal."

"You're saying Spacer can really read the future?" Diane asked.

"No," Ta Shaa Ta replied. "I doubt that any being can read accurately what has not yet occurred. What he can do is read people—hearts, minds, and tendencies. He can subconsciously extrapolate from these to tell you more about yourselves . . . and not what your future will be, but what it *might* be."

"Uh-uh. I can read the future," Spacer said stubbornly. "It's in the cards! I can tell you who your enemies are!"

"That might be interesting," Jarrett said. "Go ahead. Draw us a portrait in the cards. We'll tell you if we recognize the picture."

Spacer sat down at the workstation, gathered up the cards, and shuffled them. "What I just did was a single card reading on each of you—not very accurate, not very detailed, just a sketch of where you happen to be at the moment. If you want to know what forces are standing against you, we need a more detailed reading." One by one, he began laying out the cards, face down on the table. "I'm laying out a simple Celtic Cross," he said. "I'm focusing on whoever or whatever is opposing you." The array consisted of a central card first, with another card laid crossways on top of it, followed by four more cards to left, right, below, and above.

Diane watched him then glanced at Ta Shaa Ta. The fraal had been with her for a long time, had been through a lot with her, and she'd thought she knew the fraal as well as any human could. He still managed to surprise her, however, on an almost regular basis. Did he really believe in something as far-fetched as fortune-telling cards? She watched with considerable interest as Spacer turned over the first one.

"The center card represents your enemy," he said as the image sprang to life.

The Nine of Pentacles. A tall, slim, dark-haired woman walked in a rich garden. Nine golden pentacles bloomed like flowers among thick-clustered grapes on the vine. She wore a yellow gown decorated with flowers that recalled cross-and-circle female symbols. Her upraised left hand was encased in a falconer's glove. A bird of prey, chapeled and jessed, rested on her hand. Two tall trees rose in the distance against a gold-yellow sky, while a castle appeared against the horizon.

"That's one hell of a space pirate," Jarrett said. Maricia laughed.

Spacer flipped over the cross card. "This is what your enemy has been struggling against . . . what's holding her back."

The Lovers. Adam and Eve stood in the Garden beneath a winged angel rising from the clouds and spreading his hands in blessing against a sky ablaze with light. Behind the woman was the Tree of Knowledge, complete with forbidden fruit and a sinuously coiling serpent. Behind the man was a tree with twelve leaves. A high, steep-sided mountain rose in the distance, squarely between the two human figures. In a moment, the second holoimage merged seamlessly with the first. Now, the tall, dark woman in the first card stood against the mountain and between the two nude lovers, shifting first one way and then another as though unable to decide which way to go.

"The Lovers is about choices," Spacer said. "Your enemy has had to make some tough decisions in her life. Some of them are tying her down, right now . . . or maybe she thinks she made the wrong choice."

"Why do you say it's a she?" Maricia wanted to know. "That first card doesn't literally mean we're up against a woman, does it?"

"Not necessarily," Spacer said, "but that's what it feels like to me—a very strong, confident woman with considerable resources, money, and skill."

"Who can't make decisions," Jarrett added with a laugh.

Spacer glared at him but turned over the card to the left. "This is her past, where she's coming from," he said.

The Eight of Swords: The bound and blindfolded woman stood alone on the muddy field, fenced in by upright swords.

"Fear," Spacer said. "She was very afraid, once. Overcoming her fear led to her being what she is today." He turned over the lower card. "Her base. Where she's standing now."

The Seven of Wands. A young man stood on a hilltop, a living wand in his hand as he battled enemies at his feet. He had the advantage of position, but the issue still seemed in doubt.

"She's fighting for what she believes in," Spacer said. "She's battling against . . . competing interests, someone she thinks her enemy . . ."

"Us, in other words," Diane said. She thought she was beginning to get the hang of the cards' subtle symbology.

"Maybe." Spacer turned over the card above the others. "This is where she's going, what she wants out of life."

The World. A woman danced within an upright wreath, naked except for a purple banner draped across her arm and groin. The rich fabric swirled behind her shoulders as she spun, curling about her legs. She held two batons that she moved about as part of her dance, snapping them this way and that to the tiny ebb and flow of rhythmic music.

Surrounding her were four images—a man, an eagle, a bull, and a lion.

"The World?" Maricia said, reading the name of the card beneath the feet of the shifting, swirling figure. "She wants it all, huh?"

"She wants to go into real estate," Verdoss suggested, "maybe buy herself her own planet."

"She wants fulfillment," Spacer said, "achievement, self-act—self-actual—"

"Self-actualization?" Diane finished for him. She wondered how much of the card imagery Spacer had simply memorized from a book or grid feed . . . or simply learned from his grandmother.

"That's it, yes. She wants to be herself, growing out of all of her past experiences. She wants freedom, to be her own boss."

"Don't we all?" Diane said. "What's the last card for?"

"That's what's in her near future," Spacer replied.

The Ten of Machines. A man in long robes stood on a frozen, ice-locked plain. He held two of the glass-eyed mechanical devices high above his head. Eight other complex devices seemed to lock-in close to his body from either side, as though he were becoming a part of some strange and rigid, perfectly symmetrical mechanism . . . one part of a larger, more complex machine. His face was shining, and he looked radiantly happy.

"Okay . . ." Maricia said, drawing out the word, uncertain. "I give up. She's going to be eaten by robots?"

"They look more like floater eyes," Verdoss said. "Maybe she'll get picked up by security, and we can get on with our business."

"Spacer?" Diane asked. "How do you interpret it?"

"The number ten always means change," he said, "a change of position, possibly within some sort of large group or organization. It also usually means success or completion, so my reading would be that your enemy is going to get what she wants."

"Oh, great," Maricia said. "We haven't even started yet, and you're telling us we're going to fail!"

"She wants freedom and self-expression," Spacer said, pushing ahead, "but as part of some much larger enterprise or business." He looked at Maricia. "It means she might win, not necessarily that you're going to lose."

"Part of a large organization, huh?" Jarrett said, thoughtful, "like one of the major pirate families, maybe?"

"Or one cog in a much bigger machine," Verdoss said. "Maybe she's a rival in some other Rigunmor corporation. She's going to kick our tails, then get a promotion."

"You have enemies in other Rig businesses?" Jarrett asked him.

"Hell, yes! That goes without saying. Business rivals, competitors, hostile take-over attempts . . . There's this one company—Ad Astera Corp—that has been trying to acquire my family business for years. If I fail at Storm, they may get what's left of it. If I can't keep up with the debt payments. . . ."

"I do get the impression that this woman is in a kind of business competition with us," Spacer said. "Money *is* involved, I know that much. A lot of it."

"Well, Ad Astera's CEO is a man," Verdoss said, "Loran Denicek, a slimy bastard who'd sell his own mother to VoidCorp if he thought he could get a decent price. He's also one of the thirty or forty richest people in the Consortium. He hates my guts and I hate his."

"VoidCorp?" Spacer said. The name . . . tugged at him.

"One of the big stellar nations," Diane told him. "A commercial consortium, actually . . . like Rigunmor."

"Yeah, but if you think the Rigunmors worship the almighty Concord Dollar," Jarrett said, "well, you haven't seen anything until you've had a run in with the Corpses. Together they're richer and more powerful than God, everyone in their orbit is an 'Employee,' and they all have numbers instead of names."

"Oh, I've heard of them," Spacer said. "We call 'em 'Voiders' on Lison. I was just wondering . . ." What? Why did he feel that there was something important here?

"Well, we can be happy we're not involved with *them*," Jarrett said. "At least the Rigunmors stand for

good-old fashioned private enterprise, eh, Mr. Verdoss?
Mr. Verdoss?"

The Rigunmor appeared preoccupied, staring off into
space for a moment and unaware of the others. He shook
himself. "Eh? Oh, yes. Definitely." He scowled, as though
thinking of something unpleasant. "Look, we're not going
to believe this crap, are we? I mean, we can't base our
decisions on superstitious nonsense like *card* reading, I
don't care *what* your fraal friend says about symbols and
right-brained intuition!"

"Doesn't much matter whether we believe it or not,"
Jarrett told him. "It still sounds to me like we're dealing
with pirates, and Spacer's tall, dark lady in the garden
doesn't strike me as all that helpful."

"Maybe the symbolism is just getting too obscure,"
Diane suggested. "I mean, Spacer thinks we're up against
a woman, but it's not necessarily so. She might be a business competitor or just be an enemy . . . or maybe she's
just looking out for herself." She waved at the cards. "All
of this could really apply to anybody."

"Which, of course, is how fortune tellers, astrologers,
and other charlatans make it seem like they can work miracles," Verdoss said. "Ambiguity, coincidence, and selec-
tive memory. That's all it takes."

"If your enemies aren't pirates," Spacer said, ignoring
the barb, "then doesn't that mean you can talk to your
pirate contacts about getting another ship?"

A stunned silence hung in the room for a long beat.

"I mean . . . that's why we did the reading, right? To
find out if it was the pirates who were out to get you. If
it's not, if it's somebody else, maybe Tom Kind can charter you a ship. The different pirate families all do a lot of
charter work on the side. Some of them are almost completely legit."

"Out of the mouths of babes . . ." Maricia said softly.

"We'll still have the port authorities to deal with,"
Diane said. "Customs might try to impound our gear like
they did the ship. We'll have to move fast on that."

"And the local police don't want us going anywhere."

"The hell with that," Diane replied. "Someone's using the system to keep us here and out of the way. I say we get a little help from *outside* the system. Let's not just push the envelope. I say we tear the damned thing wide open."

"Chartering a ship could be expensive," Jarrett pointed out, "and if you do this, you'll never be able to come back to Lison."

"Look, it's a direction to move in," Verdoss said. "Personally, I'd rather pay a pirate to get us all off this rock and on our way to Storm than to pay room and board for as long as they decide to keep us here, all the while doing nothing! Jarrett, you must have some contacts. Private charter pilots, perhaps?"

"I know a few. You're in favor, then?"

"Absolutely! I say go! Go!"

"Hell, yeah," Maricia said.

"Agreed," Ta Shaa Ta said.

"Hey, don't tell me we're all agreed on something for a change!" Maricia laughed.

"We have one remaining vote," Ta Shaa Ta said. "Spacer, you are a part of this expedition now. What do you say?"

"What? Do I want to stay in Tribon or find a ship and get the hell out of here? You lockin' me out?"

"I assume that is an affirmative response."

"We'll still have to watch ourselves," Diane said. "Dealing with pirates . . . it's not like we can complain to the local business ethics bureau if we don't like the service."

"Trust me," Jarrett said. "In Tribon, the pirates *are* the business ethics bureau."

"Pirates are always preferable to bureaucrats," Maricia added. "I'd rather be shot than slowly strangled in red tape."

"That," Diane told them, "may be exactly the choice we're being given."

Chapter Eight

THEY STEPPED OUT of the tubecar in front of the Hot Nose. Spacer looked up and down the street, scanning the crowds moving along the walkways in shoulder-to-shoulder mobs. No goldies . . . and no sign of his friends. His *former* friends, he corrected himself.

He still wasn't sure it was a good idea to be out on the streets with the authorities searching for him. The constant public broadcast of his image had ceased, however, and when Jarrett Aylen had pulled a deep gridsearch of the Tribon Legal Authority database, he'd turned up nothing, either on Spacer's warrant or on the death of wealthy off-worlder Sennis Thorne.

It was almost as though the whole incident had never happened.

"Something weird is going on," Jarrett had said. "I'm wondering if whoever is trying to stop us from getting to Storm isn't trying to cover up the murder now."

"Why would they do that?"

"Maybe calling attention to it would reveal that the

rhodium aboard *Serendipity* was a plant. Maybe it would make the authorities look in all the wrong places." He shrugged. "Hell, maybe they caught the real murderers, and they're embarrassed about admitting they were hunting for the wrong guy."

Spacer had spent the night with the party in their hotel suite, sacked out on the lounge sofa across the room from the fraal, because both tiny bedrooms were full—Verdoss and Jarrett in one, Maricia and Diane in the other. By the next morning, there was still no word on Thorne's murder, no indication that a warrant was out for Spacer, so they'd decided to risk his going out. After all, he had to leave the Blue Star Arms sometime, if only to grab his one change of clothes from his box up in First Tier B-5 and meet the others at the spaceport once they'd chartered a ship. While Jarrett knew a lot about Lison and Tribon, he didn't know the city labyrinth a tenth as well as Spacer did, and he'd never even heard of the Hot Nose, so Spacer had volunteered to take him there.

They took some precautions first, of course. He went out with his cloak arranged as a cowl to cover his sandy hair and help hide his features, and he wore one of Jarrett's black synthleather jackets, complete with Verge Ranger insignia on breast and sleeve. "Most people never look past the uniform," Jarrett had told him, "even when there's nothing to the uniform but a couple of patches anyone could buy in a surplus goods shop." Once they left the hotel, their first stop was a footwear store to buy Spacer a decent pair of boots. By the time they boarded the tube train for the Refinery District, he felt like a completely different person.

"Anything?" Jarrett asked him as he checked out the crowd.

"Looks clear," Spacer replied. "Don't see anyone I recognize, anyway."

Besides serving as guide for Jarrett, he'd been told to keep an eye out for any of the three thugs he'd seen in the alley with Thorne. So far, he'd seen nothing that indicated any interest in himself or the Verge Ranger at all.

"Is that the place?" Jarrett asked, pointing at the massive bulk of the Hot Nose.

"That's it. If we can't find a charter pilot with his own ship in there, we'll at least get a recommendation from Siggy, the bartender."

"Let's go, then."

The Hot Nose was a popular bar at the edge of the Refinery District, a kilometer from the Lower Halls, tucked against the sheer, granite wall of Tribon's deepest level. Originally, it had been a Mark XIX Mole, a massive, squat, six-tracked vehicle fifty meters long and twenty high, shaped like a trio of dull, rusted-iron spheres trailing behind the ugly, triple-headed snout of a nuclear-thermal torch. The hull was rusted and battered, streaked with acid corrosion that had etched out scratches and dents that made the thing look like it had been through a couple of major wars. The name *The Hot Nose* could just be seen in faded, acid-pitted letters on the huge machine's blackened prow.

A century and a half ago, the Hot Nose had been one of a number of Rigunmor mole tunnelers, employed to burn out the tunnels through solid rock that let the miners get at the richest veins of rhodium and iridium . . . and to open up the caverns in which they eventually built Tribon. The thermal torch plied heat against the end of the tunnel, raising the temperature to the melting point until solid rock flowed, sluggish and plastic. As the mole pressed forward, the near-liquid rock was packed, shaped, and cooled into a dense, glassy surface that helped support the tunnel roof. On a good day, a mole like *The Hot Nose* could open up two or three hundred meters of new tunnel.

The Hot Nose and her sisters had been retired after the Lison Revolt in 2373, though. They were aging by that time and becoming dangerous. This particular machine had rusted at the Ortis Refinery for a few decades, before finally being purchased by an entrepreneur who'd moved her to her present location and turned her into a restaurant-bar. Sigmund Nakamura was the latest in a long line of owners who'd run the place ever since.

Spacer and Jarrett walked up the ramp leading through the mole's armored side. They ducked to clear the low seal and entered a dark and smoky room filled with noisily eating and drinking people. A working mole had open space within sufficient for a crew of twenty in starkly claustrophobic conditions, but the Hot Nose had had her thermal reactors and particle projectors stripped out, half of her thermal armor yanked, her main and secondary coolant systems salvaged and sold for parts, and her main power plant scrapped. The interior consisted of several interconnected rooms, a space large enough for two main eating halls, a bar and lounge, and a fair-sized kitchen.

Most of the patrons, logically enough on this world, were miners, and the interior decor reflected the mining theme. The walls were hung with shovels, picks, old power scoops, rusted vibrohammers, lanterns, e-suits, breather masks, diacarb drill heads, air tanks, gas sniffers, vent tubing, boots, safety line, and even an ancient hand trolley hung by chains from the ceiling. The floor was finished in some areas with something that looked like naked rock and in others with a mole deck's steel plate. Counters, tabletops, and chairs were trimmed in faux-rhodium stripping. Even the waiters and waitresses in the place had adapted to the mining theme—at least in their head- and footwear; they were garbed in little more than knee boots and full breather helmets, with the opaque visors closed.

"Think any of your friends are here?" Jarrett asked as they stood at the threshold, looking down into the sunken lounge. The place, as always, was crowded. With no day and night among Lison's cycles of time, one person's morning was another's evening revel. Music thumped from overhead speakers, and people had to shout to make themselves heard. Several couples were dancing on an open stretch of deck, but most were talking or getting down to the business of serious drinking.

"I doubt it," Spacer said. "It's a pretty fancy place—three dollars for a beer? But a lot of pilots hang out here, not just miners."

Spacer had held a job here once, telling fortunes for ten dollars apiece and paying a percentage to the house, but not that many of the patrons had been willing to shell for Spacer's patter and fuzzy-feel-good platitudes, and even fewer had wanted to pay for the truth. When the goldies had moved in and demanded that Nakamura get an entertainment license for Spacer's "act," Spacer had decided to leave. He and Siggy were still on good terms, though.

Siggy had always claimed that some of his regulars were pirates. Hell, according to him, Thomas Kind himself showed up from time to time, though Spacer didn't think that was too likely. Spacer figured the old guy had just been taking advantage of a kid's lust for adventure, dangerous people, and far-off places. Still, there was a post board for charter ships and pilots inside, and he knew for a fact that a few freelance pilots hung out here between jobs. Hell, most of those guys, and gals too, operated on the thin, ragged edge of piracy and smuggling already, so maybe Siggy's stories had been true after all.

He spotted Siggy behind the long bar at the far end of the lounge and walked over. "Hey! Siggy, remember me?"

Sigmund Nakamura was a beefy, large man with long, dark features and eyes that showed his Asian ancestry. His face registered no emotion at first . . . and then his eyes widened suddenly. "Spacer!" He looked back and forth, as though checking who might be listening in, then leaned closer. "Hey, man! It's been a long time! You okay?"

Spacer grinned. "Never better."

"Yeah?" Siggy glanced at Jarrett, standing behind Spacer, then leaned even closer, dropping his voice so no one else could hear. "Listen, Space! Was that really your mug and stats they were beaming last night? I mean . . . you didn't *really* scrag anyone, did you? Especially an offie!"

"Grep, no! They had me confused with someone else."

"Good to hear it. You never struck me as the psychopath type. Crazy, yeah, but not psychopathic. Whatcha want? Lookin' for a job?"

"Got a gig, thanks. We're looking for a pilot, actually. Somebody with his own ship. Know anyone?"

Siggy considered this. When he didn't answer right away, Spacer assumed he was waiting for a touch of grease for the referral. "Look, I don't have much on me, Siggy, but I know some people who could—"

Siggy waved him off. "Ferget it. Remember me if your gig pays off. Yeah, I do know a guy. He's here now, in fact." He pointed to the last in a row of booths. "Back there. Number fifty-two. Name's Jean-Paul Duprés, but everybody calls him Smilin' Jack."

"Thanks, Siggy."

"Don't mention it. But . . . you watch yerself, kid, okay?"

"Will do."

Spacer and Jarrett walked over to the indicated booth. There were two people there: an attractive, black-haired woman in synthleather and a computer gauntlet sat beside a hard-muscled, rugged-looking man with a scar down the left side of his face from hairline to squared-off jaw. The scar dragged at the man's mouth, twisting it into an uncomfortable leer, and it was easy to see why he carried the name he did. The irises of his eyes gleamed pure silver; Spacer couldn't tell if they were implants, or if some of his ancestors had indulged in a bit of gene manipulation.

"You Smilin' Jack?" Spacer asked.

The man looked him over with something like distaste. "Who wants t'know?"

"We're looking for a ship," Jarrett told him. "We hear you have one."

"Maybe. What's the cargo?"

"A scientific expedition," Jarrett said. "Six people and about three tons of equipment—base camp gear, computers, stuff like that."

"And you're goin' where?"

"Loman system. A place called Storm."

Jack looked at the woman beside him. She frowned. "I don't think . . ." She tapped something into her gauntlet, and studied the screen mounted on the back of her hand. "Loman," she said after a moment. "Okay, there is a listing. Just over twenty point light years from here. Red dwarf, two gas giants . . . and some crap." She looked up and met Spacer's eyes, then Jarrett's. "Nothing there of interest. No colonies, bases, or outposts of any kind. An open system."

"My navigator and first mate," Jack said, nodding at the woman. "Michelle Vaughn. So . . . what's the idea? A wilderness jaunt?"

"As I said, a scientific expedition. We're with the Terran Xenarchaeological Institute. We want you to put us down on Storm, one of the moons of a gas giant called Salamanca. We expect to be there for anywhere between a week and two months. We'd like to hire you for that whole time, though. We may need transport within the system or from one part of Storm to another."

The woman was keying in data again and reading the flow of data on her gauntlet screen. "It's hairy, Jack. I don't like it."

"We'll pay the usual expert pilot's percentage."

"And a hazard bonus," the woman said, "up front! Jack, you will not believe this place! Radiation fields, asteroid and ring debris, magnetic flux up the inductors, extreme vulcanism and seismic activity, electrical storms . . ."

"This Storm place doesn't exactly sound like prime real estate," Jack said.

"It isn't. Will you take us?"

Jack leaned back in the booth's padded seat, stretching out his long legs. It was hard to read what he was thinking through those pale silver eyes. "Why come to me? You couldn't have come all the way out to the Verge figurin' on hiring a ship once you got here."

"Well, no, actually," Jarrett said. "We had an Institute ship, *Serendipity,* but we've run into some . . . bureaucratic delays."

"He means their ship was impounded," the woman said, still reading from her display. "A smuggling charge. Half a ton of rhodium, apparently."

Jack whistled appreciatively. "Not bad! Too bad you were caught!"

"We didn't smuggle anything," Jarrett said. "Obviously some sort of official mix-up."

"Yeah, those can be bad news. You or your people hot?"

"I beg your pardon?"

"You on the run? Wanted by the authorities?"

"No. Nothing like that. We just need a ship to take us and our gear out to Storm."

"Okay, well . . . I'll tell ya what. Happens I'm free now, and I could use a short hop, so here's the deal. CD one hundred per person per light-year. That's forty an' something lights, there and back, plus a thousand a day loiter. We'll call it, oh, say, ten days, and renegotiate later if you want longer, but ten days minimum. Plus five thousand for your gear and supplies. Plus fifteen percent expert pilot's fee. Plus fifteen percent hazardous flight fee. What's the tally, Mike?"

The woman checked her screen. "Fifty-one thousand, eight-hundred fifteen, point fifty-five Concord dollars," she said.

Smilin' Jack's smile grew broader and a bit more crooked, if possible. "Tell ya what. Make it an even fifty thousand. I'm offerin' a special today to scientific expeditions heading to Verge wilderness worlds."

Jarrett's eyebrows arched high. "Fifty thousand! You're a pirate, right?"

"Only when business is bad, pal. Take it or leave it."

"We'll leave it. You're charging a hundred a light-year? The going rate is twenty-five, unless you're offering first-class luxury accommodations! What's the name of your ship, the *Galactic Queen*?"

"Don't you go knockin' ol' *Questar*, mister. She might not be luxury class, but she'll get you where you're goin'."

"I'm sure she will, but not at a hundred a head. We'll pay twenty-five a head, that's the going rate, plus two thousand for the gear and five hundred a day loiter. We'll pay your bonuses."

"What? Are you serious?" Jack looked at the woman. "Mike?"

"Pathetic, boss. Sixteen thousand, one-oh-two point oh one three."

"You heard the lady. That's pathetic! Sixteen thousand? I don't even come close to making expenses with that! Forty-six."

"Twenty thousand. Hell, I'll have to gridcomm my principles and check to see if the budget can stand even that much!"

"Your budget ain't my affair. Forty-five."

"You want our business or not? Twenty-one."

"Twenty-one! Twenty-one! That's not an offer! That's an insult! Look, you seem like nice folks, and I'd like to help you out, but I *can't* go a damned CD less than . . . oh, let's say forty-two fifty. Otherwise I'd have to hock my ship, and I couldn't live with myself then."

Spacer listened as the bargaining proceeded. Jarrett, he thought, was doing a pretty slick job, but Smilin' Jack was a real pro, letting his face get red and his strange silver eyes turn wild as he threw himself into the exchange . . . or dropping back to calm and sympathetic tones and a closed expression at will.

He wondered if Smilin' Jack was a pirate. The man certainly looked and sounded the part—overbearing, swaggering, cocky, the sort of guy you'd expect to meet in a bar fight and just hope to hell he was on your side.

Spacer had nothing against pirates. They were thieves, sure, but so was he. So was any government he'd ever heard of, and in some places it was an open question as to which side was the worst crook, the pirates or the government.

More often than not on the Frontier, it was groups like Kind and his band who provided the revenue, stimulated the economy, and looked out for the public welfare better than the government could possibly manage.

As far as Spacer was concerned, everyone had a right to look out for themselves the best they were able. More than that, piracy could only exist because it was *permitted* to exist by the locals . . . who allowed it to become a stable institution by providing markets and bases. Pirates did not—*could not*—exist in a vacuum. They needed ports on which to land, refit, repair, refuel, and resupply their ships, markets to sell stolen goods and captured vessels, liberty ports for recreation, homes for families between raids and ventures. It was widely rumored in Tribon that Thomas Kind was personal friends—or at least a hand-in-gauntlet business associate—with Michael Kevik, the president of United Lison. Kind and some of the other better-established pirate families were hovering on the verge of respectability . . . if not outright legitimacy.

Smilin' Jack Duprés was typical of the small-time corsair, as opposed to the big boys like Kind. He probably worked with larger pirate families from time to time, but most of his income must come from borderline legit stuff and occasional smuggling, with the odd intercept course on a target of opportunity. In the Oberon system at least, piracy was widely considered to be a relatively innocuous form of taxation . . . a variant on the age-old protection racket. The real piracy came when he tried to gouge unsuspecting clients for four times the passage price he had a right to expect.

Spacer wondered how Verdoss was going to take being hustled off to Storm aboard a corsair. The Rigunmor hadn't been happy at the idea when they'd discussed it yesterday, or again this morning over breakfast.

As for Spacer, he didn't mind at all. A pirate raider or the *Galactic Queen* . . . one way or another he was getting off this damned planet.

"Done!" Jarrett said loudly, interrupting Spacer's thoughts. He sounded exhausted.

"And done!" Jack added. "Make a note, Mike. Thirty-eight five with five hundred per for loiter, half in advance, half upon return to Lison."

"I can arrange for a cash transfer at once," Jarrett said. He pulled out his data pad and typed an entry. "Where do you want it?"

"Point it at me," Mike said. "I handle the banking."

Jarrett used the pad's link to beam the transfer to Jack's account.

"You in a hurry?" Jack asked as the link was broken.

"We need time to transfer our cargo from Bay Seven to

wherever you keep your ship, Captain. But as soon as we can get loaded aboard, we want to raise ship."

"You've got someone after ya, don't ya?"

Jarrett grinned. "Someone doesn't want us going to Storm, that's for sure."

"Yeah? Maybe I should've charged combat pay too."

"It shouldn't come to that, Captain, but the sooner we lift, the better."

"Okay. Well, *Questar* is in Bay Three. I'll pass the word down there and have your gear transferred for you."

"Thank you. We appreciate that."

"Be at Bay Three at oh-seven-fifty tomorrow. We'll raise ship by nine hundred."

"We'll be there." They shook hands.

"Nice meeting you, Captain," Spacer said as they rose to leave.

He was wondering which tarot card would best categorize Captain Smilin' Jack Duprés. The Chariot, perhaps? Associated with travel, protected by the stars, but forced to make his own victory through strength and fortitude. Stamina, victory through adversity, success and conquest, a blend of black and white, good and evil . . .

Yeah, he would associate Smilin' Jack with the Chariot.

The chariot that would take him to the Star. . . .

*   *   *   *   *

Jean-Paul Duprés traced the ragged scar on his face as he watched the two go. "We got a couple of live ones, Mike," he told his navigator. He wasn't sure how much truth had been in the story those two had been peddling. They were both wearing Verge Ranger jackets, but anyone could get those. What was certain was that they had money, and they were desperate.

The perfect business combination, so far as Smilin' Jack was concerned.

"Hope you know what you're doing, Jack," she replied. "This Loman system is no easy walk in the park."

"We can handle it, and we need the money."

"We *always* need money."

"Yeah, but not like this. Thirty-eight five? That'll pay off Kind, so we get to keep the ship. Not bad for a morning's work!"

"Assuming we come through this in one piece."

"Ah, you worry too much, Mike."

"Someone has to. You don't worry enough."

He started to rise. "We'd better get back to the *Quest*. I want to make sure there aren't any complications with their gear. If their ship was impounded, there could be a problem there."

"Captain Duprés?"

He looked up. A very tall, very thin man with deep-set eyes and a shaven head blocked his exit from the booth. He wore a computer gauntlet on his left arm, and a gridcomm mike and earset appeared to have been grafted to the side of his head.

"Yeah?"

"I wonder if I might inquire . . . have you just agreed to transport those people who were just here to anyplace in particular?"

"I don't think that's any of your damned business. You wanna let me by?"

The man did not move. Instead, he laid his gauntleted hand on Jack's shoulder. "You misunderstand me, Captain. It is possible that we could do some business, you and I. Those two represent some people trying to travel to the Loman system, where some associates of mine have a personal interest. It would be worth a considerable amount of money to us if these people did not leave Lison."

Jack glanced at Mike. She was sitting quietly, her own gauntlet on the table. She'd positioned her arm, however, so that the carefully hidden laser in the forearm was aimed directly at the stranger's gut. Her eyes were steady on Jack; if he gave the slightest sign, a simple nod of his head, she would close her fist to trigger the laser and burn the stranger down where he stood.

Smilin' Jack always preferred to negotiate from strength.

"I don't know about you, mister," he said easily, "but where I come from, an agreement is something worth keeping."

"As I say, we can make it worth your while." The man paused as if to consider the matter. "You could even lift with them. Take their money. Just see to it that they don't reach Storm. That way, you get whatever they paid you in advance, plus the bonus that my associates will pay. Say . . . triple what they've already paid you?"

"What do you suggest I do? Space 'em?"

"It doesn't really matter. You could suffer a breakdown and not be able to leave the Oberon system. You could arrive at the wrong system, put them down on the wrong world. Yes . . . that would be most satisfactory! You could maroon them. . . ."

Jack stood up suddenly, coming face to face with the stranger, his glare so hot it made the other back off two steps. "Now you hear me and you hear me good," he said quietly. "I don't care what your associates are offering. I accepted this charter in good faith, and I'm going to carry it out. Now get the hell out of my way."

"What are these losers to you? We can offer—"

"I don't care what you offer, slekhead." He elbowed the man aside and stalked past, Mike hurrying along in his wake.

"You're making a big mistake, Duprés!" the man shouted behind them.

"I've cleaned up bigger mistakes than you!"

"You take them to Storm, and none of you will be heard of again. Your bones will dissolve in that radioactive hell, and there won't be enough DNA left to run an ID check!"

Jack banged through the front door then stood for a moment at the top of the ramp leading to the entrance of the Hot Nose. He was breathing hard. Mike emerged and stood beside him silently.

"I don't like it when people try to shove me around, Mike," he said.

"I didn't say a word!"

"No, but you were thinking a few."

"Sure. I'm thinking that guy's friends might not be the sort of people you want to have ticked off at you."

"So? I'm not workin' for them."

"I've noticed. I've also noticed you have this damned soft spot for strays and orphans."

"That's a negative! I just don't believe in goin' back on my word. If it gets around that you screw your clients, it can affect your reputation, y'know?"

"Whatever you say." She shrugged. "What now?"

"Back to the ship. And you get hot with that arm of yours. I want all Grid defenses up five minutes ago. These boys play rough. I don't want no surprises."

"They're already in place and running, boss. Set 'em as soon as I got a look at that guy's hardware. And I've already told the *Quest* to start warming up."

"Good girl."

"And . . . boss?"

"What?"

"Don't worry. I won't tell anyone you have a conscience."

"You do and I'll space ya. C'mon. Let's hustle."

They hurried toward Tribon's main tube access to the spaceport level.

Chapter Nine

THEY HAD A fifteen minute wait before the next tubecar arrived.

"I've got to go up to B-5," Spacer said. "I can't go back with you right now."

"Is that wise?" Jarrett said. "Your old pals might be hanging around up there. You said you thought they were trying to turn you in to the authorities."

"Maybe. I can always slip 'em, no sweat. But I gotta get my stuff." He paused. They were standing on an elevated platform not far from the Hot Nose, which gave them a magnificent view of the lights of Tribon's lower level. It was a familiar sight for Spacer—the base-lit towers and buildings, the broad domes, the high, rocky ceiling almost lost in darkness overhead. It was a view that he'd known for as far back as he could remember. "I don't ever want to come back to this place."

"No?" Jarrett looked doubtful. "What are you going to do instead? Dr. Strang and Dr. Radlevich will be heading back for the Institute, I imagine. There's no place for you there. And you'll need a job. You won't be able to get by without money."

"I don't know. I'll think of something." He shrugged. "Maybe I can find one of those stormfire stones. That'd be worth something, I bet!"

"Maybe so. You might have to argue the point with Mr. Verdoss. I think he wants them all for himself."

"Is that why you didn't tell Smilin' Jack about the stones? He might not have charged you so much if he'd thought he could come back with a pocket full of those."

"Maybe. We can always talk about that later. For now, though, the fewer people who know about stormfires, the better. If news started spreading, we might find half the people in the Verge camped out on Storm by the time we got there."

"I guess so. A rhodium run, huh?"

"Rhodium run?"

"You hear stories about 'em here. Back in the old days, when a strike would make someone rich, it would cause a stampede of hungry miners." He thought about it for a moment. "I wonder what the stormies would think of all those humans dropping in on 'em?"

"Another good reason to keep this to ourselves."

"Yeah . . ." He hesitated. "Jarrett?"

"Hmm?"

"Is that all that this is about? The stormfires, I mean? Just money?"

Jarrett laughed. "A few trillion dollars is hardly what I'd call 'just,' but, yeah, there's more. Verdoss is in it for the money, that's obvious. The ladies, though . . ."

"I know they're interested in the stormies."

"They're looking for the ruins—Diane and the fraal, are, anyway. Maricia is coming to help communicate with the stormies and try to learn more about them."

"What ruins?"

"Ever hear of the Precursors?"

"Sure. The tunnel ghosts."

Jarrett blinked. "Tunnel ghosts? That's a new one on me."

"Oh, it's just stories. You know, the sort of thing parents scare their kids with to make 'em behave, or the kind of story the guys'll tell at the end of a cycle, standing around a barrel fire and passing around a bottle of cheap alga-hol—all about aliens who used to live on Lison, millions of years ago before topside died. There are lots of tunnels in Lison *we* didn't dig. Some folks claim they've seen the ones who did . . . or their ghosts."

"I see." He smiled. "Well, there an awful lot of ghosts among the stars, Spacer, and a lot of debris left by different civilizations who were here a long, long time before we arrived on the scene. We call 'em all Precursors, though most of them didn't have anything to do with any of the others. Diane has told me about civilizations going back hundreds of millions of years ago. Others were flourishing just a few thousand years back.

"Diane is a xenoarchaeologist. Her specialty is Precursor civilizations. She tries to find whatever they left behind, to learn about them . . . and about what happened to them." He chuckled. "She calls it 'picking through other people's garbage.' I guess that pretty well describes what an archaeologist does."

"She thinks the stormies are Precursors?"

"Let's just say there are some significant mysteries about the stormies and about the planet's history. The Rigunmor Expedition found some ruins on the planet that the stormies obviously didn't build. You know the secretary you stole from Sennis Thorne?"

Spacer nodded slowly, uncomfortable. "Yeah."

"Sennis had been researching some stuff for us on Earth, and he found something important—a map, drawn by the captain of that Rig expedition, of a large cluster of ruins on Storm's surface. He was able to scan that map and was coming out to Lison to show it to us."

"A map? What was it doing on Earth?"

"Excellent question. It turns out that the Rig expedition never made it back to the Consortium. They were attacked, the ship captured, looted, and destroyed."

"Why?"

A shrug. "It was the beginning of the Second Galactic War, remember. Apparently, Verdoss's great-great-whatever grandfather made it to a lifeboat with nothing much but his memories and that one stormfire. Eventually, he got back home, but all he could tell anyone was that the records of the place they'd visited were at the Rig colony on Lison. And with the war, well, no one was interested in Storm at the time, and old Grigor apparently didn't want to let anyone outside his family know about the gems.

"The ship that looted the Rig vessel, though, was apparently a VoidCorp raider, but it never made it home either. It might have suffered some damage in the fighting; we don't know. But the ship and its contents were later salvaged by a research vessel and taken back to Earth. Ended up in a space flight museum, I gather."

"And Sennis Thorne tracked it down there?"

Jarrett chuckled. "Some of the contents of that ship were still classified even after all these years, but money talks."

"I still don't understand why a bunch of old ruins would be that important to anyone."

"Knowledge is always important. For Diane and Ta Shaa Ta, though, it's something more."

"Yeah?" Spacer was interested. Of the others in the expedition party, he was most attracted to Diane and in awe of the fraal. They'd been interested in him, had seen something in him worth knowing. It was a new experience for Spacer, and one that he found he liked more than he could say.

"You'll have to get Ta Shaa Ta to tell you the whole story," Jarrett told him, "if he will. It's kind of a private matter for him. He's on a quest, you see."

"What kind of quest?"

"He's looking for his homeworld. You'll have to ask him if you want more information than that."

Spacer's eyebrows raised. He'd spent most of his own life wishing he could lose the world of his birth. He wondered what the story was with Ta Shaa Ta.

A tubecar glided into the station, humming softly.

"You want me to go up to your level with you?" Jarrett asked. He sounded concerned.

"No," Spacer replied. "No, I just need . . . to get something. I'll meet you back at the hotel in about an hour."

"See you there."

Spacer watched him climb into the car. The pod levitated with a low hum then slid swiftly away from the platform and down the tube.

Spacer took an uptunnel to First Tier and made his way across and over to B-District complex. He was thoughtful as he pushed along through the crowded streets. He was determined that this would be his last time home.

His box was still there. Inside, untouched, were his bed pad and blanket, and the small, age-tattered travel case that held his extra clothes . . . and the real reason he'd come back.

When he touched the power-on key set into the metal frame, a holopic materialized. He stared for a moment into his mother's face, wondering why he felt nothing. So long ago . . .

Another touch of the button, and the image of his grandmother watched him from the frame, eyes bright, jaw set. He could hear her voice again, speaking in his mind. *If a tunnel rat is all you want to be, a tunnel rat is all you'll ever be. There's more to life than stone tunnels, and you can find it if you know yourself . . . and if you want it bad enough!*

"I'm workin' at it, Grandma," he told her softly. He touched the button again, changing the holo.

For a moment Spacer could imagine himself *there*, staring into infinite depths of luminous, star-strewn night. The shot was a commercial holo taken from a liner in deep space, and it showed the Star. It was a souvenir view of Titania, but Spacer never thought of it any way but the Star. He'd seen that image, known it, *loved* it long before his grandmother had given him the holotarot deck. He was certain that that picture had strongly influenced his choice of the Star as *his* card in the set.

Titania was a blue-white giant, dazzling partner to Oberon, Lison's far cooler, smaller, and less boisterous sun. She shone against the black firmament, imbedded in a twisted, nebulous veil of blue glory, radiating in fierce defiance against the night. Sometimes, you could see Titania in Lison's sky, a dazzling white gleam of a pinpoint low above the horizon, bright enough even in Tribon's eternal twilight to cast shadows and edge the cloud-wrack with silver.

She was a beacon to Spacer, a brilliant pinpoint of hope, a promise that there was life beyond the narrow confines of crowded Tribon.

He replaced the holopic in the satchel, took a last look around, and crawled out of the box.

The flyer was waiting for him.

It was small, the size of a big man's fist, with a glittering array of optical and thermal sensors circling its equator. Spacer could hear the tiny hum of its onboard microinductors, which held it suspended two meters off the ground. "Grep!"

He started to run, but the hovering sphere followed. Spacer didn't know if it was a police surveillance model or a private job, but he knew it was relaying his image *somewhere*, and someone was controlling its flight.

Spinning, he whipped off his cloak and snapped it at the flyer, hard, whipcracking the sphere out of the air and sending it smacking into a nearby wall. He didn't stop to see if he'd damaged the thing but ran down the alley as fast as he could go, the cloak fluttering behind him like a tail.

"There he is!" someone shouted.

"Stop him! *Stop him!*"

Spacer veered to avoid a sudden shape lunging at him from the shadows beyond the alley's mouth. Hookie was there, shouting, pointing . . . and then he saw the goldies, one of them already pointing an ugly black stutter pistol in his direction.

There was a loud *thud*, and something hit Spacer in the side of the head. He felt himself spinning backward onto the pavement.

After that, he didn't remember anything. . . .

*   *   *   *   *

"Damn it, where *is* that kid?" Verdoss was pacing back and forth in the hotel suite's sitting room. "We should be at the docking bay now!"

"Patience," Diane said. Verdoss was starting to get on her nerves. If they didn't need his backing for this expedition . . .

"Jarrett's in the Lower Hall database now," Maricia said. "He should get some answers."

"He's the reason we're in this mess," Verdoss said, scowling. "He should never have let that tunnel punk out of his sight. Hell, we shouldn't have let him out of this room. We shouldn't have taken him on in the first place. We shouldn't—"

"*Will* you shut up!" Diane said, exploding. "We don't need the stress of listening to your yapping, thank you very much!"

"If I didn't need you people for this expedition . . ." he muttered.

"Got something," Jarrett said, and the others turned to look at him.

Jarrett was seated at the workstation, a gridcaster helmet on his head, gridware gauntlets on both hands. His face was masked by the hazy glow of a holofield. His arms reached out, moving, touching, sliding back and forth in the empty air before him, the motions interacting with the virtual reality he was experiencing through the helmet.

They'd agreed not to try the v-sphere again, not with the enemy waiting to strike, but the headset could maintain only a shadow of the v-sphere's linkage to gridspace, and it was almost impossible for an enemy on the Grid to hurt him before he had a chance to bail.

"I'm into their main records," Jarrett said, pushing some immaterial object aside, then opening an unseen door. "They have Spacer in custody, but no charges have been filed. Nothing yet, anyway."

"They can't hold him without charging him, can they?" Maricia asked.

"They can do pretty much whatever they want," Diane

replied. "The United Lison Charter basically says they're
operating under a constant state of emergency."

"Such is usually the case," Ta Shaa Ta said, "on worlds
with such extreme conditions as prevail here. When air and
water and even living space have to be rationed, there can
be no room for your so-called democracies."

"Can you tell if he's told them anything about us?" Verdoss asked. "If he's said anything about the stormfires?"

"Don't see anything," Jarrett replied. He shoved something aside, reached out, and closed his fist on something
only he could see. "Funny. The case is marked 'special
handling.' "

"What does *that* mean?" Diane asked.

"Dunno. There are several names here—people who
wanted to be alerted when he was captured. Don't recognize the names, though. Lemmid Dorlan? John Garth?
Wolfgang Krueger? They may be aliases. Uh-oh."

"What is it?" Maricia wanted to know.

"Wolfgang Krueger. He's also listed in here as KL945
72YKV."

"VoidCorp!" Diane said.

"Well, well," Verdoss said. "It's nice to put a face on the
enemy at last."

"They would certainly have the resources to find and
penetrate the old Rigunmor files," Ta Shaa Ta said, "and
they would be able to purchase favors from the local government easily enough. I would be interested in knowing
their motives, however."

"Maybe they found out about the stormfires, somehow," Diane said. "Or maybe," she added, unable to keep
the acid out of her voice, "they're out to exploit the natives,
like they did the sesheyans."

VoidCorp's rigid power structure, its sometimes dicta-
torial management structure, its near legendary greed were
well known throughout human space. Their enslavement
in all but name of an entire alien species had branded them
in Diane's mind as genuinely evil, though VoidCorp had
more than its fair share of apologists.

Every person within VoidCorp's domain was an

Employee, not a citizen, assigned an identifier that began with a double-letter rank, ranging from AA to ZZ, and with almost seven hundred steps in between. Krueger's rank of KL placed him well below the management levels but quite high in the hierarchy of skilled workers—high enough to be trusted with his own, independent command.

Why would VoidCorp be interested in Spacer? What were they doing on Lison in the first place? Why were they trying to block the expedition's departure for Storm?

"Damn!"

The exclamation jolted Diane from dark thoughts. "What is it, Jarrett?"

"If I'm reading this right, they're going to lock him out! He's already in the transport!"

"What do you mean?" Diane said. "What's lock out?"

Jarrett moved his arm, and a holographic image appeared above the algae pool. There, playing over a tertiary newsfeed, was a steel-hulled vehicle of some kind. Spacer, his hands shackled in front of him, was being led between two heavily armored troopers. The left side of his face was badly discolored, purple with a massive bruise, and both of his eyes were black.

"My God!" Maricia said. "What have they done to him?"

"It's what they're about to do that worries me," Jarrett said. "He's listed here as scheduled for a lock-out this morning. That means they drive him out into the topside desert and push him out the airlock. The termination order is stamped EP."

"Which means?" Diane prompted.

"Extreme Prejudice. Apparently that's at Krueger's specific orders."

"How can they get more extreme than pushing the poor kid out an airlock without an e-suit?" Diane wanted to know.

In the holodisplay, a fourth figure entered the pick-up, a tall and lanky man with shaven head, a computer gauntlet, and a face so fleshless it looked like a skull's. He leaned over Spacer, grinning. He was saying something, though no sound was coming across with the picture.

"Doesn't that look like the man Spacer described?" Maricia pointed out. "The one who killed Sennis?"

"What do you want to bet that's Krueger?" Jarrett said. "Or, rather, our good friend KL945."

"We've got to do something!" Diane said. "We can't just let them kill him!"

"There's nothing we *can* do," Verdoss pointed out. "If he hadn't run off by himself—"

"Can it," Diane snapped. "Jarrett, see if you can access Lower Hall Administration."

"I'll try," Jarrett said, "but there's not much time. These images here are recorded. According to the newsfeed, they left nearly a half hour ago. They should already be on the Sunrise Flats."

"What does that mean?" Ta Shaa Ta asked.

"It means," Jarrett said, "that they're almost at the place they perform most of their executions, and they're going to reach it within the next few minutes."

*   *   *   *   *

Krueger leaned closer, teeth showing in a death's head imitation of a smile. "You still have a chance, my young friend," he said. "I want to know why your friends are interested in Storm. We know that the story of a scientific research expedition is a cover for something else. We want to know what that something else is."

"I told ya, I don't know!" Spacer cried. "They was talkin' about aliens—stormies, they called 'em. I don't know anything more than that!"

Spacer's mind was racing, his heart hammering in his chest. He knew what they were about to do to him—the one punishment guaranteed to strike sheer terror into any Lisoner's soul: topside, without an e-suit.

He wondered if they wanted to know about the storm-fires or about the Precursor ruins Jarrett had been talking about. It didn't much matter. He wasn't going to tell them anything, not when telling might mean the death of Diane, Ta Shaa Ta, and Jarrett, the only people he'd known since his grandmother who'd ever really cared about him.

"You know, kid," Krueger said, "you just aren't running with the program. You need to be a corporate player. If you cooperate, I could make you a very lucrative offer—more than being allowed to live, even. You could be *rich*, and maybe with a K or L prefix to your number!"

Spacer didn't know what he was talking about, but he did know he was being asked to betray his friends. He inhaled sharply through his nose, gathered a mouthful of phlegm, and spat in Krueger's face.

"All right," Krueger said, wiping his face with a gloved hand. "If that's the way we're going to run the program, that's the way it is. Time for some attitude adjustment. Hold him!"

The armored troopers grabbed Spacer's arms. He tried to kick, but they dropped their polymer-encased legs over his, pinning him in place. Krueger left the compartment for a moment and returned holding a breather mask, a translucent cup molded to fit over nose and mouth, with small bottles attached to either side. Krueger was pouring a dollop of some viscous liquid from a small bottle onto the face seal, carefully smearing it with the applicator tip to cover the seal completely.

Spacer tried to whip his head away, but Krueger grabbed the hair at the back of his head with one hand, and with the other pressed the mask into place, covering his nose and mouth completely. He held it there for a long count of ten.

"That's a molecular bonder," Krueger told him, giving a painful tug at the mask before releasing him. "Industrial strength. It'll keep you breathing for maybe three hours. After fifteen minutes, though, you'll wish you *weren't* breathing. That I promise you!"

He tugged the mask again. The seal yanked at the skin of Spacer's face, pulling his head forward. "Yeah, that'll do. Now . . . there's a small radio transmitter inside that thing. If at any time in the next couple of hours, you decide you want to cooperate, well, all you have to do is give me a call. We'll come out, pick you up, and bring you back inside. We'll have a lovely little chat, and if I like your answers, I'll take the mask off and we'll all head back for Tribon together. If I don't like the answers, well, we'll just have to let you enjoy Lison's topside recreational benefits. Understand?" He sounded cheerful. "All right, time to—"

"Mr. Krueger?" a voice crackled over an intercom.

"What? I'm busy!"

"You'd better come up here, Mr. Krueger," the voice said. "We got a gridcall in from HQ. You oughta talk to 'em."

Krueger sighed and made his way forward, vanishing through a low, narrow hatch.

Spacer tried to pull free, but his two guards held him in grips of steel polyalloy. His breath came in short, hard-drawn gasps. He couldn't get enough air through the face mask, and what air there was stank of bonder fumes. His head was aching already, and he felt dizzy.

"Look, I don't know who that guy is," he told his guards, "but he ain't a Lisoner! You don't have to do what he says!"

"Shut up," the one on his right said, the voice rasping through an external speaker on his helmet. "We got our orders, and those orders are to do what *he* says, to the letter! Besides, you offed an offie, and you're scheduled for EP termination, simple as that."

"This isn't a termination! He just wants to make me talk!"

"Not our concern. Now shut up, or we'll toss you out right now."

Minutes dragged past . . . and more minutes. Spacer was sweating heavily now. Maybe this was part of the treatment, he wondered? Maybe they figured he'd break, being forced to wait and think about what it was like top-side without an e-suit.

Krueger re-emerged from the forward hatch. He looked grim. "Well, it seems, that some of your friends tracked you down and are trying to help you. They talked to some people back at your government center, trying to get your execution stayed. But you know what? It's not going to help you one little bit." He nodded at the troopers. "Do it."

"Hey, wait!" Spacer shouted.

The inner hatch of the vehicle's airlock sighed open, and the troopers squeezed through, holding Spacer locked between them.

"Wait, you can't do this! Listen! Your bosses must have given an order not to kill me, but he's trying to do it anyway!" He groped wildly, trying to find an argument that would make sense, would make them listen. "*You guys are gonna be in a lot of trouble!*"

One of the armored troopers laughed at that as the inner hatch slid shut, closing off Krueger's grinning face. "I'm shakin'," he said. "I'm also *rich*, thanks to Mr. Krueger. I think we'll go ahead and do what he says, right Tom?"

"Works for me. EV checkout. Gauges green and sealed."

"EV check out. Set for EVA."

"Go."

One of the troopers palmed a press-plate on the bulkhead, and the outer hatch slid open with a scaldingly hot, vile, inward blast of air. Lison's atmospheric pressure was slightly higher than the normal pressure maintained within the sealed cities underground.

"Ready?" he heard one of the troopers say. "One! And two! And . . . three!"

Suddenly, Spacer was sailing through the air. He hit hot, raw sand with his arm and shoulder, rolled, and came to a sitting halt.

"Hey kid!" one of the troopers called. "Watch out for the rain!" The transporter's external lock closed off the laughter.

The air was hot, and it prickled his skin, a tingling that made him wonder if he was already picking up excess rads. A steady wind was blowing from the direction of the sun, a small orange eye hanging in the sky just above a horizon of sand-blasted, black mountains. Four meters away, the transporter squatted on its immense tracks, a black, hull-pitted teardrop with an upper turret. Scrambling to his bare feet, he staggered across the sand and started pounding at the outer hatch. "Hey! Lemme in! Don't do this!"

He might as well have been trying to gain entry to a sheer rock wall. He pounded until his hand was raw, his knuckles bleeding, with no response from within.

He turned and looked up . . . and then the full nightmare horror of where he was and what was happening descended on him like a rockfall. The sky, cloud-wracked and gloriously lit, was descending, encompassing him, crushing him into the burning sand.

In all of Spacer's twelve Lison years of life, he had never, *ever* been outside on the surface. His views of topside had always been encompassed by vidscreen boundaries or safely held within the square of a holopic frame. He'd grown up inside the rock-bound world of Tribon, always surrounded by people and rock, never without the comforting sight of the ceiling of cavern or tunnel.

The rawest terror of being dumped topside he'd never before imagined.

Windblown sand rasped at the exposed skin of his face and hands. The wind was a living thing, hot, violent, and palpable, laden with sand that cut like broken glass, and droplets of various liquids from the witch's brew of Lison's native air—sulphuric acid, nitric acid, and others.

He screamed, a long, drawn-out shriek of fear and pain and nightmare expectation, as the horror of topside closed in on his mind.

Chapter Ten

SPACER CROUCHED ON the downwind side of a boulder, huddling against the rock and trying to keep his face out of the wind. How long had he been out here? He glanced at the tattime on his wrist, but the skin was already so raw and abraded, blood-slicked and coated with sand, that he couldn't make out the dermal-implant numerals.

It actually wasn't too bad so long as he kept out of the scouring blast of the wind. His clothing offered some protection, though they'd taken his boots, and his feet were already blistered and bloody. Still, the stories he'd heard about this sort of execution whispered that offenders were usually tossed out here naked, and though they'd taken his cloak, jacket, and boots, his tunic and trousers still offered some protection.

That wouldn't last for long, though. Every few minutes, a pattering of raindrops pelted the area, each drop thumping into dry sand and dust and steaming for a moment before being absorbed into the thirsty ground. Drops striking his tunic began to steam and smoke. The sleeves had torn already in several places and were starting to fray and unravel at the cuffs. Drops falling on unprotected skin itched, the sensation building to an intolerable prickling all over his hands, his face, even in his hair.

Still, the worst was the terrible, yawning openness all around him. It almost was bearable if he kept his eyes squeezed shut, kept his body pressed against the comforting shelter of rough, acid-etched rock. Better to keep his eyes closed in any case, to keep out the sand and acid rain.

Each sound, each fresh pattering of raindrops, each change in the howl and keen of the wind, jerked his eyes open, and he was confronted again by vistas uncontained by walls or vidscreen frames, a complete inversion of what he thought of as the natural order of things—the comfortably enclosed world of Tribon's caverns, concourses, and tunnels.

How long . . . how long . . . *how long*? . . .

How much oxygen remained in the pressure cylinders on his mask? The device used external air, mixing it with a trickle of oxygen as it hissed in through louvered microvents with each breath he took. Theoretically, he knew, the device filtered out everything but nitrogen, but the air still stank of sulphur. A stifling, vinegar smell tasted hot in his mouth. The air also contained a higher level of carbon dioxide than the caverns, and that was contributing to the pain hammering behind his eyes, his increasing grogginess, and the tightening band of pressure about his chest as he dragged in each breath.

Once, he knew from the safety sims every citizen of Lison experienced, the air had been breathable, and topside had been a paradise as perfect as the legends of Old Earth. What had happened? No one knew. Conventional wisdom stated that the planet was so old its rotation had gradually slowed until the world had become tidally locked with Oberon, its sun. The oxygen in its atmosphere had rained out on the frigid night side—but that theory didn't explain the poisonous brew of acids suspended as multicolored clouds in the green and purple sky. He'd heard stories about how the temperature dynamics of

Lison's atmosphere were all wrong, that the entire planet ought to be a frozen lump of rock and ice.

He'd never given much thought to the composition of the topside atmosphere—a matter of interest only to someone who never expected to experience it at first hand. Not that his knowledge of Lison's atmospheric chemistry did him any good now. A raindrop hit the dust nearby with a soft plop . . . followed by another, and another, and then a steady drizzle pricking and stinging as it splashed across his hands and the back of his neck and in his hair. He hunched over further, protecting his face. He felt the polyplas weave of his tunic tear across his shoulders, felt the sudden sting of rain hitting the bare skin of his back.

Better there than on his face, in his eyes . . .

He chanced a quick look around, despite the rain. Strange, but he wasn't as terrified by the open expanse around him as he'd been earlier. Maybe he was getting used to it, strange as that thought seemed. He still had to keep his vision focused on things relatively near to avoid that mind-searing panic and dizziness he felt when he tried to take in too much, too quickly.

Twenty meters away, the transport squatted in the sand, its huge, black form nearly obscured by the swirling dust and muddy rain. All he had to do was promise to answer Krueger's questions, and he would be whisked back inside the comfort of its armored, sealed cabin. He would be able to breathe. . . .

Maybe it wouldn't hurt if he did tell Krueger what he knew. Even though he didn't know what the time was, he did know that *Questar* should have raised ship by now. His friends were probably already on their way to Storm.

Unless they were still in Tribon, trying to stop his summary execution?

No. He couldn't risk talking, couldn't risk revealing the little he knew about the stormfire gems . . . or the map in Thorne's secretary. The thought of Diane in these people's hands burned in his thoughts worse than the acid splattering across his skin.

He thought about sprinting for the transport crawler and slipping into the dark shelter between the tracks and beneath the huge machine's belly. Grep! He should have thought of that sooner . . . except that the sudden, hard rain was already starting to turn the omnipresent dust into mud, and it was pooling in low spots, steaming in the humid air. Besides, Krueger would just have them move the machine anyway, and he would have to crawl through the puddles to stay under cover.

He just didn't have the energy anymore.

Something caught his eye a meter away, pressed up against the boulder. As the rain continued, the wet sand quickly trickled away, exposing more and more of the object—an oblong, bone-white sphere the size of his head.

In a few more moments, enough was revealed. A skull grinned at him from the mud, the bone polished clean and deeply etched by acid. The curdled remnants of a plastic mask and a pair of copper-colored oxygen cylinders lay close by. It must have been a recent execution for the skull still to be recognizable as such.

He wondered who it had been. Their bones would be sharing this spot, soon, dissolving together a bit more with each rain. It would be nice to know, in a morbidly nightmarish way.

His clothing was soaked, now, the intolerable itching and burning spreading now over his entire body. His tunic was literally dissolving, falling away in half-dissolved clumps of plastic fibers, and the itching on his back was becoming unendurable. He could feel the burns, the blisters forming on the tender skin of his exposed back. Maybe he *should* try for the shelter offered by the crawler.

He blinked, trying to see through tearing, burning eyes. The crawler was gone!

No. There it was. It had moved, rumbling off to the side a bit farther away. Krueger was telling him that his hope of survival was getting slimmer, that he'd better talk if he wanted to live.

Spacer struggled with the thought. Suppose he did talk? Wouldn't Krueger just extract every bit of information he had then toss him back out here to die? Did he even know enough to satisfy the man? These people probably already knew about the stormfires. Why else would they be so interested in the TXI party? They probably knew about the map, too. Surely that's what Krueger had been looking for when they'd grabbed Thorne and forced him into that alley.

If he betrayed his friends, they would die, and he would die as well. Better if he died alone.

Another thought occurred to him. Somehow—he still wasn't sure why—he was important to Krueger, important enough at least that the man was spending a lot of effort trying to get him to talk. That suggested that he was Krueger's only lead, the only hold he had on the rest of the party.

"You know," he said aloud, "you're wasting your time."

The sound of his own voice sounded strange in his ears—thick and rasping. The fumes seeping in through the filters had burned the lining of his mouth and throat to the point where he could scarcely speak. He coughed, swallowed, and licked his dry lips inside the mask.

"I'm not going to tell you anything when I know you'll just kill me afterward anyway . . . *and* kill my friends."

The rain was letting up. In another moment, the deadly drops had stopped falling, and the clouds overhead were tattering in the planet's constant, high-altitude winds, spilling golden shafts of sunlight across the barren, boulder-strewn landscape. Spacer let himself stretch out a bit, savoring the respite.

There was no answer from the squatting, black crawler transport.

They'd not given him a receiver, so he couldn't bargain with them. All he could do was try to convince them that they were throwing away their one chance to get any information, because he was willing to die to protect his friends.

"Yeah," he said. "Don't imagine I have much time left out here. When I'm dead, you guys'll have to start all over, right? By this time, my friends must already be on the way to Storm. How you gonna stop 'em *now*?"

He wished he had his cards. They'd taken them from him—along with his cloak, his borrowed jacket, new boots, and his travel bag—at the Lower Hall after he'd been captured last cycle. Not that he could have done a reading out here . . . or that he expected the cards to turn up anything except Death—or the Nine of Swords with its bleak message of despair, depression, suffering, and loss.

If he did convince them to come out and take him back inside, it wouldn't do that much good, not in the long run. In fact, they might come up with something worse than exposing him topside.

What if they used him as a bargaining chip with Diane and the others?

The Two of Minds. Confusion. Double-mindedness. Uncertainty. Two clear directions to move in, and an inability to decide . . .

Maybe it was better if he died now. Anything else that happened would almost certainly be worse, maybe a *lot* worse.

What if they did use him as a hostage? Would that stop the TXI party? It wouldn't slow Verdoss, he knew, not for a moment. Maricia? He didn't know her well enough.

But Diane and Ta Shaa Ta, he thought, really cared about him, cared about what happened to him. Jarrett, too, he thought . . . though the Ranger didn't seem to be one who'd be swayed by sentiment.

He couldn't betray them. He didn't even dare try to bargain with Krueger, not if there was a chance that the man would find some other, more efficient means of using him to get at his friends.

"You bastards can just all go to hell!" he screamed into the mask. "I wouldn't come back in there if you wanted me to!"

The wind was picking up again now that the rain shower was past. Dust and grit swirled through the rain-cleansed air and began clotting the small puddles of water on the muddy ground. Soon, visibility would be down to almost nothing once again.

In the southwest sky, however, high above the dayside mountains and well clear of the golden, horizon-hugging blaze of Oberon, the Star was gleaming through a green-purple gap in the ragged clouds. It was growing brighter as he watched, a dazzling pinpoint agleam in a beauty impossible in so stark and barren a landscape. Titania seemed to pulse and shimmer in the dusty atmosphere, a radiant beacon touching the nearby clouds with jagged brushstrokes of silver and blue.

The Star. Hope and faith. The promise of something better.

There was something to cling to, even as the clouds thickened and the silver gleam of the star began to fade.

The wind blew harder, keening and wailing now as it lashed across the boulder field with its deadly burden of grit and sand. Titania faded completely from view, lost behind a mountain of brown and red clouds piling high against the tortured sky. The ground, muddied by the rain only moments before, was already dry, the puddles smothered in fresh, windblown sand or evaporated beneath the wind's hurricane caress. The skull nearby was already gone, sunken once more into the hungry sand.

Spacer struggled to his feet, his eyes still on the spot where the Star had appeared so briefly and with such fervent hope. As he emerged from behind the boulder's shelter, the wind clawed at him, alive and shrill. His tunic fluttered wildly behind him, then tattered and shredded away, clawed from his body by that living, shrieking, sandblasting wind. In seconds, the tender skin of his chest and stomach and upper arms was scoured raw. The pain was terrible but somehow easier to bear than the terror and helplessness that had clutched at his throat and mind earlier.

Deliberately, he turned his back on the crawler and took an unsteady step forward. He had to lean forward against the wind, had to close his mind against the rasping pain, but he managed another step, and then another. He would face his death, not try to wiggle away from it cowering behind the illusory safety of a rock. He would face it, holding the image of the Star in his thoughts until the last possible moment.

His eyes were burning so badly now that he could hardly see through the tears. He blinked furiously then turned slightly, holding his arm across his face. He thought he heard something and turned completely around, staring back the way he'd come. He could just barely make out the shape of the crawler . . . and of the two armored troopers trudging through the wind-lashed sand in his direction.

So Krueger had decided to bring him back inside, if only to prolong the torture for a bit . . . or because Spacer had called his bluff, and Krueger knew he would have to try something else.

Or . . . what if Authority Headquarters had intervened? Maybe they'd convinced Krueger to bring him back alive.

Unlikely. Spacer *knew* people, his one genuine talent—the key to reading the holotarot. Krueger was more likely to kill him than to pretend it had all been a mistake.

He turned again and kept moving, pushing into the wind, into Dayside. He was angry with himself. He'd deliberately provoked Krueger into bringing him back in, but now that the tactic had worked, he didn't want to go. He *wouldn't* go.

He would make them kill him first.

The wind's velocity kept increasing, sandblasting his skin, clawing at his face and arms and chest. Windblown droplets of rain were mixed with the grit, stinging as they hit raw skin. He could hear thunder in the distance, just audible above the howling of the wind. A lightning storm coming. . . .

His feet were burning. When he chanced a look down, most of the bare skin was blood-slicked, and blisters were forming between the toes. Each step was agony, and he had to stop, stop and turn and look back through streaming eyes. He didn't think he could keep moving, not fast enough to outrun those goons in battle armor. They were a lot closer now, pressing ahead through the swirling sand.

How could he stop them from simply knocking him down and dragging him back to the crawler? He had to keep moving.

The roll of distant thunder he'd heard earlier, he realized, had never let up. It had grown, in fact, as though sweeping across the boulder-strewn terrain from the dark blue clouds looming above the eastern horizon. The two guards stopped their pursuit and turned to face the east.

A shadow materialized out of the dust and mist.

Spacer stopped and stared, gaping, the pain and itching and blood forgotten. It was a ship, and a fairly large one. He didn't recognize the design but supposed from its size and general air of rugged utility that it was a small tramp freighter, three or four thousand tons crammed into an ugly, boxy, insect shape with bulging black swellings for a head and eyes and a segmented, reverse-swept tail like an upraised sting supporting paired drive nacelles and thrust pods. The hull had originally been painted in white and blue stripes, but much of the surface was now rusted red-brown and broken everywhere by spike antennae, sponsons, sensor arrays, and a pair of weapons mounts—a chin turret mounted ventral and forward, and a plasma beam pod as part of the tail array. Static discharge vanes shuddered in the wind, and the blue haze of its shielding sparkled and flashed as sand particles blew into it in tiny, vaporizing bursts of heat and light.

Lison had patrol ships of its own—a fair-sized navy, in fact, that had originally been in Rigunmor service until the revolt. Spacer didn't remember any vessels that looked like this one, though—heavy and clumsy, almost certainly a conversion job from a small freighter. It trembled as it plowed into the wind, its induction fields holding it aloft, its auxiliary thrusters battling to keep it from being turned or swept away by the gale. Atmospheric stabilizers had been deployed, but the craft was anything but streamlined. Whoever was jockeying those thrusters, Spacer thought, was *good*.

The two troopers in their assault armor fumbled with their weapons. The freighter's chin turret spun, the twin barrels of high-energy lasers dropping to track them. The guards needed no further encouragement at all; both bolted suddenly for the safety of the crawler.

The dome turret on the crawler's back flashed as it loosed a beam at the approaching vessel. The beam, visible as a sparkling thread of red light against the driving dust and sand, clawed at the freighter's hull, raising a black, zigzag gash across her primary drive housing aft and scoring across the right side of her hull.

The freighter returned fire with her chin lasers. Two flickering beams sliced through the transport's aft section, burning through armor plate in a hissing, crackling flare of light and splattering droplets of molten cerametal. The crawler fired again, targeting the ship's drive sections. A second shot from the ship slashed open the crawler's turret, silencing the gun.

Abruptly, the crawler began lumbering away, its broad tracks throwing up clouds of sand and dust as it slewed up a nearby hill, racing for the cover of the badlands. The two troopers followed it, waving wildly as they chased their one hope for a ride home.

Breathing hard, Spacer sank to his knees, his back to the keening wind as the freighter drifted closer, settling toward the ground. Landing jacks deployed like opening claws; a hatch in the vessel's belly was already open, a loading ramp extending like a white tongue. Spacer tried to rise, struggling to his feet, but he collapsed before he could manage three unsteady steps.

The next thing he knew, two figures, anonymous in climate suits, were hurrying toward him. One took his left arm, the other his right, and together they lifted him off the hot sand and carried him at a quick jog back toward the ship.

As he got closer, he had a glimpse of the vessel's name, painted in rust-obscured script above the chin turret: *Questar*.

They laid him gently on the steel deck. The figures ripped off their respirator masks. One was Jarrett, the other Diane. Ta Shaa Ta was there, opening a medcare kit.

Maricia stood nearby with a decon hose, while Verdoss watched, arms folded, from a doorway.

"Hit him," Diane said, and Maricia turned the hose on him. The water was warm, and though it struck hard, Maricia's handling of the stream was gentle. Diane and Jarrett pulled off the last of the rags clinging to Spacer's body, and the water sluiced off the burning, itching chemicals that had been adhering to his skin. Unfortunately, a good bit of skin came off with it.

They rolled him over to make sure they got every part of him, including his hair and scalp. By the time the decon shower was done, the fraal and Diane were already applying strips of artificial skin and wet bandages that molded to his body, controlling bleeding and sealing the burns and open wounds. Someone hit him with an analgesic injector, and the raw rasp of pain from every part of his skin began to fade. With Spacer on his back again, Ta Shaa Ta applied a few drops of a pungent-smelling liquid to the edges of the respirator mask. Within a few moments, the molecular bond began to dissolve, and Diane was able to pull the mask free.

"Good thing they didn't use a molecular weld on you," she said brightly, "or you'd have had to go through life with a plastic nose, eating through a straw."

Spacer couldn't reply at once. He was too busy lying on his back, gulping down cool, tasteless air and savoring the spreading sensation of the pain's *absence*, like a soft and touch-blurring blanket radiating out through every part of his body.

"That feels . . . wonderful," he said at last.

"I think we got you in just in time," Diane said. "You've got some pretty bad burns, but I don't think it's bad enough to require cosmetic repair. Your hair bleached a little, but that'll grow back."

"How . . . h-how did you find me?"

"We went to the Lower Hall first," Diane told him, "and convinced them that you weren't the murderer, while Ta Shaa Ta went to the docking bay and explained things to Captain Duprés. They told us you'd been taken to the flats for execution. We told them to keep broadcasting orders to the crawler not to carry out the sentence while we tubed up to the spaceport, climbed aboard *Questar*, and launched." She held up the mask. "If they hadn't stuck this on you though, you'd have been dead long before we got here."

"How did you manage to convince them I wasn't the killer?" he asked. "The Authority isn't exactly known for its forgiving or believing nature."

"Well, that was my fault, actually," Jarrett said. "When I was logged into the Lower Hall's datafile, I planted a little data of my own. I made them think that the people who kidnapped you were Rigunmors and that they'd bribed some officials and forced through your execution."

The fraal helped ease Spacer up to a sitting position and continued applying sealer strips to the worst of his blisters and abrasions. Spacer was aware of a dull, throbbing rumble sensed through the deck plating. "It wasn't Rigs," he told them. "It's VoidCorp. It was a guy named Krueger, working for VoidCorp."

"We know," Diane told him, "but Lison has an agreement with VoidCorp. They gave VoidCorp a contract to mine another planet in the Oberon system."

"Hux," Spacer said. "Oberon Five. That's the next planet out from Lison."

"Right. That meant there were people in your government who might tend to turn a blind eye to VoidCorp's shenanigans in this system. Maybe officials who'd been bought by VoidCorp. If they thought it was the Rigunmor Consortium, though . . ."

Spacer laughed, though the effort hurt even through the analgesic fuzz. "That," he said, "seems to fit! How'd you manage it, though? I always heard that outsiders couldn't tamper with Lison's Grid."

"You've got an antique system, all right," Jarrett said. "That's one reason we had to come out here. Information is information, whether it's fiber-optic laser, mass transceivers, or high-frequency carrier waves. Unfortunately, they're going to know soon enough that we tricked them."

"It's just a damned good thing the deception won't last long," Verdoss said from the doorway as they helped Spacer to his feet. "That lie could have hurt the Consortium's diplomatic status on Lison."

"What do you mean, it won't last long?" Spacer asked.

"I didn't have time to do a thorough job planting that incriminating evidence," Jarrett said. "I couldn't reach that many files, and there are plenty of people in the Lison government who *have* been taking VoidCorp bribes. They won't want to expose themselves, but they'll be able to unravel things pretty quickly and prove we set them up."

Maricia shrugged. "All he had to do was create enough doubt about what was going on," she said. "It got your execution stayed, not canceled. They were going to review your case, which was why they were trying to get the crawler to turn around and bring you back."

"Then, they could find out you lied any moment!" Spacer said. "What happens when they do?"

Jarrett smiled. "Not much they can do, kid. We've already left Lison."

"What?"

That explained the rumbling he could feel through the deck plating.

"Sure," Diane told him. "There's no point in going back to Tribon, especially since they might want to press charges for the damage we did to one of their topside crawlers. At the very least, it would mean a nasty legal case and maybe some questions none of us want to answer right now." She was looking at Verdoss as she said it.

"Especially since I *am* Rigunmor," Verdoss added, "and I *have* spread some money around in certain quarters. There are things about Storm we don't want anyone else to know about just yet."

"But . . . that means we're already lifting?" Spacer asked.

"Sure," Diane said. "What do you think?"

"Oh, grep! I need to see out!"

"What?"

"Please? Is there a window? A vidscreen?"

"C'mon," Jarrett said.

Spacer was a bit unsteady on his feet as they led him forward through a tight maze of passageways and compartments, and past a door that slid open when Jarrett said something into a comm pick-up on the bulkhead.

Beyond was *Questar*'s flight bridge. Smilin' Jack sat in the left seat, his first mate in the right, both of them embraced by horseshoe consoles covered by touch-screens and control boards. The overhead and bulkheads forward and to either side were masked in vidscreens, creating the illusion that they were standing in the open, with nothing above or around them but empty sky.

Spacer looked up and felt his knees start to give way beneath him. Someone—Diane, he thought—guided him down to a seat tucked in next to the ship environmental controls. His eyes never left the sky.

Space arced overhead, a black emptiness so deep it was palpable. Oberon shone brightly ahead and to the right, its orange light not dimmed or tinted by Lison's dust-laden sky. To the left was Oberon's sister, the Star, Titania, blue-white and brilliant, its light rock-steady without the characteristic scintillation imparted by atmosphere.

And behind . . .

Spacer stared up at the sky visible behind the aft bulkhead and the open pressure door he'd just come through. He'd never seen a photograph of Lison seen from low orbit, never dreamed that there was anything *to* see.

He'd been wrong.

From this new vantage point, Lison was a cracked and tortured surface of ocher, white, and myriad smeared browns, swaddled in varicolored streaks and patches and mottlings of cloud. *Questar* was rising above the planet's dayside. The terminator, where most of the cities and surface habitats were located, was a thin, sunset-colored streak against the eternal black of Lison's night. Spacer wondered where Tribon was but had no idea how to find it. Its port access lock and surface beacons must be lost by now, dwindled into clouds and distance.

Spacer's breath came in short, tight gasps. His head was spinning, and he didn't think it was from his topside exposure. He'd never in his entire life imagined that his own homeworld could be so beautiful.

"Clear of the atmosphere," Mike said.

"Right," Jack said, his fingers tapping out a rapid-fire staccato on a touch screen panel. "Stowing the airfoils and discharge vanes. Prepare to engage stardrive."

"Bringing mass reactor up to max. Forty seconds."

"Roger that."

"Hey boss?" Mike said. "We got company. Bearing three-five-zero, mark ten."

"I see 'em," Jack replied. "I make four contacts, ahead and above. Out of atmosphere and closing fast.

"You have a visual on those contacts?" Jarrett asked.

Jack tapped on the touch screen, and a window opened against the black sweep of space visible to the right, a rectangle showing the ocher backdrop of the planet and a quartet of black vessels, lean as knife-blades and seen almost point-on, angling toward them in an attempt to trap them between space and Lison.

"What are they?" Jarrett asked. "ULS government?"

"I don't think so," Jack said. "They're not squawking on the Lison IFF freaks. If I had to guess . . ."

"Yeah?"

"Pirates. Maybe someone hired by your Voider pals."

Questar jolted suddenly as a flash glared briefly astern.

"Definitely the shoot first, ask later type," Mike said. "Drive kick-over in ten seconds.

"Let's do it." Jack reached out a hand, fingers poised above the control board. "On my mark, five . . . four . . ."

"*Red light!*" Mike called. "I've got a circuit failure, port drive sponson! We're bleeding mass to energy. Powering down on the mass reactor!"

"Grep!"

Questar jolted again.

"What is it?" Diane asked. "What's happening?"

"We're not going anywhere fast, that's what's happening," Jack said. His fingers were dancing across the touchpads now. The three warships visible in the vid window were growing steadily larger.

"Drive coil failure!" Mike called. "Port side! Looks like we took more damage than we thought."

"What's the matter?" Jarrett said. "Can't you jump?"

"Get these damned nullhead sightseers *off* my bridge!" Smilin' Jack yelled.

Mike swiveled her seat, glaring at them. "You heard the boss," she said. "Everybody out!"

The vessel jolted a third time, hard. As he was hustled off the bridge, Spacer caught a last glimpse of the knife-blade warships, closing in for the kill.

Chapter Eleven

SMILIN' JACK NUDGED the joystick forward, angling *Questar* back toward the arc of Lison's atmosphere. "They've got us cut off!" he said. "We'll have to lose 'em in the clouds!"

Mike hit the ship intercom. "All hands, strap down!" she cried. "This is gonna be rough!"

Questar's nose and leading hull edges began heating as the ship sliced back into the atmosphere. A steady, rumbling thunder sounded from outside as a bone-rattling vibration began to build.

"Where are they?" Jack was fighting the controls as the ship pitched and bucked.

"Passed overhead and behind us," Mike said. "They're swinging around, coming in on our tail."

Red-brown and ocher clouds flashed past the bridge. *Questar,* plunging deeper into the planet's atmosphere, dropped into the clouds, banked hard to the right, and then left as a savage detonation rocked the ship.

"They're still on us!" Mike yelled. "Range three-seven-oh and closing!"

Questar broke through the belly of the cloud deck, still descending. Jagged mountains, black and craggy, reached for them from the tortured landscape below.

"What are you trying to do?" Mike yelled.

"Lose them!" White fire flashed from the rugged surface below. He pulled back on the joystick, letting *Questar* slew to port, dropping into a steep-walled valley. "Can you target any of 'em?"

"I'm trying. It would help if you weren't jinking all over the sky!"

Another explosion splintered a mountaintop to starboard. "Right now, Mike, my jinking is the only thing keeping us alive!"

He dropped lower still. The boulder-strewn surface of Lison was a red-ocher blur beneath them as they flashed out of the valley and across a broad, chaotically broken plain. Ahead, a wall of cloud like gray ash towered across the horizon, a solid curtain from ground to overcast sky.

"Wha—you can't take us in there!" Mike exclaimed.

"The Magma Sea," Jack said, gripping the ship's controller. "If we can pull 'em all in on our tail . . ."

A succession of explosions jolted the hurtling ship. Mike tapped out a series of commands on her console. "I've got a lock!"

"Take him!"

"Firing!"

Questar's dorsal turret loosed a bolt that seared into the cliffs behind the nearest enemy vessel. Then they were plunging through darkness as they entered the cloud wall, a black and murky ocean aglow with sullen, ember-red fires. Lightning flared overhead.

"They're still with us."

"Okay. Hang onto your stomach!"

He wrenched the stick over, standing *Questar* on her port side, arrowing now within a few meters of that deadly, molten surface. Hot air rose in billowing torrents, and *Questar* screamed protest as Jack yanked her nose over, then up.

Astern, one of their pursuers tried to match Jack, move for move, but with just a hair too little energy coming out of the tight turn, he sideslipped, dropped . . . and then one wing dragged in boiling, liquid rock.

In an instant, the pursuer flipped nose-down into the magma, exploded, and was gone. *Questar*, climbing almost straight up, howled through billowing gray murk to emerge once again in a dazzling, sun-lit expanse of sky and cloud.

Smilin' Jack kicked in full throttle.

*   *   *   *   *

Spacer felt another wrench and jolt and clutched the arms of his chair. "What is he doing up there?" he said.

"Trying to save our necks," Jarrett replied. "Just be glad his inertial compensators are working okay."

There was a large vidscreen up and running in *Questar*'s lounge, a small compartment aft of the bridge and forward of the passenger quarters. Spacer lay in one of the reclining chairs, staring at the screen that was showing the view aft of the ship. For the last several moments, he hadn't been able to see much of anything but blurred landscapes alarmingly close, then roiling gray clouds.

Now, *Questar* appeared to be heading straight up and away from Lison, and Spacer found himself staring into the Magma Sea, the near legendary ocean of molten rock steaming and simmering on Lison's dayside equator where Oberon shone directly overhead. As the ship rose higher, knifing into space, he could see a vast, pinwheel swirl of black and ash-gray clouds edged by Oberon's golden light, like a hurricane the size of a continent. Staring hard, he could see the sullen flicker and pulse of lightning storms buried deep within the storm, but there was no sign of the molten sea itself.

Ancient images of various hells could have been set beneath those clouds. No one knew why the Sea was there, but it, not cool and distant Oberon, was responsible for Dayside temperatures that approached three hundred degrees.

Spacer had always wanted to see the Magma Sea, which every Lisoner knew existed but very few had seen. Surface runners, scientists . . . but few had ever returned to tell of what they'd seen.

Spacer wished he could have seen the equally fabled, equally impossible Oxygen Sea on the Nightside, then decided that he'd had quite enough brushes with death for the day.

"What power!" Maricia said quietly from her chair nearby.

"Did we lose the bad guys?" Rom wanted to know.

"Can't tell," Jarrett said. "We'll just have to wait and see what the captain tells us."

Lison was dwindling fast astern, the curve of the horizon closing rapidly on itself from an arc of ocher and sunset to a closed disk, made lopsided by the slender reach of the night side as Smilin' Jack adjusted the ship's course.

Spacer lay still, watching the planet dwindle and vanish as the others finished tending to his injuries. Diane and Ta Shaa Ta applied the last of the artificial skin strips to his burns, while Maricia hooked up a needle to his left arm. They were running an IV drip from a plastic bag—antirad serum to counter the effects of his exposure to Lison's deadly topside environment.

Someone had dug up a robe for him, more for warmth than for any concern for modesty. *Questar*'s interior was kept a bit on the chilly side, and the stark steel and ceramic bulkheads, wiring bundles and conduits snaking everywhere, combined with utilitarian lack of creature comforts offered little in the way of physical amenities. The interior looked cold, whatever the actual temperature might have been.

He was starting to hurt, now. *Grep*, he hurt! The robe burned where it stretched across his shoulders and hung down his back, and even the analgesics they'd given him couldn't blur out all of the pain. It didn't matter, though. He was aboard a ship . . . a starship, even if the drive was disabled at the moment.

He was in space, off of Lison.

The wonder he felt, the giddy sense of detachment, was as good an analgesic as the drugs they'd given him.

Diane gave him another injection, a dose of regenecells to boost his natural recuperative powers. Spacer was scarcely aware of their ministrations, though. He watched the large, slightly curved flatscreen mounted on the lounge bulkhead, where Lison was now reduced to a tiny disk of light. It grew smaller, second by second, until it was only a bright star at the center of the screen. Without the glare to wash them out, other stars appeared, a sprinkling of ice against back velvet, crossed by a faint smudge of blue-white haze marking the galactic plane—what men once had called the *Via Galactica*, the Milky Way.

Spacer had never seen the stars before, save in holopics. Their cold, distant beauty was inexpressible.

He also found the sight a terribly lonely one. It was an unnerving jolt, realizing that his homeworld, all of Lison, everything he'd ever known, was now nothing more than a spark all but lost against the night.

He had to wrench his mind away from such thoughts.

It took him a while to realize that they'd stopped taking fire from the enemy ship. There'd been no more bounces or thumps from near-misses for some time, now.

"Are we outrunning them?" he asked.

"We're in open space now," Jarrett told him, glancing up at the screen. "That means Captain Duprés can open up the inductors and go to max acceleration. What happens next depends on who has the better acceleration—us or them."

"With the stardrive down," Diane added, "we can't jump to drivespace. We have to outrun them."

"Where can we go? There's not a lot in the Oberon system except for Lison, and we can't go back there."

"These little independent freighters are usually pretty self-contained," Jarrett said. "Captain Duprés will have an engineering crew aboard, and probably some repair 'bots working on the damage now. Unless he's gone and burned out an entire drive coil or blown the mass reactor, he should be able to get us running again. If not"—he shrugged—"I imagine we'll face that when the time comes. There are other cities on Lison that aren't quite so tightly under Tribon's thumb—Raphal, for instance."

"Now *there's* a thieves' den," Spacer said.

"Coming from you, that's quite the compliment," Verdoss said.

"Hardly. Raphal is part of United Lison, I guess, but it's run by Thomas Kind and his friends." He frowned. "Trouble is, if those ships chasing us are Kind's or allies of his, we won't be able to go *there*, either."

"Like Jarrett says, we'll worry about that when the time comes," Diane told him.

Spacer looked at her. "I—I haven't had a chance to say thanks. You guys risked a lot coming after me like that."

"Hey, we couldn't leave you," Diane said. "We're partners, now!"

"Profit! Give me a break!" Verdoss said, staring up at the overhead.

"Don't mind *him*. He helped convince Duprés that we should come find you."

"It seemed the best way to protect my considerable investment in this expedition."

"Besides," Maricia pointed out, "Ta Shaa Ta would've burned out our brains and handed them back to us on a platter if we'd left you."

Spacer turned and looked at the fraal, who'd been standing motionless on the other side of the lounge, watching him. He had the feeling the alien was studying him with an unnerving depth and clarity of focus.

"Thank you," he said.

"Thanks are not necessary," the fraal replied. "I wish to know your mind better."

"I'm not sure there's that much to know."

"You underestimate yourself by a considerable margin, or else you employ false modesty, which serves no purpose beyond invoking further statements of praise and is therefore pointless. I have been intrigued by your mind since we first met." The fraal paused. "The rest of you should know, by the way, that Spacer told his captors nothing of importance or value, despite the fact that doing so might have saved—or at least prolonged—his life. He didn't want the VoidCorp operatives to get us."

Verdoss started. "What? You faced down a VoidCorp KL-level Employee, went through all that and didn't break? That's not bad." He said it grudgingly, but he *said* it.

Spacer's ears burned.

"Like I said," Diane added. "We're partners now. We look out for you. You look out for us."

Spacer sighed. "I just wish I had my cards. They took all my things before they shoved me aboard the transport."

"Ah," Jarrett said, grinning. "About that." Rising, he walked from the lounge and returned a few moments later. In his hands were his spare jacket, Spacer's boots, cloak, travel bag . . . and the red pouch holding his holotarot deck.

"My cards!" Spacer cried, reaching for them. "How did you. . . ?"

"We claimed them at the Lower Hall," Diane said, "acting as your next of kin. We thought you'd want them back."

"You thought right!" He opened the pouch, spilling the card into his hand. "Maybe I can find out who it is that's chasing us!"

Shuffling awkwardly—his hands were numb from the analgesics they'd given him, and the blisters made him clumsy—he flipped out a single card and dropped it on the tabletop next to the sofa.

The Nine of Pentacles. The tall woman walked in her garden, a hooded bird of prey perched upon her out-stretched hand. . . .

"Her again," Jarrett said. He laughed. "We just can't shake that witch, can we?"

"Kid," Verdoss said, "you have *got* to be dealing from the bottom of the deck!"

"I'm not," Spacer said. "I just take the cards that come up."

Diane looked at Ta Shaa Ta. "What do you think?" she

asked him. "Is he unconsciously manipulating the cards somehow?"

"I can't say," the fraal replied. "I don't yet understand what's happening. I can follow his thoughts, but his right-brain operations are still obscure. I can't make them out."

"Right brain," Spacer said. "Like what you were saying last cycle? About people having two brains?"

"In a manner of speaking, Spacer. At least, it's a useful model. Your psionic abilities reside, primarily, in your right cerebral hemisphere. They surface as hunches, as flashes of inspiration, as intuition, even as dreams. You seem to use these cards to focus these hunches into something tangible, words and sentences more concrete than feeling. The question is whether you also affect the cards unconsciously. You could be a low grade telekinetic."

"Whadda you mean by that?" Spacer demanded, suddenly angry. Grep! He'd thought the fraal *liked* him!

"Watch your language, Ta Shaa Ta," Jarrett said with a grin. "What you just called him could get you killed on Lison."

The fraal hesitated, the large eyes blinking twice. "I apologize. How did I give offense?"

"Mining culture," Maricia said. "A lot of their shared imagery and linguistic forms are drawn from mining. High grade means good, as in high grade ore. I imagine low grade must be a pretty bad insult."

"It means worthless," Spacer said. He let himself relax. Offies could be so damned strange sometimes. "Guess it shouldn't hurt. I've been called that a *lot*."

"I apologize," Ta Shaa Ta said quietly. "I spoke in ignorance of your *Umvelt*. I meant merely to say that you may possess rudimentary telekinetic talents, which, like your intuition, are focused through your cards."

"S'okay. You didn't mean it. What . . . what was that oommie thing you said I had?"

"Umvelt," Maricia said. "It's a German word used by behaviorists, psychologists, and xenoculturalists. It means the specific worldview of an animal or person—of any being, in fact—based on what it perceives through its experience or senses. Ta Shaa Ta sees the world differently than we do. His eyes can see further into the infrared, but he can't see the colors blue and purple. His hearing's not as good as ours, but his senses of taste and smell are *much* sharper. And he takes for granted various mental powers, like telepathy. Most humans can never know what that's like. So, it stands to reason, his understanding of the world is a little different from ours—not *too* different. You can imagine some nonhumans, though, whose senses are so alien we can't begin to imagine how they view their world."

"The stormies," Diane said. "As near as we can tell, they're blind. They see their world through touch and hearing, a sonar sense."

"Right," Maricia said. "A completely alien Umvelt. Anyway, all Ta Shaa Ta was saying was that you grew up in the tunnels of Tribon. Your senses are the same as ours, but your experience and your background is a lot different. It makes you see things in different ways from us. Sometimes, that's going to catch us by surprise."

Spacer shrugged. "No problem." He'd not really wanted a lecture on xenoculture. He was more interested in what the fraal had said about his having telekinetic abilities. Did that mean he could make things float in the air, maybe pick a mark's pocket from across the room?

With training, Ta Shaa Ta said, *any rudimentary psionic power can be deepened, strengthened, and extended.*

He looked at the fraal . . . and then with a burst of surprise, he realized the words had been spoken *in his mind*, that Ta Shaa Ta had not spoken aloud at all.

How much of him, of his past, of his memories, could the alien read that way? It made Spacer distinctly uncomfortable.

Hours passed, and Spacer's medical treatment was completed. Maricia unhooked the IV anti-rad drip. The artificial skin strips were carefully checked for signs of inflammation or rejection, but none were found. Ta Shaa Ta carefully scanned Spacer's mind again, searching for

signs of shock or traumatic stress, and pronounced him
stable. His burns and blisters, the patches where his skin
had been abraded raw by blowing sand, still hurt, especially as the analgesics wore off, but he was able to get
about and even wear the robe without wincing at its
touch.

"For someone who spent almost two hours topside on
Lison," Diane told him at one point, "you're in pretty good
shape."

Had it only been two hours? It had felt like much
longer, but the memory of those hours was already fading,
the edge of the pain almost gone. Even his visual
memory—the terror of being outside with all of that sky
pressing down from above—was losing its crystal-sharp
clarity and focus. Was that the effect of the drugs, or had
Ta Shaa Ta tampered with his mind somehow? He didn't
know, but he was grateful in any case. It was not an experience he cared to repeat . . . even in his thoughts.

After a time, Smilin' Jack appeared. He looked drawn
and haggard, with circles beneath his eyes that even that
scar-dragged grimace of a grin couldn't relieve. He was
wearing coveralls, and his hands and sleeves were stained
black with silicon lubricant and patch sealer.

"Didn't have a chance to ask earlier," he said, leaning
into the doorway with his arms pressed against the pressure seal above his head. "You okay, kid?"

"I'm fine," Spacer said. "Thanks for coming after me."

Duprés grimaced. "It's gonna cost you people. We
took a bad hit back there, and it's not good, but I'm glad
you're okay."

"We're all in your debt," Ta Shaa Ta said. "I'm sure we
will find a way to repay you."

"I'm sure you will too." He sighed. "Okay, people," he
continued, "here's the story. We took some damage duel-
ing with that crawler on the surface, and we burned out
one of our stardrive power coils when we were powering
up for our jump. We can fix it, we have the necessary
spares on board, but it's gonna take time to install the new
coil, and even more time to balance, sim, and test it. It

would be a *lot* better going back to Lison and doing it at a real shipyard.

"Now, normally I don't bother with democracy. It's my responsibility to make the decisions, and on this ship, what I says goes. Under any other circumstances, I'd be flipping *Questar* end-for-end right now and accelerating right back to Lison, where we came from.

"But I'm going to give you folks a choice. We've got us a kind of a special situation here."

"Those three ships that jumped us," Jarrett said.

"Yeah. Those friends of yours are damned persistent. One of them broke off a while ago, but the other two are still following us, and it looks like their inductors are as souped up as ol' *Questar*'s. Normally, we can outrun anything in space, but those guys are sticking with us. They're not getting any closer, but we're not losing them, either." He shook his head. "Who the hell did you guys tick off, anyway? Any self-respecting pirate would've given up hours ago and turned around to go hunt for slower game. Makes me wonder just what your real story is."

"I imagine," Ta Shaa Ta said, "that how much of the truth you learn may well depend on your decision regarding this vessel's destination."

Jack gave the fraal a long, hard look. "Maybe. And maybe I don't want to know, anymore. I thought at first those guys were old business partners of mine, people I owed some money, but they've already invested more in chasing us than I owed them, so that can't be the reason. I figure it's you they want, and someone is going to a hell of a lot of expense and trouble to get you."

"We suspect that it may be VoidCorp," Diane told him.

"Yeah?" Jack grinned. "I was figurin' it had something to do with the Riggies. I've crossed photons with the Voiders a time or two. Those people have *no* sense of humor. Makes sense, though. That ship that split away from the others looks like it's vectoring for Hux. There's nobody there but the Voiders' mining complex and the pirates who make a living off 'em."

"You said something about us having a choice to make, Captain," Verdoss said.

"Right. I can't just start decelerating for a straight run back to Lison. Those two wolves back there would be on us inside of half an hour. I don't have a positive ID on them yet, but their performance envelope suggests they're hyped up corvettes, Starrunner class possibly, or maybe Blood-hawk if we're really unlucky. *Questar* could hold her own against one of those ships, but not two. They haven't responded to my comm hails. I have to assume that if I try to go back the way we came, they're going to jump our tail and blast us.

"There's one other thing we can try, though, and that's where the choice comes in." He looked, he *sounded* tired. "We're on a vector that will take us close to Titania in another three days. If those jokers stick with us, we could use Titania's gravity to loop around without much deceleration and head back the way we came. If they stick with us, they'll still be on our tail. Then all we have to worry about is whether someone back at Lison is gonna be waiting for us when we get there."

"That's it?" Verdoss said. "That's our choice?"

"No. In the next couple of days, my gang is going to be yanking out the old coil and putting in a new one, balancing it, and checking it five ways from Founder's Day. Like I say, that's a job better done in a shipyard, but doing it here gives us our choice.

"If—and I can't emphasize this enough—*if* everything checks out in the sims, we might be able to jump into drivespace and get to Loman. Then, of course, we don't have to worry about the guys on our tail."

"That sounds . . . risky," Verdoss said.

"It is. Damned risky. We either loop around Titania—and that won't be a walk on the Concourse, lemme tell ya!—head back for Lison and straight into the arms of whatever reception committee they have waiting for us, or we hit drivespace with what amounts to makeshift repairs to our stardrive. We could explode. We could come out someplace completely different from where we want to be.

We could just disappear, and no one would ever know what had happened to us. There's another risk, too. We could emerge on-target, but if the new power connections don't take the feed, we could blow the drive again . . . and we don't have another back-up. We'd be stranded in the Loman system until someone came by to look the place over, and from what you've told us, the place doesn't get many visitors."

He straightened up, dropping his arms from the doorway and spreading his hands. "That's why I'm giving you folks some input into what ought to be a command decision. You know more about whoever is chasing us than I do. You also know how important getting to Loman is for you. Now you know the risks. What's it gonna be?"

"If we are correct about our pursuers being VoidCorp," Ta Shaa Ta said, "it seems unlikely that we will be able to negotiate."

"Oh, they'd negotiate, all right," Verdoss said, "but only if it suited them. If they want us dead, we're going to be dead, no matter what."

"Even if we got in touch with them," Diane said, "we couldn't trust what they said. They might agree to us giving up, then blow us out of space anyway."

"They'd have to," Verdoss said. "They're not going to want people to know that they've been playing pirate in Lison space, blowing up registered Lisoner vessels, bribing Lison officials. Obviously, they were trying to frighten us off before, or simply hamper us. The game has escalated too far now, though. I suspect those ships back there have one set of orders—destroy us by any means necessary."

"So you say we should try the jump to Storm?" Maricia asked.

"Definitely."

"Makes a hell of a lot of sense to me," Jarrett said.

"At least that way we have a chance," Maricia said.

"There's also whatever is going on at Storm to consider," Diane pointed out. "If VoidCorp is planning on exploiting the stormies somehow—"

"Does that mean there are Voider ships waiting for us at Loman?" Jack said, eyes narrowing.

"We don't know," Ta Shaa Ta said. "It is a possibility, certainly."

"Grep," Jack said. "Trapped between a cliff and a swarm of blackworms."

"At least we will have options."

"Yeah. Damned few, but options." Smilin' Jack looked at each of them in turn. "How about you, kid?" he asked Spacer. "You just got your life back. What do you want to do about it?"

"I—I was just wondering what it would be like to see the Star . . . Titania, I mean."

"You'll see it, okay, one way or another, but do you want to loop around or grab for night?"

"I don't want to go back to Lison!"

"Hmm. Can't say I blame you, after what you've been through. Okay, that's the consensus?"

"You must make the decision, Captain," Ta Shaa Ta said, "but so far as we are concerned, we *must* press on. There is no turning back. For *any* of us."

"I figured that's what you all would say. Okay . . . but it *is* still my call. If three days from now I get less than, oh, let's say an eighty percent success probability when we balance out the coil and run her through the sims, we just flat ain't goin'! I'll take my chances with trigger-happy marauders over a crabby drive coil any day!"

Spacer hardly heard him. After Smilin' Jack had asked his opinion, he'd pulled out his holotarot deck, shuffled them, then extracted a single card. He'd been thinking about the flight, their future, about what they should do . . . a vague enough request, to be sure. With Ta Shaa Ta's talk of psionic powers and telekinetic potentials, he felt his confidence in his ability to read the cards slipping. He wasn't sure he was up to formulating a more precise question about the future.

He dropped the card on the table, staring into the haze of the holoprojection that formed above it, holding his breath.

The reply to his vague question was equally vague, and rightly so, but at least it was a positive sign, not Death or the Tower or the Nine of Swords or any of the other harbingers of doom it might have been. In fact, the draw was quite a promising one.

The Star.

There was hope.

Chapter Twelve

AFTER AN ACCELERATION that would have converted all aboard to a thin red gruel without the induction drive's dampening effects, *Questar* soon reached a cruising velocity that let her tick off astronomical units at the rate of one every fifteen minutes. Sheltered by the ship's induction drive field from the discomfort of high acceleration, the passengers quickly settled into a shipboard routine that consisted largely of sleeping, eating, and reviewing their datafiles on Storm from Sennis Thorne's secretary.

They met the other members of the crew, Engineers Ron Carlyle and Nared Tartaglia, who for the most part stayed out of the passengers' way and seemed to expect the favor to be returned.

Spacer's blisters were nearly all gone after twenty-four hours, and even the rawest parts of his hands, arms, and back, still swaddled in artificial skin, were no longer hurting. He could get dressed again and stopped wandering around in a robe.

He had little to do. While the others studied the Storm

files, Spacer wandered those parts of *Questar* that weren't off-limits—there wasn't a whole lot to see—and spent a lot of time in front of the vidscreen, watching the stars. A touchpad gave him access to different sensors on the ship's hull, and he soon found the one mounted on the bow, staring straight ahead into the quickly brightening blue-white beacon of Titania. He spent most of his time in the lounge, watching the star and dropping holotarot cards into different spreads, trying to discern the future.

The cards, however, were largely silent—that, or his own mind was closed to their message.

It was as though he could no longer feel the story they were telling, even when the meaning should have been obvious. Each time he laid out a Celtic Cross while concentrating on whether or not the expedition would be successful, the Tower appeared—the forked lightning blasting apart a high tower, overturning a crown and sending two men, a king and another, hurtling headfirst and shrieking into the abyss.

The card indicated surprise, a singular, unexpected event, the bolt from the blue that could completely change one's life, but how to interpret it *here*? It could mean a rude awakening from complacency or the commonplace. It could mean an unchanging situation suddenly reversed, an old way of life abruptly changed, a shock, the sudden end of an enterprise . . . or even the beginning of a whole new way of life. It wasn't *necessarily* bad. . . .

But Spacer could get no feeling from the card at all, no emotion, no intuition.

He wondered if his experience topside had somehow changed whatever it was about him that let him read the cards' message.

He tried meditating on the card he'd drawn for the expedition before—the Star. He stared at the nude woman emptying her two containers upon water and earth as a man might stare at the holopic of a lover. Had she simply appeared as a message of hope, or did she literally represent the star they were approaching? If so, what did it

mean—that they should continue with the expedition to
Storm or whip around Titania and return to Lison?

He didn't know, and the cards were silent.

Spacer began to wonder if something was wrong with
him.

"So," Jarrett said late on the evening of their second day
out, "you're glad to be leaving Lison, huh?"

"Did it show that much?"

They were alone, the others in the party having retired
to their small cabins. It was almost impossible to find privacy aboard the tiny freighter. Spacer was used to crowding—all of his life had been spent sealed within the
crowded warrens of Tribon—but that just meant he valued
the time when he could be alone that much more.

"Well, a little." Jarrett sat down next to him. On the
screen, as always, the star gleamed brilliantly, the blue
nebula in which it was imbedded just now becoming
visible as a wispy tracery of strand-twisted fog. "You
weren't exactly hesitant about wanting to sign on with us.
I'd like to know why you're so eager to be out of there."

"You kiddin'?" Spacer snorted. "It's dull! *Nothing* ever
happens there. I would have died of boredom if you guys
hadn't shown up."

"Ah, but we *did* show up. Something must happen there
once in a while. We're the proof!"

He tried to suppress his growing exasperation. Jarrett
was playing word games with him. "Lison has got to be the
deadest planet in the galaxy. It's too crowded, there's no
work, most of the good mining jobs are taken, and the bad
ones aren't worth having. There's no place to go, no future,
and nothing you can do makes the slightest difference."

"So how do you figure it's going to be better on another
planet?"

"You've got to be skiploading me, right?"

"No, I'm not. What makes you think it would be better
anywhere else?"

"It couldn't be any worse!"

"Oh, I'd have to disagree with you there. Storm is going
to be a *lot* worse, a lot like living topside on Lison, but

with natives, lightning storms you wouldn't believe, floods every six days, and a whole cargo load of surprise dangers that we haven't even guessed at."

"Surprise dangers?"

"The Rig expedition barely scratched the surface of the place. This is a whole *world* we're talking about, not one of your tunnels in lower Tribon. Every time we go over a hill and see a new piece of the landscape, we'll be facing new dangers—maybe lots of them, maybe things we can't even dream of now."

Spacer thought about the Tower.

"At least there's the chance of a new direction, y'know? And . . . well, at least it won't be boring!"

"I guess you're right there."

Spacer touched the control, and the vidscreen switched to the view astern. Oberon was visible now, a brilliant orange star too small now to show a disk. Lison had vanished entirely, lost in the distance and glare of its star. The strange thing was that as fast as they were traveling now— something like a hundred and sixty thousand kilometers every second—there was absolutely no indication from the view outside that they were moving at all.

Spacer had heard that at high percentages of light speed, the view fore and aft became distorted as the very light waves from the stars were crammed together and stretched out astern, but there was no distortion he could detect yet. Was Titania a bit bluer now, or Oberon a bit redder? He couldn't tell, not with the naked eye, at any rate. As far as he could see, all of the stars remained motionless, unchanging, and very, very far away.

Questar seemed poised midway between the two brightest of those stars, hanging motionless, the blue giant ahead, the orange dwarf behind.

"There's no future there," he said aloud, half to himself. "No future, no hope, no mystery . . ."

Jarrett laughed, startling him. "No mystery? About Lison?"

"No. How could there be? The place is as dull as shaft tailings."

"Depends on your point of view, I guess. Lison is one of the most bizarre planets in the Verge. There's a whole planetological research institute on Aegis devoted to studying Lison's mysteries. They even have a local base in Tribon. You never heard of it?"

"Is that the Lison Institute?"

"Sure is. The Lison Planetological Anomalies Research Institute. LiPARI, for short."

"Well, I've heard of it, sure. They sometimes hire locals to do fieldwork topside." He grimaced. "You gotta be *nuts* to take on a job like that! I never knew it was an offworld thing, though. Figures."

"Why's that?"

"Crazy offies. No accounting for what they're interested in. No offense."

"None taken. The problem is, we thought we understood a lot about planets—how they evolve, how they grow and age, what happens to them when they die . . . but the universe seems to be specifically designed to throw us for a loop every time we think we have a part of it figured out. I guess it's good for us. Keeps us from being too complacent."

"What's so strange about Lison? It's locked to Oberon because it's so old. That happens to lots of planets, doesn't it?"

Jarrett shook his head. "Lison is one big package of anomalies and scientific impossibilities. At its distance from Oberon, Lison's day side ought to be a balmy minus fifty degrees Celsius. With that thick atmosphere, the night side shouldn't be much colder than minus one-fifty or so. The planet shouldn't be tidally locked, either. Leen, the next planet in, isn't, so the system isn't *that* old. The big mystery is that blue star, Titania."

"What about it?"

"It's young. Blue giants like that don't last more than about twenty million years before they use up so much of their hydrogen that they explode in a supernova. But Oberon is old enough to have spawned planets, complete with life . . . that takes billions of years. So Titania must have wandered into the area thousands of years ago. The planetologists think that a close passage by Titania might have caused some of the oddball effects—like slowing Lison and Hux so that they became tidally locked, and maybe melting Lison's dayside—but it doesn't explain it all, not by a long shot. And then there's the problem with—"

"Stop!" Spacer said, raising his hands. "Please! You'll have me believing I don't exist at all, pretty quick."

"Well, that's the trouble with physics. Just when you get a handle on the universe, someone goes and proves that you're trying to open the wrong door. We're presented with the facts, the objective reality of the situation, but what we see just doesn't fit with what we know about how the universe works." He laughed. "Sometimes I think God creates planets like Lison just to keep us humble. My point is that there's all kinds of mystery right in your own back yard. You don't have to go all the way to another star to find more than your fair share of the stuff."

Spacer shrugged. "Well, life's still life in Lison, y'know? All that stuff you were just talking about, it doesn't really have anything to do with getting through a day or finding a job."

"I know what you mean."

"How do you know all that stuff, anyway? About Lison and stuff?"

"That's my job. I'm a Verge Ranger."

"That means you have to know about all the systems out this way?"

"Among other things. We get hired out to research and exploration groups like this one who need local experts on just about everything—from planetography to native life to dangerous conditions to unpleasant politics."

"Yeah? How do you become a Ranger?"

Jarrett smiled. "A very great deal of very hard work. There's a school on Aegis, almost like a military training center."

Spacer sighed. "I know. And that takes money, right? Probably a lot."

"Yup."

"Figures."

For a moment Spacer's mind had been racing. Jarrett Aylen, as far as he could see, had the perfect career, a job that routinely took him to different worlds to meet different people, to experience different things. Spacer wasn't entirely sure how he would handle some of those experiences . . . like being out of doors, but he would have loved to have had the opportunity to try.

Not that *that* was ever very likely.

On the third day, *Questar* began her long deceleration toward the blue sun. Captain Duprés announced with obvious pride and pleasure that both of their pursuers had fallen some distance behind. Apparently, the modifications he'd made to the ship's drives had given the freighter a considerable edge in both acceleration and maneuverability. Her speed falling, *Questar* dropped toward Titania as the blue fog of the stellar nebula grew thick and knotted in her viewers.

Early on the morning of the fourth day, they all were crowded into the lounge, watching the display screen. Titania was close enough now to show a disk, but so bright that the ship's computer had to step down the fierce light from the star to prevent the optical circuits—or the watchers' eyes—from being blinded.

What the computer could reveal, however, was an essence of beauty, a perfection of form and light and color unlike anything Spacer had ever been able to imagine. The holopic souvenir given to him by his grandmother paled in comparison, as effective in conveying the reality as a description of a sunset to a man blind from birth.

The star nestled within its nebula, which appeared to be multiple layers of gossamer fog. It wasn't a true nebula, of course. What they were seeing, Jarrett informed them, was the outer layers of Titania's atmosphere as it was constantly being blown off into space, a steady hurricane of stellar wind. Stellar prominences arced and reared and sprayed into space, loops expanding upward through Titania's intense magnetic field in slow, graceful explosions of plasma, cool only by comparison with the searing blue-white heat of the star's corona.

The surface of the star itself, a pale, radiant blue with a faintly visible granulation, was mottled by black patches, each a magnetic storm, a sunspot as big as Oberon. Titania, Jarrett told them, was sixteen times more massive than Oberon, four and a half times larger, two thousand times brighter. It was a litany of superlatives, impossibly beautiful, and impossibly deadly. At a distance of sixty million kilometers out from Titania, *Questar* was plunging through oceans of high-energy radiation, and her magnetic screens were being driven to the limit. She was receiving so much heat from the star that her outer hull, Smilin' Jack informed them, was now at nine hundred degrees, a temperature climbing minute by swift-passing minute. The ship was now moving slowly enough that Titania's gravity could catch the vessel and twist her course around, a hairpin fall that would send her looping about the star and back toward distant Oberon.

"Last chance to change your mind, people," Smilin' Jack told them. His shipboard coveralls were drenched with sweat. The temperature aboard had been climbing steadily as *Questar*'s life support gear struggled to keep pace with the blaze of heat from outside. The air was now as hot and humid as the inside of a sauna. "The new drive coil's mounted and balanced. The sims say we're *probably* okay, but . . . well, we're takin' a mighty big chance, dropping into drivespace without having that coil fully tested and simmed groundside. Now's your chance to back out and do the *sane* thing, even if it means fighting those jokers behind us."

"There's no going back for us, Captain," Diane said. Both she and Maricia had stripped down to briefs. It was too hot for anything else.

"You have our decision," Ta Shaa Ta added. He didn't appear uncomfortable in the steamy, sweat-stinking air, but then, fraal rarely appeared to be bothered by anything. He had removed his *sarabel*, however, so perhaps even he was feeling the heat.

Verdoss slumped in the sofa, a towel over his bare shoulders, his naked belly and chest glistening with sweat. He'd even removed his gridlink monocular. "When can we jump?"

"We can't, yet," Jack told him, "not this deep inside Titania's gravity well. We'll have to complete the slingshot course-change, accelerate for another five hours, and then we can drop into drivespace. *If* the drive works properly."

"If it doesn't," Jarrett said, "we continue back to Lison?"

"Assuming the attempt doesn't blow us to pieces or drop us with a burned-out coil somewhere a million light years from anything, yeah."

Spacer scarcely heard them. He was transfixed by the star, grown from a gleam against the eternal twilight of Tribon's sky to a heaven-filling radiance of blue-white glory.

*   *   *   *   *

"What's the answer?" Mike asked.

"We're go for jump."

Jack settled back into the comfortable embrace of his control seat. *Questar*'s command center was now bathed in the liquid blue radiance of Titania, burning in the sky above the bridge work stations. Even stepped down by the computer, the light was bright enough that he was beginning to have trouble reading some of the instruments. He considered shutting of the screens, but he hated not having the visual input. It was like flying the ship while being sealed in a box. Once, many years ago, Smilin' Jack had been a true Lisoner, with a Lisoner's dread of wide vistas, a far horizon, and an open sky. Almost fifteen years of crewing and piloting starships had changed that. Now he felt claustrophobic if he was seated in a tiny, dark room with no connection with the cosmos outside.

"Coming up on time for our roll maneuver," Mike told him. "Sunside hull temp now eleven hundred."

"Rog."

"We shouldn't do this, you know."

He looked across at her. "Why not?"

"The best sim we ran gave a seventy-two percent chance of success with that new coil."

"Pretty good odds."

"You said you wouldn't go unless it was eighty percent."

"Close enough."

"Look, what are these people to us? We don't have to risk our lives this way for the likes of them!"

"They're enemies of VoidCorp, that's what they are. You think those ships back there would have chased us this far if the Voiders weren't *real* interested in nailing them?"

"All the more reason not to be too close to them. When the axe falls—"

"Look, the Voiders at Hux already have the active sensor signatures of *Questar*, many times over. By now, they already know who we are. You think the Voiders are going to let us go if we swing around this star and meekly fly back to meet them? 'Oh, excuse me, Mr. Voider, sir. Here are the people you wanted. Please let us go!' "

"We have to go back to Lison sometime, whether it's now or when they're finished at Storm."

"Sure. I'd just rather it was later, that's all. We can't face those two ships on our tail, and there are going to be a lot more waiting for us on the way back!"

Mike shrugged and checked her sensor readout. "Sunside temp twelve hundred degrees. We'd better roll."

He looked back and up, checking *Questar*'s high, curving tail arcing above the ship's main hull, heavy with weapons pod, drive sponsons, and the broad fan of the unfurled heat radiators.

The radiator sail was glowing a dull red now, its heat transfer coils stressed to their limits as they attempted to deal with the fury of Titania's radiance. One of the toughest aspects of starship engineering was getting rid of heat— both the heat arriving from outside the vessel and that generated internally by drives, equipment, and warm bodies.

"Do it," he said.

Mike's long fingers caressed her control screens, and the sky above the command center spun suddenly as the ship rolled. The star slid behind the curve of the ship's upraised tail, and suddenly the bridge was plunged into a much cooler, dimmer light. The outspread radiator sail, no longer able to keep up with the demands of leaking *Questar*'s excess heat into vacuum, was now being pressed into service as a sunshade.

Almost immediately, it felt cooler as the main hull fell around the huge star, riding inside the shadow of her own radiator sail. It was a temporary measure only. All too soon, the temperature would begin rising again, since the sail could no longer radiate the onboard heat. Worse, the overload was now melting the panel's heat-pump circuits. It wouldn't be working as a radiator sail at all until Jack and his crew could perform some repairs. That was why he'd waited until the last possible moment before performing the roll maneuver.

With the direct blaze of Titania blocked from the vidscreens, the computer could step up the detail on the background light. The knots and curls and twisting filaments of gossamer blue spilling off the huge star's surface filled the sky now, a radiant glory as ethereal and beautiful as the silent ghost play of an aurora.

Light danced and played along the curve of *Questar*'s magnetic screens, fierce storms of free protons and electrons deflected in bursts of electrical brilliance before they could pierce the ship's thin hull and fry those aboard.

The temperature continued to climb.

Swiftly, the sky rolled once more, this time by itself as *Questar* whipped around Titania's far side and Mike engaged the inductor drive to full, adding the ship's drive acceleration to the gravitational boost imparted by their slingshot spin around the star.

Within the next few hours, the blue light began to dim noticeably. By shipboard evening, Titania was much smaller, dwindling into the pearly, outflung sprawl of its corona.

"Local gravitational field curve is falling below one point three times ten to the minus three," Mike said. "We can jump whenever you give the word."

"Right."

Smilin' Jack was watching a small screen on his console where the courses of *Questar* and the two pursuing ships were drawing themselves out in red and green lines. The pirates were closing now, very quickly indeed as *Questar* raced back to meet them even though they were now decelerating at max. If this didn't work, *Questar* was going to flash past the pirates in another few hours, traveling so fast relative to them that they would only have a chance for one or two shots in the instant of passing. If they hit though, there was a good chance that not much would be left of *Questar*.

He touched a comm control. "Ron?" he said. "What's she look like?"

The lean face of Ron Carlyle, *Questar*'s engineer, appeared above the comm projector, a disembodied head. "Everything checks out, Captain," he said. "The radiator pumps are done for, but we knew that going in. The new coil's behaving itself . . . so far, anyway."

"Okay," Jack said. "Let's bring up the mass reactor to full."

"Sixty percent and climbing. I can give you full output in ninety-five seconds."

Time crawled. "Mike?"

"Hmm?"

"What do you think they're after, out there on Storm?"

"Cosmos knows!" She snorted. "Scientists!"

"Gotta be something pretty hot for them to want to risk this."

"Maybe. I just want to see the ship come home in one piece."

"You and me both. Retract radiator sail."

In the darkening night above the command center, the accordion-pleated radiator, now blackened and fused in places by its mistreatment over Titania, folded silently and was withdrawn into its storage compartment on the weapon pod.

"Are we ready to jump?"

"Mass reactor to full output in twenty seconds. All non-essential systems secured. Ron reports active systems online. Vessel ready for jump to drivespace, Captain." She sounded cool and disapproving.

No matter. It was worth the risk. It *had* to be.

"Reactor to full output in four . . . three . . . two . . . one. We're clear for jump."

He took a last look at the intercept paths of the oncoming pirate ships. Sorry fellas, he thought. We're the one who got away!

"Engage stardrive."

The night around them exploded in a dazzling blaze of color and light.

Chapter Thirteen

"THE TARGET SHIP has just dropped into drivespace," the tall, gaunt man with the death's head face said. He was trying to hide his fear but not with complete success. "They're gone."

Employee PK349 98TVR stared at Employee KL945 72YKV from high up at the center of the room and measured her options. This was not good, not good at all.

She sat astride her electronic throne in the center of a spider's web of cables and data feeds. At a touch to her control pad, the chair descended, drifting with a low hum of inductor fields until it came to rest two meters from the trembling KL-level Employee. Somewhere in the dark-shrouded boundaries of the compartment, metal clanked on metal. Her bodyguard, anonymous in heavy battle armor, stirred slightly, shifting to afford himself a clear shot from his station ten meters away. Other Employees watched from the shadows, awaiting their own interviews with emotions ranging from greed to concern to terror.

"Whose is the responsibility for this . . . scheduling set-back?" she asked, her voice a low, almost sultry purr. She touched the side of her communications headband, and the gridlink monocular covering her left eye pivoted away with a tiny, shrill whine. Project reports and progress analyses could wait for a few seconds, at least. She wanted to see the Employee with both eyes.

"It could not be anticipated, PK," the man said. Beads of sweat were standing out on his forehead, glistening in the thin lighting of the Project Management Center. "We did not foresee Duprés' refusal of our offer. Before we could move to block his departure from Lison, he had lifted from Tribon's spaceport."

"Stopping on the way to steal your prisoner."

"Y-yes, PK." He gulped down a couple of hard, quick breaths. "The responsibility was . . . the responsibility was mine, PK. Analysis: I should have moved more aggressively against Duprés and neutralized him and his vessel rather than concentrating on the boy. In retrospect, I should have arranged for ground support for the crawler against just such an attempt to rescue the boy. I should also have ordered Talon to lift sooner. Perhaps he could have caught and destroyed Duprés' ship before it left Lison space."

"You've failed me on several levels, KL. You have failed the Corporation. There will be payback."

He looked as if his knees were about to fail him. "Yes, PK."

A voice crackled in her headset. "Excuse me, PK, but we're ready for the next run."

"Very well." She glanced at KL945 72YKV as she closed the monocular back over her eye. "Wait."

"Yes, PK."

She touched a control and raised her chair again, pivoting to face the vidwall. "You may begin."

The broad, curving sweep of the vidwall flicked on. Orbital Blast-Mining Facility 287N hung vast and complex against the backdrop of the small, frigid world of Hux, the scene relayed from an outlying, unmanned remote. A mottled ruggedness of dark red, ocher, and brown, with thick-cratered plains and broken mountains, Hux showed the savage scars of decades of heavy blast-mining. In the old days, Lison miners had dropped nuclear explosives from orbit, churning up the surface to reveal veins of precious rhodium. Several years ago, however, VoidCorp had negotiated a contract with the United Lison State, trading high technology for mining rights to the small planet. Now, blast-miners like 287N used drilling beams to fracture and pulverize surface rock so that extractor vessels could land and sift through the rubble for pay dirt—strip mining on a planetary scale.

They were coming upon a part of Hux's surface that robotic surveys had pegged as a possible high-yield target zone.

PK349 98TVR had been partly responsible for negotiating the Hux contract. She had been OS349 then, and her advancement over seventeen intervening grades and her assignment as assistant project manager at Hux had been her reward.

"Beam control to automatic," the voice whispered in her ear. "Firing position in twelve seconds. Ten . . . nine . . ."

She listened to the countdown as the station orbited low across the surface of Hux. As the count reached zero, the drill beam blinked on, silent in space . . . but she could feel the throbbing rumble of its raw power through the station's structure. A quasisolid pillar of blue-white, intolerably brilliant, connected the central focusing lens of the drilling station to the surface of the planet one hundred five kilometers below. As the beam struck, a shock wave visible as a silvery-white disk flat against the landscape, expanded rapidly through Hux's tenuous carbon dioxide atmosphere. The beam's three megaton per second output slashed into the planet's tortured surface, leaving in its wake a gaping, red-glowing trench of molten rock beneath a widening pall of black, high-flung dust.

What a splendid weapon that would make, she thought. Such power, and all at my command.

Ten seconds after the beam's initiation, it flicked off.

"Firing run complete, PK," a voice said within her comm unit. "Results appear nominal."

"Very well. Prepare the extractors for descent. I'm increasing quota on this run by three percent. I have not been satisfied with overall performance. If I cannot get people to deliver full quota on time, I will find myself people who can. Pass that to the extractor commanders."

"Yes, PK."

She touched her chair controls and descended once again to the waiting KL.

She was pleased with her performance as assistant project manager on the Hux drilling operation, at least so far. Her star was rising within VoidCorp. Another coup would firmly establish her in the lower ranks of upper management . . . and then her career track could only lead higher.

Once she'd been called Julia Lynn King, but she rarely thought of herself by that name any longer. She'd been an Employee of VoidCorp since her father had sold her contract to the Entertainment Division when she was ten standard, and her corporate rank and contract number were far more important to her identity than anything as maudlin as a personal name. That had been a hard time. Her memories of those days were mercifully fuzzy, though she wasn't sure if that was because of the long hours, the abusive customers, or the electric shocks.

What mattered was that she had endured. She'd worked her way up from AJ table bus to AQ gropie to BN fun girl to CC erodancer to DY companion all in the course of ten years. Her income had gone into an education fund, and with a break provided by an enthusiastically grateful client, she'd been able to sidestep into a premanagement track.

The rest had been damned hard work, long hours, determination, and a ruthlessness born of fear and pain and loneliness, emotions long ago buried in her relentless climb up VoidCorp's alphabetical hierarchy.

"So," she said to KL945. "Where were we?"

"We . . . *you* were determining my punishment."

Her eyes widened slightly. She wasn't used to that much of a show of individuality or defiance from her workers.

She considered the mitigating factors in this case. His plan had been well developed and had failed only because of unforeseen circumstances—Duprés's refusal of KL945's offer, and the TXI expedition's determination to rescue the tunnel rat. And he had vectored here to Hux to report in person rather than attempting to flee . . . or to continue an obviously hopeless chase.

But the debit side was not easily reconciled with the credits. He had killed Sennis Thorne and risked exposing the entire operation. He had managed to pin the murder on the tunnel rat, which could have exposed VoidCorp operations in Tribon if the boy had survived. His determination to capture the tunnel rat had been based on shaky probabilities. It was not at all certain that the boy knew enough about the TXI expedition or their plans to be a useful information source. Bad judgment there . . . and clumsiness. That sort of thing could *not* be tolerated.

"Your actions have resulted in a schedule setback, necessitating redistribution of key assets," she said. "It has also put several VoidCorp covert operations on Lison and in this system at risk. I would rate your failure at least as a Class Seven."

His eyes closed. His fists clenched at his side, the knuckles of his ungauntleted hand showing white.

"What is the standard disciplinary action for a Class Seven failure?" she asked him, pretending she couldn't remember.

"C-contract termination, PK," he replied.

"Indeed. I thought so. And . . . have you sufficient assets to transport you off Corporate property?"

He shook his head, a miserable twisting of his head back and forth on his skinny neck. "No . . ." it was a whisper, soft as death.

"Not even to Lison?"

"You have my financial statement, PK."

Of course she did. The figures were scrolling down her monoptical eyepiece screen. At the moment, KL945 had corporate credits totaling just under nine hundred Concord

dollars, enough to buy him passage if a commercial inter-
planetary transport was available.

Unfortunately, the only vessels on-station were Void-
Corp shuttles, and the next run to Lison wasn't scheduled
for another eight days. By that time, his assets would be
nearly exhausted, and he wouldn't have enough left to pay
for a seat.

The numbers were there, in black-on-green.

"That's too bad," she said. "I'm very sorry for you."

Termination of contract meant simply that. He would no
longer be Employee KL945 72YKV, but simply plain
Wolfgang Krueger, a null, uncontracted with no income, no
chance of employment, and he would be occupying quarters aboard a VoidCorp field facility. Every Employee paid
for the food he ate, the water he drank, the life support and
sanitation services he used, the very air he breathed. These
costs were automatically deducted from his computer
financial records each time he made a purchase by placing
his hand tattoo in a scanner, whether he was buying a meal
or using the toilet. Estimated air usage costs were deducted
at the end of each day, as were costs for quarters, non-
business conversations, and work breaks.

Null-Krueger would have to pay his own way with his
own assets. He could go without eating for eight days, of
course . . . but with breathing and quartering costs he still
wouldn't have enough for a ticket to Lison at the end of it.
If he was lucky, someone aboard might be willing to open
a new contract with him as a level AA or AB laborer,
though most Employees didn't have anything like the
assets necessary to support another as well as themselves.
Much more likely, he would be spaced as soon as his
assets hit zero. A VoidCorp mining facility was a finely
tuned business operation after all, and not a charity institution. They couldn't afford to hand out free air and water
to uncontracted nulls.

She studied KL945 for a moment. He kept his eyes
squeezed shut, his fists tight, waiting for the hammer to fall.

"My position here," she told him at last, "permits me a
small amount of latitude in disciplinary cases. You will be

broken to rank JR and assessed a fine of five thousand Concord dollars."

His eyes popped open, and his knees very nearly gave way. "Th-thank you, PK!"

"You're still at attention," she gently reminded him as he reached out to a nearby support to steady himself.

"Yes, PK. Sorry, PK."

She watched, amused, as he pulled himself together. It would take him a long time to pay off that debt, especially at 18 percent interest, but he was just now realizing that he would *live* and have a chance to pay off the debt.

"Now . . . as to your assignment," she continued. "I *could* assign you to the extraction teams mining Hux. We're falling behind quota on the operations here, and adding some more muscle to the ground teams might help us get back on track."

She watched his eyes closely for reaction. What she'd just suggested was little short of a death sentence. The statistical life expectancy for low-rank manual laborers shoveling raw ore into the loading hoppers beside the half-molten pits blasted into Hux's surface was currently ten point six days, and that would be going down as she kept increasing the quota.

"Whatever you say, PK."

Good. He wasn't resentful . . . or, if he was, he was hiding it well.

"On the other hand, there is a special project, one which might interest you. I'm going to need to reinforce our operation on Storm now. I had in mind sending Talon with another platoon of mercenaries. You would go as Corporate liaison to make sure the intruders are dealt with and that our interests in the Loman system are secure. Do you think you could manage that?"

His eyes lit at that. "Yes, ma'am!"

"The assignment technically requires management-level personnel with a rank of at least MA. If you perform well, I will promote you to MA and negate the five thousand debt. You'll be on the management track. What do you think of that?"

"You're . . . you're being very generous, PK. Thank you!"

"I believe in motivating my people, JR. Speaking of which . . . I don't think I need to add that I *will* revoke your contract if you fail. You won't have another chance after this."

"No, PK. I won't fail! You can count on me!"

"Good. Since we don't have direct drivespace relay communications with our operations on Storm, you will carry my report and my warning to NV112 48YTY. You will be directly under his command and carry out his orders. You will also see to it that the intruders are killed or in our custody. The scientists among them, especially, may have information of value to NV112 in his operations."

"Yes, PK."

"I want Jack Duprés terminated. His ship has been positively matched to one of the pirate vessels that has raided us at Hux. I want an example made for the others. I will not tolerate these pinprick marauder assaults against Void-Corp assets."

"Yes, PK."

"Finally, you'll be my eyes and ears on Storm, JR. You'll be looking out for my interests, as well as those of the Corporation. I don't entirely trust NV112. He may be trying to cut me out of the Storm operation, and I won't stand for that. I discovered the old Rigunmor records on Lison. I discovered the significance of Storm. I will not be cheated out of my profit margin!"

"I will see to it that you receive full credit, PK," he replied. "Thank you for the opportunity to prove myself!"

"There's no profit in thanks, only in results. You will depart for Storm as soon as Talon's vessel has been checked out and the mercenaries loaded aboard. Get to work."

"Yes, PK!" He turned and strode from the command chamber, leaving PK349 98TVR with her thoughts.

JR945 was an excellent subordinate, and she was glad she'd found a way to keep from having to space him. It was a win-win situation. He got to live, she retained the services of a useful Employee, and his motivational factor had just hit high orbit. It would be tough on him straddling the jurisdictional knife's edge between her orders and those of NV112, but if anyone could do it, JR945 72YKV could.

She returned her attention to the mining operation on the surface of Hux. The first of the extraction vehicles was approaching the stretch of planetary crust smashed open by the drilling beam.

If the survey had been wrong about rhodium deposits in that sector, she could think of half a dozen J, K, and L contracts that were about to be terminated.

* * * * *

Questar fell through the nothingness of drivespace, a tiny bubble of light and life awash in the surging currents of energy that made up the mathematical abstraction that was an alternate realm to the normal space of mass, gravity, and reality.

"Okay," Diane told the others, crowded into *Questar*'s lounge. "This is what Storm looks like, as near as we can work it out from the stuff we downloaded at Lison and from the files Sennis had in his secretary."

The holoprojector on the lounge table switched on, and a wrinkled globe of mottled brown, white, green, and blue appeared above the table top. The blue, with a few scattered exceptions, formed a band all the way around the world, stretching from pole to pole and back again.

"Actually, you can rarely see the surface like this," Diane went on. "The atmosphere is dense and averages eighty-four percent cloud cover. This is what the planet usually looks like from space."

She touched a control, and the wrinkle of mountains and blue of oceans was replaced by a ragged girdle of cottony gray white. One side of the world darkened to night, but the globe was still easily visible as deep-buried pulses of yellow and orange flared and flickered deep within the cloudy layers.

"Is that lightning?" Spacer asked.

"It certainly is. Storm came by its name honestly. The weather is, to put it mildly, unstable."

"Why?" Spacer asked. "You said it's like Lison, only worse. What makes it worse?"

The planetary image dwindled away, becoming a bead on a circular string. Another planet appeared in the holo— vast, golden-ringed, horizontally banded, and brooding— a huge gas giant. Other moons appeared, including one large one farther out than Storm The gas giant dwindled as well, taking its complex system of moons into invisibility, shrinking to become a marble-sized ball circling a much larger, sullen red star.

"Storm is a moon of a large gas giant named Salamanca. Salamanca, in turn, is the innermost planet of the star Loman, a Class M1 red dwarf. Storm is an Ionian world."

"Ionian?" Verdoss said. "What's that?"

"There is a gas giant named Jupiter in the Sol system. One of its moons is named Io. Io is so close to Jupiter that it's literally stretched and pulled by tidal forces between Jupiter and some of the more distant satellites.

"Now, the case of Io is pretty extreme. The whole moon is only something like thirty-six hundred kilometers across, and the tidal pull is literally turning it inside out through constant volcanic eruption.

"Something similar is happening on Storm—not as drastic, because Storm is farther from Salamanca than Io is from Jupiter, and it's a lot larger, over eighty-three hundred kilometers across, but there's still some pretty extensive volcanic activity. That large, outer moon is called Taliafiero. It plays God's own tug of war with Salamanca, with Storm as the prize. It also helps keep Storm's orbit stable, but I'll get to that in a moment.

"Now, Salamanca is something of an oddity too." As Diane kept speaking, a greenish cone formed next to the marble representing the gas giant, always pointed away from the red star as the planet followed its orbit. "Once upon a time, long before we started going to the stars, it was always assumed that gas giants would only be found far out in the outer reaches of a star system. Once we got telescopes strong enough to make directly measure stellar perturbations from Earth, we discovered that quite a few stars had gas giants tucked in very, very close to their stars—impossibly close really, since it isn't a stable configuration. Even now, we don't entirely understand the processes that are going on in these types of systems.

"Anyway, Salamanca is only thirty-three million kilometers from Loman—that's just over two tenths of an astronomical unit. That happens to place it squarely in the middle of Loman's habitable zone, which is why we won't find extremes of temperature on Storm, but it also means that Loman's stellar wind blasts away at Salamanca's upper atmosphere, literally blows it away. Salamanca is losing atmosphere—hydrogen mostly, which gets stripped of its electrons, becoming a very thin but very highly charged plasma. It forms a tail, almost like a comet's tail, extending back and away from the star.

"As you can see from this model, every four days Storm passes behind Salamanca and goes through the tail. Storm is already an electrical motor of a sort, circling Salamanca inside the gas giant's magnetosphere. We estimate it's generating some hundreds of trillions of volts. All of those charged particles entering Storm's magnetic field result in a great deal of power being transferred from Salamanca to Storm—a *great* deal of power. Those constant electrical storms are only a tiny part of it."

The holographic model expanded again, centering once more on Storm.

"So . . . on the surface of Storm, we have constant volcanic eruptions filling the air with ash and dust and various noxious brews, kind of like the Magma Sea on Lison, only worse. We have the atmosphere highly charged from the electrical flux around Salamanca, discharging as lightning. We have hydrogen entering the upper atmosphere, again from Salamanca, and explosively combining with oxygen in the air to form water—a lot of water. It rains a *lot* on Storm."

Diane touched the controls, and the cloud cover on the holographic model vanished, taking the disturbing, rapid-fire pulse of lightning with it.

"It's hard to see on this model unless you look close," she said, "but Storm is less a sphere than it is an ellipsoid. That tug of war between Salamanca and Taliafiero has literally stretched it. See how the sea follows a band all the way around the planet, between the Salamanca and the anti-Salamanca hemispheres? The Twilight Sea. The stretching resulted in those lowlands, which over millions of years have filled with water. The two end caps are actually so high above the topographical mean that the air's very thin up there—less than a hundredth of a bar. We think the sea must be growing, too, with all that new water coming in. There's a lot of photodessication going on, so Storm is losing water almost as fast as it's coming in, but there is a net gain, and over geological periods, it adds up."

"What we have here," Jarrett said quietly, "is an extremely dynamic system—lots of energy, lots of change."

"Right. And that energy expresses itself in the weather."

"One thing I don't understand," Jarrett said, pointing. "That really doesn't look like a very stable system. Every time Storm passes over Salamanca's night side through that tail, it must lose energy. Friction. It ought to fall into Salamanca."

"Right you are. We think Storm started a lot farther out and has been slowly spiraling in closer over the course of the past few million years. It's been slow, because Taliafiero out there is in a resonant three-to-two orbit with Storm. Every other pass, it gives Storm a bit more orbital energy and loses some of its own. It's kept the system going for as much as a billion years, but that can't last much longer. As you can see, Storm has very nearly reached Salamanca's outer rings—the meteor showers are gorgeous, when you can see the sky. In another million years or so, Storm will begin to break up as it approaches Salamanca's Roche limit. That's the distance at which tidal forces will shatter any large body."

"Is there anything like landing facilities on that nightmare?" Smilin' Jack asked.

Both he and his navigator had joined the expedition party in the lounge for the planetary briefing. It was the first time since coming aboard that Diane had seen either of them off the bridge for more than a moment or two. During the maneuver around Titania, they'd been sharing watch on the command deck, and much of Duprés' off-time had been spent in engineering. In drivespace, however, the flight systems could be left on automatic, and he'd been more visible these past few days, and perhaps a bit more approachable as well.

"The Rigunmor survey left a landing beacon," Diane told him, "but their landing area was just an open plain. We don't know if the beacon is still there. Given surface conditions, we're not even entirely sure the *plain* is still there. Geological formations on Storm are in a state of flux, and it's been a hundred and fifty years, after all."

"Then how can you expect to find anything there?" Mike asked. "Like those ruins you're looking for . . . ?"

At Diane's touch, a green light winked on, close beside the girdling sea. "Some formations are relatively stable. This is the area explored by the Rigunmor survey—a level plateau overlooking the ocean. The cliff is almost a thousand meters high, here at Solitaire Point. There are volcanoes nearby, but no major ones, and the plateau appears relatively stable. We think that's why Storm's native sentients live here and apparently nowhere else on the entire planet. And . . . this is where the Rigunmors found the ruins."

"A single small island of stability in all that chaos," Ta Shaa Ta said, "a mathematical probability, expressed as sea and mountain."

"It looks like a world of surprises," Spacer said. He sounded worried.

"That," Diane told him, "I can guarantee. We're going to have to watch ourselves to make sure the surprises don't kill us!"

"The surprises killed several of the original survey team

members," Verdoss pointed out. "I'm more concerned about the surprises my ancestor didn't encounter."

"What might those be?" Duprés asked him.

"VoidCorp," was the reply. "VoidCorp wasn't interested in Storm a hundred fifty years ago. They didn't even know about it then. With their obvious interest in the place now, I think we have to assume they have something going on there. And that could be the most unpleasant surprise of all. . . ."

STORM
Twilight Zone trailing-equatorial

Caldera

"Stonehenge"

Central Lake

VoidCorp Base

← Salamanca

Anti-Salamanca →

Thunder Plateau

Questar Landing Site

Ancient Ruins

Solitaire Point

Twilight Sea

N

0   5

Kilometers

Chapter Fourteen

ONE HUNDRED TWENTY-ONE hours after dropping out of normal space near Titania, *Questar* emerged from drivespace with Storm and Salamanca just ahead.

Captain Duprés had thought he was jaded, that *nothing* he saw among the stars could surprise or impress him any longer. He'd flown over the blue-crystal beauty of Blue-fall's ocean and navigated the impossible, diamond-dust spectacle of the Arch of Lucullus. He'd seen doomed, brilliant Tendril ablaze in space and witnessed the delicate, ethereal beauty of the Lightning Nebula. He'd walked among Babel's golden towers, survived the natural laser sting of a crystallis on Polyphemus, and once had even glimpsed the surreal nightmare of a horror on Yellow Sky.

Nothing he'd seen or experienced anywhere had prepared him for the sheer spectacle that was Salamanca and Storm.

The holographic images the scientists had shown in the lounge had not prepared him for the reality. Salamanca loomed huge just ahead, visible as a fire-rimmed black disk eclipsing the granulated red glare of Loman, its rings edge-on and only just visible as a straight-edge slash of black haze. As they fell silently across its night hemisphere, strange lights and colors pulsed and throbbed deep within that murky dark—whole continents of light shimmering and flickering in eerie pinwheels and shapes that seemed somehow geometrical in their propagation. Was it life or some purely physical phenomenon, like auroras or lightning? He didn't know, couldn't tell.

He did call his passengers' attention to the phenomenon. The kid especially seemed transfixed by the light show, a spectacle of impossible, world-girdling dimensions.

Just ahead, a red-silver crescent facing the sun, the world-moon of Storm hung against the darkness, its night side alive with a different kind of light and motion. Lightning flashes stuttered and flared in cloud-muffled silence. The moon's poles glowed in the eerie greens, blues, and yellows of rippling auroras.

It could never be completely dark there, Jack thought.

It was hard to make out details, though. Loman might be a red dwarf, a feeble stellar candle compared with brighter suns like Oberon or exuberant Titania, but at this distance it was still bright.

Something flared off *Questar*'s magnetic screens high and to port, a sand-grain–sized speck from the giant's rings.

"Lots of crap in this system," Mike said. She seemed unmoved by the spectacle. "I'm reading the gas giant's magnetic field at . . . call it five point one gauss. Electrical potential between Salamanca and Storm is two hundred thousand volts. Current at seven million amperes—that's a power field of ten to the twelfth watts." She looked up briefly from her console and stared into glory. "If it weren't for our magnetic screens, the radiation out there would have fried us to a crisp already."

"You got that beacon yet?" he asked Mike.

"Negative. Nothing there to receive."

"Great."

"We have the map coordinates at least," she reminded him, "and that plateau will have a distinctive radar signature."

"Good thing, too. We'd never find it on our own under that soup."

Questar was dropping rapidly toward Storm's night side. The moon had recently emerged from its eclipse behind Salamanca, and the planned landing area was on the trailing hemisphere of the world, now in darkness. As Storm swelled larger and larger in the command center vidscreens, Jack touched the intercom control.

"Okay, I'm piping the view forward to the lounge monitor," he said. "I strongly recommend you all strap yourselves in. This could be a *very* rough ride."

The red glare of the sun vanished behind the world's horizon, and Salamanca, a slow-growing crescent, filled a glorious quarter of the sky. Storm's dark horizon flattened out. Even over the night side, the cloud tops remained illuminated by the light from Salamanca's crescent and from the ghostly play of the auroras. Slowing steadily, *Questar* dropped lower, then lower still. A thin, high keening filled the command deck, accompanying a faint, steady vibration as they hit the first tenuous traces of Storm's upper atmosphere. Moments later, the sky outside was swallowed by orange flame, and *Questar* drew a long, down-curving scratch of ionization across Storm's sky.

Below, lightning flashes pulsed and strobed, the bursts muffled and spread by cloud banks the size of small continents.

Moments later, *Questar* plunged into the clouds, and the real ride began with the ship bucking and yawing in the sudden high wind. The same fields that protected the ship's passengers and crew from body-pulping accelerations in space continued to muffle the worst jolts, but Jack was steadily cutting back on the inductor drive power to allow *Questar* to "feel" the atmosphere.

A blue haze ignited around them, *Questar*'s reduced induction field intersecting with windblown rain and dust particles. Lightning flared close by, and Jack felt the jolt of the shockwave.

"Extending electrostatic vanes," Jack said. "Airfoils deployed."

"I've got a solid return," Mike said, "bearing zero-one-five, range two-zero-one. Looks like a sheer slope, a kilometer high. I think it's the Thunder Plateau."

"Hope you're right. I'd hate to spend the next couple of hours poking around in this soup looking for it."

The ship rolled heavily to the right. Jack reached for the manual controls, but the ship's AI was faster.

"Remind me again why we're doing this," Mike said.

"The money, my dear. *Always* the money."

"Radar image matches our mapping data. Close enough, anyway."

"Altitude?" Jack's hands played over the control screens. The ship's AI was doing the actual flying—no human reactions could be fast enough—but he was inputting his own recommendations as the situation changed from moment to moment.

"Twenty-seven kilometers. Expect cloud base at fifteen hundred meters."

Still they fell, dropping through swaddling, cottony blackness illuminated only by the shimmer of their induction field and the occasional stab of lightning.

"Uh-oh."

"I hate it when you say that, Mike. Whatcha got?"

"Someone just pinged our IFF, looking for an ID. Must not have liked the answer they got, because now we're being painted. Looks like a weapons lock."

"Weapons lock? You sure it isn't the beacon?"

"High-energy, narrow beam, and it's tracking us. Bearing zero-zero-five."

"Grep!" Jack cursed.

"Launch! Missile launch! Active tracking!"

"Okay! Don't grepping panic. Give me a range read-off."

"I'm not grepping panicking. Range one-nine-zero. One-eight-zero. One-six-zero. One-two-zero . . ."

Jack held *Questar* dead on course, continuing their descent. The missile was coming up from almost directly ahead, accelerating fast—a ground-to-air missile with an induction drive. What kind of warhead? A small nuke? Conventional explosives? Or something cute like a cloud of bomblets designed to shred *Questar*'s skin and riddle her sensitive electronics with shrapnel?

"Nine-zero . . . five zero . . ."

Jack cut the inductor fields and simultaneously released a double load of chaff, twin clouds of aluminum fragments blooming huge on any watching radar screens. With luck . . .

Questar plunged through the clouds in free fall . . . and then those clouds lit up with a day-bright light flaring overhead. The shockwave shuddered and rumbled through her hull seconds later.

"That," Mike said, "was just a little too damned close for me!"

They emerged beneath the cloud deck, slowing sharply, *Questar*'s re-engaged inductors shrilling their protest at such cavalier treatment. It was raining, a furious lashing of wind and water, as lightning stabbed across the horizon. A cliff loomed skyward to starboard, huge and black—Solitaire Point and the Thunder Plateau. A trio of waterfalls hurtled from the plateau's crest and arced out into the air, plunging a long, rock-bound kilometer before vanishing into fog and rumble. At the cliff's base, the sea crashed across bare rock, the spray leaping far higher in Storm's gravity than it would have on Lison . . . assuming Lison had ever had an ocean of liquid water. Spindrift turned the surface of each marching wave and swell into a labyrinthine chaos of foam and wind-whipped spray. Inland, an erupting volcano showed a jagged smile of orange against black.

Ghostly lines of green light sprang up against the vidscreens, overlaying black rock, revealing the three-dimensional topology of the cliffs ahead. Mike pointed.

"That looks like what we're looking for. Looks like artificial structures—at three-five-zero."

"Got 'em."

"And a flat patch right there."

"I see it." Jack tapped out a command, and *Questar* banked left, shuddering with the effort as it turned into the howling wind. "Anything more from our friends?"

"Negative. I think we dropped off their screens. I'm picking up broadband search pulses, but it's fringe stuff. They don't see us."

"Not in this gunk, anyway. They'd need a radar beam powered by a small thermonuclear detonation to cut through this stuff."

Questar swept across the edge of the cliff, slowing now to a ground-track speed of a few meters per second.

"Hit the landing lights."

White light exploded beneath and around the ship, illuminating the steady downpour outside. Jack saw mud, black rock, and the improbable shapes of pillars or towers of some sort, almost invisible against the night.

"Landing jacks."

"Jacks extended. That looks good over there."

Questar gentled out of the sky, landing legs touching solid rock, then yielding under the vessel's weight as the induction fields slowly died away.

"Cutting gyros," Mike said. "Inductors off. Drift at zero, zero, and zero. We're down."

"Thank God." Jack slumped back in his seat. Lightning flared, backlighting a pyramidal structure a hundred meters away . . . or perhaps it was just an unusually regular hill with something like pillars at the top. In the distance, a volcano burned and muttered in a sullen glow of magma.

"Welcome to Hell," Mike said.

*   *   *   *   *

Spacer felt strange—light-headed and almost buoyant. With the ship's induction fields switched off, he could hear the wind and thunder outside, a muted, ongoing rumble. He unsnapped his safety harness, stood up quickly . . . and cracked his skull against the lounge overhead.

"Watch out, Spacer!" Diane said, laughing. "You don't know your own strength!"

"What . . . happened?" He rubbed the top of his head, glaring ruefully at the power conduit he'd just collided with. Normally, he had a good ten centimeters' of clearance under even the lowest of *Questar*'s overheads. Then the answer hit him, almost as hard as the blow. "Oh. Lower gravity."

"Standard gravity for Lison is one point six four Gs," Jarrett told him. "Here it's only point six G. You'll find things on Storm only seem to weigh about a third of what you're used to . . . including yourself."

Verdoss rose cautiously from his seat. "I thought he was supposed to be our expert on hostile planets?" he said. "Be a shame if he knocked himself out because he forgot something as basic as G-differentials."

"Right now," Spacer told the Rigunmor, "I feel strong enough to kick your fat Rig tail the length of this ship. Want to give it a try?"

"That's enough," Diane said, "both of you. We need to get our bearings."

Maricia and Ta Shaa Ta were already at the lounge vidscreen. A miniature holoscene winked above the table—a three-dimensional map showing blocky structures that looked just a bit too regular to be natural formations.

"We've certainly landed near a city or complex of some sort," Maricia said. "That pyramid over there is definitely artificial, but I can't see enough to tell if it matches with any of Thorne's maps."

"He only mapped one set of ruins," Diane pointed out.

"Sure," Verdoss said. He gestured at the vidscreen. "But just *look* at conditions out there! There could have been whole cities a few kilometers from where my ancestor was exploring, and he'd never have known it."

"Unlikely," Ta Shaa Ta said. "Given the radar surveys of the area made by the Rigunmor survey, the Thunder Plateau appears to have only a single cluster of artificial structures."

"That was a hundred fifty years ago," Verdoss said. "The stormies could've been busy as binies since then."

"From the information your ancestor left us," Diane said, "it's hard to see how the stormies could have built even *one* city complex, much less anything else."

"Well, what do we do now?" Verdoss asked. "Doesn't seem to be much point in waiting for the rain to end. It's supposed to rain all night, and night here is three and a half days long!"

"We'll have to go out and make our initial survey," Jarrett said. "Let's break out the suits."

The first EVA, they'd already decided, would be fairly limited in scope. Jarrett would go as commander because of his experience with e-suits and unfamiliar worlds. Maricia would go with him as science specialist, wearing her backpack linguicomp just in case they encountered any of the natives, though as hard as it was raining, any encounters with anything other than lightning seemed unlikely.

Half an hour later, they stood in *Questar*'s main cargo bay, surrounded by packing crates and shipping canisters, as Jarrett and Maricia finished suiting up. Both were donning Sunrunner 60 climate suits—tight, form-fitting complexities of fiber bundles, ceramic composites, and plasweaves that gave them the look of ungainly, bipedal insects. High-endurance e-suits, they could be worn for thirty days before the power cells needed recharging. Onboard water, food, and elimination systems let the wearer stay suited up for days at a time.

"All right," Jarrett said, "everybody remember. It's vital that we keep the capacitor screens up and at full at all times. The ionization field will help dissipate any charge build-up out there . . . enough to ward off a lightning bolt before it hits you."

"We hope," Maricia said. "Yeah, I'll remember." She pulled her helmet on over her brown hair, which she'd pulled back in a severe pony tail to keep it out of the way. The Sunrunner suits were normally worn with respirator masks, but conditions outside were extreme enough that they were using full helmets instead.

"It's still a good idea to try to stay clear of anything that might attract lightning," he continued. "Tall trees, the ship . . ."

"The ship should be pretty well grounded," Jack said, "and I haven't seen anything out there like a tree yet."

Maricia asked Spacer to help her with her linguicomp.

"Will this thing let you talk to the stormies?" Spacer asked as he handed her the backpack-sized strap-on computer.

"Well, it'll help," Maricia said, shrugging into the harness and making the lead connections with her helmet's comm ports. "We're a long way from developing a true translator machine for nonhuman languages, but this unit is pretty smart. It'll store vocabulary and phrasings and even suggest meanings of unknown words, based on context. Mostly, it means I don't have to remember a few thousand words in the vocabulary myself . . . or the pronunciation of sounds no human throat was ever meant to make."

"Yeah?" Spacer was intrigued. "What do the stormies sound like?"

Maricia touched a control on her suit gauntlet and Spacer heard an unpleasant muttering growl that sounded like nothing so much as the rumble of a hungry stomach mingled with something like the chirp of a rusty hinge.

"There are growls in there too low for your ears to hear," Maricia said, "and some squeaks that are too high. The stormies have a really astonishing range."

"But you can talk in Standard, and they hear you in their language?"

"More or less. I have to be careful to stay within the vocabulary range already in memory, of course, or they just hear noise. The stormies aren't technologically oriented. If I make a funny noise, they *might* think I'm being rude."

"It would be damned nice if talking with a nonhuman was as easy as just having a new vocabulary," Jarrett said. "Right, Ta Shaa Ta?"

"Indeed," the fraal said. "Even within human cultures, meaning does not necessarily allow comprehension."

"How come?" Spacer asked. If he understood what Ta Shaa Ta was saying, two men could have a conversation in a language known to both and not understand one another.

"Remember *Umvelt*?" Maricia asked him.

"Oh, yeah. You mean how people and aliens with different kinds of senses see the world in different ways."

"Right," said Jarrett. "The word smell means one thing to us, and something very different to Ta Shaa Ta, who has a sense of smell that would make a trackerhound or a dog envious. And fraal don't know what we're talking about when we say the word blue; they can't see that color."

"Actually," Ta Shaa Ta said, "I suspect that what I perceive as green is close to the color you humans call blue. What you call red, I see as shades of yellow, and I see five other specific families of colors in what you call the infrared—*doka, na-doka, anah, adah*, and *zimf*. You are blind to all of these."

"I wish I could see those," Spacer said. The thought of a color unknown to humans seemed impossible, yet exciting.

"Well, no matter how hard we try," Jarrett said with a smile, "we'll never know exactly what it is he's seeing when Ta Shaa Ta says something is *zimf*."

Their preparations complete, the two locked out through *Questar*'s cargo bay airlock while the rest of the party returned to the lounge. A second monitor had been set up next to the first, and each was tuned in to the EVA team's camera transmissions, one from Jarrett, the other from Maricia. The two images moved with their movements, tracking as they turned their helmets to take in the rain-lashed panorama outside.

"This rain is really something," Maricia's voice said from a speaker in the lounge. "Visibility is down to, oh, I'd say ten meters. We should have brought our swim fins, Jarrett."

"Just watch the mud holes," Jarrett replied. "We don't know how deep some of them are."

"Hell, it's *all* mud. How do you avoid them?"

Spacer sat close to the monitors, his chin on his folded hands, watching everything. It was a bit disappointing, actually. Here he was on another world at last, something he'd been dreaming of for years, and he couldn't see anything but rain.

Even the rain wasn't a total loss, though. It never rained in Lison's sealed tunnels, and the rain topside was pretty sparse compared to this. Still, it got boring after a while, and he wanted to see what was beyond those dark, sleeting curtains.

"It's raining so hard," he said. "Won't that corrode their suits?"

"The acid concentration in the rain here isn't anything like what you had on Lison," Diane told him. "In fact, there's so much more rain that most of the corrosives are being constantly washed out of the air. You won't have to worry about getting burned like you were on Lison."

"I'll be able to go out there?"

"Of course. What did you think? We didn't bring you along just so you could tell our fortunes!"

"But what can I *do*?"

"Don't worry. We'll find plenty to keep you busy!"

Spacer wrestled with conflicting emotions. He still wasn't entirely sure he liked the idea of being outside, and the downpour he was witnessing on the vidscreens only reminded him that he was a creature of the indoors, of sealed caverns and underground habitats, of made-to-order air and a *controlled* environment.

But to set physical foot on another world, upon a world other than Lison . . .

"Look at that!" Maricia said. "Can we get closer?"

Spacer was beginning to wonder if there was even a point to having the helmet cameras running. With Jarrett in the lead, he occasionally caught a glimpse of the back of the Verge Ranger's e-suit from Maricia's camera, but there was little else to see except for the smear of suit lights in the rain. And the snatches of conversation he was catching were more mystifying than enlightening.

"Definitely artificial," he heard Jarrett say. "Look at those walls!"

"The facing on the stone has been worked somehow," Maricia's voice said. "Very intricate designs."

"Yeah. What do you think, Maricia? Is it writing, art, or just decoration?"

"Maybe none of the above. We can't even guess at their artistic modes or aesthetics."

"I'm wondering about blind beings who put artwork on their walls."

"It's relief work. They might see it by touch—or sonar, if they have a fine enough sensory resolution."

"*Grep!*" Spacer said. "What are they looking at? I can't see!"

"They're at the pyramid," Diane told him. "They're moving too fast for me to see a lot of this stuff. We'll have to wait to replay their suit memories before we can analyze what they're seeing."

"Looks like steps," Maricia's voice said. "Shall we?"

"I'm a bit worried about that lightning."

"Nothing's happening close to here. Besides, if we wanted to stay safe, we wouldn't have come out here."

"Hell, we wouldn't have left Lison, and even that wasn't all that safe," Jarrett said. "Okay, but watch your footing. That stone is wet."

"Got news for you, Jarrett. Nothing out here isn't."

For several moments, all Spacer could hear was the hiss and rasp of the team's breathing inside their helmets. He could see something that might have been a wall, glistening in the rain and lights.

"Huh," Jarrett said, a sudden breath of surprise.

Then from Maricia, "My God, look at this. . . ."

"EVA, this is *Questar*," Diane said, using a headset radio. "Don't keep the stay-at-homes in the dark."

"Sorry, *Questar*," Maricia said. "Are you getting this?"

On the screen, the rain suddenly vanished. It looked as though the party had just stepped into an alcove or a small room, though the helmet cameras were still picking up little that Spacer could recognize.

"There's an entrance in the face of the pyramid," Maricia was saying, "about halfway up. We're inside now, moving down a narrow corridor. There's a room at the end—completely dark, except for our lights. Well . . . that follows. The people who built this must have done it all by sound and touch."

The camera view swung left, then right. Spacer caught a glimpse of a silvery something glistening in the moving beams of illumination. For a moment, it looked like a man in an e-suit.

He heard Maricia's sharp intake of breath. "God!" Then, "*Questar*! Can you see any of this?"

"I wish I didn't," Jarrett said. "Careful, Maricia! Don't touch a damned thing!"

"Believe me! I won't!"

Both cameras finally held steady. Five man-sized shapes appeared to be hanging in the air, suspended midway between floor and ceiling in a broad semicircle. As Maricia moved closer, her helmet lamps focused more tightly on one shape alone, the one hanging in the middle of the array.

Spacer and the others leaned closer, trying to see. As details became clearer—silvery fabric, corroded fittings, faded red helmet—he suddenly realized what he was looking at and jumped. "*Damn!*"

A human skull, still partly enveloped in the rags and tatters of long-dried flesh, grinned gape-mouthed from behind the helmet's visor. A name was easily legible above the visor and on a patch sewn to the front of the e-suit.

The name was VERDOSS, S.

Chapter Fifteen

Dᴵᴬᴺᴱ ᴸᴱᴬᴺᴱᴰ ꜰᴏʀᴡᴀʀᴅ, pointing to the holographic image of Sergei Verdoss's body. The e-suit appeared immaculately clean . . . except for a dinner-plate-sized patch on the front that looked like it might have been melted open. The silvery outer layer was blackened and charred, and what might have been cooked or mummified remains were visible inside.

"You're both sure you didn't touch anything?" Diane asked.

"Absolutely," Maricia said. "it was obviously a B-RECUM situation."

Maricia and Jarrett had rejoined the rest of the party in *Questar*'s lounge. Smilin' Jack was there as well, along with Mike, Carlyle, and Tartaglia. The lounge was crowded, but everyone aboard wanted to hear the first EVA's experiences first-hand.

" 'Be wreck 'em'?" Spacer asked.

"Burial or religious customs motif," Diane told him. "Throughout history, most human societies we know of have fairly elaborate customs surrounding the disposal of their dead. That's not universally true of the nonhuman cultures we've met, but it's true of a significant number. Primitive societies tend to take death very seriously."

"Not just primitive societies," Ta Shaa Ta said.

"Very true."

Verdoss looked closely at the holo. "This isn't their dead. They took my ancestor's body and strung it up on a wire! Maybe it's a trophy or something."

"That's just it," Diane told them. "We don't know *what* is going on here! Maybe they display the bodies of their enemies. Maybe they hang them up and worship them as ancestors—or gods. Maybe this is the stormie equivalent of a museum, with the bodies of the Rigunmor survey people on display in the 'Strange Visitors from the Sky' exhibit. *We* don't *know,* and we're going to have to be damned careful until we do."

"It might help if we knew more about what happened here a hundred fifty years ago," Jarrett said. "Rom? You told us five people were killed. How did they die, and what happened to the bodies?"

"I can't really help much there," the Rigunmor said. "I know their names, of course: Edmund Thomassen, Kathy Yu, Vasily Kubrinin, Nicole Rothheim—of the Bazaar Rothheims, you know—and Sergei Verdoss. Grigor's father, my great-to-the-third grandfather.

"Anyway, old Grigor's journals mention the deaths, but the only one he described in detail was Sergei's. He said Sergei was killed by what he called 'charge grass.' I assume that's one of those fulgivores you saw in the Storm simulations. I don't know for sure. As for the other four, he mentioned that Kubrinin was killed by lightning, but he doesn't say what happened to the others. It does sound like all of the deaths were separate incidents—not a battle or anything like that—and he doesn't say anything about trouble with the natives. In fact, according to him, the natives were all very friendly, very cooperative. The survey party was able to learn some of their language, as you know. As for the bodies, he did say that funeral services were held for them before the expedition left to return to Lison."

"Then they were buried?" Jack asked.

"That's right."

"In their e-suits?" Mike asked. "I thought you Rigs were more frugal than that."

Verdoss scowled. "Stereotypes, Miss Vaughn. Mindless, vicious stereotypes. Besides, would you want to reuse an e-suit someone had been rather messily killed in?" He pointed at the charred area on the front of the hanging suit. "Especially one with a hole in it?"

She winced. "Point taken."

"But that means," Spacer said, disgusted, "that those monsters dug up the bodies and then put them on display!"

"How do you dispose of bodies on Lison?" Maricia asked.

"Huh? Oh . . . you know those algae tanks they have all over?"

"Sure. That's how you recirculate your atmosphere, partly . . . and a lot of your food comes from those vats as well."

"Well, what do you think the algae grows on?"

"There are some cultures," Diane said, "that would find that disgusting, Spacer."

"I don't see why. It's just efficient."

"Of course. And you *need* efficiency to have as many people as there are on Lison survive, and under rather cramped and inhospitable conditions. You just don't have the room for agromanufactories or farms, and you don't have the technology for forced-culture bioproduction."

"*Profit!*" Verdoss said. "I was eating local food the whole time I was there!"

"Hey, we're all worm-food," Jack said. "On your worlds, you die, worms or the local equivalents eat the remains, then fertilize the soil for your farms and bioprocessors, right? We Lisoners just eliminate the middle man!"

"You're barbarians," the Rigunmor said in a dark mutter. "Why don't you just serve the bodies up as main courses and be really efficient?"

"Enough," Diane said. "Rom, you must know that there are cultures that do just that! And if it works for them, it's valid. Now let's stick to the problem at hand. We need to learn more about the stormie culture. In particular, we need to know if they're venerating those bodies somehow . . . or if they're more like trophies."

"I see what you mean," Verdoss said, thoughtful. "If that was some kind of chapel in that pyramid, if they were worshipping those bodies, maybe, then we could appear like gods to them. *Living* gods!"

"Let's not get carried away," Maricia warned. "I, for one, will not be involved in a god-scam. Even if we wanted to, we couldn't pull it off. We have no idea what the cultural context we're working with here might be."

"God-scam?" Spacer asked. He'd run a number of cons and scams in Lison and was always interested in hearing about others.

"Sure," Diane said. "Basically, that's like what Void-Corp did when they discovered the sesheyans. The seshes were quite primitive. The VoidCorpsers came in, showed off a few simple technological tricks that must have looked like magic to the locals, and set themselves up as gods. Next thing the poor sesheyans knew, they were all Employees." She gave Verdoss a hard look. "Maricia's right, Rom. None of us is going to stand for that kind of garbage."

"Of course, of course." He looked thoughtful. "But the decision might not be ours to make, you know. If VoidCorp is already here, they may be employing such tactics already. What worked on Sheya, after all, would work elsewhere."

"How about it, Captain?" Jarrett asked. "You said earlier someone tossed a missile at us during our descent. Was it VoidCorp?"

"No way to know," the man said.

"You know, Rom has a point," Diane told the others. "We know VoidCorp is interested in Storm . . . and that means they're probably already here. And that means they must have already begun interacting with the natives. This could complicate things."

"How?" Jarrett wanted to know.

"Filters," Ta Shaa Ta said. "The natives will have already formed an impression of humans, based on their contact with those who have already landed here. It is a matter of some importance to us just how the natives now perceive VoidCorp."

"You mean, because they won't be able to tell we're any different from the Corpses," Verdoss said.

"You humans have an expression you often use with other species," Ta Shaa Ta said, " 'They all look alike to me.' That mindset works both ways."

"The stormies aren't going to understand differences in human ideology," Maricia said, "or conflicting philosophies, or anything at all about different stellar nations." She sighed. "Damn. All we know right now is what we *don't* know."

"Don't take even that for granted," Ta Shaa Ta said. "What we know and what we know we don't know are two entirely different sets. The nonintersection can kill us."

"What can we do about it?" Diane asked.

"Learn," was the fraal's reply.

* * * * *

Four hours later, the second EVA prepared to exit the ship. The team this time consisted of Jarrett, Diane, Ta Shaa Ta, and Spacer. Spacer had to wrestle with the mounting turmoil of excitement and outright fear that was making even a relatively simple task like donning an e-suit into a thumb-fingered battle with the different sections. The suit was a smart garment, which meant it sized itself and automatically handled the various medical, life support, and sanitary connections more or less without active input from the wearer, but he still had to get the thing on right-side out and right-side up for the fittings to do their job.

"Let me help you with that," Diane told him. He dropped his hands and let her close the suit's vest across his chest. Smart hooks grabbed hold and pulled the garment snug, front and back.

"Thanks. Are you sure I'll be of any help out there?"

"You don't have to go if you don't want to," she told him. "We thought you'd enjoy seeing a world other than Lison."

"Oh, I will! I *do* want to go . . . at least, I think I do."

"I know. Pre-first-step jitters."

"I guess so."

"Just stick close to the rest of us. Make sure you keep your SCAM on and set for high. If we do meet with any natives, let us do the talking."

"We will be very interested, however," Ta Shaa Ta added, "in your thoughts and intuitions about the natives." The fraal was wearing a suit similar to those worn by the humans, save that it had tailored itself down to the slender, long-limbed proportions of his body.

Spacer looked at the SCM-20 control on his left-sleeve gauntlet as Diane helped him pull it on and seal it at the shoulder. "Will this thing really keep lightning from hitting me?"

"It should. It'll help, anyway, though a strike nearby could still stun you."

"Weapons," Jarrett said. "Captain? What are your people using?"

"My people have been carrying K-SAT one hundreds while doing outside inspections. We have some heavier stuff in the armory: nine-millimeter Bulldogs, and a couple of Aggie-Sevens."

"Charge weapons."

"That's right, but they're rugged. They'll stand up to that slop out there."

"Good point. We don't want to kill the stormies, unless it's a matter of them or us. I think we'll break out some stutter guns."

"Do we have to carry guns at all?" Maricia wanted to know.

"We'd better, until we know what we're up against. Remember that stormies might not be our only threats out there."

"If you're referring to the VoidCorpers," Diane put in, "then something more along the lines of a quantum minigun wouldn't be a bad idea."

"Actually, I was referring to the local equivalent of predators," Jarrett said, "There is also the problem that not all of us have military service backgrounds. If there are going to be any friendly fire incidents out there, I'd rather they were with nonlethal weapons."

Spacer wondered who in the party had been in the military. Jarrett, almost certainly. The ranger carried himself with the poise and confidence that Spacer associated with the Air Guard and similar military units in Lison.

Of course, so did Diane, and to a lesser extent, Maricia. Ta Shaa Ta, too, for that matter.

When they cycled through *Questar*'s cargo bay airlock, Spacer carried a stutter pistol in a thigh holster. Diane and Ta Shaa Ta were both carrying the same, while Jarrett lugged an AAMG-12 mass rifle, a monster he affectionately called an am-gee.

The pistol didn't make Spacer feel all that safe. A stutter gun essentially fired a very tiny, very tightly packaged chunk of compressed air, which unfolded as it left the weapon's muzzle to stun the target—so long as the target was not armored and wasn't much more than thirty or forty meters away. Jarrett had shown him how the weapon worked before they'd finished suiting up, but Spacer just wasn't that confident with firearms. He'd never fired one, had never even held one in his hands before.

Even if he had, he wasn't sure that a compressed-air pistol was going to help much against whatever had burned a hole in Sergei Verdoss's chest . . . or against a combat-armored Voider, for that matter. He decided he was going to have to rely more on wits and fast reflexes than firearms . . . and hope to hell he didn't need any of them.

The ground squished beneath his e-suit's boot as he stepped off the boarding ramp. Beyond the overhanging shelter of the ship, the steady, pounding rain had thinned to a gentle drizzle, almost a mist turned to shifting, translucent silver by the powerful exterior lights of *Questar*.

Lightning flared on the horizon, an almost constant pulse and throb of murky light. He understood now why the Rig survey team had named this place Thunder Plateau. Even with his external suit pick-ups muted, he could hear the steady background rumble and mutter of ongoing thunder. Some, Diane had told him earlier, was real thunder, caused by the lightning flickering and stabbing in the night all around them. There was also an erupting volcano nearby, however, visible in the west as a jagged patch of red light stark against black clouds, and to the south, unseen but heard, three separate rivers catapulted from the top of the Plateau into a free-fall through space into the sea a kilometer below, and the roar of those falls formed a constant, muted thunder.

It was a little unnerving for Spacer, who'd never in his life heard either full-sized waterfalls or volcanoes, and for whom meteorological thunder was kept safely topside, away from inhabited areas. The realization contributed to his unease as he again stepped into a world unbounded by comforting rock or metal walls. In a way though, the dark and the rain helped by shutting off the full force of the encircling panorama. It helped the world feel a bit more like Lison—close, small, and bordered—and therefore safe.

Even so, his spine and the hairs at the base of his neck pricked and crawled as he followed the others out from under *Questar*'s comforting bulk and into the semidarkness beyond the hot white circle of the ship's external lights. He felt as though he were trying to grow an extra set of eyes in the back of his head as he kept stopping and turning to see if anything was following the group across the muddy plain. Diane was carrying a biodetector that was supposed to be able to pick up any life forms within twenty-five meters or so. Spacer wasn't sure how much he trusted the device, however, especially since the party didn't have any recorded scans of Storm life. Either the Rigunmor survey hadn't had the equipment to make biosniffers, or their records hadn't survived. Spacer did his best to watch in every direction at once.

Ahead, shadows loomed out of the mist—huge pillars or columns carved from black, basaltic stone, and a flat-topped step pyramid rising at least seventy meters into the sky.

Spacer felt a thrill of awe and fear looking at those ruins, unlike anything he'd ever seen before. They appeared to be manufactured from huge, rectangular stones piled atop one another. As someone who'd grown up in mines and around miners, he knew just how tough that black, volcanic rock was, and wondered how the locals—primitives, according to Diane and Maricia—had managed the trick of cutting, shaping, and transforming blocks that even in Storm's low gravity must have weighed five or six tons apiece.

Some of the structures had tumbled down, as though in a powerful seismic tremor. Many—the upright pillars, most covered with enigmatic shapes and forms worked into the stone in three dimensions—had no possible purpose that Spacer could imagine. Were they signposts? The foundation stones of something far larger, now vanished? Advertising? He couldn't tell.

"Hold up," Diane said. "I'm getting something peculiar here. A life reading . . ."

"What kind of life reading?" Jarrett asked.

"Damned if I know. Not like anything in this thing's memory, anyway. That way." She pointed almost straight ahead, toward the pyramid.

Spacer couldn't see anything obviously alive, although there were things rising from the mud here and there like spiky antennae made of gold or copper foil that might have been the Storm equivalent of plant life. Lightning flared in the clouds directly overhead, momentarily turning the scene silver-white and stark with shadows. Thunder boomed and rolled.

"Wait!" Jarrett called. "I hear something! What the hell is that?"

Spacer heard them first in the emptiness following the thunder, an eerie, piercing ululation, high-pitched chirps and squeaks and sounds unnervingly like human screams mingled with deeper, bass rumblings and growlings like those of some monstrous beast of prey.

Then Spacer saw them—a dozen or more creatures moving toward them through the uncertain half-light, some coming down off the pyramid, others from around it from either side. They moved with a peculiar, rolling gait that should have been comical but seemed to match their bodies with an elegance that could only be termed graceful. Each stood nearly three meters tall, not counting the two to three meters more of whiplike tentacle questing and snaking from the top of the creature's elongated body. Spacer had seen holopics of the stormies during *Questar*'s passage out from Lison and had an idea of what to expect, but no picture could possible do justice to the reality.

The nearest snapped out its tentacle, flicking it through the air centimeters from Diane's e-suit.

"Diane!" Jarrett called.

"It's okay!" she replied quickly, holding very still. "It's just checking me out. I think."

It was almost as though the rubbery-looking being was tasting the air around her. Several more creatures did the same, and one began tasting the space around Jarrett's suit. Spacer saw a faint flicker of blue light each time the appendage moved near one of the suits, more like a quick-fading glow than an actual spark.

"I think they're sampling the SCAM screens," Jarrett said. "My sensor gauntlet is picking up pretty strong electrical fields around each of them. I think these folks are electrofield sensitive."

Other stormies moved closer. Spacer steeled himself as tentacle tips flicked and quested about his e-suit, each snap eliciting a momentary faint blue glow.

"I'm getting a feed from the translator," Diane said, keying something on her gauntlet. "I'll punch up it up on the HUD feed, so you can all see."

Words began crawling up the right side of Spacer's heads-up display inside his helmet. His mastery of written Standard was poor, and he had trouble puzzling out the words as they moved. Had they been part of a more complex statement, he knew he would have missed it entirely.

BAD . . . BAD NOT FOOD <UNKNOWN> OTHER <UNKNOWN> WARNING <?>

"Diane!" Maricia's voice called over comms. "We're getting the translation here. You'd better pull back. Are any of you doing anything that could be interpreted as a hostile gesture?"

"How do we know what a hostile gesture is to these people?" Jarrett asked.

Spacer wasn't sure what to do. As still more stormies glided closer, he drew his stutter pistol from its holster, but he didn't aim it, assuming that that would be a definite hostile gesture. Then he realized that the stormies probably didn't recognize the gun as a weapon. They didn't seem to have any of the accoutrements of technology themselves, so maybe they didn't recognize a pistol for what it was.

"Spacer!" Diane said. "Don't—"

"Let him," Jarrett said, interrupting. He'd unslung his own, heavier weapon. "Everybody start moving back . . . slowly . . . slowly . . ."

BAD . . . BAD NOT FOOD <UNKNOWN> OTHER <UNKNOWN> WHAT IS <QUERY> . . .

Still more stormies were approaching, streaming around either side of the pyramid, tentacles whiplashing back and forth in an agitated exploration of the air ahead of them. Spacer could sense their excitement, their anger. Reading emotion into the manner of a creature that didn't even have a face was a risky proposition, he realized, but there was no mistaking the mounting fury in their blind movements.

A spark crackled, arcing from the tip of one of the tentacles waving close by Jarrett's helmet. Spacer didn't think it connected with the ranger's suit, but Jarrett staggered back a step, his knees folding beneath him.

DANGER/WARNING<?> NOT FOOD <UNKNOWN> PAIN/AVOID <UNKNOWN> BAD . . .

Spacer raised his stutter pistol then, aiming at the stormie closest to Jarrett and dragging back on the trigger.

A sharp clap of sound blended with a paper-tear hiss sounded, and the stormie twisted away, shrieking. Other stormies halted their advance, milling about as if suddenly uncertain. Most, Spacer saw, had unfolded the rings of tissue encircling their bodies, revealing a bewildering array of feathery, wildly groping antennae.

Diane was at Jarrett's side, trying to pull him up off his knees with one arm while aiming her stutter pistol with the other. Spacer darted forward, helping her drag the stunned ranger to his feet. Together they herded him back from the pyramid and the hostile stormies, leaving the mob in a seething but confused frenzy. Some of the natives were standing rooted to one spot, trembling, their feathery antennae folding and unfolding in and out like panting tongues, others shifting back and forth, tentacles lashing, the image of outraged uncertainty. When several of them started moving toward the retreating party, Spacer loosed another shot.

"Wait!" Diane cried. "His gun!" Jarrett's mass rifle was lying in the mud in front of the screaming stormies.

"Can't do anything about it now!" Spacer yelled back. He wasn't about to go back toward that quivering, keening, whiplashing mob.

They kept moving, falling back toward the ship. The natives followed, but at a distance. Spacer didn't think their shots had more than bruised any of the natives. None had fallen when hit, and he wondered why they didn't rush the party and overwhelm it.

Then they were back beneath the overhang of the ship, and Maricia, Smilin' Jack, Mike, and Rom Verdoss were all there, brandishing weapons, closing in on Spacer and Diane and taking Jarrett from them, shepherding them back up the ramp and into the startlingly homelike embrace of the cargo bay.

The natives, by that time, were gone, vanished back into the wet mist as suddenly as they'd appeared.

Chapter Sixteen

SPACER SAT IN *Questar*'s lounge, slowly laying out his cards. The others were talking in low voices, discussing the unexpected attack.

"They must have seen us enter that temple or sanctuary or whatever it was," Maricia was pointing out.

Jarrett seemed to be recovering okay, though he said his hands and feet were still tingling from the shock he'd taken. He was sitting across the table from Spacer, wrapped in a blanket.

" 'Seen' is the wrong word," he said. "Did we leave a bad smell behind the first time or something? If they heard us, how did they know we were the intruders?"

"They were almost certainly responding to our SCAM capacitor fields, somehow," Diane said. She was studying one of the monitor screens, where a vid of their encounter was playing itself out, looping through the same scenes over and over. She pointed. "Do you see how their tentacles keep moving around our e-suits? Not touching . . . but kind of tasting the air around us."

"Stands to reason," Jarrett said. "If they can generate a shock like the one that decked me, they can probably sense electrical fields, maybe even use them to navigate or for communication."

"I thought those SCAM units were supposed to protect us from lightning," Verdoss said. "Doesn't look to me like we got our money's worth there."

"The capacitor fields can prevent a charge from building up that might cause a strike," Jarrett said, "but those guys were actually channeling bolts off the tips of those tentacles of theirs."

Smilin' Jack was leaning against the lounge doorway. "I imagine the SCAM fields helped dissipate their charges a bit. Otherwise, you might not be here to tell us about it."

"Most life on Storm appears to get at least some of its energy directly from lightning," Maricia said. "The Rig survey recorded at least twenty varieties of sessile organisms—call them plants, for lack of a better word— that actually store electrical energy in organic batteries growing underground. Storm's equivalent of animals, most of them, seem to live by digging up those batteries and ingesting them, utilizing the stored energy directly. At least, that seems to be the pattern for the stormies. We don't know of any other motile, animal forms yet. I guess it's a short step from there to creatures that are living electrical storage cells, who can channel a jolt of power like a weapon."

"There are numerous examples in nature of life forms evolving organic batteries and using electricity for hunting or defense," Ta Shaa Ta pointed out. "Lightning eels on Reliance, Corvalen voltangs, there were electric eels, electric rays, and an odd little creature called a stargazer, all in the seas and rivers of Earth, as I recall. With lightning a near-constant phenomenon on this world, it would be surprising if the native life did not find a way to utilize some of that energy in its metabolic processes."

"Well, the question is how we're going to communicate with creatures that try to fry us when we go to shake hands," Verdoss said.

"Worse than that," Jarrett said. "They have my mass rifle now. I wonder if they can figure out how to use it?"

"That could be a problem," Jack said. "A lucky shot could damage our hull."

"I doubt that, Captain," Jarrett said. "An am-gee can punch through battle armor, but I doubt it can hurt *Questar*'s hide. Still, if they figure out how to use it, they could kill any of us from a distance instead of having to get close enough to touch us."

"What is it you are doing, Spacer?" Ta Shaa Ta asked.

Spacer had been only half listening to the exchange. He'd laid out three cards in a line and was studying the holoprojections glowing above the table.

The Two of Minds. A nude couple stood back to back, taking the first steps away from one another. Stars burned blue-white above their outstretched hands.

The Knight of Swords. A man in armor sat astride a horse, leaning forward as he entered a full gallop, brandishing a sword.

The Nine of Swords. A woman sat upright in bed, sobbing hysterically into her hands. Nine swords hung in horizontal display behind her, one close above the other.

Spacer looked up. "I thought I'd try a reading on the stormies," he said, "just a three-card spread, enough to answer simple questions."

Diane came closer, looking at the spread. "What was the question?"

" 'What do you want?' I figured that's the first question you ask someone, if you want to get to know them, right?"

"And what's the answer?"

Spacer passed his hand through the first image, the Two of Minds. "I . . . I kind of get the feeling that this represents the stormies, somehow. That this is how they think of themselves—divided, going in two directions, or maybe it's more literal than that. Maybe they can't make up their minds about something, something pretty important."

"Okay," Diane said.

"I feel like that most mornings," Maricia added.

Spacer indicated the galloping knight. "They want to

talk, want to communicate, maybe give us a specific message, but they can't. And the message . . . it's important. I don't know what it is or what it's about, but it's very important, whatever it is. Maybe life or death."

"Whose life or death?" Verdoss wanted to know. "Theirs? Or ours?"

"Maybe both." Spacer pointed to the Nine of Swords. "*That* one means loss of hope, of dreams, of plans. It means despair, pain, loss, depression, anguish. It means they're hurting and don't see any way out, that they're desperate."

Smilin' Jack rolled his eyes at the overhead plating. Maricia and Verdoss shared an instant's skeptical grimace.

"How are you getting these interpretations, Spacer?" Diane asked. "From what you've said before, each card has quite a wide variety of possible meanings. But when you give these readings, I've noticed you tend to narrow down the list of choices, make things more specific."

"I'm not sure," he admitted. "It just kind of . . . well, comes to me. I have to be in the right frame of mind. I don't just read one meaning but all of them together, and sometimes I just get a feeling that a particular reading is *right*."

"Intuition," Ta Shaa Ta said, "information acquired through abstract means by the right side of your brain, channeled through to your analytical left." The fraal looked at the others, his large eyes blinking once. "I submit that Spacer may be our single greatest asset in our attempts to communicate with the natives."

"What?" Verdoss said, puzzled. "You mean like telepathy?"

"Not telepathy," Ta Shaa Ta replied, "not as you understand the term. Call it, rather, *telempathy*, an understanding of what the other being is feeling, is perceiving. A glimpse, if you will, through his umvelt."

"How about it, Spacer?" Diane asked. "Would you be willing to use your cards to try to talk with the stormies? Is there a way you could so that?"

"I can try," he said. He felt again the sharp, rising fear as he remembered the Storm natives closing in around the party, but he fought the image down. "It would be better if I could see them face to face, though. It's kind of hard to get a feel for them sitting in here."

"That can be arranged," the ship's captain said. He pointed at one of the monitors, which was set to show the view from a camera mounted on the hull of the ship, near the cargo bay ramp. The ramp was raised now, of course, but the muddy ground was still bathed in hot, white glare from the ship's external lights. At the edge of the light, a number of tall, elongated shapes could be seen moving back and forth, a growing number of natives gathering in a ring about the ship.

Swiftly, Spacer scooped up the three cards on the table, shuffled them back into the deck, and laid out three more, studying the new images.

Ten of Minds. Ten dazzling, blue-white stars hung in the night, a blazing semicircle of light. A man and a woman, Adam and Eve, stood nude on the plain beneath, each with one arm around the other's waist, the other arm uplifted. Both wore golden crowns, and their faces were raised to the heavenly radiance, smiling, at peace. At their backs grew the Tree of Knowledge, its fruit illuminated by the light of the stars.

Three of Wands. A man in green and red robes stood alone on a precipice, looking out to sea. He held upright one living wand in his right hand, while two others grew from the ground to either side. The sky was golden, the light reflecting from the sea beneath, where three sailing vessels slowly beat their way into the harbor.

The Ten of Swords. A man lay dead, face down on a barren plain beneath a gold and black sky. Ten upright swords pierced his back from thigh to neck as blood pooled on the ground.

"The question," Spacer said slowly, "was, 'Do they want to communicate?' " He pointed to the Ten of Minds. "I think this one means a definite yes. In knowledge is completion. They want full knowledge. They want to know everything, and they want to tell us everything." He pointed to the next card in line. "This one indicates a

partnership, two very different people working together on
some project to their mutual benefit. It . . . well, it suggests
they'll rise or fall together. I think the stormies want to
work with us."

"They have a damned funny way of showing it," Verdoss pointed out.

"The attack could have been a mistake," Spacer said,
"or maybe they weren't attacking. Maybe they were trying
to communicate."

"What's that last rather depressing scene?" Maricia
asked. "Come out and talk or we'll stab you in the back?"

"The Ten of Swords always indicates the end of a cycle
of some sort," Spacer replied. "It can mean a sense of loss.
I think the stormies have lost something . . . maybe their
way of life? Something like that. The card often means an
old way of life is dead, and a new one is going to begin. I
don't think this card applies to us at all, really. I think it
applies to the stormies."

"Just so it's not a threat," Jarrett said. " 'Do what we
say, or we'll kill you.' Are you really in communication
with them now, do you think?"

"I don't know. I don't see how I could be." He looked
at Ta Shaa Ta, but the fraal's expression lacked any emotion or information that Spacer could read. He still wasn't
sure he trusted Ta Shaa Ta's explanation of how the cards
worked. As far as Spacer was concerned, the cards themselves read the future . . . or the feelings and desires and
personality of another person. The idea that he might
somehow be tapping into other people's minds—or in this
case, the minds of beings as alien from him as Lison's
night side was from its day side, left him feeling uneasy,
almost as though he'd just been caught trespassing in a forbidden area. For Spacer, lifting a mark's wallet was just
business. Breaking and entering—deliberately invading
another person's precious personal space—was something
else entirely. Not that it didn't happen in Lison . . . but that
kind of robbery was just plain *wrong*.

Was he really reading other people's minds, using some
mystic power of mind over matter to influence the shufflings

of the cards? No. No, he rejected that completely. Still, the cards themselves might be able to reveal the stormies' thoughts. The question was how to communicate in the other direction, to tell them what the human party wanted.

"Communicating our thoughts to the natives *will* be an interesting problem," Ta Shaa Ta said. Spacer's eyes widened. It was eerily as though the fraal were looking into his mind right now. "The linguicomp may help. Spacer's intuitive translation should help us make sure they are hearing our words as we want them to hear."

"You can read minds, fraal," Verdoss said. "Why can't you just use telepathy on those things? Talk to 'em directly, instead of using this hocus-pocus crap?"

"I have tried," Ta Shaa Ta said. "I was trying just now, when the three of them were out there. The more different, the more alien the mind, the harder it is to see and understand, the harder it is to generate understanding. I can read very little of the stormies' thoughts . . . emotions only, and those scattered and disjointed, a kind of background noise, from which it is nearly impossible to extract meaning. I do not think they could understand my thoughts at all."

"So how is Spacer's fortune telling going to help?"

"Young Spacer is our one hope to establish meaningful communication with the natives, and in a short time. I fear their, ah, current agitation will preclude the usual lengthy process of learning their language, a word or a phrase at a time."

"I'll do it," Spacer said. He tried to put more confidence, more determination into the words than he actually felt. "But I'd rather be there, in their presence. I can't tell if I'm really reading them here at all."

"We will talk to them together," Ta Shaa Ta said, "and I suggest that high on our list of questions for them be a request for information about other human activities on Storm. I have a feeling that the stormie attack earlier was directed at a different enemy entirely."

* * * * *

Hours later, Spacer descended *Questar*'s ramp as it slowly lowered into the mud and wet outside. The gathering throng of natives had moved back as the ship's main cargo lock started to cycle open, but they moved closer again as Spacer, followed closely by Ta Shaa Ta and Maricia, reached the end of the ramp and stopped.

All three were wearing their e-suits with the charge dissipating SCAM fields up. Maricia was wearing the linguicomp. None, however, were carrying weapons. There was still no way of knowing whether the stormies even recognized human weapons as such—there'd been no indication that they'd been more than stung by the stutter gun shots earlier, and they hadn't appeared to feel threatened by them at all.

Spacer sensed a kind of rustling or stirring among the waiting aliens, an *expectancy*, but none of the agitation they'd shown during the earlier attack.

Squatting on the ramp, Spacer unfolded the red cloth on the steel decking and began shuffling the cards. He'd left the e-suit's gauntlets off, preferring to handle the cards with his bare hands. The temperature was warm, the air wet. The suit's internal breach seals kept the poisonous atmosphere from leaking inside.

"Are you ready?" Maricia asked.

"I guess so. . . ."

Maricia asked the first question. A series of bass growls coupled with a high-pitched chirp sounded from her suit speaker. At the same time, Spacer's heads-up display inside his helmet showed the translation scrolling up the side of his visor, the words in green.

WE FRIEND. WE WANT TALK.

He wondered if the sounds the stormies were hearing were as flat, as stilted, as pidgin-language clumsy as the Standard words felt. At least he was better able to read them, now. He'd asked Jarrett for help and learned how to slow the march of the words up his helmet visor display.

One of the stormies stepped into the circle of harsh light, barking and whimpering something from all three upper mouths. The translated words scrolled up Spacer's

HUD in white letters. Some were words he didn't recognize, words too long to puzzle out in an instant. No matter. He could *feel* them, somehow. . . .

NOT-FRIEND <DENIAL/REFUTATION> TASTE WRONG SMELL WRONG <UNKNOWN> BIG CONFUSION/ANTICIPATION <?> <QUERY>

At the same time, Spacer drew a single card and laid it on the cloth.

The King of Machines, reversed. The image hung suspended upside-down, a regal-looking man in robes and crown, seated on an inverted throne. He held in his hand a mechanical device of some kind, an orrery with a central, living eye. Above and behind him was a vast whirlpool of stars, the Galaxy—but in the inverted position, the king appeared to be dropping headlong into its swirling vortex.

What was the card telling him? The stormies had little to do with machines; Spacer could sense that much just by looking at them. There was, however, the sense of a grand and intricate plan, a plan that had been delayed or even overthrown. The fact that the card was part of the minor arcana suggested that the issue was a serious one, but one that could still be salvaged—that was in their power to salvage, in fact.

The king could also be a person standing in the way of stormie plans. Who? The TXI party, or someone else?

"Okay," he said, speaking over the general comm channel. "The stormies have some sort of a plan or a project under way, but it's been upset by someone or something. It has them confused . . . and very upset." He drew a second card.

The Five of Swords. A young man with a sly grin on his face carefully picked up a sword. Two other swords lay on the ground, while he carried two more on his shoulder. Two men stood in the distance, their backs turned, while the sky boiled and seethed at the brink of a thunderstorm. The first man, by his expression and by his attitude, was clearly stealing the swords from the other two.

The card usually involved a lack of concern or sensitivity for others and could literally refer to cunning, theft, unethical coercion, a bad reputation, or simply destructive attitudes or behavior.

"Someone has been hurting the stormies," Spacer said. "Either they've been stealing something from them, or they're engaged in behavior that could destroy them or whatever it is they're working on."

A third card.

The Seven of Swords. A young man in a colorful print tunic carried five swords away, leaving two standing point-down in a field. In the distance, banners waved from the tents of a military encampment. The man looked back over his shoulder, a smug grin on his face.

"Third card," Spacer said. "It just reinforces the second. Someone is stealing something important from the stormies. There may be deception involved, or it could be a literal theft. I can't tell yet." He thought about it a moment. The Seven of Swords often meant a deception was being practiced. "I think . . . I think maybe they think we're trying to deceive them."

"That could explain the attack," Diane's voice said.

Maricia's suit barked, growled, and whined. Green words on Spacer's HUD gave the translation.

"NOT NOT-FRIEND. FRIEND ALL. GIVE TRUTH. WANT TRUTH. NOT HURT. WHO/WHAT HURT. QUERY."

The stormies appeared to digest this piece of linguistic intricacy. Spacer hoped they were getting some sense out of it, because he certainly wasn't.

The reply was quicker in coming this time.

TASTE WRONG <QUERY> HARD OUTSIDE WRONG/BAD <UNKNOWN> <QUERY> TOUCH WRONG TASTE WRONG <UNKNOWN> BAD

Quickly, Spacer shuffled the cards back into the deck and drew a fresh one, laying it on the cloth.

The Five of Cups. A man in a black cloak stood alone, looking down at three overturned cups, their contents spilling on the ground. Two cups stood upright behind him. In the distance, a bridge crossed a river, with a castle on the far horizon beneath a leaden, purple-gray sky.

"Loss," Spacer said, translating. "Terrible loss and sorrow."

He drew again.

The Eight of Swords. A woman, tightly bound and blindfolded, stood in the muddy field surrounded by the hedge of eight upright swords.

"Fear. The stormies are afraid. They also don't know what to do. They may be too weak to fight for their own rights or protect what is theirs. They feel helpless."

A third card.

The Seven of Swords . . . again. Once more, the smiling man stole five of the seven swords from the encampment.

"Deception." The feeling was stronger now. He was learning how to relax and ride with his intuitive feelings. "They think we're trying to deceive them somehow."

Suddenly, the nearest stormie took several rolling steps closer. Spacer froze, unable and unwilling to move as that three-meter tentacle snaked through the air and slid back and forth, only centimeters from his e-suit. Blue light glowed as the tentacle tip slid across Spacer's SCAM capacitor field.

Spacer tried to make himself relax. It wasn't an attack.

Intuition took over, and he drew another card from the center of the deck, thinking as he did so that it would tell him what the strange being was trying to say.

The Knight of Wands. A heavily armored knight, a blossoming wand held upright in his gauntleted hand, sallied forth on a leaping orange horse. The red plume on the knight's helm, his red hair, and the portions of his streaming red cape visible behind his body looked like curling tongues of flame. He rode through a desert featureless but for three pyramids on the horizon, representing body, mind, and spirit. The tabard, the sleeveless tunic he wore over his armor, was bright yellow and decorated with salamanders—a motif symbolizing magical protection.

"He's anxious, even eager," Spacer said. "He wants to set things straight, once and for all. Stress . . . difficulty . . . winning through . . ." For some reason, Spacer's thoughts turned to the salamanders on the holo-image and to the idea of protection. . . .

"Wait a minute!" he called. "I think I know what the problem is!" Deliberately, Spacer reached for the control on his left sleeve that would switch off his SCAM-20 capacitor field and pressed the touch plate with his bare finger. A green light showing at the upper left of his helmet HUD winked out.

"Spacer!" Jarrett called from inside the ship. "You've switched off your capacitor field!"

"It's okay," he replied. *"I'm* okay. I just wanted to see . . ."

The stormie jumped as though poked by a stick. It stood several meters away, mouths alternately gaping and closing, its tentacle whipping back and forth, touching the ground on all sides and intermittently snapping back to Spacer and lightly caressing his e-suit.

The being growled and chirped. White-lettered words scrolled up Spacer's HUD as Maricia's linguicomp translated.

<UNKNOWN> TASTE DIFFERENT NO BAD TASTE TASTE GO <?> BAD NOT-BAD <QUERY> TASTE BAD <REFUTATION/ DENIAL/NEGATION> FRIEND <QUERY> NOT-FRIEND IS FRIEND <QUERY> TASTE STRANGE

Spacer drew a card.

The Two of Minds. Nude lovers parting, back to back, each holding a glowing star representing thought and mind.

"Two people the same . . . but completely different," Spacer said. "Confusion between two paths, two courses of action . . . No. Confusion over two things that look alike, but aren't!" He hesitated. Was it that simple? "Our armor," he gasped. He was thinking of the Knight of Wands, and the protective salamanders on his tabard. "Our e-suits. I think this guy is telling us that our e-suits taste like someone he doesn't like or doesn't trust!"

"The capacitor fields," Diane said. "That's what they mean by bad taste. With the capacitor fields on, we taste bad to them!"

"Either that," Jarrett added, "or we taste like someone they don't like. I'm wondering . . . those five Rigunmor strung up in the pyramid. We know they didn't use capacitor fields, right? One of them, at least, according to Rom, was killed by lightning. I'll bet to a stormie, sensitive to electrical fields, we look . . . uh, we *taste* a lot more like a VoidCorper than we do like the Rigunmor survey personnel."

"I concur," Ta Shaa Ta said, from his position behind Spacer. "I am probing this one's thoughts now. There is still a great deal of noise—the way they think is really quite alien to anything I've encountered before—but I'm definitely picking up surprise that Spacer seems to have abruptly changed from one shape or form to another. It would be the same surprise you might feel if you saw a weren suddenly transform itself into a fraal."

"That's a pretty weird thought," Spacer said. He'd never seen a weren in the flesh, but he'd seen vids of the creatures—great, hairy, long-tusked, hulking brutes as obtrusive and loud as the fraal were delicate and retiring.

"Uh . . . how long can I stay out here without my field switched on?" Spacer asked. He was remembering that it not only afforded protection against lightning, but against the far more pervasive and unseen threat of radiation as well.

"You're okay, Spacer," Diane told him. "We're monitoring the rads from in here. The planet's ozone layer and the ship's fields are protecting you right now. The ship should also protect you from any nearby lightning strikes."

"Good. Just thinking about it, I was starting to feel itchy all over."

The stormies were in motion again, shifting uncomfortably along their perimeter about the ship. Suddenly, the one serving as spokesman turned and stumped away without another word. For a moment, Spacer wondered if they were all leaving, but that didn't seem to be the case.

Another stormie was approaching.

At first, it looked identical to the others. All of the Storm natives, Spacer had noticed, looked pretty much alike to him, save for slight variations in size and the shape of the black patches on their dark, rubbery skins. As it grew closer though, he saw that this one was different.

It had an eye.

The eye—large, wet, and quite similar in design to a human eye with a richly textured brown and gold iris—

stared at him from a swelling on the left side of the creature's body, just below the sensory ring girdling the stormie's body. There was an unusual swelling there, a lumpy and discolored mass that didn't look entirely healthy, as though the being's body had developed a large and misshapen tumor on its otherwise sleek frame. A dark bluish fluid leaked from places where the rubbery hide had stiffened and cracked, and from the tissue surrounding and holding the eye itself.

There was another difference besides the purely organic. A stormfire crystal was imbedded in the creature's skin above the sensory girdle, beneath the base of the tentacle—a kind of badge or emblem. It seemed unusual in a species that, so far, had shown no differentiation at all from one being to the next.

For a moment, the newcomer stood there a few meters from the end of *Questar*'s ramp, its lone eye rolling back and forth as it openly studied Spacer, Maricia, and Ta Shaa Ta.

Spacer had thought the eye surprising. The being startled him even more now, when it spoke. "You . . . are . . . not . . . VoidCorp."

The voice was flat, utterly without inflection, but the words were precise and clear in carefully enunciated Standard.

"We are *not* VoidCorp," Maricia said, her words sounding over her suit speakers.

"Your . . . skins . . . are . . . like . . . VoidCorp," it said, "but . . . VoidCorp . . . does . . . not . . . talk. They . . . only . . . tell."

"How is it you speak our language?" Maricia asked.

"We . . . learn . . . from . . . VoidCorp. Learn . . . or . . . die."

"Did VoidCorp give you the eye, as well?"

"The . . . words . . . come . . . from . . . VoidCorp," the creature said. The hesitation between each word felt like a groping, as though it had to go through a list to find the one that would fit. "The . . . eye . . . and . . . the . . . second . . . brain . . . are . . . from . . ."

The final word was an explosion of sound, as though the native had reverted to one of the barks of its own language rather than using Standard. A single word appeared in white, however, as translation on Spacer's HUD. The word was "Salamanca."

But the *feeling* that came with that name was quite different, not the name of a world at all. Spacer drew a new card and placed it on the cloth. The image confirmed the feeling, his intuition given form and substance.

To Spacer, it felt as though the native had just casually told them that its eye and brain were from God.

Chapter Seventeen

Dawn was slowly breaking over Thunder Plateau as the expedition party, following the stormie who called itself Touches Far, wended its way down a gently sloping plain toward the northeast across a tortured, twisted, and bewildering alien landscape. Storm's fifty-three-hour night was drawing to a close. The night-long rain had let up, the clouds had begun to fragment in red, blue, and purple-gray tatters, and the first traces of daylight were exploding skyward from the jagged eastern horizon in vast, luminous shafts of pink, red, and orange.

Diane Radlevich was in the lead as they walked single-file along a narrow path that appeared to have been worn into rock and soil over the course of thousands of years. South, the volcano they'd named Sunbreak Mountain grumbled beneath a towering ash plume, gray beneath and golden-lit at the top. The steady, crackling thunder of the night had given way to a muted, distant roar—the deep-seated mutter of the volcano, and the far-off rumble of the waterfalls cascading into the sea.

Everywhere, plant life exploded from black, wet soil, plumes and spikes and catcher nets uncoiling so quickly the growth of each organism could very nearly be noted by the naked eye. There were two main types of plant life on Storm, their guide explained. "Catchers" unfurled semi-rigid sheets of purplish membrane to the morning's eastern wind, thereby collecting moisture from the warm, damp air. Condensation beaded from the ends of the huge leaves, eventually running down into the mouth at the plant's base. The membranes also caught microscopic, sulphur-based organisms borne on the wind and channeled them in a thin but constant soup to the plant's metabolic process-ing centers underground. "Eaters," on the other hand, uti-lized energy stored in large, underground organic batteries to swiftly grow spikes, rods, and bizarrely twisted shapes glittering with traces of metal tapped and concentrated from deep beneath the soil. They would be full-grown by the time of Eclipse, when Storm's lightning would return. Fulgivores, they attracted bolts of lightning in a one-time meal of incandescent destruction, channeling some frac-tion of the skyborne current into tubers and storing it against the next cycle of growth and reproduction.

It had been two days now since their landing on Storm. Storm's weather, according to Touches Far, was actually fairly predictable: rain throughout the fifty-three-hour night, partly cloudy to clear during the day, and hell unfet-tered for the hours of Eclipse, when Storm passed through Salamanca's ionized "tail" and lightning fell from the sky like rain.

Salamanca was visible above and behind Diane's left shoulder as they descended the plateau. It was partly masked by Storm's clouds in the thick, wet atmosphere. She and Maricia both had closely questioned Touches Far and determined that Spacer's original pronouncement was essentially correct. Salamanca, the giant planet hanging in Storm's sky, was their god.

Spacer. Diane still wasn't sure what to make of his eerie ability with the cards. Ta Shaa Ta seemed to trust his talent though, and she trusted the fraal's judgment completely on all matters psionic. Even Rom Verdoss had been forced to admit that Spacer had paid his own way on the expedition by successfully opening communications with the stormies.

They'd learned a lot more about Storm and its natives in the past thirty hours. Sleeping in shifts, Diane and Maricia had used the linguicomp to increase the device's vocabulary and begin the laborious trial-and-error process of smoothing out the grammar into something the stormies wouldn't assume was coming from a mentally deficient juvenile. Touches Far didn't seem to need sleep but was always waiting for the human researchers when they emerged from *Questar*.

The sighted Storm natives, they'd learned, called themselves the Chosen of the Eye—"Eye" apparently another name for their god. The word was a compound phrase, a series of barks and squeaks that translated directly as "touch-with-no-touching." Maricia had supplied the word "eye" for the fast-growing stormie vocabulary. For obvious reasons, the stormie language had no references to vision, to seeing, to sight, or to the organs of sight.

Like so much else about this system, about this world, the stormies presented a host of questions—far more questions than the small expedition could possibly hope to answer. Ta Shaa Ta, Maricia, and Jarrett all agreed that the Loman-Salamanca-Storm system was not stable, nor could it be terribly old. The gas giant could not have existed in its current orbit for more than a few million years at most—just as Storm was not in a stable orbit around Salamanca. How long ago had intelligence evolved on Storm . . . and how?

Diane found the ramifications of that question tremendously exciting, both from a theoretical standpoint and even more from the perspective of her career as a xenoarchaeologist. She was on the trail of the Precursors, and it was just possible that the stormies were evidence of Precursor activity in this part of the galaxy.

The galaxy was at least ten billion years old, twice the age of distant Sol and the world that had spawned humanity a cosmic heartbeat or two ago. When Earth was still gathering out of a swirling cloud of dust, other worlds had already given rise to life, intelligence, and technology—had already grown old and died, had already given to the universe their particular legacies of wonder, thought, and mind.

In the popular mind, the Precursors were a species of godlike intelligence that had flourished in the galaxy long ago then passed on . . . elsewhere, leaving behind their enigmatic ruins and artifacts. Whole religions had been raised on the premise that the Precursors were gods who would one day return.

There had been many Precursor races, most separated from one another by gulfs of time and space at least as vast as those that separated humanity from any of them. In fact, at least a hundred distinct Precursor races were known among the worlds explored so far by humankind. Eight or ten, depending on how you counted, existed in the Verge alone . . . from the Stoneburners to the magnificent Glassmakers. Several life forms on Verge worlds were suspected of being bioartifacts created by one or another of the ancient intelligences who'd once strode among the stars of the Verge like giants.

Diane strongly suspected that the stormies themselves were such artifacts. While there was a rich biodiversity on Storm, there were few animals and no large ones at all. The stormies were the largest motile and predatory species on the planet, and the fact that life appeared to have evolved over the course of a very few hundreds of millions of years suggested that the stormies were something special—either an evolutionary leap far beyond the relatively primitive forms now living on Storm, or an artifact, a species literally engineered from similar forms for reasons long ago lost.

It was that possibility that had drawn Diane to Storm like a black hole drawing down infalling matter.

The stormie called Touches Far had been a godsend. Since meeting it—stormies appeared to be parthenogenetic, though that was not absolutely certain yet—they'd more than tripled the available vocabulary, though they still had trouble communicating with the ordinary stormies. Those not of the Chosen, while clearly intelligent, seemed to organize their thought in ways peculiarly different from human mental processes. They did not have names for themselves, either as a species or as individuals. They did not know of "God" or think in religious terms. In fact, most of their speech appeared to be short, staccato bursts of feeling or of emotional judgment—"good," "bad," "wrong," "right." They tended to be passive; their "attack" on the first day hadn't been aggression, because stormies—with no natural enemies, no tribal rivalries, no competition with others—literally had no concept relating to "aggression" or "fighting" or "war." The electric arcs that had stunned Jarrett, and a hundred fifty years before, killed one of the Rigunmor Survey Team members, had been frustrated attempts at communication, nothing more.

A peaceful, gentle people, in fact, the stormies grazed for tuber-batteries buried in the soil where fulgivores had grown, stored a bolt of lightning, and died. With a lifestyle about as exciting and demanding as that of bovines or terrestrial cattle, there seemed to be little point to their intelligence—a fact that, in Diane's mind, strongly suggested that they were bioartifacts.

The stormies, according to Touches Far, had not built the temples, the pyramid, and the other large and elaborately engraved buildings on the Thunder Plateau. Those ruins had been built by Someone Else in the inconceivably distant past—a Precursor race.

The Chosen of Salamanca were something else . . . stormies transformed from pastoral grazers to shepherds of a sort. According to Touches Far, there were only a few Chosen among many stormies—the Storm natives didn't seem to have mastered the concept of numbers or counting beyond "few" and "many"—and those few apparently appeared at random from among normal, sightless stormies.

Diane glanced over her shoulder at Salamanca, looming huge above the western horizon. It seemed obvious now that they thought about it: the stormies had never known of Salamanca's existence in their sky. There was no way they could see it with their awareness limited to sound, smell, taste, touch, and two other senses Touches Far called *warm-tasting* and *flow-tasting*, which almost certainly referred to sensing electrical and magnetic fields.

According to Touches Far, God Itself had reached down and provided a few stormies, the Chosen, with a whole new sense—vision, which they called "far-touching"— and, weirdest of all, with a second brain that let them use it. Suddenly, with the eruption of physical eyes on the bodies of some of the stormies, their world had been transformed. Vision had given them access to a flood of new information, a literal view of things they'd never dreamed existed before.

Diane wished they had a xenobiologist with them. Both she and Ta Shaa Ta had training in the field, but this was something utterly new and totally beyond her comprehension. The Chosen simply grew the eyes in what appeared to be lumpily misshapen tumors erupting from their bodies. Most grew from their torsos; a few, apparently, grew on one of their legs or inside a mouth. Sometimes the individual Chosen was crippled by the growth. Sometimes they were driven insane—she was pretty sure that that was what Touches Far meant by the phrase "touch-but-feel-things-wrong."

The tumors, she was almost certain, were literal second brains, somehow hardwired with the neural necessities for processing visual imagery, but also allowing an extension or an elaboration of their normal way of thinking. The thought processes of the Chosen, if Touches Far was any indication, were much closer to those of humans than to ordinary stormies.

She thought again of their discussion of umvelt aboard *Questar*. It was as though the Chosen's worldview, their way of perceiving their surroundings, was enough like that of humans that the two could communicate.

She was also reminded of the card Spacer had drawn, the one he'd called "Two of Minds." The Chosen were literally two-minded, and in a grossly distorted way, shared that fact of existence and thought with humans. Ordinary stormies, she was beginning to understand, were emotive, intuitional, and feeling. The Chosen seemed more analytical, more rational, more idea-driven, though she was willing to admit that that could be anthropocentric prejudice on her part.

None of which explained where the eyes were coming from. Something like that—an eye, complex, full-blown and working—*couldn't* be a disease, an essentially random process. Maricia thought the eyes were an expression of some long-buried fragment of stormie DNA, something in their past evolution long suppressed that was now occasionally expressed in certain types of cancer-like growths.

Diane disagreed. She wasn't sure what the answer was, but she sensed intelligent design behind the randomly appearing eyes and second brains. The party's trip down off the Thunder Plateau this morning had only reinforced that for her. Three times as they'd walked along the trail through patches of rapidly unfurling vegetation, she'd seen plants that sported eyes and cancerous lumps exactly like those borne by the Chosen. It was positively eerie to walk past what was obviously a catcher plant, but with a lone, sad, brown eye and brain growing off-center in the upright membrane. The moisture trickling down the plant membrane tended to collect around the tops and sides of the eyes then drain off below, an effect uncomfortably like crying.

With no means of speech, there was no way to talk to them . . . if, indeed, there was a mind behind those tragic gazes. Hell, did they even *have* a language? Chosen speech was obviously based on the native stormie language, even if the difference in umvelt meant their use of it was more intelligible than that of their blind brothers.

Touches Far was unable to say anything about the sighted plants, other than that they were, like him, "Chosen of the Eye," somehow singled out by God Itself.

"What if it *thinks*, like you do?" she'd asked Touches Far the first time she'd seen one of the odd, sighted plants. "Does it know it's going to die the next time there's a storm?"

Touches Far's response had been an enigmatic rippling of its tentacle, as though it were groping for something in

236 WILLIAM H. KEITH, JR.

the air. "It does not matter," the being had told her. "God creates, and God destroys. It will destroy us all very soon. That is how things are."

That streak of fatalism seemed strange . . . perfectly in character, perhaps, for the blind and passive stormies, but not for the more dynamic Chosen.

Obviously, they still had a lot to learn about these oddly bicameral beings.

She was sure of one thing. Those eyes *did* speak of a designer and not of evolution and natural selection across hundreds of millions of years.

But if there *was* a designer, who—or what—was it?

*   *   *   *   *

The Heirophant. A man in regal red and white robes and a high, golden triple crown, raised his right hand in benediction. In his left was a crosier, while at his feet were crossed, golden keys. The crown symbolized the kingdom of heaven, the red of the vestments the kingdom of Earth, while the white trim revealed the purity of God. He sat on a throne between two massive pillars while two tonsured priests knelt before him.

Spacer had never heard of the Pope—the figure who was the basis for the Heirophant of the holotarot. Maricia had explained to him later the idea of the Catholic Church and its leader, the heir of the throne of St. Peter.

According to his grandmother, the Heirophant in holotarot symbology represented authority, conformity, and social structure. It symbolized a teacher and the concept of unity through a single language, religion, or government. Spacer's feeling that the card represented *God* had been based more on the intuition of the moment than on accepted tarot understanding. Salamanca, to the sighted stormie, was the source of life, of knowledge, of the order of all things . . . as good a definition of *God* as Spacer, an agnostic by default, could imagine.

But their subsequent conversations with Touches Far had convinced them all that the gas giant Salamanca was, in fact, a kind of god . . . at least to the Chosen. Spacer still got a bit of a shiver up his spine when he remembered the moment, some hours ago now, when the clouds had first broken and Salamanca had appeared in the west—huge, filling a vast sweep of the sky. The planet was nearly full, its rings, so golden and glorious from space, were invisible here, but the bands and storm-whorls and striations of its sun-tortured day side were clearly visible. Touches Far had turned and watched the spectacle with its single large, brown eye, as all three mouths gaped wide with a shrill cacophony of wailing harmonies blended uncomfortably with guttural and atonal rumbles.

Maricia's linguicomp had crashed, unable to manage a running translation. Later, Touches Far had explained it had been "greeting" the god, and telling it in formal song what the Chosen had learned since the last time God had been made manifest.

A prayer? Worship? Spacer wasn't sure. Later, when he'd had a chance to consult his cards, he'd turned up the Six of Minds, indicating adjustments in thoughts and attitudes, bridging gaps, communication . . . and a need to touch someone far-removed.

He knew he'd seen an answer to his question, but he wasn't sure if he understood the answer or not.

After a long and welcome sleep, Spacer had awakened to preparations for a new venture into the wilds of Storm. Captain Duprés and his crew were now engaged in repairs to the starship. Jarrett, Diane, Maricia, and Ta Shaa Ta were planning on following Touches Far to see something the Chosen stormie wanted them to see. Spacer had immediately volunteered to go along; his communications skills might come in handy, all agreed. Besides, Rom Verdoss was staying with the ship. He claimed to want to keep an eye on Smilin' Jack and his party, but Spacer thought the Rigunmor was afraid of the stormies. No matter. Spacer decided he would much rather be where the Rigunmor was not, and that meant he was going with the rest of the party to see what Touches Far had to show them.

They'd been walking now for nearly three hours,

crossing rugged, broken ground that was gradually dropping in altitude. He'd not been bored during the trek. Twice, mild tremors had reminded them that this was a seismically active planet, caught in a gravitational tug-of-war between Salamanca, the huge moon Taliafiero, and the sun. The sky was startling in its intensity and strangeness, alive with clouds similar to the storm clouds of Lison, but more brightly colored. In the north, even after the sun began its long, languid crawl up from the horizon, Storm's auroral displays burned and shifted like cold, living flame. Meteorites periodically streaked and flared across the sky. Jarrett explained that Storm circled Salamanca close to the outer edges of the gas giant's ring system, and the planet-sized moon was constantly skimming fist-sized chunks of ice and rock from the sky and devouring them in flaming, shooting-star bursts.

Closer at hand, the native plantlife presented a bewildering array of life and strangeness. The catcher plants they'd passed with eyes had been unnerving. It was bad enough to be watched by a grepping *plant*, worse still that the trickling moisture on the catching membranes made the things look like they were crying. Spacer thought that he could feel the entities trapped inside as he passed— minds without voices, without expression, trapped immobile and helpless for the four days of life they had available, with nothing to do but *think*.

The eyes had followed Spacer as he passed each sighted plant, leaving him each time with a crawling sensation beneath his skin.

The path Touches Far led them along leveled off eventually, then began rising once more, winding up the face of a broad, low mountain. Jarrett transmitted a topological map to all of them, linking it through their helmet HUDs. According to that, they were now ascending the outer slope of a very old, very wide volcanic crater.

"Diane? Where the grep is he taking us?" Spacer asked, petulant and impatient. He'd never walked this much back in the tunnels of Lison, and his feet were starting to hurt.

"It wouldn't say," Diane replied. She'd been walking just ahead of Spacer the whole way, with the long-legged stormie in the lead and Ta Shaa Ta, Maricia, and Jarrett following behind. "It just told us it wanted to show us something bad."

"My guess is that it's VoidCorp," Jarrett said. "We're headed in the general direction from which those missiles came, anyway. I suggest that we keep talking to an absolute minimum. Our suit radios are set for short-range transmission only, but we don't know if VoidCorp has automated listening posts set out—or maybe sentries in those rocks up there."

They completed the climb in silence, trudging at last to the crest of the hill. Ahead of them was a long, broad, absolutely flat plain adorned with a circle of standing stones.

Spacer felt a deep-seated tickle of awe . . . and a little fear. The main circle, composed of pairs of upright stones as tall as *Questar* and capped by massive lintels that surely weighed ten tons apiece, must have been nearly a kilometer across. Other stones stood as lonely sentries beyond the inner ring. As the red sun rose in the east, the sunward side of each stone glowed red and gold, while the rest was etched black in shadow.

Several lintels had fallen to the ground, and a couple of the uprights as well. Seismic quakes, Spacer thought, would present a problem for anyone building large structures on this world.

"My God," Diane said. "It's Stonehenge!"

"What's that?" Jarrett asked.

"A megalithic monument on Earth. See how the standing stones are laid out in a huge ring with other stones laid out on the ground in and around the circle? On Earth, it's actually a kind of astronomical computer for celestial objects—marks the rising and setting of the moon and sun at key times of the year. I'm betting this does the same, though it's much larger. See how that one stone off by itself is casting a long shadow with the sunrise, right into the stone circle? This is incredible!"

"Do you mean this stone place on Earth was built by these guys?" Spacer asked.

"Hell, no! But I think it was built for the same reason: to measure the sky very accurately!"

Touches Far barked something, a lengthy speech. Spacer tried to read the translated words, but they were moving too fast for him. Maricia translated, however.

"He says the stormies built this place for measuring. He calls it 'length-touching,' and says that *this* was why God gave the Chosen eyes . . .this, and something else he calls the Gateway of God."

"It seems hard to believe the stormies raised these stones,"Jarrett said. "Those tentacles of theirs seem so delicate."

"You'd be surprised how strong they are," Diane replied.

Touches Far was still speaking. "He also says that the 'bad ones' have stopped all of God's work here," Maricia said. "He says he can show us what happened just a little farther on."

"Great," Spacer said. "More walking."

"I'm getting worried about these 'bad ones,' " Jarrett said. He unslung his am-gee rifle—returned to him by the stormies, who'd had no idea what it was or what it was for—and gave the entire, encircling horizon a good looking over. "I feel kind of naked out here."

They passed by the stone circle. Spacer stared at the vista beyond, holding up his gloved hand to shield his eyes from the red-gold glare of the sun that was just peeking above the black, saw-toothed silhouette of the distant mountains. From the center of the circle, the sun appeared to be rising just to the left of one particular outlying stone, which was casting a long, straight-edged shadow into the center of the ring. He wondered if that meant anything.

The tumbled-down stones suggested that the circle had been neglected for a time. Was that what Touches Far meant when he said the bad ones were interfering with God's work? Spacer knew rock well enough to wonder how the stormies, each slender and rubbery, could have cut, shaped, and moved those titanic blocks of stone. They didn't appear to be designed for such demanding heavy labor, and he'd seen no sign at all that they possessed anything like machines—even machines as simple as the block and tackle.

Beyond the stone circle, the ground began to rise again, but only gradually, a hillock atop the far larger swelling of the main mountain. The terrain also became much more broken and torn, with huge cracks slashed deep into solid black rock, and boulders the size of houses tumbled about like children's scattered blocks. The ground here was barren and almost all solid rock, gravel, and ash. Nothing grew here, as though the land were cursed.

Once, they passed the body of a stormie, its rubbery hide torn open and the blue and purple organs within hideously visible. The wound looked like it had been burned into the being, possibly with a high-powered laser. A steel shackle with a snapped-off length of chain still encircled one of the being's three legs.

Touches Far gave its dead compatriot a brief, rolling glance with its sad, brown eye and passed on without comment. The humans and lone fraal followed.

The Chosen stormie led them onward, winding through the labyrinth of broken stone, and then they reached the cliff.

They emerged in the shadowed crevice between two huge boulders standing on the rim of the pit. Spacer had to reach out and place his glove against one of the boulders to steady himself.

The view was spectacular . . . and dizzying.

At their feet, the ground dropped away in steeply terraced steps into a vast, volcanic caldera at least four kilometers across. The crater was an ancient one, long cold and dead, but a heavy mist was rising from a lake at the caldera's center, creating the illusion of active volcanism.

Spacer had some trouble making out other details. Though the sky was fully light by this time, the crater floor itself was still lost in shadow. Still, there was a cluster of bright white and orange lights perhaps a kilometer from the foot of the cliff they were standing on, and those, clearly, were not the work of stormies. Nearby was a dark, cigar-shaped shadow that looked like the hull of a small freighter.

Beyond the encampment, in the center of the lake, something like an arch rose above the still, blue water. It was hard to see in the dark, but to Spacer, it looked like it was made of glass.

Jarrett was studying the scene below through a monocular viewer. "VoidCorp, all right," he said. Thoughtful, he handed the monocular to Maricia, who in turn took a quick look, then passed it to Diane. "What's that archway, out in the middle?"

Touches Far said something explosive, and Diane translated. "He says it is the Gateway to God."

Spacer dropped into a crouch, squinting. He could see movement down there . . . and something that looked like a very large, very irregular pit. There was a lot of activity inside.

Diane handed the monocular to Ta Shaa Ta, who held the viewer close to his helmet. "I can see stormies working in that pit," he said. "There are armed guards nearby. What are the natives looking for?"

Touches Far burbled something, the tip of its tentacle curling back to touch the stormfire imbedded in its rubbery hide.

Spacer didn't need the translation on his HUD or Diane's explanation. "He says they are looking for eyes-of-the-gate. I think he means those gemstones."

"Figures," Jarrett said. "That must be why VoidCorp is interested in Storm."

Ta Shaa Ta handed the monocular to Spacer, who brought the viewscreen up to his helmet visor. At maximum magnification, the figures in the bottom of the caldera looked as though they were only a few meters away. He could see a vast mob of blue-green and black stormies slowly widening the meter-deep pit with flicks of their long tentacles, filling buckets with gravel that other stormies carried in an unending procession out of the pit and across the broken plain to a small mountain of debris well clear of the camp.

Guards were everywhere, standing about in black combat armor and lugging potent-looking weapons. Spacer could see the black, gray, and red emblem of VoidCorp on one upthrust stabilizer of the freighter. The encampment was a collection of habitat domes encircled by a field fence. A narrow bridge had been constructed across the lake, leading to the archway at the center. Through the monocular, the arch looked like a glittering mass of many small pieces of glass, as though laboriously constructed of tens of millions of marbles. Several VoidCorpers, wearing e-suits much like those worn by the TXI party, were taking measurements of the archway with electronic devices of some sort.

Spacer guessed that there were twenty or thirty Void-Corpers down there . . . and at least two thousand stormies.

"There are so many natives," he said. He looked up at Touches Far. "How come the stormies don't just overrun the Voider base and kill them all? There's enough of them down there!"

Touches Far's answer, translated by Maricia, was puzzled. "We work, or we are ended. What are these words about what we should do?"

After a few more exchanges with the native, Maricia was able to add, "They really don't have concepts like 'kill' or 'overrun.' I don't think Touches Far has any idea of what we're talking about."

"It's damned well about time they learned!" Diane said.

"Why is it," Ta Shaa Ta said, "that humans tend to see violence as the answer to everything?"

"We don't," Diane replied, "and it's not. But sometimes, nothing else will deliver the message."

"Okay," Jarrett said. "How do we go about teaching the idea of *kill* to a bunch of blind natives who don't even know the meaning of the word?"

A tone chirped in Spacer's helmet headset. "EVA Team, this is *Questar*! EVA Team, *Questar*! Do you copy?"

It was Smilin' Jack's voice. Spacer felt a stirring of fear. The ship was supposed to maintain radio silence. All transmissions were being scrambled, but if the ship's call could be picked up by the team, it would be picked up by the VoidCorp encampment.

"EVA Team," Jarrett replied. "Go ahead."

"We got trouble," Jack's voice said. "Picked up three bogies incoming just a few minutes ago. I'm readin' them as a Fury-class corvette and two transports, probably Merchanter class. Looks like they're coming out of the west right on top of your position!"

"Roger that, *Questar*. What's their ETA?"

"Hell, the fraal can probably smell them already!"

Spacer glanced at Ta Shaa Ta. Fraal had a reputation for a fantastically keen sense of smell, but Smilin' Jack couldn't have meant it literally. Even so, Ta Shaa Ta had stepped clear of the boulders and was scanning the sky in the direction of Salamanca. After a moment, he pointed. "There."

Three specks coming out of the west just above the swollen disk of Salamanca, swiftly grew into distinct objects, toylike with distance but growing larger fast. Two of the ships, flattened cylinders made clumsy by massive vanes, sponsons, and nacelles, slowed and turned, drifting toward the VoidCorp encampment. The third vessel, twin-bodied and dangerous looking, flew almost directly overhead, the thunder of its drives following behind it as it moved toward the southeast.

"*Questar!*" Jarrett shouted over comms. "It's headed for the ship!"

"They must have picked up Smilin' Jack's transmission," Maricia said.

"They would've seen him anyway," Jarrett replied. "Furies have Hyperdine Mark XIIs in the scanner suite. They probably spotted *Questar* by her heat and long-wave emissions!"

"What can we do?" Spacer asked.

"I'm not sure there's anything we can do," Jarrett replied, a grim edge to his voice. "*Questar*'s all but helpless on the ground. This does *not* look good at all!"

Chapter Eighteen

THE FURY CLASS corvette drifted slowly above the plateau, the rumble of it inductors adding to the thunders of volcano, lightning, and waterfalls. Static crackled from its discharge vanes. The VoidCorp flag-logo was prominent on its atmospheric stabilizer surfaces. A pair of ugly, 200mm ventral laser mounts had swung to aim directly at *Questar*'s main power coupling outriders. At point-blank range, they couldn't possibly miss.

Smilin' Jack stood on *Questar*'s command deck, cursing furiously. Mike, the engineering crew, and the repair robots were still cycling in from outside where they'd been carrying out repairs to the ship's radiator sail. His power mains were offline, his reactor scrammed. His auxiliaries could power the ship's dorsal weapons, but only for a shot or two. It would take a full twenty minutes to cycle through the start-up procedure and get the ship skyborne.

He was helpless . . . grounded and helpless.

"Questar, this is VoidCorp DE 710," sounded over his headset. "Respond, please."

That was bad. If they had a solid ID on him, they knew who he was and probably knew he'd been one of the raiders who hit the VC facilities and freighters in Hux space every so often.

"Questar! You are ordered to surrender your ship at once. Any delay will result in the immediate destruction of your vessel and the death of you and all of your employees! Respond!"

He doubted that they would destroy *Questar*. She was too valuable, either as a prize or even just sold for parts and scrap, but a shot or two from those lasers would leave her defenseless, and he was under no illusions as to what would happen to him and his crew.

There was absolutely nothing else he could do. He opened the comss channel. "Yeah, yeah, I hear ya. Quit your yappin'! You got us."

Mike stepped into the command center, her eyes wide. She was still wearing her e-suit, minus the helmet, and was carrying a charge rifle. "Boss . . ."

He shook his head.

"Questar, do you surrender your ship?"

"Listen to me first! You got us in a box, all right, but first ya gotta guarantee me you won't hurt my people!"

"We guarantee nothing. Surrender or be destroyed."

"Boss," Mike whispered furiously, "we can take 'em when they come aboard! Ron and Nared are breaking out the Ronin!"

It was almost tempting. *Questar* carried one Ronin 900 semiportable sabot cannon in her aft weapons locker. That weapon's 20mm sabot ramjet rounds could punch holes in almost any small target, even the best personal armor, but it wouldn't more than scratch the ship hovering out there, not unless they pulled down some fantastic luck. It was simply too big.

Smilin' Jack had been around too long to believe you could ever rely on luck, especially in a tight situation like this.

"Very well. We surrender!"

"Boss!"

"We can't, Mike," he said softly.

Outside, the corvette was slowly lowering to the ground, the faint haze of her inductor fields shimmering as dust roiled up from the drive's invisible footprint. The corvette was half again longer than *Questar* and designed for fighting. She had twice the weapons, three times the armor, and a hell of a lot more power to draw on. Even in a stand-up fight in open space, she would be able to swat *Questar* like a buzzerbug.

"*Questar!* You, your crew, and your passengers will assemble outside your vessel immediately. You will make no attempt at communication with anyone outside your vessel. Do you understand?"

He hesitated. He was trying to think of a way to save Mike and the others. Three seconds passed, and then there was a dazzling flash against *Questar*'s hull. Bits of half-molten hull and fragments from the number two high-gain antenna spun through the air.

"*Do you understand?*"

"Yes! Damn it, yes! Yes! Hold your fire! We give up!"

Landing legs unfolded as the corvette settled onto the surface a scant hundred meters away. A cargo bay ramp was already lowering. Six black-armored figures spilled out of the lock and jumped to the ground, bounding forward under Storm's sixth-tenth of a G gravity.

Rom Verdoss stepped into the control center. "What's happening? I heard—"

"I've just surrendered to VoidCorp, Mr. Verdoss," Jack replied.

"Profit! Can't you fight?"

"Not and *win*, Mr. Verdoss. No. Mike, go aft and tell the boys to stand down. No weapons. Everybody is to suit up and go outside. Do what they say."

She said nothing, but her eyes spoke volumes. She left, seething.

"What . . . what will they do to us?" Verdoss asked.

"If you're lucky," Jack told him, "you'll become an Employee of VoidCorp. Guaranteed security for the rest of your life. Of course, they don't offer much in the way of retirement benefits."

"And if we're not lucky?"

"They'll shoot you in the back of the head and send the bill for the bullet, the time, and any mental trauma inflicted on the shooter to your next of kin."

The armored figures were advancing toward *Questar* now, laser rifles at the ready. Jack knew that he was dead, no matter what.

He just hoped he'd be able to talk them out of killing his people before they killed him. . . .

* * * * *

"What's happening?" Spacer asked. "What the grep's going on?"

The others had been talking in tense, low monotones for several moments, their suit radios cut to minimum power to avoid their being picked up by the VoidCorp base. They'd pulled back from the lip of the caldera and were huddled in the shadow of a house-sized boulder. He could taste the fear in their voices, in the way they held their bodies.

"We can't raise the ship," Diane told him at last. "After their warning . . ."

"Duprés wouldn't have had a chance," Jarrett put in. "We have to assume *Questar* has been taken . . . or destroyed."

Touches Far abruptly turned and began walking back toward the ring of standing stones visible on the open plain to the southeast.

"Wait!" Maricia called. "Touches Far! Where are you going?"

"I must not be taken by the bad ones," it said. "They use the Chosen to talk to the others, to make them work. That is wrong."

"Wait," Diane said. "Wait just a moment, please! It can't end like this! It can't!"

Touches Far kept walking.

"Our suits are good for thirty days," Jarrett reminded her. "We'll be able to recharge the water tanks, of course, but by that time, we're going to be in a bad way, needing food." He nodded toward the VoidCorp camp. "Those two transports just brought in a bunch of troops, a company's worth, at least. We can't hold out against them."

"Maybe they won't know we're here," Spacer said.

"Oh, they know," Maricia said. "They would've heard Duprés' radio call to us, even if they haven't picked up our short-range conversations. The signal was scrambled, but they'll know he was talking to someone."

"Besides," Jarrett said. "There's Verdoss. To save his skin, he'd probably give them our exact location, names, comm numbers, and Grid addresses."

"We don't know that," Spacer said, "not for sure." He wasn't certain why he wanted to give the Rigunmor the benefit of the doubt, but for some reason Spacer felt as though the man had more to him than he'd shown in his words and actions until now. "The Voiders can't know how many of us are out here, right?"

"Spacer may have ascertained a key truth," Ta Shaa Ta said. "If Verdoss does not give them a list of our complete party. . . ?"

"They'll know," Jarrett said. "They'll search the ship, find out records. Unless we can—"

"TXI expedition personnel!" a new voice said, cutting in over their helmet headsets. "This is JR945 72YKV of VoidCorp! Your ship has been captured, and the pirate who commanded it and his crew are in our hands. You will surrender yourselves immediately, or you will be killed as trespassers on VoidCorp property! This is your only warning! Respond at once!"

"Well, well," Diane said, recognizing the voice. "Our old friend Krueger . . . except it sounds like he got a demotion."

Jarrett held up his hand then punched in a command on his gauntlet, adjusting the output on his e-suit transmitter. "VoidCorp!" he called. "This is Jarrett Aylen of the Verge Rangers. Your claim on this world is not recognized by either Concord or Verge Confederacy law. Therefore, you have no jurisdiction over us. We demand that you release our ship and its captain and crew, safely."

"You're hardly in a position to demand anything, Ranger Jarrett," the voice replied.

"Jarrett!" Maricia cried. "Look!"

With a shrill, fluttering howl, a pair of fighters were rising from the volcanic caldera. Painted red and black— stubby, flattened darts with bulbous forward canopies that gave the look of ungainly insects—they hovered for a moment as though tracking an elusive scent, then in perfect unison dipped their right wings and shrieked almost directly toward the hidden party.

Jarrett stood up, hefting his mass rifle and snicking back the charging lever.

"Wait, Jarrett!" Diane cried. "What are you doing?"

"The rest of you get back into that boulder field!" he snapped. "I'm going to convince them that there's only one of me!"

"We're not leaving you to them!" Maricia said. "Do you know what the damned VoidCorpers do to—"

"I'm not going to argue with you! Get the hell out of sight!"

Trailing twin peals of thunder, the two fighters boomed overhead, banking hard as they passed over the boulder field and swinging low over the plain beyond. Spacer could see the golden sunlight flash from their canopies, could see the twist and turn of air brake and stabilizer surfaces unfolding.

"*Run!*" Jarrett yelled.

Stepping into the open, he shouldered the mass rifle, took aim, and opened fire, snapping off five three-round bursts as the fighters swung around in their tight, shrieking turn. Spacer couldn't tell if Jarrett had hit the targets or not. They didn't seem hurt as they leveled off and roared back up the shallow slope of the hill, coming directly toward the party.

Jarrett loosed two more bursts, and then the ground on either side of him erupted in flame and clumps of gravel and earth. Multiple explosions tore the ground between the ranger and the boulder field. The split-second echo rang among the boulders in shrill claps of sound and raw concussion. Spacer felt himself picked up and slammed against unyielding rock. His e-suit absorbed much of the impact, but his ears were ringing and he tasted blood. More explosions ripped through the stone labyrinth, toppling several boulders as the ground beneath them tore and shifted.

Then the fighters were gone, roaring back over the caldera, slowing before swinging about for a second pass. Smoke roiled between the boulders as rock heated to incandescence hissed and popped.

Jarrett was laying in the open, face down.

Rising, trying to clear the singing in his ears, Spacer raced out from the illusory shelter of the rocks and into the open. The weapons those fighter used had torn the ground in savage gouges and pits. Jarrett's e-suit looked intact, but he wasn't moving. Spacer dropped to his knees and tugged on the still form, rolling him over, terrified at what he might see.

"Let me help!"

Maricia was there with him, helping him roll Jarrett onto his back. There was blood on the ranger's face, smearing the inside of his visor . . . but his eyes fluttered open.

"What. . . ?"

"Don't move, Jarrett," Maricia said. "That was pretty stupid, taking on a couple of Raptors with a rifle!"

"S-seemed . . . like a good idea at the time."

Spacer looked past her. "Where's—?"

Maricia cut him off with a sharp shake of her head. "It's just us now."

Spacer heard an approaching roar. "They're coming back! We have to get him under cover!"

It wasn't the fighters. A quintet of skybikes, the fluttering sound of their inductor engines rattling the air, angled in low above the smoke cloud that still cloaked the boulder field.

"Drop your weapons!" an amplified voice boomed from one of the nimble, single-man vehicles. They were circling like carrion fliers above a kill. The fighters banked and turned in the distance, bearing on sun-flashing wings the promise of instant annihilation if the party tried to fight it out.

Maricia stood slowly, unholstered her stutter pistol, and tossed it onto the ground. Spacer did the same, and they stood there with their hands up as the skybikes lightly grounded, one by one, and the armored pilots dismounted.

"Diane!" Spacer cried, looking at Maricia. "Is she. . . ?"

"We're alone now, Spacer. There's no one else."

Stunned, Spacer stood helplessly as armored troopers closed on them, knocking them down, roughly searching them for weapons, and locking their wrists behind their backs with durasteel cuffs. Minutes later, a skycar grounded nearby, and the three of them were hustled aboard.

The flight down into the caldera and the VoidCorp camp took only a few moments. They were herded out of the skycar at gunpoint and forced to walk through part of the base. The ranger was still dazed but able to walk with assistance from Maricia.

It was still dark beneath the towering, encircling cliff wall, though the sky was bright—a deep purple lightening to deep green at the horizon. Within the camp, however, night was banished by powerful arc lights and spots.

All around, stormies were at work under the watchful eyes and guns of black-armored guards. Most of the natives wore metal bands on one of their legs, and many had been shackled together to keep them in groups of five or ten, moving along in single file, the chains between them clinking sadly. In the pit outside of the camp, humans in sealed trenching machines broke up the hard-packed soil and rock. Hundreds of stormies worked side by side, picking through the rubble, filling buckets and carrying them off to be emptied—a vast project being carried out almost entirely by backbreaking labor.

At one point, the prisoners and their guards skirted the lake at the center of the caldera, giving Spacer a much closer and better view of the pulsing glass arch. Here in the twilight depths of the caldera, the arch definitely appeared to be glowing with a deep, blue-white inner light. He looked more closely. The arch wasn't made of glass after all, but of thousands of stormfire gems, carefully pieced together in a glittering mass.

He noticed something else, too. Each time the inner light pulsed, a ripple spread outward from the central island on which the arch was constructed, disturbing the otherwise motionless mirror of the lake's surface. The throbbing light, the glow, the ripples in the water, all spoke of tremendous power somehow trapped within that lone, enigmatic structure.

"Move on!" a guard snarled, and the butt of his charge rifle cracked painfully against the back of Spacer's helmet. He stumbled forward.

Forced into a cramped coffin of an airlock, the prisoners were taken inside a large habitat dome beside the water, and they were locked inside a room empty of furniture save for a single, bare cot and a portable toilet. A window in one curved wall gave them a view of the lake and the glowing arch.

"Helmets! Gauntlets!" one of their captors snarled. "E-suits too! Snap it up!"

"What are you going to do to us?" Maricia demanded, helping Jarrett lie down on the cot.

"For now, darlin', nothin'," the trooper said. He'd removed his helmet, exposing a hard, angular face, short-cropped blond hair, and an unpleasant sneer. "You're all going to wait right here until the boss can see you. After that"—a shrug, almost lost within the heavy armor—"it's probably gonna be the pit. We need all the fresh labor we can get."

"This man needs help." Maricia pointed at Jarrett.

"Too bad. We don't have any to give him. Let's move it with the gear!"

The three stripped down to skin under the watchful gaze of their captors. Two troopers carefully went through each e-suit, checking for hidden weapons, microcircuitry, anything that might pose a threat or a potential means of escape. They found a small laser pistol in Jarrett's torso shell, and a small, slim-bladed knife in Maricia's left boot. The search was unpleasant and humiliating, but at least the

Voiders returned their e-suits when the checks were complete. They kept gauntlets, backpacks, and helmets, though.

"You'll get 'em back later," the blond guard said. "You'll need 'em."

"Hey!" one of the other troopers said. He held up the red cloth encasing Spacer's cards. "What's this?"

"Those are mine!" Spacer said. "They're just cards."

"What, playing cards?"

"That's right."

The trooper opened the cloth, looked at them curiously, then shrugged. "They belong to us now. Just like you."

"Hey!" Spacer advanced, furious. "You can't—"

A rifle butt swung, catching him painfully in the chest and knocking him down. As he lay on his back, clutching his chest and gasping, the blond trooper strode over and stood above him, fists on hips. "You're wrong. We can do anything we want with you three."

Spacer sat up, then struggled to his feet. "Why are you doing this?"

The man smiled, death-cold. "Business. Simple business. You're not leaving this planet alive, you know. The Boss would never let any outsider who'd seen this place leave with the information. But until we terminate your contracts, you belong to us, and if you want to avoid a lot of pain, you'll do exactly as you're told."

The prisoners donned their e-suits again, and the guards left, locking the door behind them. The one window, constructed of tough, transparent plastic, was unyielding as steel.

"Diane and Ta Shaa Ta," Spacer said quietly. "Are they really. . . ?"

Maricia shook her head once, sharply, and pointed to her ear. Spacer understood. Any room the Voiders used to hold prisoners could be expected to have a few listening devices scattered about. Did that mean that Diane and the fraal were alive?

He wished he had his cards. Not that he could divine whether or not his friends had survived the Voider attack, but simply, Spacer admitted to himself, for the comfort. He hadn't seen Touches Far since the attack either. Maybe they'd all escaped, and Maricia was trying to give them a chance to get clear of the caldera and the VoidCorp encampment.

Even if they did escape, where could they go? What could they do? The Voiders were holding all the cards right now.

Spacer walked over to the window, leaned against it with folded arms, and stared out across the lake at the arch. There was something . . . *something* tugging at his mind there. . . .

The King of Minds. A man in golden robes and wearing a crown sat upon a high throne. His hands were raised, and a single brilliant, blue-white star floated in the air just above and in front of his head. Illuminated by the star, the king seemed to radiate a light of his own, a light of logic, thoughtfulness, and stern will. A naked sword lay across his lap. Other objects—a pentacle, a wand, a cup, a machine—rested on a table visible through an archway at the king's back, while a sacred ibis piped its tune from a tree in the distance. . . .

The vision came so strongly to Spacer's mind that he thought at first he still had his holotarot deck, that he was staring into the illusion of light and warmth projected from the card's surface.

Then he blinked and found himself staring at the glowing arch. Where had *that* come from?

The tug was stronger somehow, a prickling at the back of his neck, a shiver down his spine. It was almost as though something was *calling* him from the other side of that arch.

Chapter Nineteen

WHAT ARE YOU people doing here? And, more to the point, what am I going to do with you?"

Spacer stood with the others in a small, bare room, identical to the hab quarters they'd been imprisoned in, except that this one had a desk with full computer and holographic interface instead of a cot.

The man behind the desk was Wolfgang Krueger, the man who'd glued an airmask to Spacer's face and shoved him onto Lison's topside not so very long ago. Spacer watched the gaunt-faced Voider with intense fascination. There was no mercy behind those glittering eyes, only a ruthless hunger, and perhaps, a cold and calculating interest.

"We are a legitimate scientific expedition," Maricia told Krueger, "partly funded by and operating at the behest of the Terran Xenoarchaeological Institute. People know we are here. If we don't return, they will come to find us, and they'll find you."

"I hardly think so, Dr. Strang. By the time a relief expedition can be assembled, we will be long gone, and your

bones will be bleaching beneath that red sun out there.
That is, of course, assuming they come at all. Six people,
hiring a pirate to take them to a deadly, unknown world?
They'd scarcely know where to begin looking, especially
if my fellow Employees plant some misleading information in the data files at Tribon."

Two hours after their capture, the corvette they'd seen
earlier had returned, touching down next to the lake in the
center of the caldera. They'd watched, grim and unspeak-
ing, as armored soldiers had marched Jack Duprés, Mike,
and the ship's two engineers down the ramp and into the
encampment.

There'd been no sign of Rom Verdoss. Spacer wondered if the Voiders had killed him.

Duprés and his people had been marched to another
habitat dome. There'd been no opportunity to speak with
them.

It was nearly twenty hours later when the guards had
finally come for them, prodding them to their feet, order-
ing them to clamp helmets and gauntlets in place, and
again shackling their wrists behind their backs.

They were led back into the early Storm morning.
Clouds had moved in, and it was raining, a thin, gray
drizzle obscuring the swollen face of Salamanca low in the
western sky. Spacer was just as happy he couldn't see the
giant world, though. There was something about that
ringed and banded world that was gnawing at him, something relating to the odd feeling of being called. He tried
not to look at the arch as they were marched past, but the
compulsion drew his eyes and his thoughts.

There was something there, and Spacer thought he
could feel it watching him.

They were taken to a gate in the fence surrounding the
inner buildings of the camp. The fence appeared to consist
of no more than glowing, upright poles set along the
perimeter every ten meters or so, but Spacer could sense
the crackle of electricity between each upright. He'd heard
about such things. Anything that tried to break through
would receive one hell of a jolt. Even the stormies with

their natural resistance to lightning would be stopped by the charge stored in that thing's underground capacitors.

The prisoners were ushered through a closely guarded gateway to the largest of the habitat domes. Helmets removed but hands still bound, they were herded along from the airlock to the office where they'd again met Wolfgang Krueger.

The VoidCorper studied them a moment longer, as though trying to decide what to do with them. Then he moved his hand in the holographic field above his desk display while apparently reading something on his monocular.

"There are three of you missing," he said. "Dr. Diane Radlevich, xenoarchaeolgist, Rom Verdoss, Rigunmor businessman and entrepreneur, and a fraal mindwalker." He looked at Jarrett. "I presume these individuals were all with you on your EVA?"

"You *killed* them."

"Perhaps. We searched up there, but none of their bodies were found."

"The way those boulders were tumbling around when your fighters attacked us," Maricia said, "it's a wonder you found *any* of us afterward."

"It's possible. We will continue to search. We can't have unauthorized personnel bumbling around our operations area. It would be unsettling for the natives. Bad for business, you know." He looked at Jack Duprés. "You, Captain, are easily disposed of. Some high-ranking corporate officers are going to want to have a long, and I assume, painful conversation with you back at Hux. You've been loudly proclaiming that your crew had nothing to do with your attacks on our assets there, that they weren't even with you on the dates in question."

"Damned right! If you're gonna kill me, Voider, fine, but my people had nothing to do with that grep."

Krueger appeared to study Mike and the two engineers for a moment. "Well, we don't need to arrive at a final decision now. All four of you will be returned to Hux. They have mindwalkers there in Corporate employ. If you're telling the truth about them, they might be allowed to live . . . as VoidCorp Employees, of course. Take these four back to their cell." He signaled to the guards. Two of them advanced, took the *Questar* personnel by their arms, and led them away. "You know, don't you, that none of you can go free again, knowing what you know about our operation here?"

"Damn you!" Spacer exploded. "You can't do this to us! It's not right!"

Krueger chuckled. "You'll find, my young friend, that there is very little in this cosmos that even remotely qualifies as right, at least in a moral sense. The cosmos belongs to those strong enough to *use* it, those strong enough to take advantage of the opportunities they find there. You three, it seems to me, represent a unique opportunity for us."

"Why should we help you?" Jarrett said. "You as much as said yourself you're going to kill us anyway."

"Not necessarily. There *is* a way out for each of you. If there weren't, you would already be dead. It's as simple as that. It costs money keeping you alive, you know. Every dollar must be accounted for. If you decide to cooperate, you'll live. In fact, you could all have very bright futures within the Company.

"Refuse me, of course, and you're all dead. And, believe me, I can make your deaths last a long time. It's expensive, true, but the spectacle of one of you taking a long time to die can be of use in persuading the others."

"What is it you want us to do?" Maricia asked.

"My technicians have been going over your ship, examining your computer files and records. It seems that you have made startling progress in learning the native language. You can be of invaluable assistance in communicating our orders to the work force."

"We needed a linguicomp for that," Maricia said. "Dr. Radlevich was wearing ours when . . . when she was killed."

"Not a problem. We have translators that can read your data. What we primarily need is your understanding of the way the natives use language." He shook his head. "My people here are having trouble understanding the locals.

They don't seem to think the same way we do, and meanings and intents are garbled, even when we know the proper words. You, Dr. Strang, are well known as a xeno-linguist. You will work with us. These two"—he nodded at Spacer and Jarrett—"will be the guarantees of your perfect compliance and the accuracy of your translation. If anything goes wrong, they will suffer. Do we understand one another?"

"Yes."

"Very well," Krueger said. "As prisoners of VoidCorp, you automatically become VoidCorp Employees. Each of you now carry the designation AA, which puts you at the very bottom of the Corporate hierarchy." He moved his hand in the holofield, flexing his fingers as though typing on an invisible keyboard. "The computer has allotted identifiers. You, Dr. Strang, are now AA498 93QQN." He looked at Jarrett. "You are AA929 77MCV. And you," he added, looking at Spacer, "are AA981 14BRK. Those are your permanent numbers. Memorize them."

"We're not grepping numbers in your system," Spacer said.

"*Everyone* is a number in the system," Krueger replied. "From the lowest AA to the supreme ZZ-CEO. The sooner you learn that, the sooner you will find a fulfilling niche for yourself within the Corporate family.

"Terms of Employment. You will do everything you are ordered to do, without question, without fail. If you complain or do not work with maximum required zeal, you will not eat. If you resist, refuse to work, or engage in anti-corporate activity, your contract will be terminated. That means you're tossed out with no e-suit. Not very pleasant, I assure you." He looked at Spacer and grinned. "It's actually a lot more hospitable here than on Lison. The air will actually keep you alive for a little while, long enough to appreciate the benefits of loyally serving the Corporation without selfishness or reserve. Do we understand one another?"

There was no response from the prisoners, but Krueger appeared to accept silence for assent.

"Good. AA498, you will begin work with the senior natives immediately." There was a pause. "That means you, Dr. Strang."

"Huh? Oh . . . right."

"Learn your ID numbers! I will see that you have print-outs to work from."

"Just what is it you want me to tell them? What is it you're making them do?"

For answer, Krueger reached into his desk and extracted a small bag. He spilled the contents onto the desktop, a glittering cascade of thumb-sized crystals, each exquisitely shaped, each aglow with an inner blue light.

"Beautiful, aren't they?" he said. "The first survey to Storm found a few of these. 'Stormfires,' they called them, but then, I suspect you already knew that. Why else would you have come all the way out here, eh?"

"To study the native civilization, for one," Maricia said, "without destroying it in the process."

"Nonsense. There's no profit in that." Krueger poked at the stones with a forefinger, moving them about, eliciting sparkling gleams and rainbows as they caught the light. "When we first established our base here, we expected to find outcroppings of these crystals so that we could begin mining them commercially. It's not as simple as that, however. The natives find them by digging, and we haven't been able to learn how they know where to dig. They simply point vaguely and say, 'Dig there.' So far, we haven't found more than these few, and most of these were taken from dead natives—the strange ones with the eyes. They wear them as a kind of decoration or emblem. They say it lets them talk to their god." He snorted.

"Maybe the natives don't know where to get more," Jarrett said.

"Have you seen that curious arch out there in the lake?" Krueger asked. "It's made of some hundreds of thousands of stones just like these, all laboriously fitted together into a single structure, using a kind of organic glue or secretion as cement. Our first survey found that. It's why we set up our base here, because we expected at first to take all the stormfires we needed simply by demolishing that arch. But if we do that, we fear the natives may become, um, *demoralized*. They're placid creatures, really, but we don't want to risk an uprising. The arch seems to have some sort of religious connotation for them, so we're going to wait until the last moment before we take those stones.

"More than that, though, is our discovery that the arch appears to be a focus for some considerable power. We don't know what it's for or how it works, but our scientists have been studying the phenomenon for some time now, and so we maintain our base here. Our scientists continue to study the arch, and in the meantime, we have organized the natives into a sizable workforce. Our planetologists tell us the stones could be of volcanic origin, like diamonds, so we have been concentrating our search here in this extinct volcanic crater. As our workforce expands, we will begin investigating other possibilities.

"What I expect from you, AA498, is to encourage the natives to keep looking, and to try to get a better idea of what they know about where these stones can be found. I intend that we leave this world with no fewer than five metric tons of these stones. We estimate that the arch contains three tons all together, so we need to uncover two tons more."

"What the hell are you going to use five tons of stormfires for anyway?" Jarrett demanded.

"Well, that depends on what our scientists learn, actually. By themselves, that many stormfires will purchase a very large chunk of the gross product of the stellar nations, leading to VoidCorp's supremacy throughout known space. We're more interested, however, in the effect we've discovered within this arch, a possible resonance between these crystals and certain natural sources of power. What might happen if a large crystal structure were hooked up to a mass reactor, I wonder?" He smiled and spread his hands. "We will find out. Whatever the result, VoidCorp's divisions of energy are going to be *very* interested in this discovery. Again, it could make VoidCorp the pre-eminent stellar nation in control of all humankind's destiny!"

"Grep *that*," Spacer said.

"The only reason the rest of mankind would follow *you* guys," Jarrett added, "would be out of morbid curiosity."

Krueger's smile, the easy manner, vanished. "Silence. AA498, you will be given a translator and access to your shipboard database. You will begin work immediately. You two," he added, pointing at Jarrett and Spacer, "will join the natives in the pit, for now. Nothing too taxing. You are to retrieve any stormfires you find and load the rest of the rubble into buckets for removal. Perhaps we will find other work for you later, if you behave yourselves in the pit." He signaled to the guards. "Take them away!"

It was the beginning of a nightmare, a nightmare that had no ending in sight but death.

*   *   *   *   *

"No, no, no!" Diane cried, exasperated. "To kill someone, you stop them! You stop them hard, *very* hard, so hard they die!"

Touches Far spoke briefly with the other stormies gathered in the clearing among the gently waving catcher plants and fulgivores. The creatures rumbled and chirped back and forth for a few moments, with the linguicomp on Diane's back only picking out a few words here and there. Clearly, the stormie language was much more complex and intricate than anyone had guessed before now.

She wished Maricia were here. The xenolinguist had a talent for sorting through alien phonemes and striking the root of what the speakers were trying to convey.

"We are not understanding," Touches Far said at last. "You say when bad ones stop stormies running away, that mean 'kill.' But bad ones use strange stones to stop stormies. Use light to stop stormies. They stop us. We no stop them. We are not understanding."

By "strange stones," Diane assumed they meant guns. "Light" probably referred to laser beams or other energy weapons. In the past forty hours, she and Ta Shaa Ta had learned so much about the stormies and stormie language. The creatures were actually remarkably intelligent and quick. They'd already picked up a number of Standard words and used them in their attempts to speak with her—their use of the word "stormie" for themselves was a case in point. She felt like she was actually beginning to get to know them.

And yet some concepts seemed impossible to communicate.

Was it some twist of their alien mindset? If she was understanding the way they thought, just because humans did something to stormies didn't mean that stormies could do the same thing to humans. Reciprocity meant nothing to them, nor did concepts like "revenge" or "getting even." Instead, things simply *were*, to be accepted. Death by a VoidCorp trooper wielding a plasma gun was no different than random death by lightning. It just *was*.

Math was a problem for them too. Stormies did not have a counting system and didn't seem able to grasp the concept of numbers. Stormie math was strictly relational. You had "more than," "less than," or "the same as," but they couldn't seem to focus on finer detail than that.

This last was especially puzzling to Diane in light of the stone circle they'd seen on the way to the caldera. Touches Far said that the circle was for measuring astronomical events. "Yes! Yes! Measure!" it had said, tasting the new word. "Circle measures moons in sky. Measures sun. Measures where sun rise, where moons rise, where sun goes down, where moons go down. Measures all for God!"

Time after time, just when she thought she was getting a handle on things, the stormie discussion would veer back to the concept of God . . . *the* God who hung forever in the western sky, watching the stormies, sending its fires, and telling them all what to do through its servants, the Chosen.

For Ta Shaa Ta's sake, Diane had been willing to accept that Spacer had some psionic power connected with his cards, but the stormie concept of a literal god embodied as a planet was simply too much for her to swallow.

And the concept of *kill* seemed especially hard to communicate.

She looked at Ta Shaa Ta. *Are you getting anywhere?*

she thought, focusing her mind so that the fraal mind-walker could pick up her thoughts and know she was speaking to him.

No, was the fraal's response. *You must remember that these beings have nothing in common with humanity. They are gatherers—harvesters, if you will—not hunters. Even their bodily coloration proves that they have never had serious natural enemies. You cannot take it for granted that they share* any *human qualities of conceptual thought, logic, or rationality.*

I know, she thought back, *but if we don't come up with something soon, we're going to have to see what we can do on our own.*

That would be unwise, Ta Shaa Ta replied. *We have no effective weapons. We must find a way to enlist the active cooperation of the stormies.*

"Listen," Diane said aloud, trying a different tactic. The linguicomp transformed her words into the booming chirping speech of the stormies. "That ring of standing stones on the mountain, how did you build that?"

"We cut stones, using parts of plants that call down God's fire."

"Lightning. Yes, go on!"

"Lightning. Yes. Lightning cracks the stone. We then carry stones to place where they are to be set up. God tells Chosen exactly where to put stones. We Chosen tell others what God says, and they do what God says."

"Okay, stop right there. How do you carry those stones? They must weigh ten or twelve tons apiece."

"Not know 'tons.' Not know 'ten or twelve.' "

"They're heavy!"

"There are many stormies," Touches Far said gravely. *"Many* stormies. Enough stormies move rocks."

"Exactly! Many of you together are strong! Together, you could overrun the bad ones' place! Tear down fences! Overturn vehicles! Hurt bad ones!"

"Many . . . strange words . . ."

She sighed and said, "I don't know what else we can do, Ta Shaa Ta."

"You show kill," Touches Far told her. "You show other words. Show kill."

"I can't. There's no one here to kill! Look . . ."

"What is 'look'?"

"I mean . . . listen to me." She picked up a smooth, water-worn rock the size of her fist. "Let's say this is one of the bad ones."

She was starting to reach for another, bigger rock when Touches Far said, "No."

"What?"

"That is not bad one. That is rock."

"I mean, imagine that it's a bad one. The rock represents a bad one."

"Rock nothing like bad one. They are not the same."

"What I mean is—"

"Bad ones are alive, like humans, like stormies. Rocks are *not* alive." It was hard to read expression into that single large, brown eye, but Diane had the feeling that Touches Far was trying to patiently explain a very simple concept to a three-year-old. "Rock not bad one."

"Okay. Forget the rock." She dropped her visual aids. "The bad ones are humans, like us. If you wanted to hurt us, wanted to *kill* us, there are lots of ways you could do it. You're much bigger than we are, much stronger. Those long tentacles of yours . . . you could hit us, hard. You could grab us, pick us up, slam us down! You could throw a heavy rock—"

"What is 'throw'?"

Angry, Diane stood up suddenly, snatched up the rock she'd been using to represent a bad one, and threw it as hard as she could at a catcher plant watching them all in mournful silence five meters away. "Throw! Throw! *That* is throw!"

The rock had punched a ragged hole squarely through the center of the catcher's membrane. The plant's eye twisted comically, studying the damage done to it, and for a horrible moment, Diane wondered if she'd lost her temper and hurt the poor thing.

Then she wondered if she'd done something to upset

the stormies. They were agitated now, shifting back and forth, rumbling to themselves, their long tentacles coiling and uncoiling, the sensory antennae in their torsos fluttering like feathers in a stiff breeze.

Ta Shaa Ta stepped forward. "Stormies can hurt the bad ones, as Diane has hurt the catcher."

"Hurt . . ." Touches Far said. He sounded . . . amazed, as though suddenly presented with a magnificent truth. "Kill . . ."

"That's the idea," Diane said. "Simple, isn't it?"

She felt terrible inside—the serpent in Eden. No, Cain, the bringer of murder to an innocent world.

* * * * *

Rom Verdoss stopped for a moment, clinging to an out-thrust ledge of rock. He was panting so hard that his e-suit's visor began fogging faster than the cool air stream directed across the surface could keep it clear. He heard the suit's heat pumps kick in and wondered again if he was going to survive this trek.

Maybe this hadn't been such a profitable idea after all. . . .

All he'd known was that he wasn't going to meekly walk out to those VoidCorp thugs and surrender, no matter what Captain Duprés decided to do. Duprés was interested in his ship and crew, nothing more. Rom Verdoss was trying to save considerably more than that—his reputation, his business, his fortune, and his family's hierarchical standing within the Consortium.

After donning his e-suit, he had snagged a laser rifle from the armory and found a place to hide in the cargo bay. Crouching inside an empty foamplast casing that had held a half ton of the expedition's food, he'd watched as the others filed out. It had been terribly risky. If any of the invaders had been carrying a biodetector they would have spotted him, but Rom was gambling that these competitors had been caught by surprise and wouldn't be all that organized yet. The careful search would come later, especially if Duprés—as thoroughgoing a mercenary as Rom had ever had the pleasure of working with—pointed out that there was one missing from the ship's compliment.

He'd waited for his opportunity, hiding until he'd heard the VoidCorp ship lift again with a deep bass rumble. Several troopers had been left behind with *Questar*, but none were in the cargo bay. Rom had slipped out of his hiding place, down the ramp, and into the veritable forest that was growing so rapidly outside.

The things the others had referred to as "catchers" were growing everywhere, springing up from the wet soil and growing centimeters by the hour. By that time, they were taller than a man and afforded plenty of cover as he made his way clear of *Questar*. A few of the things bore gruesomely sad, weeping eyes that watched him with eerie, silent contemplation. He tried to ignore their stares and kept moving.

For the next thirty hours—with occasional breaks for rest and short, uncomfortably fitful sleeps—Rom had trekked across a bewilderingly alien landscape, following the EVA's path toward the north. He couldn't get lost. His suit had a built-in inertial tracker, and he'd downloaded the electronic maps recorded by the EVA team. With Sunbreak Mountain behind his right shoulder and Salamanca behind his left, he couldn't go wrong.

Of course, he *had* gone wrong, and more than once. Clouds had moved in, obscuring Salamanca, Sunbreak, and the rising sun. His inertial tracker gave relative bearing, but he soon got confused as to how that related to absolute position. When he called up the downloaded map on his helmet HUD, he could make very little of the glowing tangle of elevation lines and point data, and he found it impossible to relate the information on his HUD to the real-world terrain around him. The jungle of catcher plants and other, stranger vegetation closed in around him, slowing his march, and before long he had no idea *where* he was.

Verdoss had found the caldera at last by almost stumbling into it. He'd been making his way through a tangle of house-sized boulders, sometimes leaping from one rock to another, at other times squeezing through narrow passages between sheer, basaltic walls, until he'd suddenly rounded a corner and found the ground dropping away beneath his feet, giving him a spectacular panorama of the dead volcanic crater, the lake, and the VoidCorp base.

By this time, the rain had ceased, and the rising sun had cleared the caldera rim, illuminating the interior. Rom had approached the caldera from the western side, and the red-gold sun was so squarely in his eyes that he had trouble making out any details. Using a vidscanner, he'd been able to make out the bulk of the VoidCorp corvette grounded beside the far shore of the lake. He'd seen the armies of laboring stormies, the dozens of heavily armed troops, the freighters disgorging equipment, the field fences ringing the habitat domes that were almost certainly VoidCorp's inner sanctum on this world.

What was he supposed to do now?

He wouldn't be able to find the others in that ant's heap below; he knew that much, but he couldn't do any good hiding in the wilderness outside the camp. Through the vidscanner, he could see a number of VoidCorpers wearing e-suits, some in ordinary breather masks, others in high-tech and conveniently anonymous helmets like the one he wore. Perhaps he could slip in among them and pass himself off as one of VoidCorp's finest.

It was a long shot, a terrible gamble, but Rom Verdoss couldn't see any alternatives. Besides, his whole career had been based on taking the long shot that had ultimately paid off. This attempt to find the source of old Grigor's stormfires had been nothing less than a long-odds bet against the turning of the wheel. Up here he could do nothing but watch and eventually die or be captured. Down there, he might at least find some useful information, and information could nearly always be used as a weapon.

Carefully, watching his footing on the wet rocks, he'd begun his descent.

That had been three hours ago. The cliff, he'd guessed, was only half a kilometer high . . . five hundred meters of rock cracked and pitted enough to afford plenty of hand-holds, especially for the high-friction gripper surfaces on his e-suit's fingertips and boots.

What he hadn't counted on was years of sitting on his tail behind a desk or in virtuality simulations. After ten minutes, he was puffing. After twenty, his knees were trembling every time he shifted to another foothold. He'd done a fair amount of rock climbing as a kid on his birth-world of Alhambra. He knew how to lean into the rock, to become a part of the cliff, how never to release more than one hand- or foot-hold at a time, but after the better than day-long hike, he was beginning to realize that his days of intense physical activity were long over.

Maybe this hadn't been such a good idea after all. . . .

He allowed himself a glance down. In two hours, he'd managed to descend perhaps fifty meters. He was pretty sure the way would be easier during the second half of the descent, because it looked as though at that point the cliff face opened up into a gentler, less vertical slope of fallen rock and scree.

He still had at least two hundred meters to go, and he was beginning to think he was never going to make it.

Chapter Twenty

I T WAS A dream. Spacer was *sure* of that.
At the same time, he could not shake the sense of
unnerving reality that suffused his surroundings. The light,
the color, the texture, the detail of everything around him
seemed heightened, more intense, more real than reality
itself.

Yet the imagery was completely surreal, defying logic,
forcing him to accept the fact that this *must* be a dream.

He was naked, kneeling at the side of a pond, holding
two pitchers of water which he was slowly spilling—one
into the pond, the other onto the shore. In the sky overhead, seven stars gleamed brightly in the deepening twilight. One was brighter than the others, blue-white and so
dazzling that it was like looking into the heart of a stone-
cutter arc.

He sensed someone watching . . . a presence . . . a threat
. . . a terror. Rising, turning, he saw a lone woman in the
distance, the woman of the Nine of Pentacles wearing her
long yellow and red robe, the bird of prey perched on her

falconer's glove. She was coming toward him. Small with distance, she grew rapidly with each gliding stride, until her head seemed to scrape the sky, scattering the stars. She gestured, and the bird took flight, wings outstretched, a screech like thunder in its throat. It wheeled, banked, and dived toward him . . . not a bird now, but an orange and black Raptor fighter, wing surfaces and canopy flashing in the light.

Spacer ran.

"Spacer." Ta Shaa Ta stood just ahead, his odd, slender body silhouetted against the glare of the blue sun. "Spacer, this way."

"Ta Shaa Ta!" he cried. "Are you dead? Where are you?"

"Close by. Always I am close by."

"Am I dreaming?"

"Yes."

"Then what are *you* doing here?"

"Speaking to you."

"The cards. I can't find my cards."

"Your psionic abilities reside primarily in your right cerebral hemisphere. They surface as hunches, as flashes of inspiration, as intuition, even as dreams. You seem to use these cards to focus these hunches into something tangible, words and sentences more concrete than feeling. . . ."

"You . . . that's what you told me before. On the ship . . ."

"This way, Spacer. Follow me."

The arch pulsed and throbbed just ahead. It seemed much bigger than it had when he'd been awake, a vast span of blue-white light, as vast as the arc of Salamanca's rings.

"Where are you taking me?"

"Through the arch. Someone is there, calling you. Calling *us*."

"Who?"

"That is what you must find out."

He stepped through, feeling the heavy throb of power in and beneath and around that enigmatic construct. The stormfires blazed, as brilliant as Titania against the curl

and glow of its own nebula. The woman of the Nine of
Pentacles was gone, as was the fighter, and Ta Shaa Ta as
well. He was *alone*. . . .

He was flying.

The view opening up ahead, below, above . . . all around
. . . was astonishing, a vista of golden clouds piled one
atop another in towering majesties, sun-dazzled at the
peaks, plunging into purple shadow in the unfathomable
depths, lost in distance and sheer scale.

He was fleeing the sun, that burning red-gold Eye just
above the cloud-bright horizon. He wasn't entirely sure
how he was moving, only that he had to continue his fight,
both literal and figurative, racing across the world's terminator into the comforting depths of Night.

He couldn't see himself, but he found that he could see
in all directions, a strange blending as if from millions, no
billions of separate points of view, all seamlessly folded
together somehow, though he couldn't quite tell how the
trick was done.

All around him were clouds. There was no land below,
only the blue-purple depths that he instinctively feared.
Above, the sky was a deep and perfect royal blue, lighter
behind him where the sun was setting, darker, richer,
deeper, more alive ahead. He could see stars . . . and a
silver-gold sliver of an arch . . . vast and glorious frozen
flame etched across Heaven. Beyond, a scattering of
moons, those closer to the sun in crescent phase, those
overhead in half. He recognized Storm, a cloud-swaddled
half-moon of blue, white, and ocher, tiny, *tiny* with distance, almost lost behind the brilliance of the ring-arc.

He struggled to understand. His perception was . . .
scattered, somehow—broken, impossible to really grasp.
He felt like a solid, massive body, long and broad and very
thin unfurled against the sky, but he was aware, too, of
myriad glittering points of dust above and beneath and all
around his central core, flying free, distinct and separate,
yet the same.

What *was* he? What had he become?

He tried to focus on one of the dust motes, concentrating

his will and his understanding on seeing. What he saw shocked, like ice water dashed in the face. A single golden mote was a free-flying creature—he sensed its size, somehow—as big as *Questar*, bigger perhaps, a delta shape with trailing tail and fleshy, outstretched wings. At the rounded snout where a head should have been was a single huge, brown eye, identical to the eyes he'd seen on the Chosen stormies and on the catcher plants during the hike to the caldera. The main body of the thing—vast beyond comprehension—as big as a continent, as big as a *planet* perhaps, rippling slowly in the winds that shaped the towering clouds around him and beneath. It was a part of the fliers as the fliers were a part of it, a titanic, extended, rippling complexity too huge to be taken in and understood at once.

Clouds everywhere. No land, no rest, only clouds and light and the matchless glory of the sky. As his surroundings grew darker, Spacer was increasingly aware of the subtle glow of planetary auroras smeared and shifting across the southern sky, of the pulse and throb of lightnings buried deep within the cottony layers below.

Spacer remembered the vast and alien continent of light he'd seen on Salamanca's dark side, pointed out to him by Smilin' Jack . . . and for the first time he began to understand what it really was. . . .

He was aware of the light that he himself was giving off.

He was a composite being, an organism of astonishing size and organization with dissociative fragments extending far beyond his immediate physical limits in a vast and roiling cloud. At will, by simply thinking of it, those myriad fragments could glow. As the cloudscape around him grew safely darker, he extended his will and light flowed and rippled across the sky, a display of living light, a declaration of existence against the profound depth and loneliness of the night.

"Spacer?"

That loneliness of that dark and seemingly infinite cloudscape struck Spacer like the sharp bite of a knife.

A name . . . from another world, another existence. It seemed . . . familiar.

There'd been others. Diane, Ta Shaa Ta, Jarrett . . . They'd all been aboard a ship, *Questar*. . . .

Lights spanning a planetary hemisphere glowed around him, shouting upward into an empty sky. There were Others out there somewhere. He had to reach them. . . .

Spacer remembered the lights he'd seen from *Questar*'s lounge as they'd entered the Loman system, and he now knew their source.

"Spacer!"

He came wide awake, starting from a deep sleep. Jarrett was leaning over him, shaking his shoulder. "Spacer?"

"Huh?"

"You were having a bad dream."

He blinked, shaking his head. "No. No, it wasn't a dream! I was *there!*"

But of course it *was* a dream, not real at all. He'd fallen asleep leaning against one wall of their cell. Outside, the sun stood almost directly overhead, reaching into the depths of the caldera, painting them with ruddy light. The arch of stormfires still shone above its own reflection in the lake, but its inner light was lost in Loman's brighter glow.

Spacer groaned and eased himself into a sitting position. After the interview with Krueger, he and Jarrett had been hustled away to work in the pit, a vast shallow excavation teeming with laboring stormies. The labor had been backbreaking, unrelenting, and exhausting, bent over on their hands and knees, sorting rubble into buckets so that waiting lines of stormies could carry them away. They'd worked for hours without let-up, before finally being taken back to their cell where they were fed emergency rations and allowed to sleep.

Then up again, more work . . . and eventually sleep. Spacer was beginning to lose track of time. His helmet display showed the passing hours, but their steady march was meaningless in Storm's long, drawn-out day. He wasn't sure how long they'd been here. He did remember that Storm had a day of over a hundred hours as it revolved about Salamanca. When they'd been captured, the sun had been rising in the east; now, the sun was edging toward Salamanca in the western sky. The gas giant was showing a vast emptiness over most of its face, edged by a brilliant crescent of silvery-gold light that seemed almost to touch the slow-moving sun. Jarrett had told him that when the sun went behind Salamanca, it would get dark again and there would be storms—what they called the "Storm Passage."

Spacer wondered if they would be allowed to wait out the lightning and rain inside, or if the Voiders would keep them working.

"You okay, Spacer?" Maricia asked.

"Just sore," he said. "Man, I feel like someone's been working me over with a club."

"Not enough physical activity," Jarrett said, grinning. "You're out of shape." He rotated his own arm to demonstrate, then winced and grabbed his shoulder. "Ow."

"I don't know why you're smiling. Damn it, what are we gonna do?"

Jarrett shrugged. "For the moment, nothing." He glanced at the ceiling and tugged hard on his ear . . . a reminder that there might be eavesdroppers. Spacer nodded understanding.

"I . . . I was dreaming about Ta Shaa Ta," he said.

"Oh?" Maricia seemed interested. "What did you dream?"

"That he was talking to me . . . guiding me, somehow." Standing, he walked to the window, then pointed at himself, and then at the arch. "It was like he wanted me to go somewhere. I didn't really understand."

"Just a dream, Spacer," Jarrett said. "We all miss them." He was obviously thinking hard.

Their guards brought them more rations and stood nearby while they ate. Then they were given their helmets and gauntlets and led outside into the ruddy sunlight. As before, Maricia was led off in a different direction to continue her translation efforts with the stormie Chosen. Jarrett and Spacer were led to the pit.

Spacer was thinking about the dream as they left the VoidCorp field enclosure and were led past the water—still rippling with each passing pulse—surrounding the stormfire arch. He could still feel that . . . that *thing* beyond.

It had been a dream, right?

Somehow, he knew that the creature he'd seen—the titanic flying beast with its incredible swarm of fliers all around it—was real. Moreover, he knew what he'd seen was a glimpse of life on Salamanca, a huge creature adrift on the winds among the planet's cloud tops.

"Hey, Jarrett?"

"Yeah?"

"Remember those lights we saw on Salamanca's night side?"

"Sure."

"It's something alive. Something *very* big, and . . . I think it's intelligent."

"Did the fraal tell you that?"

"I saw it . . . in my dream."

"Hey, you two!" a guard snarled. "Shut up and keep moving!"

In the pit, Spacer found himself clawing at the gravel broken up by one of the VoidCorp bulldozers between two stormies. One of the stormies, he saw, was a Chosen with a large, sad brown eye located just above one of its three rubbery legs. Spacer noticed a puckered wound beneath the base of the tentacle, oozing pale blue blood. Krueger, it seemed, didn't just take the stormfires off *dead* Chosen.

He wished he had a linguicomp so he could speak to the being. He tried Standard once. "I know Touches Far," he said, trying to keep it simple. The stormie rolled its eye at him but continued flicking through the gravel with its single tentacle. If it understood any Standard at all, it wasn't admitting it . . . and, more likely, it had no idea what he'd just said.

Hours passed. Loman crawled ever closer to the narrowing sliver of the Salamanca crescent. Eventually, the two touched, and then, minute by dragging minute, the brilliant orb of Loman slipped farther and farther behind the giant planet's bulk.

A shadow raced across the land, sweeping from east to west. In another few moments, the caldera began growing dark. With a final flare of golden light, Loman vanished completely behind the giant, and the night of Eclipse returned to Storm.

In the east, lightning stabbed, followed long moments later by a roll of thunder. A storm was gathering already.

Spacer . . .

Spacer stopped working and looked around. Who had called him?

Spacer!

That was Ta Shaa Ta's voice speaking in his head!

"Ta Shaa Ta!" he cried.

Think your thoughts silently but slowly, the voice said. *I will hear them. It is difficult, because I am far away, but I can hear.*

I hear you! I hear you! You're alive!

I live, was the reply. *How close are you now to the stormfire arch?*

Uh, pretty far. Four hundred meters, maybe. And there are guys here with guns who won't let me out of the pit.

They should be distracted soon as the storm gathers strength. When you can, make your way to the arch. I will tell you what to do.

Okay. Um . . . where are you, anyway?

Atop the cliff to the south. Diane is here with me . . . and others, but it will take time for us to get down. You will buy us that time!

Okay. I'll try. . . .

Diane was alive! He was so excited by that one bit of news that he almost leaped out of the pit right there.

"You!" A guard barked. "Back to work!"

Lightning crackled overhead, jaggedly forked and branching, and thunder pealed. The guard ducked, an involuntary flinch.

That was about as much distraction, Spacer thought, as he had any right to expect. He leaped out of the pit and started trotting toward the Arch. *I'm out,* he thought, hoping Ta Shaa Ta was still listening. *I'm out and running for the arch!*

Flash after flash of lightning snapped across the sky, dragging cracks and peals of thunder with them.

Do not run, the fraal's voice said in his mind. *The e-suit you wear looks like those worn by other VoidCorp personnel. Walk and you will not attract attention.*

Spacer slowed to a walk. Other VoidCorp personnel, he saw, had stopped what they were doing and were looking at the ominous sky. Clouds were gathering rapidly, though the vast bulk of Salamanca could still be seen, now almost invisible save for a ghostly ring of ruby light encircling its night hemisphere. Spacer could see the flicker of golden lightnings inside Salamanca's night. It was as though the two worlds, Salamanca and Storm, were connected in searing, random pulses of electric violence.

In the darkness, when they weren't obscured by the lightning flashes over Storm, the lights of Salamanca were becoming visible, a rippling, flickering motion like waves in a phosphorescent sea.

We've learned so much about the Storm natives, Ta Shaa Ta told him as he walked. The bridge leading to the island and the bright-glowing arch was just ahead. *We now think that the being you saw flying in Salamanca's sky is an extremely large, extremely intelligent being—what xenosophontologists would refer to as a meta-intelligence, an intelligence arising from the composite minds of many billions or trillions of separate thinking creatures. When you touched the mind of this intelligence while you slept, I was able to let my thoughts ride along, and I touched that mind as well.*

Were you able to talk with it? Spacer asked.

Not really. That's what we want you to do now.

Huh? How?

You must let your right brain show you the way.

What . . . what do you want me to tell it?

We need you to tell it that we know it's there, that we understand, that we know what it's trying to accomplish here on Storm, and that we can help it.

But I don't *understand!* Spacer protested.

Don't worry. I will help you.

Spacer was passing the VoidCorp encampment now. There were lots of guards about, but none were paying any attention to him. Most were staring at the sky and the lightning display there. He could feel their growing fear and restlessness.

What is *it trying to do?* he thought.

Imagine that you are a brilliant mind, adrift on the winds of a gas giant, the fraal told him. *Perhaps you evolved out of the symbiosis of trillions of flying creatures joined together. You can never land, for there is no land. A gas giant is simply air, atmosphere growing thicker and denser and inconceivably hotter the deeper you go, until you reach its hot, high-pressure core of metallic hydrogen. If you evolved on such a world, you would circle endlessly in the sky, never able to stop, never able to be still.*

Imagine now, Ta Shaa Ta continued, *that you have eyes much like fraal or human eyes and a mind able to wonder at the things you see in the night sky. You would see the moons in their passage around your world, watch the rising and the setting of the sun . . .and perhaps guess at what they might be.*

Finally, imagine that you are possessed with a curiosity almost human in its intensity, in its determination to know the reason why. You have no machines, no industry, no fire, no spacecraft . . . and yet you learn to grow very tiny creatures within yourself, manufacturing tiny machines out of the very substance of your own body—machines like bacteria or smaller. Viruses, minute packages of biological nanotechnology cast into space on powerful magnetic winds . . .

Most of those tiny spores would be caught up in the stellar wind and blown into the depths of interstellar space, forever lost. A few, however, might fall upon nearby worlds, on the larger of the moons circling your world, for instance.

Storm. Spacer understood at last.

Yes, on Storm. Where these spores land, they begin to change their surroundings, to multiply, to make living tissue—the fraal hesitated, searching for the proper word—*change, to grow along carefully laid-out plans, a program, of sorts, hard-wired into the nanotechnic package from the beginning.*

"Eyes!" Spacer was so startled he spoke aloud. *You're saying the eyes on the stormies were grown on them by the thing on Salamanca?* He repressed a shudder of raw distaste. *That's . . . horrible!*

It depends on your point of view. How better to explore another world than to give eyes to the beings there—beings which, quite by coincidence, were blind to begin with?

But . . . but how do they communicate?

The stormfires seem to augment the telepathic effect, though only slightly, Ta Shaa Ta told him. *The Chosen wear the stones because they think it lets the Salamanca Intelligence hear them more clearly. In any case, telepathic contact between the Salamanca Intelligence and the stormies has not been perfect—far from it, in fact, since the stormies have developed the idea that the Intelligence is God. The nanotechnically grown brains worked for visual processing and for some analytical thought. Their impulses merged, however, with the original stormie brains, which are almost entirely intuitive and feeling. The blend is . . . imperfect.*

Spacer was up to the bridge now. No one was on the island. He looked around to see if anyone was watching then stepped onto the metal deck plating above the water. Lightning flared, dazzlingly bright. The thunder followed close behind, an explosion of raw noise.

How did you learn all of this? Spacer asked the fraal.

Diane and I have been talking with the stormies for several standard days now, and I have been probing their minds, trying to understand how they think. Diane actually hit upon the idea while she was thinking about the stone circle.

Those big, stacked up rocks outside the caldera?

Correct. The Salamanca Intelligence directed the placement of those boulders so that through the Chosen it

*could take extremely precise measurements of the sky from
a fixed position on the ground—something that doesn't
exist in Salamanca's upper atmosphere. I believe it was
trying to deduce the laws of orbital mechanics, of gravity,
and of motion by recording the rising and the setting of
Salamanca's sun and moons.*

Well, did it?

*I'm not sure. I do not believe so, since Touches Far
indicated that the measuring was not yet complete. Perhaps you'll be able to help us learn that.*

Spacer had nearly reached the arch, which flared brilliantly in the twilight, alive and aglow with seething, pulsing inner life.

"Okay," he said, both aloud and in his mind. "I'm
here!"

*You must contact the Salamanca Intelligence. It should
be easier for you this close to the arch.*

Yeah. I can . . . I can feel it, just on the other side!

Spacer cleared his mind, reaching out.

What had Ta Shaa Ta said? That his psionic powers
resided in the right hemisphere of his brain, that he could
hear what it picked up through hunches, intuition, or outright guesswork. And dreams. And maybe visualizations
as well? He tried to picture the Intelligence as he'd seen it,
as he'd experienced it in his dream.

?

That was all. No words, just a feeling, a feeling of
questioning.

He wasn't getting through. Clearing his mind, he tried
again. He sensed Ta Shaa Ta there with him, inside his
own mind, steadying him, helping him to control his
thoughts.

*The Two of Minds. A man and a woman walked away
from one another, each holding a hand out, a dazzling star
afloat just above their palms, representing mind and division. Two courses. Two paths. Two peoples, sundered by
distance and alien ideas . . .*

He'd just been wishing that he had his cards. Spacer
found, however, that the cards' familiar imagery came

easily to his mind, helping him to narrow his thoughts, to focus them, and to project the ideas behind the symbolism.

We understand the division between the stormies and the Salamanca Intelligence, he was saying. *We understand this duality of minds. It's part of us, and what we are.*

He sensed no response from the other side of the arch, nothing but a deep and abiding Watchfulness.

The Knight of Minds. A golden armored knight rode forth astride a white horse. His right hand was held high, the flaming orb of Mind aloft like a banner in the sky. In the distance, men squabbled, all speaking at once, none hearing. Like fiery tongues, the letter Yod rained from a gray and overcast sky, words from God. In the remote distance was a thriving city and a well-tended orchard . . .

The knight always represented communication, the Yod symbol the Word proceeding from the mouth of God and an indication of God's protection. The struggling, shouting men in the distance presented discord and a failure to communicate. The orchard and the city were the potential results of working together in harmony.

We want to talk, the card was saying in Spacer's mind. *We want to work with you, the Two of Minds. We have information for you, things you want to know. Talk to us, and we can help!*

Spacer searched for an indication that he was being heard. Thunder boomed and crackled. Most of the sky was shrouded now in clouds, but the ruby-lit circle of Salamanca as it eclipsed the sun was still visible.

The Ace of Machines. A hand, the Hand of God, extended horizontally from a cloud, holding an orrery, and an eye gazed from the machine's heart. Above the machine was a golden crown from which hung the olive branch of peace and the laurel of victory. Six Yods surrounded the sword, three to a side, symbolizing God's Word and His protection.

The Ace of Machines was a powerful card, a card of decisiveness, of focused action, of *victory*. Like the Ace of

Swords, which it resembled, it indicated power and control, reason and logic, new ideas and swift action.

It indicated a literal *deus ex machina*, deliverance from on high, a device to capture the mind and the heart and transform conditions of evil below.

Help us! The card was saying in Spacer's mind. *Give us a sign, something delivered through your Chosen—the Two of Minds—to help us now as we battle the enemy that threatens us and your people!*

Spacer waited then, listening, trying to weigh his own thoughts for some sign, for a hunch, for a flash of intuition, something, anything that would indicate that he'd been heard.

Nothing . . .

He heard a shout.

Turning, he saw several armored troops at the far end of the bridge. They had seen him and had been coming for him, but something had stopped them. They were looking toward the west above the caldera rim, staring up at Salamanca and pointing.

"My God!" one shouted. "What *is* it?"

Thunder rolled. Turning, Spacer looked up at Salamanca, and his jaw dropped. There was . . . *something* happening there, something alive within the depths of the Salamancan night.

The lights he'd seen during *Questar*'s pass above Salamanca's night side were there, but they were now far vaster, far more brilliant than they'd been before. It was like looking at an image poorly formed on a black-and-white monitor, a rippling, swirling effect, now like a whirlpool, now solidifying into marching spokes of light rotating around a brilliant center.

And then the light coalesced, steadied, and opened once more. There was a background of gray-white, luminous against Salamanca's night. A central black disk was centered on the white, almost like the pupil of a titanic eye.

Spacer gasped. It *was* an eye! Or rather the crude image of one, precisely like the eye on a holotarot orrery . . . or like the ones growing on the Chosen. The mirage shimmered a bit as clouds in Storm's atmosphere continued to gather, but even as visibility faded, it seemed to stare down from Heaven upon the fast-panicking humans gathered in the caldera so far below.

Chapter Twenty-One

T HAT'S IT!" DIANE said. "Let's go!"
From the south rim of the caldera, it appeared that pandemonium was spreading across the VoidCorp encampment like ripples in a pond. Everywhere, humans were stopping what they were doing, standing in small, uncertain groups, and staring up at that impossible, awful Eye hanging in the sky above them.

Along the caldera rim, nearly one hundred stormies had gathered, four of them Chosen. The sighted stormies boomed and whistled a command, and the entire small army of natives began slipping over the edge of the cliff.

Ta Shaa Ta clung tightly to Touches Far, while Diane had mounted a Chosen that called itself Warm Motions. She couldn't help a smile at the picture they must present: a human and a fraal riding piggy-back upon these tripedal creatures that, properly speaking, *had* no backs. Warm Motions had used its tentacle to hoist her high enough up its body that she could lock her arms all the way around its torso just beneath those gaping, alarming mouths. Hanging

on was entirely up to her; the Chosen couldn't support her
with its tentacle . . . not and manage the descent of the cliff
face. She locked her legs around the rubbery hide, clung
left-wrist to right as hard as she could, and tried not to look
down as her ride swung itself out and over the cliff's edge
and started down.

The stormies seemed so awkward sometimes, like cartoon animals or caricatures, but they moved with astonishing grace and confidence down the sheer rock wall.
Surprisingly, the sighted ones appeared to have no advantage over the others. Stubby legs stretched as needed, toes
finding recesses and footholds easily. The long tentacles
tautened like ropes as the creatures rappelled down the
cliff, loosing their grip every few seconds, snaking about
for another purchase, then catching hold once more.

Peering out of the corner of her helmet visor, Diane
watched the stormies nearest her and marveled at their
agility. They no longer seemed comical or awkward but
majestically graceful.

"Ta Shaa Ta?" she called over the radio. "What *was* that
thing, that big eye? How did Spacer do that?"

"I am not sure. I *thought* he was trying to do something
else entirely and have the Salamanca Intelligence communicate with the Chosen. I'd hoped to have it tell the
stormies that it would be with them, would help them
somehow."

"God is on our side, huh?"

"That was the idea. Apparently, Spacer and the Intelligence came up with something else on their own. It
appears to have acted as a nice distraction."

Careful to maintain her grip to Warm Motions's body,
Diane twisted herself far enough around to see into the
encampment. In the dark, it really wasn't possible to make
out much except the glare of lights that had come on automatically with the sudden advance of the eclipse. With
each stab and flare of lightning, she could see small groups
of e-suited or combat-armored men standing in the open
and looking up at Salamanca. Originally, they'd planned to
try the descent with the darkness of the eclipse as cover. It

might have worked, but there'd been a terrible risk that some alert guard would have looked up at the cliff and seen a small army of moving shapes flowing down the rock. If they'd been seen, and the VoidCorp troopers had opened fire . . .

But the full attention of every VoidCorper in that crater was riveted on the sky. Diane felt a curious sense of exultation as her tiny army charged into battle.

*   *   *   *   *

Spacer felt his knees giving out beneath him, and he sagged to the steel plate surface of the bridge. The Eye appeared to be staring directly down at him, staring into the innermost depths of his soul.

He *knew* what he was seeing wasn't real. The Salamanca Intelligence was made up of huge organisms, with discrete parts scattered in a vast cloud across much of the gas giant's night hemisphere. Clearly those parts could control electric, magnetic, and phosphorescent phenomena in Salamanca's upper atmosphere to create patterns of light and dark.

On Tribon's lowest level, the Bjorn Sports Arena occupied one of the largest of the habitat domes, with seating for half a million Lisoners. Once Spacer had snuck inside for a glimpse of a kickball game. At one point in the festivities, the entire mass of spectators on the far side of the stadium had held up cards printed black on one side and white on the other. Each spectator had also been given a card and a small bracelet with two lights on it. They'd been told that when one light was lit, they were to hold up their card with the black face out; when two were lit, show the white face.

The entire display had been controlled by an AI with cameras watching the scene below from every angle. With each spectator controlling only two bits of data, they'd created startlingly lifelike images of the faces of each of the star players in the game, one after the other . . . along with such keen and pithy observations as "WIN! WIN! WIN!" and "Drink Narcola."

Something of the sort was happening in Salamanca's upper atmosphere right now, though how the immense intelligence was coordinating so much raw data, how it was checking itself for accuracy, how it even knew what it looked like from space were all mysteries. The effect was working, and that was what counted. The Eye, so obviously drawn from Spacer's mental image of the machine eye in the holotarot, continued to study the VoidCorp encampment, like the eye of some incredibly vast, cosmic bioresearcher peering down into the noisome slime of a petri dish culture.

Spacer felt as though it was studying him, dissecting his soul.

The strangest part about it was that *this* wasn't what Spacer had been trying to do. At Ta Shaa Ta's urging, he'd been trying to communicate the idea of victory and strength, of God reaching down and helping His Chosen. It had been meant as a kind of pep talk, a rallying speech to goad the stormies into an attack against the Voider base. Somehow, he'd been misunderstood. Possibly the Salamanca Intelligence was just too alien to comprehend such human subtleties. Maybe he and Ta Shaa Ta had been thinking in terms too *human* for the vast intelligence to comprehend.

Or maybe the Salamanca Intelligence had understood more than they'd realized and had simply carried out an idea of its own. . . .

Spacer found his feet again and started jogging back across the bridge. The VoidCorp troops at the other end had vanished, two of them dropping their weapons as they'd fled—cut rate hirelings, no doubt. Spacer stopped and picked up one of the weapons, a laser rifle. He wasn't sure he could use it with any accuracy, but it made him feel a bit bigger and a bit stronger to carry the thing.

He started back toward the camp.

There was a hell of a lot of screaming and panicking going on there.

*   *   *   *   *

The stormies reached the bottom of the cliff in a surging rush. Diane continued clinging to the stormie, unable to see very much but aware of the bucks and twists and ripplings of powerful muscles as the creature nimbly leaped from boulder to boulder across a huge spill of broken rock at the cliff's base.

She let go as the charging stormies approached the huge pit outside the VoidCorp camp where thousands of other stormies were milling about in confusion. A trio of humans in black armor, shocked perhaps by the appearance of the new stormies, took aim with their laser rifles.

Almost as one, the charging stormies reached down with questing tentacles and snatched up rocks the size of human heads. The barrage was poorly aimed—a wild scattering of missiles, most of which missed.

But those stones that struck did so with the incredible force. Those three-meter tentacles, swinging hard in an overhand slash and uncoiling from the rocks as they descended, imparted terrific speed to the missiles.

One trooper shrieked as he was smashed backward, his chest and right arm crushed. Another had his rifle torn from his arms, along with one hand. A third had his visor smashed by a grazing blow. All three were dead seconds later as the stormies surged over and past their bodies.

The newcomers boomed and shrieked, their message spreading among their captive comrades. First one by one, then in small groups, then in surging masses, the captive stormies poured out of the pit, shredding chains and leg shackles as they joined the charge. A bulldozer near the edge of the pit was picked up like a cork in a raging sea—picked up, tipped, and toppled as the VoidCorper inside the cockpit screamed and struggled.

Diane was swiftly left behind, the stormies moving much faster on their short trio of walking limbs than she could manage on her two long legs. She saw Ta Shaa Ta nearby, standing alone near three crushed and mutilated bodies.

What have we done? The fraal's voice said in her mind.

"Come on," she told him. "We started this. Now we're going to have to see it through to the end."

They followed the booming thunder of the stormie mob toward the VoidCorp encampment.

*   *   *   *   *

Spacer stood in the open, uncertain as the stormie army bore down on him. Some VoidCorper troops tried to stand and surrender; he saw them go under, struck by volleys of stones or simply run down by the furiously charging creatures.

He suddenly felt very small and vulnerable. How were the oncoming stormies supposed to know that he wasn't a VoidCorper?

Impulsively, he tossed aside the laser rifle, but he could see that most of the Voiders being run down weren't armed either. The nearest stormies were racing straight toward him, some holding large rocks in tightly coiled tentacles.

Spacer remembered his e-suit's capacitor field.

Swiftly, hand trembling, he reached over to the arm control to check. Yes, it was still off. He'd left it off while he was working in the pit, despite the danger of lightning. But would that be enough? He stood very still as the rampaging creatures swarmed closer. A dozen tentacles lashed out, probing, touching, tasting all over his suit. He squeezed his eyes shut and waited.

When he opened them again a moment later, he saw the stormies flowing around him to either side, ignoring him completely. Shaking, he allowed himself to draw a long, deep breath. He turned and looked up, but Salamanca and the Eye were lost now, vanished behind the roiling clouds. Lightning exploded, forking across the sky, stabbing at the caldera rim. Scarcely able to control the shaking in his legs, Spacer started following after the charging stormies.

*   *   *   *   *

"The field fence!" Diane cried. "They're hitting the field fence and can't get through!"

She watched, horrified, as a mass of stormies hit the apparently open space between two of the glowing uprights of the field fence that surrounded the inner compound. Artificial lightning flashed and crackled, stabbing from one upright to another, and a dozen stormies writhed and twisted as the electrical charge shot through their bodies.

"I thought they would be immune to lightning!" she said. "I mean, living on this world, using electricity the way they do . . ."

"Other organisms here are not immune," Ta Shaa Ta pointed out. "In fact, they seem to require lightning to complete their life cycles."

"Damn! They're living, walking batteries! *I thought they'd be okay!*"

Another line of stormies surged across the smoking bodies of their fallen comrades, hit the opening between the uprights, and died in coruscating bursts of artificial lightning.

It was her fault, she knew. During the planning of this attack, hours ago, Ta Shaa Ta had raised the issue of the field fence around the VoidCorpers' inner sanctum. Touches Far had insisted there was no problem with the "God's-fire wall," as he called it. They would simply go through. Ta Shaa Ta had gently suggested that the stored energies in the fence capacitors might be higher than *any* organic forms could survive. Surely the VoidCorpers had known what they were doing when they'd constructed the thing.

Diane had been so damned *certain* it would work. Now she was seeing the results of a guess made with too little information, and she felt sick. A hundred dead stormies already lay at the barrier in a grisly heap. VoidCorp troopers stood inside, firing with lasers into the seething mob outside as more and more stormies leaped across the bodies of the fallen and into the flame-shot horror between the uprights. It seemed that they hoped to overwhelm the Voider defenses by sheer numbers, to bury the terrible fence beneath the bodies of their own dead.

Diane didn't think there were enough stormies on the whole world to carry *that* off.

* * * * *

Rom Verdoss watched what was happening from the edge of the encampment, saw the attack, and knew that it was going to fail. *The idiots!*

All of the Voiders outside the inner perimeter had been killed or incapacitated, he was pretty sure—or else they'd managed to flee to safety through the gates in the field fence.

Verdoss was still groggy and terribly, terribly sore after his descent of the western caldera wall. How he'd managed to reach the bottom in one piece, he still wasn't sure. All he'd been able to do upon finishing the long climb was to find the shelter of a large boulder at the base of the cliff and collapse into a long and exhausted sleep. When he'd awakened, it was full dark with lightning crackling and flashing across the sky and a vast mob of stormies surging across the caldera floor.

Stumbling along on aching, trembling legs, Verdoss had hurried toward the battle. He reached a Voider bulldozer, abandoned by its driver near the pit, and leaned against one dirt-encrusted track as he watched the stormie wave slam into the field fence and recoil, leaving dozens dead and burned.

There was no profit to be had here, no profit at all. Verdoss was no soldier, but he knew a losing situation when he saw it, knew when continued head-bashing against an immovable barrier was simply going to result in a sore head. There had to be another way.

He looked up at the machine towering above him. Perhaps there was.

Rom Verdoss had been born to one of the prominent merchant houses of the Rigunmor Consortium, a guaranteed position of luxury and even ostentation by almost any standards. However, his father had insisted that Rom, Karp, and Anjera all learn the business of Periapsis

Systems literally from the bottom up. For a time, when he was fifteen, he'd worked as a loader at Ettelkep Hold's main spaceport, driving skiploaders and floaters and cargo lifts. He was no stranger to heavy machinery.

Mounting the track, he squeezed into the driver's compartment, a transplas bubble that had been abandoned with the hatch hanging open. He studied the simple controls. It was an old-fashioned model, not that different from an Ettelkep cargo lift. He pressed the starter button and the engine purred to life. He released the brake, engaged the main drive, then took the two track controllers in hand, pulling the right back as he shoved the left forward, sending the machine into a hard, shuddering turn.

If you want something done right, he thought as excitement surged through him, do it yourself!

He tromped on the accelerator, and the bulldozer lurched ahead, racing across the open ground toward the VoidCorp inner compound.

*   *   *   *   *

Wolfgang Krueger, wearing attack armor and clutching a hand flamer in his right gauntlet, stood in the inner compound. Ten meters away, the natives surged forward again, striking jaggedly dazzling bolts of electricity from the fence uprights as they tried to force their way through the impalpable barrier.

"Fire!" he shouted over comms. "Fire into them! Drive them back!" He raised his flamer and squeezed the trigger, sending a jet of flaming aerosol through the lightning and into those writhing bodies. The native horde appeared to be wavering now, uncertain and hurt by their losses. The Corporate forces inside the perimeter might still carry the day if they could hold out a few moments more.

They should be able to hold out. Most of his people had managed to get inside the fence when the attack had begun. His troops were breaking out crates of heavy weapons now, including a tripod-mounted grenade launcher and a couple of portable Bantams. They should have had the big guns set up from the start, but damn it all, the natives hadn't been giving any trouble—not a *hint* of unrest so far as he'd been able to tell!

He glanced up at the western sky. At least the clouds had closed in, masking that nightmare apparition. What the hell had that thing been?

Krueger didn't know how the natives had pulled it off. It was almost enough to make him believe in their gibberish about the gas giant being some kind of god.

No. Ridiculous! The TXI people were behind this, somehow. Maybe it had been a laser projection against clouds in Storm's atmosphere, a gigantic hologram designed to distract his people long enough for them to launch an attack. That was it.

He wondered, though, how he was going to explain this to PK349 98TVR. She wasn't going to be pleased with *this* turn of the Corporate ledgers, not at all.

"GM692!" he called. "This is JR945! Have the creatures entered any of the ships, yet?"

"N-no, JR!" replied the female officer.

"Is the crew still aboard DE 710?"

"Minimal crew, yes."

"Enough to fly the thing?"

"Yes, sir!"

"Order them to take off immediately. They can use their lasers and plasma guns to clean this mess up!" Damn! He should have thought of that sooner, but things had been happening so quickly!

Movement caught his eye: a squat, black and red shape lumbering across the plain, headed straight for the field fence gate. A bulldozer, one of the machines they'd had at the pit. At first he thought it was a Corporate Employee racing to the rescue, but as it drew closer, he could tell by its all-out speed and the course it was taking that the driver was going to try to take out the fence.

"GM692!"

"Sir!"

"A weapon! A *heavy* weapon! Fast!"

His assistant handed him a Bantam-5 rocket launcher.

Krueger checked the load—four programmable 30mm hunter-killers. He couldn't fire projectile weapons through the fence without triggering a discharge and detonating the warheads, but with this weapon, he could lob a few over the fence, each warhead programmed to home-in on a moving target. He balanced the weapon over his shoulder, taking aim to give the warhead's simple-minded brain a look at the target, then tilted the muzzle almost straight up and squeezed the trigger. With a shrill sound like tearing paper, the missile vaulted high into the lightning-shot sky. At the top of its trajectory, it paused a moment, then began to descend, gathering speed as it fell.

* * * * *

Rom Verdoss saw the missile streak into the sky but never saw its fall. He was less than thirty meters from the field fence when a savage explosion rocked the 'dozer, shattering the plastic canopy and slamming him painfully to one side. He felt ribs crack and tasted blood.

The 'dozer's motor was still running, and it was too late to stop now. Besides, Rom Verdoss had never backed away from a fight in his life.

Pain dragged at him. Two of the vehicle's four battery packs were shorting, but he tromped hard on the accelerator and kept the 'dozer on course.

Seconds later, the smoking vehicle slammed into the paired uprights of the fence's main gate, shorting them out in a blazing crackle of arcing current. The bulldozer's remaining battery packs exploded, flame gouting into the eclipse-darkened sky. The fence was shattered, the uprights toppled, the only sparks now coming from the sputtering shorts of the bulldozer's burning engine.

The stormies had been surging against a portion of the fence some thirty meters away. Even the blind ones sensed the sudden falling of the charge-potential near the gate. Abandoning their head-on attack over their fallen comrades, they surged back and around, spilling into the path

carved by the charging VoidCorp bulldozer, clambering
over and around the burning machine heedless of burns or
the crackling, snapping shots of the human defenders
within.

The battle, if it could be called that now, lasted only a
few minutes longer.

* * * * *

Diane ran the last dozen meters, picking her way over
the smoldering bodies and still-burning wreckage of the
bulldozer. Inside the compound, the stormie army was
busily demolishing habitat domes, destroying equipment,
and killing VoidCorp Employees.

"Stop!" she shouted, increasing the volume on her linguicomp's external speakers to project the stormie command in a booming roar. "Stop! Stop killing them!"

It was a battle no longer, but a slaughter. Everywhere,
VoidCorpers were throwing down their weapons, raising
their hands, trying to surrender, but the rampaging
stormies didn't seem to understand. It was murder now,
murder with a cold and implacable ruthlessness unlike
anything Diane had ever seen or felt.

She saw one e-suited man raised high into the air, his
arms and legs flailing wildly as he was flung into the
crackling charge of the fence. Another was picked up by
his armored legs and dashed against a habitat wall.

"Stop killing them!"

A Chosen turned its watery brown eye on her. She
thought it might be Touches Far, but in the chaos and noise
and uncertainly flickering light she couldn't be sure.

"Why stop?" the being asked her. "You say kill. We kill.
Why stop?"

"It's over! They're giving up! You don't need to kill
them all!"

"Why not kill all? No understand." The Chosen raised
its tentacle. Clutched in its rubbery coils was the blackened wreckage of VoidCorp armor, blood dripping from an
open end. She caught a glimpse of the gaunt, pale features

of Wolfgang Krueger behind the visor, eyes and mouth wide in a soundless scream.

"Because . . . because . . ." She stopped, unable to speak, unable to think. She had started this slaughter, and now it was completely beyond her control.

"Touches Far!" she said. "The battle is over. Simply . . . let them . . . *be!*"

The Chosen hesitated a moment, as though digesting this. Then it barked a command, a command spread from stormie to stormie in a rippling, expanding circle. In another few moments, the killing had stopped.

An hour later, the real storm began.

Chapter Twenty-Two

THEY'D WAITED OUT the lightning, rain, and wind of the Storm Passage inside one of the intact habitat domes in the VoidCorp camp. It wasn't so much a matter of the victors taking charge of the vanquished as it was fellow survivors huddled together against the raging elements outside.

"I never thought of Verdoss as a hero," Spacer said, listening to the howling wind, the rain striking like steel pellets.

"Rom Verdoss was a mind in pain," Ta Shaa Ta said. "Pain can twist a man, twist his thoughts, yet the twisting does not make him evil."

"I'll miss him," Diane said simply.

"I always thought I knew people, could read people pretty well," Spacer said, "and you say I have some kind of power, but I didn't read him right at all."

"A lesson, Spacer," the fraal said. "Never assume you know a person with complete accuracy. Mind—spirit, if you will—is too volatile. It changes, shifts, and grows too quickly. Even a mindwalker can never know another completely."

As they waited for the storm to pass, the TXI expedition began hammering out an agreement with the VoidCorpers. They had two choices. With two freighters on the ground, those who wished to fly back to Lison and freedom from VoidCorp servitude could do so. Those who wanted to return to Employment on Hux were free to do so. None were ever to return to Storm. The natives, under the command of Touches Far, would be in constant touch with Concord military forces in the Verge and would control all access to the planet until Loman's status as a Concord Protectorate could be legally established in the courts.

Spacer was surprised that only a handful of Voiders opted for freedom—most of them low-rank workers imported from Hux, contract violators undergoing correctional service, or mercenary soldiers hired by VoidCorp to fill out the company's military presence. The rest wanted to return to Hux. As the commander of the loyal Voiders put it, "Why should we go with you?" She was an attractive woman who identified herself only as GM692 85THY. "You have only chaos to offer—inefficiency, confusion, waste. The Corporation offers order and a proper place. Because of this, every one of us knows who we are and what is expected of us."

She'd cocked her head to one side as she'd spoken to Jarrett, then added, "Of course, you're free to come with us, if you want. I'm sure the Corporation could find positions for all of you."

"I think not," Jarrett said gently. "I've seen enough of VoidCorp's efficiency, thank you—and their hospitality."

Umvelt, Spacer thought. What was it about the Voider worldview that made them prefer life under Corporate rule to life almost anywhere else? He didn't understand.

*   *   *   *   *

In her quarters, PK349 98TVR stared into the holo for a moment, examining critically the fall of her formal dress gown, the hang of her Corporate cloak, the fit of her computer gauntlet, the placement and tilt of the discrete, magnetically levitated jewelspheres orbiting slowly behind her head. If they were going to terminate her, she wanted to look her best.

Actually, her failure most likely didn't require full termination . . . but she almost wished they would cancel her contract anyway. The disgrace of being broken to sub-MA ranks would be almost too much to bear.

Almost. PK349 98TVR was a very determined woman. She'd fought her way up from the muckpits before. She would do it again.

Satisfied with her outward appearance, she strode from her room, head high, and caught the lift up to the Administration Level.

She knew they were expecting her.

"PK349 98TVR," an electronically distorted voice announced from the darkness overhead as she stepped into a single pool of light. Corporate policy held that one *never* saw the board members responsible for administrative discipline. "You will be interested in the fact that a VoidCorp freighter, escorted by corvette DE 710, is now en route to Hux. They report the operation on Storm has been overrun by natives and shut down."

"Yes, sir." She was already well aware of the situation. GM692 85THY had already reported as much.

"In view of the situation," the voice went on, "we have decided to terminate all further operations on Storm. It will be noted in the record that this Board was never fully convinced of the value of Storm as presented in the initial feasibility studies."

"Yes, sir." Here it comes, she thought: the judgment of the Board.

"It is the judgment of the Board that you, PK349 98TVR, be given an immediate promotion to Administrative Level PQ and be transferred back to VoidCorp Home District for reassignment at your new level."

Her jaw dropped. This wasn't what she'd been expecting at *all!*

A promotion? Even a small one . . .

"Off the record," the voice added, hesitating long

enough for the recording devices to pause, "don't be so surprised. In view of the Board's contention that the Storm affair was never of serious importance, we could scarcely maintain credibility by *demoting* you. Clearly, you did your best in a difficult situation. The Employees responsible for the debacle are dead. The ledgers balance. We move on to other projects from here. Agreed?"

"Y-yes, sir! Absolutely, sir!"

"Resume recording. Very well. Further inquiries into recent events will be carried out when the returning Employees dock at the Hux facility. However, the Board is satisfied that this matter is closed. PK349 98TVR, you are dismissed."

She nearly stumbled from the boardroom and had trouble finding her way down seven levels to the O-S Level lounge. She badly needed a drink after that scare— and a chance to think things through.

She'd survived. She would *live*.

And there was so much more she wanted to do. . . .

Storm would be avenged one day, and she would make one hell of a profit doing it. Already, she thought she saw a way to do it.

Her star in the Corporation was still rising after all.

*   *   *   *   *

Questar stayed on Storm for two more weeks so that the TXI team could complete their investigation of the ancient ruins and their studies of the Storm natives. At last, the party said their good-byes to the gathered throngs of natives, and then they boarded ship. They left Rom Verdoss on Storm, buried with the bodies of the original Rigunmor expedition. The Storm natives had evidently thought the e-suited Rigunmor bodies were representatives of God. The ceremony of planting them in the Earth—like food or fire gems—seemed to impress them deeply.

Later, Spacer watched the cloud-girdled sphere of Storm receding rapidly in the aft viewscreens. Loman blazed, red-gold and brilliant, to starboard. Salamanca, visible now in half-phase, slowly grew larger ahead.

All them were gathered in *Questar*'s command center and were watching the glory of the superjovian world unfold. Smilin' Jack had rescinded his order that they stay off the bridge. After all, the TXI team had rescued him and his crew and recovered his ship.

"I believe the most unexpected development," Ta Shaa Ta was saying, "is the unusual sexual nature of the natives' life cycle."

They were discussing what they had seen, done, felt on Storm, a mutual debriefing to try to understand the shape and scope of what they'd learned on this strange and alien world.

"Not so unusual," Maricia replied. "Lots of other life forms have extreme dimorphism among the sexes."

"Still, the cycle on Storm is unusual. The motile natives—the stormies—are, in fact, female and not parthenogenetic as we believed."

"The males are the catcher plants," Maricia explained to Smilin' Jack and his crew. "They store up energy during their four-day growth and life cycle, and then store it in underground tubers."

"Which the females dig up and eat after the males are blasted by lightning," Jarrett added, "and in doing so, manage to impregnate themselves."

"We had our first clue," Maricia said, "when we saw that both the catcher plants and the stormies could grow eyes and second brains from the Salamanca Intelligence's nanotech spores. Obviously, the tissue and cell structure of the two are quite similar."

"A clue," Diane agreed, "but not a very obvious one. I don't feel too dumb that we missed it at first. Still, it just goes to prove what I've always suspected: *Most* males are vegetables at heart."

"I'd still like to know about these stormfire gem things," Smilin' Jack said. "You say those were made by the catcher plants too?"

"In a sense," Maricia said. "We'd already determined

that some plants—especially the fulgivores, but to a certain extent the catcher plants as well—concentrated certain metals in their growing parts as an aid in attracting lightning. Some catchers also concentrated lanthanides and other rare earths. The stormfires are fulgurites, crystalline formations created when lightning is channeled through certain concentrations of minerals in the ground. They seem to be natural capacitors, charged by lightning and acting as tiny batteries. That's why they glow. The stormies dug them up when they were rooting around looking for battery-tubers in burned-over male growth."

"That's rich," Jack said. "The damned Voiders were digging in the wrong place. There weren't any plants in the caldera, so no gemstones!"

"They would have had better luck digging where *Questar* landed," Maricia said, laughing. "It turns out the stormfires aren't so rare after all."

"At least, not as long as the stormies are there," Diane said. She seemed pensive. "What's going to happen to them? Storm isn't going to last much longer, at least in planetological terms. Another few thousand years at best."

"The Salamanca Intelligence seemed certain that it could handle that end of things," Ta Shaa Ta said, "if we fulfill our part of the bargain."

"Well, that's the idea, isn't it?" Jack said. A small alarm chimed on the console.

"We're coming up on our pass over the Salamancan night side now," Mike said.

"Are you ready, Spacer?" Ta Shaa Ta asked.

"I guess so." His hand strayed to the red bag at his belt, and he touched the cards inside. "I just wish I could be sure I was really getting through to that thing. That whole time on Storm by the arch I couldn't tell if I was getting through or not."

"I imagine we will know," Ta Shaa Ta said. "Go ahead."

Spacer closed his eyes, trying to reach out with his mind—with the feeling part of his mind—to touch the vast intellect adrift among the cloud tops far below. He

visualized the Knight of Cups, the messenger with an
offer of friendship, of a new relationship, of a *joining*.
    ?
"I think he's there," Spacer said.

Visible through the bridge viewscreens, phosphorescent
waves spread out from a central point, an island of interlocking bars of light.

Here is the data it needs, the fraal said, his voice filling
Spacer's mind. *Storm: diameter 8,345 kilometers. Density:
5.314 g/cm³. Mass: 1.6 x 10²⁷ grams. Surface gravity 0.63
G. Orbital inclination . . .*

The string of words and numbers went on and on, most
of it incomprehensible to Spacer as he accepted each from
the fraal and spread it out upon his thoughts for the Salamanca Intelligence to read. There was more than simple
almanac data. The fraal was also transmitting a detailed
primer in mathematics, in measuring units, in trigonome-
try, geometry, calculus . . . all carefully compiled by *Questar*'s AI, using measurements taken at the stone circle as a
basis for all measurements and constants.

Before *Questar* had completed its passage across Salamanca's night hemisphere, they'd given the intelligence
below everything it needed to calculate precisely the orbits
of Salamanca and all of the planetary and satellite bodies
in the Loman system.

Spacer could feel the being's sheer pleasure, a feeling
of accomplishment, a sense of utter wonder at so complex
and yet so simple a cosmos. . . .

He decided to add some thoughts of his own. As Ta
Shaa Ta completed his recitation—all extremely hard, left-
brain facts and figures—Spacer added some right-brain
imagery of his own.

Lison, viewed from space as Questar *boosted clear of
the atmosphere, agleam with clouds and deserts, then
dwindling into the utter vastness of star-strewn space, a
planetary mote adrift upon the universal sea . . .*

*Titania in approach: an immense blue-white sun,
swelling in magnificent glory, a stunning radiance buried
deep in the heart of its filmy, light-tattered nebula. Again,*

during close passage, as the blue-white giant filled half of heaven, as prominences arced millions of kilometers into a sky that was all seething light and heat and magnetic storm. And again, all of that brilliance compressing into a single hard, dazzling point of light as Questar *fell outbound once more. . . .*

And the view of Loman, of Salamanca, of Storm, of Taliafiero, as seen during Questar's *initial approach—a view of its home system that the Salamanca Intelligence could never enjoy, a glimpse at the impossible mystery of worlds that could not . . . that* would *not be for much longer . . .*

And he sensed again the Salamanca Intelligence's sheer sense of wonder. . . .

Outside, phosphorescent waves the size of a dozen Lisons spread across the Salamanca sky.

As Spacer opened his eyes again, Diane gasped. "Spacer! Look!"

The patterns of light and dark against the gas giant's night side were rippling together, reforming, reshaping themselves into an image. It was very crude, almost a cartoon, but Spacer recognized it at once.

The Nine of Cups. A smiling man in rich robes sat beneath a curved shelf on which nine cups were placed in a row.

"The Wish Card!" Spacer said. "But I never told him about that one!"

"It drew the image from your mind," Ta Shaa Ta said. "What is the message?"

"That I—that *we* will get all of our wishes. Love. Happiness. Fulfillment. Wealth. I think it's saying, 'Good-bye, thank you, and good luck!' "

"I agree."

Questar accelerated, inductors straining to haul them clear of the planet's huge gravity well. The image against Salamanca's night soon dissolved into random light.

"Hey, Ta Shaa Ta?" Spacer said.

"Yes?"

"All those numbers and things you were just having me repeat. How hard would it be for me to learn all that stuff?"

"Not hard. It would take time, but your mind is easily up to the task. Why?"

"I dunno. I've been thinking about what's next. Where I'm going, y'know? Grep, I have trouble just *reading* . . . and that number stuff sounded pretty complicated."

"Why would you want to learn mathematics?"

"I was wondering if it was necessary to get into Verge Ranger school."

Jarrett chuckled. "You don't need higher math to get in. They'll teach you. Reading helps, but they can teach you that, too. Why?"

"I don't know." Spacer shrugged. "I first started thinking about it when I was wondering what I could do that would keep me off Lison. Later, though, I got to thinking that seeing new worlds, meeting new life forms . . . well . . ." He tapped the right side of his head. "Seems to me that whatever I have goin' on up here, maybe it would come in handy for a ranger, y'know?"

"It would at that." Jarrett looked puzzled. "I'm surprised, though. The Rangers didn't exactly come off as winners this time. I went to talk to the stormies and got knocked on my tail. I tangled with a couple of Raptor interceptors and got knocked on my tail. Hardly an inducement to new volunteers."

"Maybe I just have some ideas about how I could've done it better." Spacer smiled.

The others laughed . . . even Jarrett.

"Well, I think he's right," Diane said. "I'll pay for his transport to Aegis, if that's what it takes. I, for one, would like to hire him out as a guide someday. Maybe the next time Ta Shaa Ta and I are tracking down Precursors?"

"Thus speaks the independently wealthy xenoarchaeologist," Jarrett said.

"Independently wealthy? I guess so. We *all* are now, of course." She reached into a shirt pocket and extracted a glittering handful of glowing gems. "I'm still a bit shocked that Touches Far gave us all of these. Almost ten kilos, counting the ones stowed away aft. Enough to take you, Spacer, where ever you want to go. Enough to finance me,

Ta Shaa Ta, and the Institute in our research for the next five years, at least."

"Well, she has lots to spare," Jack said. "Me, I'm gonna use my share to put some additions into ol' *Questar* that you guys aren't gonna *believe*!"

"Actually, she doesn't have a lot to spare," Diane said. "She told me that they were all the stormies could spare. Once God, as she calls the Intelligence, got the information we'd promised, she and the rest of the stormies were going to use every stone they could find to complete the arch. Something about joining with God . . ."

"So why'd she do it?" Maricia asked.

"She said she didn't really understand humans that well, but she *did* know that we liked these stones. She said it was her way of saying thank you and good-bye."

"We'll be back to see them," Maricia said. "I intend to get a whole research team out here just as soon as I get back to the Institute."

"I don't think they'll be here to meet you, Maricia," Spacer said.

"What makes you say that?"

"Just a hunch."

Salamanca was receding rapidly in the aft screens now.

"Your buddies'll be okay," Jarrett said, laughing. "As smart as that Intelligence is already, and as powerful . . . it'll be okay. It'll take care of the stormies, too. Man, think where it might be a million years from now."

"The Salamanca Intelligence already wields godlike powers," Ta Shaa Ta said. "At this point in its evolution, there are no purely physical restraints to what it might one day become."

"I wonder," Spacer said, "how it will see the universe, how it will see *us,* if we're still around to meet it then?"

Epilogue

TOUCHES FAR STOOD on the caldera plain, watching as the last of
her people filed across the bridge left by the Bad Sky
People. They stepped through the dazzling brilliance suf-
fusing the Gateway to God and vanished. She looked up at
the heavens past the roiling, lightning-flecked clouds, past
the brooding Presence of God, and into the Depths, and
she wondered about the Good Sky People. She hoped they
would meet again, one day.

For now though, God was fulfilling Its bargain. It was
time to leave Storm for the New Storm, a world within the
Heart of God.

She still didn't understand all that God had told her and
the other Chosen. She grasped the concept, she thought,
that the physical body of God was ten times greater than
the mass of all of the World, that within God's body there
was space for many worlds, each sealed and safe, warmed
and fertile, with air as rich as that of the World, with the
fire of God to continue the endless cycle of life.

Touches Far wasn't sure how God could do all of that,

but she was willing to trust It . . . at least for now. The Gateway that God had had them build was open now, charged by the fires above and the fires below, opening a temporary portal through the walls of the World and allowing all the stormies—each carrying the seeds for a new forest of males—to step through. Now that the measurements God had needed were complete, now that God knew the shape of Heaven, the stormies' work here was done.

A new world. The concept still seemed strange, though the Good Sky People had spoken of other worlds, scattered like sand across the heavens.

It was time to go.

Curling her tentacle about five male sprouts, she hurried across the bridge and stepped through the Gate. Lightning, bringer of death and life, flared and crackled across a new sky.

A new world.

Someday, she knew, she would *see* the Good Ones again. . . .

⊖TAR◦DRIVE®

Adventure beyond the stars with Diane Duane

The Harbinger Trilogy

Starrise at Corrivale
Volume One

Gabriel Connor is up against it. Expelled from the Concord
Marines and exiled in disgrace, he's offered one last chance
to redeem himself. All it involves is gambling
his life in a vicious game of death.

Storm at Eldala
Volume Two

Gabriel and his fraal companion are scratching out a
living among the dangerous stars of the Verge when they
stumble onto new, unknown forces. Only their deaths seem
likely to avert disaster. But an astonishing revelation from the
depths of time makes the prospect of survival even
more terrible than a clean death.

Nightfall at Algemron
Volume Three

Gabriel Connor's quest to save the Verge and clear his
name leads him to a system ravaged by war and to the ruins of
a long-dead alien civilization. Along the way, he discovers that
to save himself and all he holds dear, his one salvation may
also be his ultimate destruction.

STAR DRIVE®

*To the edge of the galaxy
and back!*

Two of Minds
Williams H. Keith, Jr.

In the urban underground hell of Tribon
on the planet Oberon, life in a street gang
doesn't offer many possibilities. That is,
until one day Kai St. Cyr robs the wrong
man and finds himself in the middle
of a power struggle that stretches
beyond the stars.

Gridrunner
Thomas M. Reid

When a black market courier journeys to the Verge, she must
enter the virtual world of the mysterious Grid. Together with an
undercover agent, she finds herself embroiled in a desperate
conflict between a crime syndicate, terrorists, and her
own boss. The solution lies in the Grid.

Available September 2000

Zero Point
Richard Baker

Peter Sokolov is a bounty hunter and killer for hire. Geille Monashi,
a brilliant data engineer, is his quarry. After Sokolov and Monashi
encounter an alien derelict in the farthest reaches of space, they
have only one chance to survive. They've got to trust each other.

On the Verge
Roland J. Green

War erupts on Arist, a frozen world on the borders of known space.
The Concord Marines charge in to prevent the conflict from escalat-
ing, but soon discover that an even darker threat awaits them.

Enter the magical land of the Flanaess, world of adventure!

GREYHAWK is the setting of the role-playing game
DUNGEONS & DRAGONS. Each of these novels is based on a
classic D&D adventure module.

Against the Giants
Ru Emerson

A village burns while its attackers flee into the night.
Enraged, the king of Keoland orders an aging warrior to lead a
band of adventurers on a retaliatory strike. As they prepare to
enter the heart of the monsters' lair, each knows
only the bravest will survive.

White Plume Mountain
Paul Kidd

A ranger, a faerie, and a sentient hell hound pelt
with a penchant for pyromania. These three companions
must enter the most trap-laden, monster-infested place
this side of Acererak's tomb:
White Plume Mountain.

Descent into the Depths of the Earth
Paul Kidd

Fresh from their encounter with White Plume Mountain,
the Justicar and Escalla depart for the town of Hommlet.
But life around a faerie is never exactly . . . stable.
Before he knows it, to save her life the Justicar is on his way
into the depths of the earth to fight hobgoblins, drow,
and the queen of the demonweb pits.